ENJOYING WINE

To
Jessie, Abby and Noelene
—

ENJOYING WINE
Don Hewitson

Elm Tree Books · London

This book was designed and
produced by The Oregon Press Limited,
Faraday House, 8 Charing Cross Road,
London WC2H 0HG and first published in Great Britain in 1985
by Elm Tree Books, Garden House,
57-59 Long Acre, London WC2E 9JZ

Copyright © Don Hewitson 1985

All rights reserved. No part of
this publication may be reproduced, stored
in a retrieval system, or transmitted in any
form or by any means, electronic, or
otherwise, without prior permission.

ISBN 0-241-11579-5

Editor: Raymond Kaye
Design: Laurence Bradbury assisted by Paula Coles
Index: Helen Baz
Filmset by SX Composing Limited, Rayleigh, England
Origination by Waterden Reproductions Limited, London
Printed and bound by Clark Constable Limited, Edinburgh

CONTENTS

INTRODUCTION
6

CHAMPAGNE
7

LOIRE
22

ALSACE
28

BORDEAUX
34

BURGUNDY
51

BEAUJOLAIS
64

RHÔNE
74

PROVENCE
80

GERMANY
86

ITALY
96

SPAIN
109

CENTRAL and EASTERN EUROPE
118

ENGLAND
121

CALIFORNIA
123

AUSTRALIA
145

NEW ZEALAND
169

SOUTH AFRICA
180

QUESTIONS OF WINE
182

THE WINE YEAR
186

INDEX
190

ENJOYING WINE

INTRODUCTION

There has been a world-wide wine revolution over the past decade. No longer can Northern Europe be automatically considered as the automatic source of the world's finest wines; there is now considerable healthy competition and this has done much to raise the overall standard of wine. The finest Riojas are fighting it out on the international market place with the wealth of excellent French wines and outstanding classics from the 'new world' wine producing countries. Also new vineyard developments in more traditional wine countries such as Portugal, Yugoslavia, Tunisia and Bulgaria augur well for the future.

The boundaries of the wine world are ever decreasing. Baron Philippe de Rothschild has collaborated with Robert Mondavi to produce 'Opus One' California Cabernet Sauvignon. The Champagne houses are investing vast sums of money in California and Australia. Cordier from Bordeaux has extensive winemaking interests in Texas. The North American distillers Seagrams own wineries in California, New York State, Champagne, Bordeaux, Burgundy, Italy, Australia and New Zealand. Spanish companies own wineries in California, Mexico and Chile . . . the list is endless.

Robin Young of *The Times* considers 'The Cork and Bottle, Shampers, Bubbles and Methuselahs have the most exciting wine lists in London.' This is a book about these wines of the world that interest me most. It is not an encyclopedia of all wines, neither is it about the well-chronicled glorious virtues of Château Margaux, Domaine Romanée-Conti, and other such illustrious names.

Ten years ago United Kingdom service stations gave away beer glasses with their petrol; now it is champagne flutes. Things *must* be improving!

Don Hewitson

Chapter One

CHAMPAGNE

HISTORY

Grapes have been grown in this northern region 130 km (80 miles) east of Paris since the Roman occupation. The tradition was carried on by the wealthy abbeys and cathedrals and the wine was famous through the centuries. Its reputation was certainly not harmed by Reims Cathedral, which was the setting for the coronations of all French kings. Foreign royalty and dignitaries as well as the French nobility all attended and consumed large quantities of the local wine. The region became a considerable exporter as these visitors took back quantities of the product and spread the message, and consequently the vineyards flourished.

There was only one small but significant problem: despite all possible care and attention, there was a tendency for a pronounced secondary fermentation to take place in the wine while in the bottle (or other 'holding vessel' in the earliest days) and for an accompanying effervescence to develop. Now sometimes, especially when the wine was very young and fresh, this effect was deemed rather pleasant, but most of the time it accentuated the acidity. Scientific research of the time confirmed the source of this problem: the mineral content of the chalky subsoil of the vineyards. It did not appear to harm the sales of the wine (or the prodigious quantities drunk at the coronations!), but the Champenois were honest enough with themselves to admit that much of their wine was preferred by merchants simply because it was cheaper than burgundy – something had to be done.

Then, in 1670, along came an eccesiastical version of the Lone Ranger, a highly intelligent, inquisitive monk named Dom Pierre Pérignon, who was installed as cellarmaster of the Abbey of Hautvillers. There is considerable academic doubt (when isn't there?) regarding the exact extent of his influence in the transformation of this rather average wine into the 'real' champagne product, but he was certainly responsible for three dramatic innovations:

1. He learned to control the secondary fermentation in the bottle.
2. He discovered the secret of blending. The Abbey was not exactly poor; it owned a considerable acreage of vines and also received taxes, often in the form of grapes, from surrounding regions. Pérignon discovered that superior wine could be produced when 'marrying' different styles of wine from different areas, and also the benefits of keeping back some of the current vintage for ageing and subsequent blending with the younger wine.
3. These bottles of fully sparkling wine needed a new form of stoppering if the by now attractive sparkle was to be retained. The Dom rejected hemp-covered stoppers in favour of the newly discovered cork type, and he tied them down extremely tightly.

So much for the history: what is amazing is how little has changed since those days!

CULTIVATION

The wine-growing slopes of Champagne have advantages of crucial importance in such a northern region: their gentle undulations obtain the maximum summer and autumn sunshine; the very harsh frosts of winter and early spring do not quite wreak the same havoc here as even a few miles away; and the River Marne meanders through much of the region adding its certain

ENJOYING WINE

degree of general and welcome warmth.

The ripening of the grapes is always a battle against the elements. The grapes are the unique Chardonnay and two reds – the Pinot Noir and Pinot Meunier. It is a source of amazement to many longstanding lovers of the wines of this region when they discover that only about 30 per cent of champagne is made from white grapes.

There is a very, very strict governmental control exercised through the Comité Interprofessional du Vin de Champagne (CIVC), who regulate everything from cultivation of vines to the actual selling price of the grapes and the production of the wine. The committee consists of representatives of both the big houses and the growers. There is a unique system of evaluating and pricing the grapes. A traditional rating of the *communes* exists with twelve '100 per cent *crus*' (*see* map) at the top of the scale, and with the least favourable regions of the Aube only mustering a low 80 per cent. Every year a price is fixed per kilo and the grower is paid the percentage according to the rating: it seems quite obvious and sensible really!

THE HARVEST

Harvest time and the pressing produces another set of variables. The production of white wine from red grapes requires the most gentle pressing. The regulations allow 4000 kg (8800 lb) of grapes to produce 2666 litres of must (grape juice) and three separate qualities are obtained:

1. *Tête de Cuvée* 2050 litres of the first and most gentle pressing.
2. *Première Taille* 410 litres of the second pressing.
3. *Deuxième Taille* The last allowable 206 litres of the third pressing. Obviously this pressing is the result of a much less delicate operation, and produces a must with considerably less depth

Vineyards by the River Marne. The number '5' is a marker for helicopter spraying

and finesse. These wines are normally sold off to the houses producing the cheaper champagnes.

At this stage of the season there is a real sense of urgency all around the region. The grapes are rushed to the *pressoirs* which are scattered around the main areas, then the must is allowed to settle before being transported to the central cellars and poured into large stainless-steel or glass-lined concrete vats where the first vigorous fermentation takes place in a carefully controlled cool temperature (air conditioning has unfortunately robbed this stage of its mystique). By December the wine has been 'racked' (rather like decanting) and left to rest until the end of January, when the important part of champagne making takes place.

BLENDING

Different wines from different areas, the products of different grape varieties, are all tested carefully and decisions are made as to what is to be 'married' to what, and in what proportions. Decisions on the contribution from the *réserve* wines of older vintages are taken. Each of the great champagne firms tries from year to year to produce a constant 'house style' with its blend. A succession of really poor vintages may upset the system slightly but the houses do achieve a remarkable degree of consistency; the personal tasting room decisions on the blending of up to thirty different wines bear a heavy burden of responsibility, linked to the past and future of the great houses. These 'clinical' *assemblages* are now put into practical action in the huge vats and the wine is bottled with an addition of *liqueur de tirage*, a blend of sugar and cultivated yeast, and capped with a crown cork.

THE SECOND FERMENTATION AND AGEING

The bottles are taken down to the chilly cellars and piled high on their sides for a leisurely second fermentation. At this stage the wine is still. Now the added yeast acts on the sugar remaining from the first fermentation and turns it into carbon dioxide. While the gas pressure is building up to 6 atmospheres, the important process of ageing continues its leisurely pace – the blend settles down and gradually a rather light, sour wine begins to bloom and soften and an accompanying unique depth of character and bouquet develops. The actual length of this process is of vital importance. Governmental law demands only one year's ageing for a non-vintage blend and three for a vintage. Many small houses without the considerable financial resources necessary for long-term stock-holding of such an expensive product will sell the wine as close to the minimum requirement as is feasible. Thousands of wedding guests have suffered acid stomachs over the years after consuming excessive quantities of this stuff. The larger houses, however, keep the wine for a considerable number of years.

This secondary fermentation has one major problem: a residual deposit is thrown which clings to the side of the bottle. Some of this deposit is relatively solid and easily moved, but the rest is much lighter, and if the bottle is shaken it merely swims through all the contents, destroying the clarity that has been so carefully attained.

REMUAGE AND DÉGORGEMENT

The bottle is now placed upside down at an angle of approximately 30 degrees in *pupitres* (sloped wooden racks) and the *remuage*, the wine's most labour-intensive operation, begins. The *remueurs*

twist the bottles every day, gradually bringing them closer and closer to the vertical position, and ever so delicately persuading all the sediment to float gently to the stopper. This process usually takes about three months, but nothing is quite that simple. Not all of the various batches react in the same manner. Some require much less time, some much more. It is interesting to hear a *remueur* talking about 'my wine', meaning the thousands of bottles that he alone is taking through *remuage*. The bottles are then carefully moved upside down and stored, awaiting *dégorgement*. Sometimes the wine is aged a little longer, sometimes a lot more (*see* Bollinger).

When ready for *dégorgement*, the bottles are moved to a room with a long bath of freezing brine.

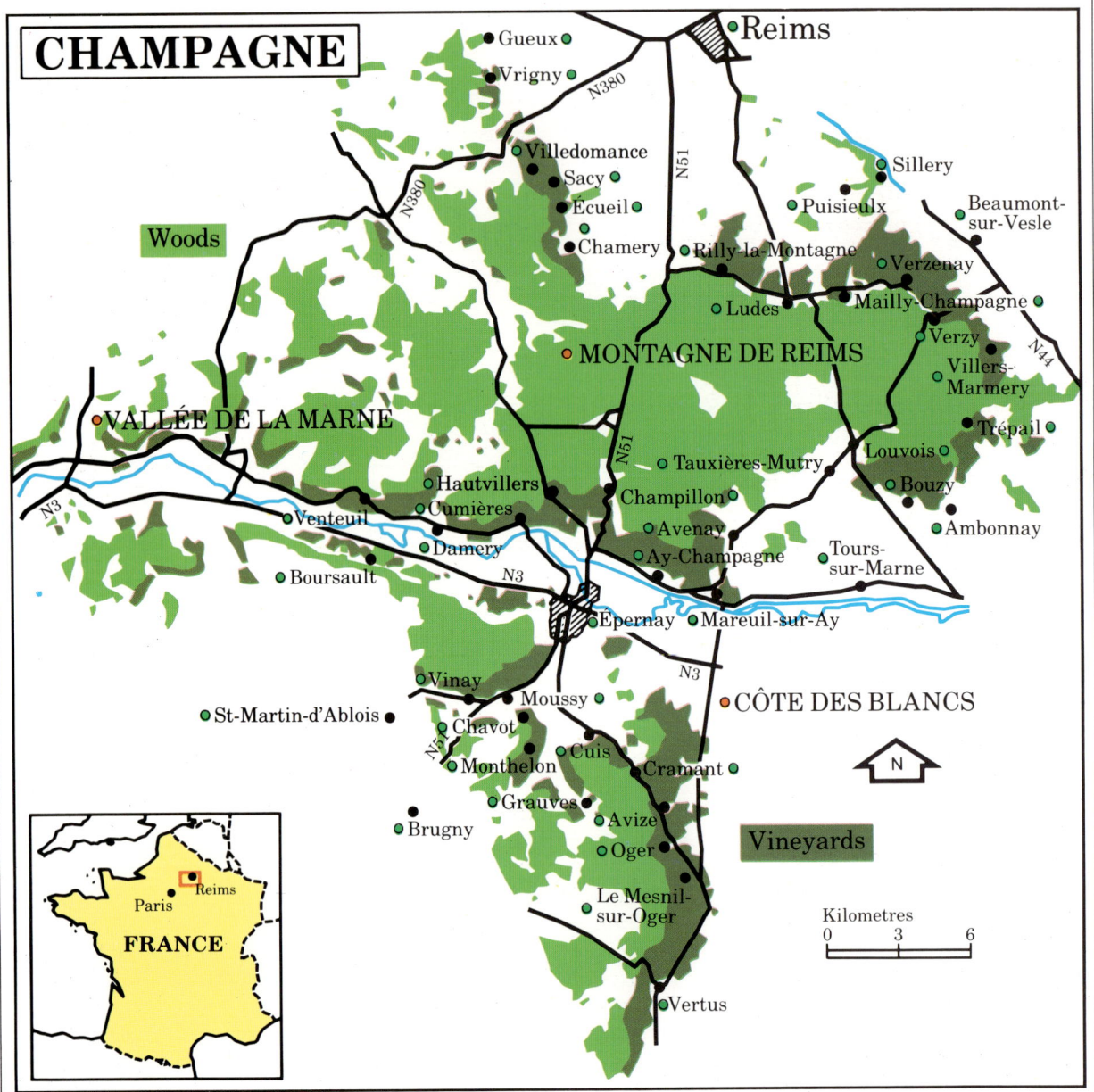

CHAMPAGNE

Ageing at Laurent-Perrier

The cap and first few inches of the neck pass through and the sediment, but not the wine, freezes. The crown cork is then rapidly removed and the pressure of the champagne violently forces out the frozen sediment. (In the old days, and still in fact with some prestige *cuvées*, the wine was properly corked after the first fermentation and the *dégorgement* then done by hand.)

The tiny amount of wine lost is now replaced with a small *dosage*, a blend of the original wine and cane sugar. It is this amount of fine liqueur that determines the style of wine: the less the *dosage* the drier the wine. There is a trend nowadays to market wine with no *dosage* as another variation of the prestige products. Such wines seem to have names sounding rather more like men's aftershave than champagne.

I don't mind the champagne firms doing this, but I wish they wouldn't serve it to me!

The wine is now corked in a method not dissimilar to pile-driving. A huge, solid, round wedge, four times the neck size, is driven in and then tied down to keep the wine in a bottle with the equivalent pressure of the tyre of a London bus!

The bottles of this unique wine are now ready to face the actresses' slippers, the bows of new ships, or simply the palates of grateful devotees.

VINTAGE CHAMPAGNE

The declaration of a champagne vintage is not quite the significant proposition of the similar decision regarding port. Many houses now produce 'vintages' with monotonous regularity. (In 1977 when I was chairman of the Champagne Academy the crop suffered from just about every possible problem – late frosts, a wet dull summer with rampant mildew – and yet one of the big houses managed to make a vintage champagne.)

In a vintage champagne the wine should be richer and more full-bodied, with a much more distinctive character: the blender's chance to flaunt his technique in a more positive manner. Over the years of regular panel champagne tastings my fondest memories are of vintage champagnes from certain houses, not of the 'prestige' *cuvées*.

Vintage champagne usually should be kept for a few years after release, despite the claims of the public relations departments of some houses, who maintain that the wine is only released when aged to perfection. This may have been the case in a time well before my involvement in the trade, but it is certainly not so now. I always work on the principle of drinking the previous vintage to the one on release. The vintages also vary considerably in ageing needs and attention should be paid to this when drinking: it was a tragedy that much of the absolutely classic 1975, which needed years more bottle age, was drunk before the lighter, forward 1976.

Pay attention to these few facts and you will enjoy simply the best value champagne of all. A lack of market awareness and the tendency for attention to focus on the 'prestige' wines have kept the cost of vintage champagne to a mere 10-20 per cent more than the non-vintage – a comparative bargain!

ROSÉ CHAMPAGNE

The attitude of both producers and consumers to this style is never constant. In the 1950s it achieved a certain notoriety as the 'débutantes' bubbly', certainly to be taken frequently but never seriously. When I was attending the Champagne Academy in 1972 very little attention was paid to the fact that the houses even made rosé; in fact I tasted more than 200 champagnes on the ten-day course – but never rosé. Well, the momentum has swung back a little in favour of this style, which is delicious when well made; even such conservative luminaries as Krug and Bollinger have launched their pinks.

There are two totally different methods used in the making. One is the standard rosé formula of macerating the Pinot skins for a short time, allowing a degree of redness, and Pinot flavour, to blend with the wine. There is another widely used method allowed by the French government only in Champagne. This is the addition of a portion of the area's red wine. The relative merits of these methods have been debated for many years and no doubt the houses will continue to be divided. These differences certainly contribute to the wide range of styles, some pale and delicate and others fuller and more flavoursome. Wine from houses using the 'maceration' method also tends to vary from year to year, whereas the 'addition' method offers a more consistent style.

I love good rosé champagne, but am irritated with the very lightly coloured ones, as I expect a distinct Pinot character – otherwise why buy it? Another irritation is the price. Surely in these modern days there is no longer the risk of spoiling the whole *cuvée*, therefore rosé does not cost a lot more to produce. Why does the wine so often have to be priced between vintage and prestige, and usually much closer to the latter? I regularly drink the excellent Laurent Perrier Cuvée Rosé Brut. It is delicately scented, beautifully flavoured and the price of the average bottle of vintage: an excellent wine for the patio or garden!

CUVÉES DE PRESTIGE

In the 1920s Moët et Chandon began production of a totally new champagne phenomenon: the luxurious and rare champagne produced from a 'super blend' of the finest wine from the first pressing. The wine was named Dom Pérignon and immediately the combination of excellence of the product and instant snob appeal marked this innovation as a resounding success. Obviously the other houses were impressed with the chance to show off and produce limited quantities of simply the finest wines they could achieve: the considerably higher sale price was also more attractive. Nowadays these *cuvées de prestige* (or, in the less fanciful terms of the retail wine trade, Premiums), play a very significant role in worldwide assessments of the relative order of merit placings of the larger houses. I never ceased to be amazed in New York, where many serious wine drinkers know little about the current release of any Moët et Chandon products other than Dom Pérignon. Similarly in Sydney the same can be said about Bollinger and its R.D. (*Récemment Dégorgé*).

The marvellous Dom Pérignon package, so different to ordinary champagne bottles and yet so simple (an adaptation of the original champagne bottle), demanded that all houses felt the need of a gimmick to accompany the wine. Louis Roederer produced its wonderful Cristal in clear bottles reputed to be derived from one created in 1876 for Tsar Alexander II, who refused to buy his favourite bubbly in bottles available to his subjects. (This prompted some of my favourite champagne advertising copy when a Cristal advertisement in the mid-1960s bemoaned the fact that after the year of the revolution their orders came to an abrupt end!)

A few years ago I was beginning to doubt the authenticity of the claims to fame of many of these premium champagnes. Packaging seemed to be of prime importance as houses chopped and changed according to the whims of their marketing people, all in an effort to join the gravy train (by the 1970s these wines were selling at twice the price of vintage). Bottles and labels appeared that looked more suitable for the bubble-bath shelves of supermarkets. The styles of the champagnes were also changed regularly; a comparative tasting of a dozen lesser-known premiums in 1979 showed wines with a distinct lack of individuality as the houses produced champagne with a soft, bland finish. Now I am pleased to say things are better.

I was lucky enough to take part in what was billed by the London *Times* as 'one of the most sybaritic tasting exercises ever': the paper's 1985 New Year blind tasting of twenty premium champagnes. There were many wines with the aforementioned faults, but the ones judged best by the tasters (myself; Jane MacQuitty, wine correspondent of *The Times*; Serena Sutcliffe, Master of Wine; Michael Broadbent, head of Christie's Wine Department; Michael Crozier, Editor of the 'Saturday' department of *The Times*; and Richard Freeman, of the specialist merchants The Champagne House) were marvellous examples of champagne at its best: not blended for the market, but made in uncompromising styles to show the wines with superb balance and weight. Definitely not frivolous bottles of bubbly. The top eight wines were:

SUPERSTARS

Dom Pérignon 1976 A remarkable effort for *the* premium wine reputed to outsell its nearest competitor by three to one, and full marks to Moët. The house has never increased the quantity at the expense of the quality. I particularly enjoyed its rich, full-bodied flavour, beautifully in balance with a delicate finish.

Louis Roederer Cristal 1979 Well, not only the bottle is unique! A superbly structured wine with a flowery nose and considerable depth. I noted: 'This is what champagne making is all about.'

Laurent Perrier Cuvée Grand Siècle A marvellous wine, classic nose, considerable depth of flavour and complemented by a soft, flowery Chardonnay finish. This wine surprised most of the panel at unveiling time because it is rarely noticed. Laurent Perrier's dogged insistence that the finest *cuvée* is to be made from a selection of vintages is admirable (and would carry more weight if the house did not produce a vintage version for the United States), but it does mean that Grand Siècle is often rather hidden among the non-vintages on both merchant's and restaurant lists. A pity!

HIGHLY RECOMMENDED

G.H. Mumm René Lalou 1979 Now this is different to previous blends. It is now much softer, with the distinctive Mumm 'frothy' style and a deliciously dry finish.

Veuve Clicquot La Grande Dame 1979 This has always been one of my favourites. A no-compromise big, gutsy wine, drinking well at the time of tasting, but with years ahead.

Pol Roger Cuvée Sir Winston Churchill 1975 Not particularly in the Pol Roger house style, with a prominent Pinot Noir character and considerable ageing potential.

RECOMMENDED

Taittinger Comtes de Champagne 1976 A *blanc de blancs* produced solely from the Chardonnay grape: very soft and elegant.

ENJOYING WINE

Not all pink champagnes look the same!

Krug Grande Cuvée I have confessed elsewhere my undying admiration for this house. Full and flavoursome, but would have scored even more highly with a little more bottle age.

ARE THESE CHAMPAGNES WORTH IT?

Some are definitely worth the incredibly high price (at the time of this tasting, all of these champagnes were about £20 per bottle in London).

CHAMPAGNE

These top wines are still value for money because of their sheer excellence; not everyday drinking by any means, but ideal 'special occasion' champagne. (I personally also marked highly Charles Heidsieck's Champagne Charlie 1976, a luscious blend of 60 per cent Pinot Noir and 40 per cent Chardonnay.)

But, now comes the worrying aspect: what about the rest? *The Times* played a sneaky trick and put in a bottle of Moët et Chandon 1978 vintage and it scored the next highest mark. The panel was not fooled. I described it as 'lacking complexity'; Serena as 'reticent and slight'; Michael Crozier as 'undistinctive'; Jane MacQuitty as 'disappointing' – and yet we preferred it to the other wines! Now this champagne was good enough in its own right to finish eighth out of twenty, and costs only a relatively modest £10 per bottle. It does not say a lot for the rest.

It was pleasing to see the two dominant brand leaders in the three top wines, but one cannot avoid the fact that, on the whole, vintage champagne offers a much better buy than premium.

THE CHAMPAGNE HOUSES

Why do I drink so much champagne with such monotonous regularity? Why don't I drink any of the multitude of sparkling wines from all over the world, even the considerably cheaper yet technically correct wines made by this *méthode champenoise*? Why don't I drink the cheapest champagnes, or the single vineyard–small estate ones so beloved by the trendy French food and wine magazines?

There is no doubt about it: I am a devotee of the larger houses, most of which are prominent members of the Syndicat des Grandes Marques de Champagne. These are the producers who pay particular attention to the most important aspect of the art of champagne making – the blending. The smaller champagne houses or growers can make satisfactory wines but rarely exciting ones, as their grapes invariably come from a small, limited area within the immediate districts. The larger houses, however, have the two crucial advantages for using the *méthode champenoise* and producing complex, well-balanced and mature wine: reserve stocks and access to the finest grapes from a large spread of the different regions. For example, G.H. Mumm owns 200 ha (490 acres) and presses at Mailly, Verzy, Verzenay, Bouzy and Avize – which is quite a spread across both the Montagne de Reims and the Côte des Blancs; the blender is certainly given the best of raw material.

I have mentioned the emphasis placed on maintaining a constant 'house' style. So what are these, and how do they vary? It really is 'horses for courses' to some extent; all of my regular favourites have their own individuality which I appreciate, admittedly with varying degrees of enthusiasm. There are also different styles for different occasions – even I would consider Krug a bit of an extravagant waste for a Sunday midday drinks party!

Broadly speaking the Grandes Marques can be divided into two categories:
1. The light, fruity champagnes from the Epernay firms.
2. The more full-bodied wines with more Pinot characteristics from the Reims establishments.

Obviously there are exceptions to the rule, especially as some houses have altered their blends considerably over the past decade. There is one point of great importance to the champagne buyer: if you can manage to keep the non-vintage wine for another year after purchase you will repay your investment considerably as the extra bottle age allows the wine to gain a little depth and concentrates the flavour.

MOËT ET CHANDON (Epernay)

The giant of the industry has often suffered unnecessary criticism, but it is an inescapable fact that in many countries of the world the name Moët is synonymous with champagne, and that the dynamism of this large organization has been a significant factor in the huge expansion of the champagne export trade.

Moët produces an attractive, fresh and light non-vintage champagne. It is not a particularly complex style, but it is easy to drink and a good example of 'the finest aperitif ever conceived by man or provided by nature' (John Arlott's words, not mine) – hence its tremendous popularity. The vintage is another ball game entirely: much more full-bodied with considerable depth of character, and yet still retaining a creamy soft finish.

ENJOYING WINE

What can one say about Dom Pérignon that has not already been stated time and time again? Around Christmas, cases of this are traded from merchant to merchant with an enthusiasm more appropriate to Reuters shares than wine. The wine itself always shows considerable delicacy and softness.

Moët's subsidiary Mercier offers an attractive 'commercial' champagne with a significantly higher *dosage*. I can remember describing it in a blind tasting as 'just the champagne to take along to the bank manager'.

PERRIER-JOUËT (Epernay)

One of my champagne trade friends always precedes his highly complimentary comments about the uniqueness of Perrier-Jouët with the words, 'Well, of course, you realize they make less champagne in total than Moët make Dom Pérignon.' I am not sure this is completely correct, but it does offer an interesting comparison of two of the top Epernay houses.

The firm has a large proportion of its vineyard holdings in the Côte des Blancs, in particular around Cramant: hence a light, flowery style reeking with what I call 'Epernay apples' (this expression does not go down well over there). Michel Budin, a superb taster and blender, is very much in control, despite the Seagram connection. The non-vintage and vintage are marvellous examples of the lighter style. I must confess that I have not been impressed with recent vintages of the 'Belle Epoque' (Fleur de France) but this has been partly compensated by the recent introduction of the excellent, soft and delicate Belle Epoque Rosé.

POL ROGER (Epernay)

Similar to Perrier-Jouët and yet so different. This family business master-minded by Christian de Billy and Christian Pol Roger produces an elegant, lightish wine, but with a marvellous underlying steeliness: definitely not the wine for actresses' slippers! I have always adored the fruity, fresh bouquet and the classic clean finish; year in, year out the non-vintage is one of the finest to be found.

The house had very strong connections with Sir Winston Churchill — not only did he always drink it, but he even named one of his racehorses Pol Roger. After the death of Sir Winston the firm added a black border to the label of the non-vintage White Foil. His son-in-law the late Lord Soames carried on the Pol Roger tradition. When he was leading the British delegation at the Rhodesian independence talks he hosted a press conference at a particularly difficult point in negotiations. Asked for an estimate of the further length of the talks he said, '30 days'. When he was asked why he thought this he replied, 'Because I only have 30 bottles of Pol Roger left.'

BOLLINGER (Ay)

Here I must plead a certain amount of bias: I will never forget my first-ever trip to France in 1972. I lunched with Madame Bollinger at her house and we drank the 1966 vintage. It was without doubt one of the finest bottles of vintage champagne I have ever drunk, rich and full with a delicious yeasty fragrance.

The non-vintage has a very mature style with considerable depth of character. It is one of the few champagnes that I happily drink with the main course.

I am intrigued by the habitués of the Newmarket Racing Club members' bars. There they never order 'a bottle of champagne'; it is always 'a bottle of Bolly, please'. The vintage rosé is wonderful, in particular the 1979, which is on sale now. The colour is the perfect tinge of reddish pink, with the most alluring nose I have ever experienced with rosé champagne; and the beautiful rich Pinot Noir flavour comes through without overpowering the elegant style. Bollinger's R.D. (*récemment dégorgé*) is a rather different *cuvée de prestige*. The wine is stored for a considerable number of years after *remuage* and allowed to age gently; the end product is a distinctive, mature 'no compromise' wine.

DEUTZ ET GELDERMANN (Ay)

This is actually marketed under the name Champagne Deutz, presumably to avoid sounding like a German sekt. The non-vintage is one of the most underrated of wines, consistently full and flavoursome, never either the cheapest nor the most expensive. The firm's Cuvée William Deutz is one of the better prestige wines and one of the less expensive.

CHAMPAGNE

The Remueur at work

LAURENT-PERRIER (Tours-sur-Marne)
One of my favourite everyday drinking wines. The non-vintage is very consistent: fresh and fragrant with a hint of boiled sweets on the back palate – just the bubbly for 'elevenses'.

CHARLES HEIDSIECK (Reims)
This wine is worthy of Oscars in the 'Most Improved Performer' and 'Best Value for Money' categories. The non-vintage 'Charlie' of the 1960s and early '70s was a very dry, austere wine. Admittedly there were many, many thousands of drinkers around the world who loved this style, but I was very pleased when the firm was taken over by Henriot, which gave it access to over 550 ha (1360 acres) of vineyards, a large proportion in the Côte des Blancs.

The reasonably priced non-vintage has been rounded and softened with a more pronounced Chardonnay character.

HEIDSIECK DRY MONOPOLE (Reims)
An enigmatic house. Often the non-vintage appears to lack character and is simply austere and rather harsh, but the vintage is of a different class altogether.

A beautifully balanced dry yet full style with the most attractive traditional yeasty bouquet and a long finish: this is one of the best champagne buys of all as it costs little more than some non-vintages.

HENRIOT (Reims)
An amazing house with considerable influence within the Champagne industry and yet Henriot has a relatively low profile for its own products. The non-vintage is an excellent, elegant and flowery wine with a well-balanced soft finish; the *blanc de blancs* is very light and smooth and yet with a firm finish. Both wines offer excellent value.

LANSON (Reims)
This house offers a light, fresh non-vintage Black Label with a very young character. I consider its vintage wines better value.

LOUIS ROEDERER (Reims)
'The wine trade's non-vintage', admired and enjoyed because of its distinctiveness. It has a fresh, racy style with almost overpowering fruit and a marked dry, almost harsh, finish. This may sound rather unattractive on reading, but it actually works beautifully in practice: there is no other champagne quite like it. And, of course, there is the marvellous Cristal – if you can find it.

G.H. MUMM (Reims)
Part of the Seagram empire, along with Perrier-Jouët and Heidsieck Dry Monopole. I consider the non-vintage Cordon Rouge, with its lightish 'creaming soda', style to be one of the most consistent champagnes of the larger houses. The vintage always has real style, but the one to search out is the Crémant de Cramant: a foaming, light and delicious *blanc de blancs*, one of the most distinctive of non-vintage champagnes. It is only made in small quantities therefore distribution is severely limited. If you are lucky enough to dine at the renowned Giradet restaurant at St-Crissier in Switzerland you should order the house champagne: it is the Crémant.

PIPER HEIDSIECK (Reims)
A house that has changed the style of its *cuvée*. I used to consider the non-vintage rather bland; now it is anything but: a dry, flinty flavour with a solid but rewarding finish. A new *prestige* has just been released (it missed the London *Times* tasting) called Champagne Rare 1976. It is an attractive blend of 60 per cent Chardonnay and 40 per cent

ENJOYING WINE

G.H. Mumm's pressoir at Avize, early 20th century

Pinot: very soft and light, but with considerable depth.

POMMERY ET GRENO (Reims)
This was formerly the house for lovers of full, rich non-vintage with so much depth of flavour that the wine was often mistaken for vintage.

Unfortunately not any longer: it is now light and fresh with a prominent acid finish.

TAITTINGER (Reims)
An exceptionally light, elegant style epitomized in the Comtes de Champagne Blanc de Blancs. This must be the only champagne that actually gives Dom Pérignon stiff competition in the international marketplace.

(The Plaza Hotel in New York does a very good deal: a bottle of this and beluga caviare for two only costs $190 – room service of course!)

VEUVE CLICQUOT (Reims)
The non-vintage Yellow Label achieves a superb consistency of style and standard, the best possible example of the 'Reims character'. It has a delightful balance between rich, full and mature Pinot character and a slight hint of sweetness on the back palate.

The vintage is my favourite most years – the same uniform high quality with extra depth and complexity but still delightfully subtle.

There are certain advantages of being a restaurateur, and regular supplies of 'The Widow' is one of them!

I could write on and on about champagnes from many other houses: the super Bonnet Blanc de Blancs; the refined non-vintage wines from George Goulet and Joseph Perrier; the attractive zippy style of de Castellane (now owned by Laurent-Perrier) the good value Charbaut and Boizel – but I must extol the many virtues of the house I have deliberately left to last.

CHAMPAGNE

Roman cellars of Charles Heidsieck

ENJOYING WINE

TOURING CHAMPAGNE

Champagne is the closest wine area to Britain and as the Calais-Dijon motorway progresses, the travelling time diminishes; soon the journey from the ferry will only be a matter of a few hours. It is the ideal place for a mini-break: superb scenery, marvellous food at all levels and, of course, the fascination of the region's product. G.H Mumm, Pommery et Greno, Taittinger, Mercier and Moët offer well-organized bilingual tours of their cellars on weekdays, and the last two houses also on Saturdays in summer. Most other houses will happily do the same, but you should telephone for an appointment. Try and visit at least two houses, one of the largest and one of the smaller: the contrast is amazing. Reims Cathedral is also a must with its beautiful stained-glass windows – a postwar Chagall is worth the trip alone. The less tourist-orientated Basilique St Remi is fascinating.

The non-driver can easily take the train to Epernay from the Gare du Nord and stay centrally, but the splendours of the region are really only revealed to the travellers by car who are in no hurry and content to meander through the villages and around the hillsides spread with vineyards. When not on official business, and especially when *en famille*, I always stay 20 km (12 miles) outside Reims at Sept Saux at the Hôtel Cheval Blanc – telephone (26) 61.60.27 Telex 830885 – run by a charming, welcoming couple who offer peaceful, inexpensive rooms and traditional *champenois* fare. The *langoustines au vin de Champagne* are often from their own freshwater stream. An added bonus is their excellent choice of claret and burgundy when a mouthful or two of red wine is required!

Boyer 'Les Crayères', Reims – (26) 82.80.80 Telex 830959 – is *the* place to dine and stay. This was formerly the Pommery et Greno château. I stayed there many times and it was gently amusing as the faded gentility became more and more faded, but by the late 1970s it was becoming all rather sad. Well, Pommery et Greno changed hands and the new owners teamed up with Gérard Boyer of the three-star Boyer restaurant in Reims and transformed this mansion into a luxurious establishment with superb food, breathtaking park surroundings and views of Reims. At the time of the renovations astronomical sums of money were whispered around the dining tables of the champagne houses, therefore it is obviously not a cheap place – but worth it! I must confess to preferring the cuisine *chez* Boyer at the old restaurant when father Gaston was more involved and the food was not quite so subtle, but that is really just carping. Don't miss a visit, and book well ahead.

First fermentation vats at G.H. Mumm

The Royal Champagne, 5 km (3 miles) north of Epernay – (26) 51.11.51 Telex 830111 – is my favourite 'special occasion' hostelry in Champagne: superb food which is inspired by the *nouvelle cuisine* but not over-elaborate, an excellent selection of the best still wines of the region as well as the choices champagnes, and a spectacular panoramic view of the vineyards. This is definitely the perfect place for a leisurely Sunday lunch. If you succumb to the *menu gastronomique* don't expect to finish before about 4.30! There are also 20 bungalow rooms away from the main building, all with splendid views.

Other hotels I recommend are La Briqueterie at Vinay, 7 km (4 miles) south of Epernay on N51 – (26) 54.11.22 Telex 842007 – and in Reims La Paix – (26) 40.04.08 Telex 830959 – and the Bristol – (26) 40.52.25.

KRUG (Reims)

The two white wines are the finest examples of the noble art of blending. They are expensive, but are in a class of their own. The individual care and attention (the first fermentation is still carried out in small oak casks) produces extraordinary champagne. The Grande Cuvée is amazing – light and soft yet with a huge depth of flavour, a wine that makes you sit and think. I like to keep the wine another few years after release, which allows the superb yeasty flavour of the Pinot to develop. Even I do not drink the vintage Krug very often (I have yet to taste the new Clos du Mesnil, the most exclusive of all 'exclusive' champagnes) but I will never forget the 1966 with its incredible flavour and depth, the product of a blending from 49 different wines. There is no doubt about it, if I am ever restricted to a mere one glass of wine a day it will be a glass of Krug!

THE FUTURE

As Jean-Marc Charles Hiedsieck says, things are changing in Champagne. Computer-controlled automatic *remuage* machines are working in many cellars. At the time of writing considerable research is being devoted to 'yeast balls' which may be inserted into the bottle and prevent the wine producing a sediment. Who knows what the future holds? But nothing will replace all the centuries of tradition and the devotion to excellence: a wonderful wine that has achieved a worldwide status unmatched by any other product of the vine.

JEAN-MARC CHARLES HEIDSIECK

Charles Heidsieck (commonly known as Charlie because one of Jean-Marc's ancestors was the subject of the well-known Victorian music hall song 'Champagne Charlie Is My Name') is one of the world's best-known champagnes. Much of this is due to this man, the most intrepid of travelling salesmen. In a business renowned for globe-trotting, Jean-Marc would rate as one of the highest mileage travellers: wherever I am in the wine world I always seem to hear, 'You have just missed Jean-Marc.'

Jean-Marc had a spell at Trinity College, Dublin, where one of his fellow students was author J.P. Donleavy. There is a wonderful moment in one of the latter's novels where the hero orders a bottle of the best in a Dublin bar and muses: 'Heidsieck, what a lovely name for champagne!'

As export director, Jean-Marc supervises all the firm's activities and personally covers Europe, Canada, the Caribbean, Hong Kong, Singapore, Australia and New Zealand. He is a charmingly philosophical *champenois* who does not allow himself to be drawn into the present conflict regarding whether the last few acres in the region should be planted – 'There is no reason to be for or against, providing local legislation is enforced regarding each delimited area'. He foresees over the years 'considerable changes in the relative strengths of the cooperatives, the growers and the small and large firms' as some of the first two become more assertive.

My suggestion that the present dramatic sales increase in two previously minor markets (the United States and Australia) may lead to a lowering of standards to keep pace with demand was refuted on the basis that, 'as in the past, price can always limit the demand for champagne as we did with the poor crops in 1980 and 1981'. Jean-Marc sees an excellent long-term future for champagne, 'as long as quality is protected by *appellation* abroad and local legislation in France'.

Jean-Marc Charles Heidsieck

CHAPTER TWO

Loire

The Loire is the longest river in France. It begins in the mountain regions of the Massif Central and wends its way for more than 960 km (600 miles) across to the Atlantic coast at Nantes. It is the most romantic countryside of France, with huge ornate châteaux crowning the gently rolling valleys. The main vineyard regions stretch over the last 320 km (200 miles) to the coast, producing a wide range of single grape variety wines.

MUSCADET
This wine comes from southeast of Nantes. It is made from the grape of the same name, formerly called the Melon de Bourgogne. The better-class

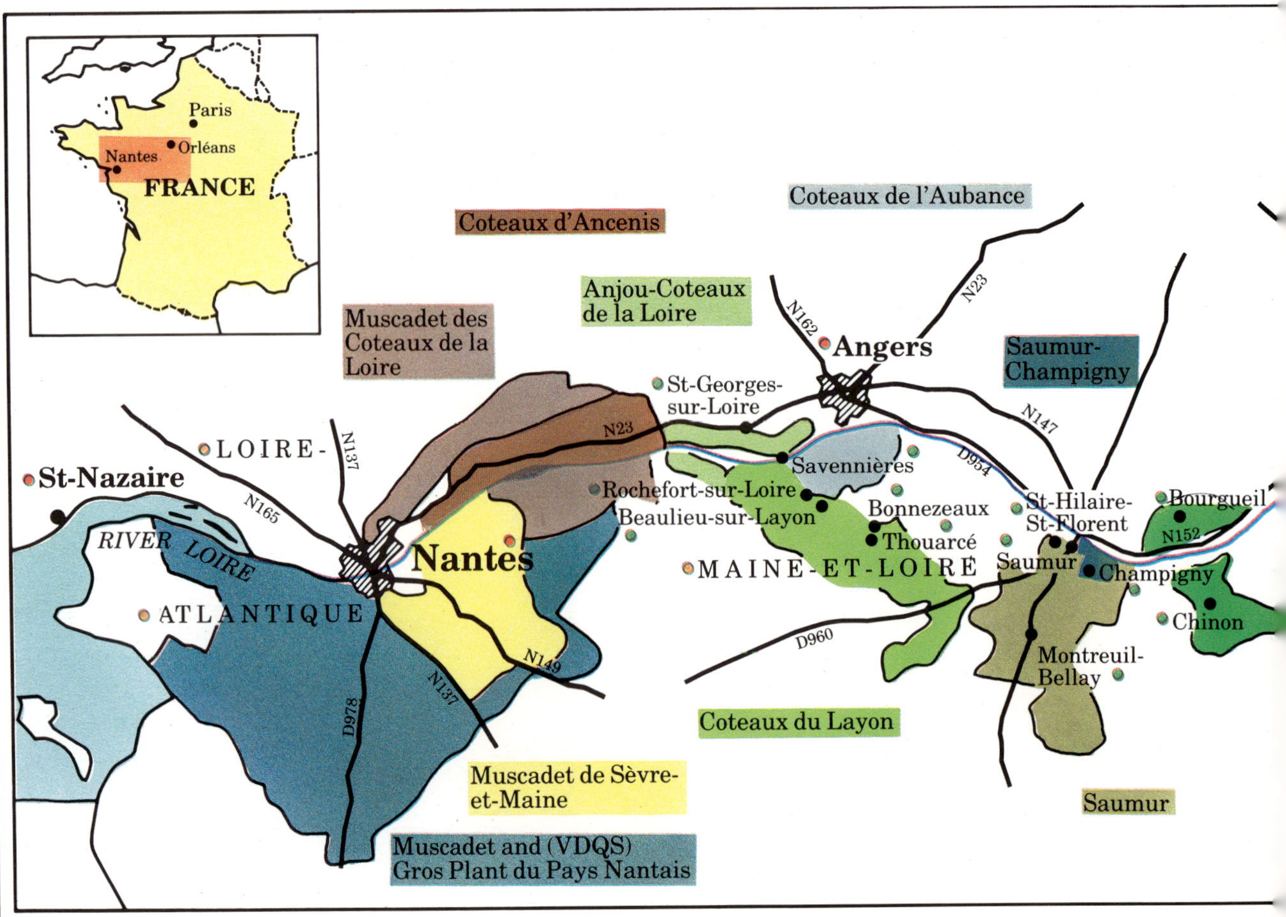

LOIRE

Muscadet comes from the Sèvre et Maine region. A certain amount of the wine is made *sur lie* having wintered in the barrel on the lees (the dense layer of sediment that has settled before and after fermentation). These wines have considerably more flavour.

Muscadet has caught the public's imagination: no self-respecting member of Parisian café society would be seen without a bottle when ordering a *plateau de fruits de mer*. It has not only conquered Paris (and, of course, Nantes), but also Great Britain, where its public image is rather that of the white equivalent of Beaujolais. Muscadet is splendid quaffing wine – light, dry with an extroverted fruit character, equally at home with shellfish, salads, white meats or simply on its own – at least that is the theory! When I taste it outside the region, it always seems to be tired, fat and flabby: an unpleasant wine with a murky finish typical of the Melon de Bourgogne which was deservedly kicked out of Burgundy.

Maybe it is true that Muscadet simply does not travel well – or perhaps the merchants only buy the really poor stuff that is all around the district. Obviously there are exceptions to prove the rule: I have tasted at the all-important Foire de Vallet right in the heart of the Sèvre et Maine, and appreciated some fine grower's and *négociant*'s wines. In England I have enjoyed wines from Auguste Braude, Henri and Vincent Chéreau, Domaine des Dorices, Château la Noë, Marquis de Goulaine, Domaine de Manoir (Madame Poiron), Domaine de la Maretière, Louis Métaireau, Domaine de la Moucherière and Sauvion, especially Château de Cléray. The region also contains small plantings of the Folle Blanche grape from

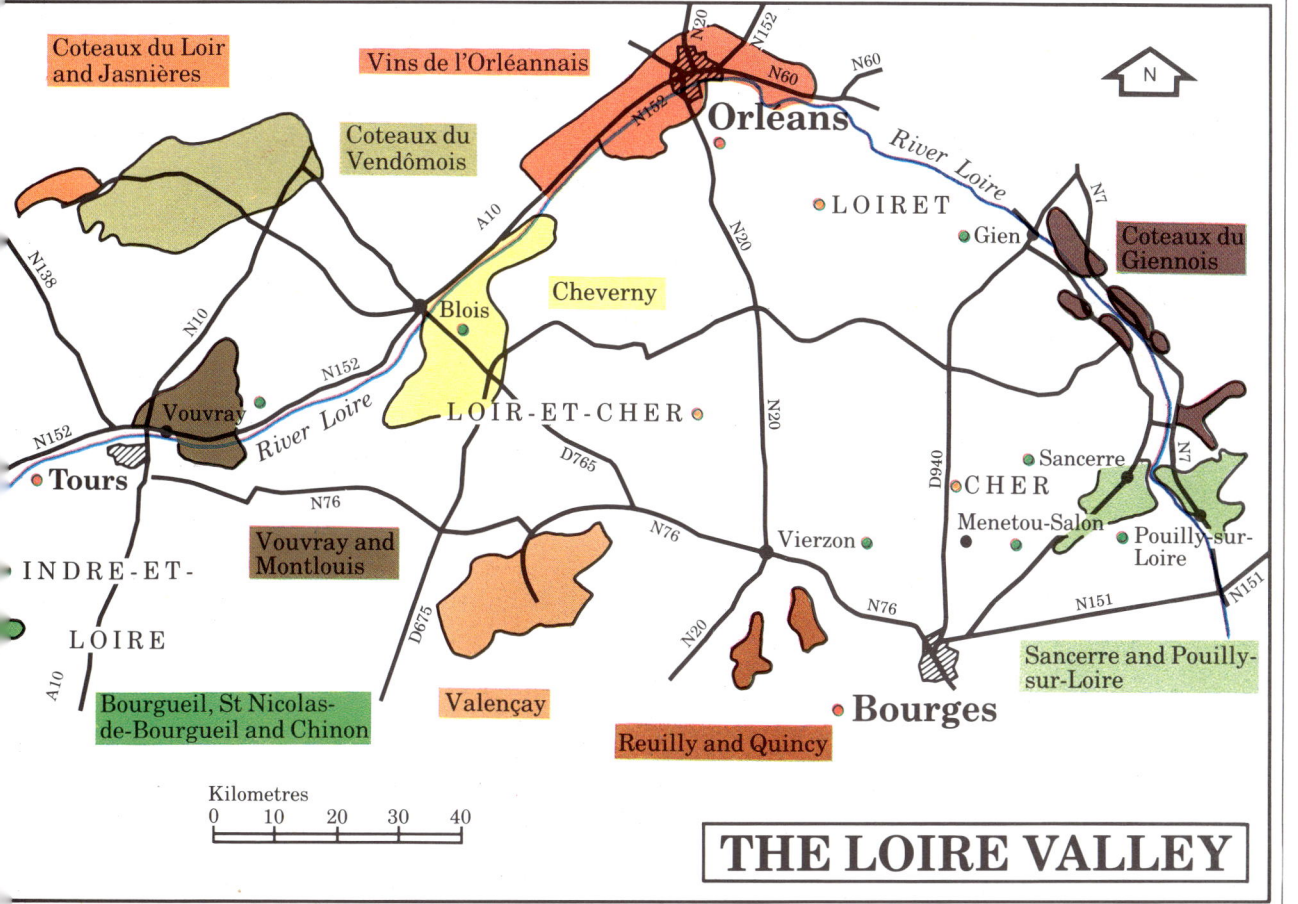

THE LOIRE VALLEY

ENJOYING WINE

Coulée de Serrant

the Cognac region, whose harsh, thin and acidic wine is fine for distillation. Well, here they use it to make Gros Plant – enough said!

ANJOU AND SAUMUR

You either like Anjou Rosé with its sweetish, cloying raspberry-scented style – or you don't. I am in the latter category, although I admit there are a few quality wines worth seeking out. But why bother with all the trial and error when you can choose from Provence with a feeling of relative reliability?

Anjou is by no means only known for its Rosé. Just outside Angers is the tiny Savennières *appellation* perched on steep, slate-covered hillsides. Here the few growers show the rest of the world that the Chenin Blanc grape can actually make elegant dry white wine of real quality. Madame Joly's estate Coulée de Serrant is only 6 ha (15 acres) but has its own *appellation*! The wine is amazing in sheer intensity of flavour, and needs quite a few years of bottle age. Jean Baumard's Clos du Papillon may lack quite the aristocratic style, but is considerably softer, drinkable within two years of the vintage – and much cheaper. He also makes a most attractive, warm Anjou Rouge Logis de la Giraudière, a fragrant Cabernet Franc. This is an excellent choice for blind tasting if you wish to deflate a pompous dinner guest: many countries of the world and regions of France are likely to be considered in the process, but never the Loire. The irrepressible M. Baumard also makes an excellent Sparkling Anjou Rosé Cuvée Coriel but you will have to travel to Savennières to buy a few bottles of this – supply is virtually limited to his closest friends.

Close by in the Coteaux du Layon, the Chenin Blanc produces some luscious sweet dessert wines. All the viticultural and financial problems experienced with the cultivation of *pourriture noble* exist here, as in Sauternes. The growers carry on year after year, despite a general decline of interest in sweet wines. The top villages, Quarts de Chaume and Bonnezeaux, have many estates that produce classy wine with just a hint of dryness at the finish: ideal with fresh fruit or simply on their own. Their unfashionable image has kept the prices down; marvellous for us wine drinkers, but rather tough on such dedicated *vignerons*.

Saumur is best known for high-quality sparkling wine. There is considerable financial interplay between Champagne and here. My favourite Saumur house, Gratien & Meyer, also owns the Alfred Gratien champagne house, and the old-established firm of Langlois-Chateau, which makes some of the most delicate sparkling wine of the area, is owned by Champagne Bollinger.

A considerable amount of still red wine is produced, mainly from the Cabernet Franc. Saumur Rouge and the higher-class Saumur Champigny are pleasant quaffing wines, which always taste better on the banks of the Loire than in the centre of London.

LOIRE

TOURAINE

Now the reds of this area are a totally different story. I loved Chinon, Bourgueil and Saint-Nicolas-de-Bourgueil from my very first visit to the Loire. Here the Cabernet Franc grape produces a totally unique style of wine: light and extroverted, with a delightful full and fragrant fruit flavour, and just a hint of crushed violets. I know this sounds pretentious, but try a bottle and see for yourself. These wines *do* travel well, but the public has been slow in appreciation and therefore the trade has been reluctant purchasers: so you may have to pester your tame wineseller (or write to Yapp Brothers, Mere Wiltshire or O.W. Loeb in London).

Names to look for are Couly-Dutheil, Raymond Desbonides, Charles Joguet, Gratien Ferrant, Gosset's Château de la Grille, Plouzeau & Fils, and Olga Raffault (Chinon); Claude Ammeux, Andebert & Fils, Paul Maître and Lamé-Delille-Boucard (Bourgueil).

Vouvray and Montlouis produce a range of white wines, from dryish through medium to reasonably sweet and rich. They have merits enjoyed by many, but not by me. I much prefer the racy, refreshing Sauvignon de Touraine, the best medium-priced wines of this variety produced in France — especially those from the Confrérie des Vignerons de Oisly et Thésée, the Cave Coopérative Onzain (if you visit be warned that Marcel Chabernaud and his son Dominique treat the continual quality assessment of their own products very seriously and you will be expected to join in and partake of liberal quantities!) and Plouzeau & Fils.

THE UPPER LOIRE

This is *the* specialist Sauvignon Blanc region. Sancerre and Pouilly Blanc Fumé have captured the imagination in particular of restaurateurs and customers alike. High-quality, distinctive white wines produced in reasonable quantities, requiring little bottle ageing, and the cost is not likely to offend the bank manager: the perfect product for today's world! But, do not be misled, as there is much more to these wines than these glib explanations of popularity.

These are my styles of drinking white wine. As opposed to most other Loire wines, they have an attractive, clean style, balancing fresh fruit. In good years the expansive rolling hillsides produce ripe fruit epitomizing the gooseberry quality of the grape, but with a delicacy not found anywhere else (although a few New Zealand and South African estates are beginning to achieve similar results). The Pouilly has the reputation for 'smokiness',

Jean Baumard

ENJOYING WINE

Chinon

LOIRE

hence the name, but it is also often noticeable in Sancerre.

Beware, there is a large amount of poor wine of these *appellations* around, especially after poor vintages. These are normally the wines of the large *négociant* houses, and only the libel laws prevent my naming them and commenting on the standards of their wines. With the exception of the remarkable de Ladoucette wines, it is better to concentrate on grower's wines. There are many top-quality producers whose wines are reasonably accessible: in Sancerre there are H. Bourgeois, Domaine Brouhard, Lucien Crochet, Dezat & Fils, Pierre & Alain Dezat, Marcel Gitton, Alphonse Mellot, Jean Vatan and the remarkable Jean Vacheron, who produces the most delicate, soft style of the region. He is also quite a forthright man who is not afraid to voice his own opinions. He recently described Gros Plant: 'The Folle Blanche grape is OK when used for distilling cognac, but when it is used for wine it is like a coffin for two people: you don't sell one very often!' In Pouilly Maurice Bailly's Les Griottes stands out. Other excellent growers are Patrick Coulbois, Jean-Claude Guyot, Masson Blondelet and Michel Redde.

Before the phylloxera Sancerre was considered a red wine-producing district. After the crisis, however, the growers discovered that the Sauvignon white grape was simpler to graft on to the American rootstock, and also the revival was more rapid this way – so out went the Pinot Noir. It is making quite a comeback, with Sancerre Rouge and Rosé very fashionable in the Parisian restaurants.

Quincy and Menetou-Salon are major areas southwest of Sancerre. Despite certain similarities I find them lacking in grace and as they are not significantly cheaper than other wines from the region, they are not really worth the money.

HAUT - POITOU (VDQS)

Not quite within the Loire Valley region, close to Poitiers. The region must be mentioned as a source of marvellous value single variety wines from the cooperative. The Sauvignon and Chardonnay are most attractive. Try and buy them as young as possible while their freshness and vivacity is still prominent.

CHAPTER THREE

ALSACE

This little gem of a region lies in the northeast corner of France bounded by the Rhine valley in the east and the Vosges mountain ranges in the west. To the north is the Palatinate area of Germany and to the south the Swiss city of Basle. The Germans and French have feuded over this narrow stretch of land. It was part of the German Empire until 1861 and then taken back in 1870 and only returned to France after the First World War. Then Germany held it again from 1940 to 1944. And yet, miraculously, Alsace has retained its unique individuality. A description of the Alsace *route du vin* may sound rather cliché-ridden: 145 km (90 miles) of road winding along the foothills of the Vosges through over 120 villages, many of them straight out of a storybook. Picturesque half-timbered houses, steep spires, cobblestoned streets and, in the warmer months, geraniums simply everywhere: nothing seems to have changed since medieval times. It also looks much more like a part of Germany than of France, with even the signs announcing wine establishments (which seem to be on every second house) mostly in Gothic script.

The region is the southernmost winegrowing part of the Rhine, but is still not particularly hot. However, it is dry as the Vosges mountains protect the area from the rain. Most of the vineyards are on the south- and southeast-facing slopes. The particular climatic balance does not guarantee Alsace consistency of vintages by any means. Few are very poor nowadays, but excellent vintages such as 1976 and 1983 can hardly be said to occur with monotonous regularity.

In Britain the wines are often described as 'the wine trade's white wines'. Many merchants representing the lesser-known houses half-jokingly claim to drink more than they sell! My wine bars and restaurant alone account for 3-4 per cent of the total United Kingdom sales – not a bad effort on my (and my customers') part – but despite enthusiasm and constant promotion, it should not be possible for me ever to achieve this proportion. Wine writers have continually enthused over the attractiveness of the wines and there is a remarkable consistency of quality. (Since 1972 Alsace has been the only *appellation* to insist on the wines being bottled in the region of production.) They do not suffer from long-winded, unpronounceable names, and they are not expensive. Why the poor sales?

I think the problem is the understandable confusion in the public's mind as to what style of wine to expect. A large percentage of wine drinkers think they are going to receive a bottle of sweetish white wine, more in the German style. Also, many wine drinkers' first experience of Alsace wine is likely to be the no-compromise Gewürztraminer, which people either love or hate – now, if they were to be introduced via a bottle of young, fresh Pinot Blanc things might turn out differently.

The Alsace winegrower basically uses the French techniques of making dry white wines by fermenting out all the natural sugar, but this is combined with the acidity and fruitiness of the Rhineland wines. Unlike the other major French *appellations*, the wines are sold under the names of the grape varieties, instead of place of origin. These wines must contain 100 per cent of the named variety, and there are seven such varieties.

RIESLING

The aristocrat of Alsace wine. The latest ripener of all, it is only the well-sited vineyards that produce these fine, elegant and rather austere wines. The cooperatives' and growers' wines listed in most

ALSACE

Riquewihr

cheaper local and Parisian restaurants are light and fresh, and for immediate consumption. Others, usually from the larger houses, require time to show their worth. I recently drank a magnum of Hugel Réserve Personelle from the excellent 1953 vintage – still full of life and flavour!

GEWÜRZTRAMINER

The Traminer variety originated in the village of Tramin in the Italian South Tyrol and was taken to Germany in the Middle Ages. There it was cloned and the *Gewürz* (which means 'spice' in German) was added, transforming a dullish, average grape into something unique, the most easily recognizable variety in the world. This is the great speciality of Alsace: intensely perfumed, a depth of spice and fruit flavour which hints at sweetness, and yet the wine is bone dry with a crisp, clean finish. It is the perfect accompaniment to the rich German-style food of the region – and it is also ideal with Asian food.

TOKAY D'ALSACE (PINOT GRIS)

The name is confusing and has nothing whatsoever to do with Hungarian Tokay. The EEC condemned the name and demanded the use of Pinot Gris, but little has been done about it as yet. The people of Alsace seem to be working on the principle that if they ignore it for long enough, it will be forgotten! It is rich, full-bodied and high in alcohol – my least favourite Alsace white.

MUSCAT

Another unique beauty, reeking with raisiny

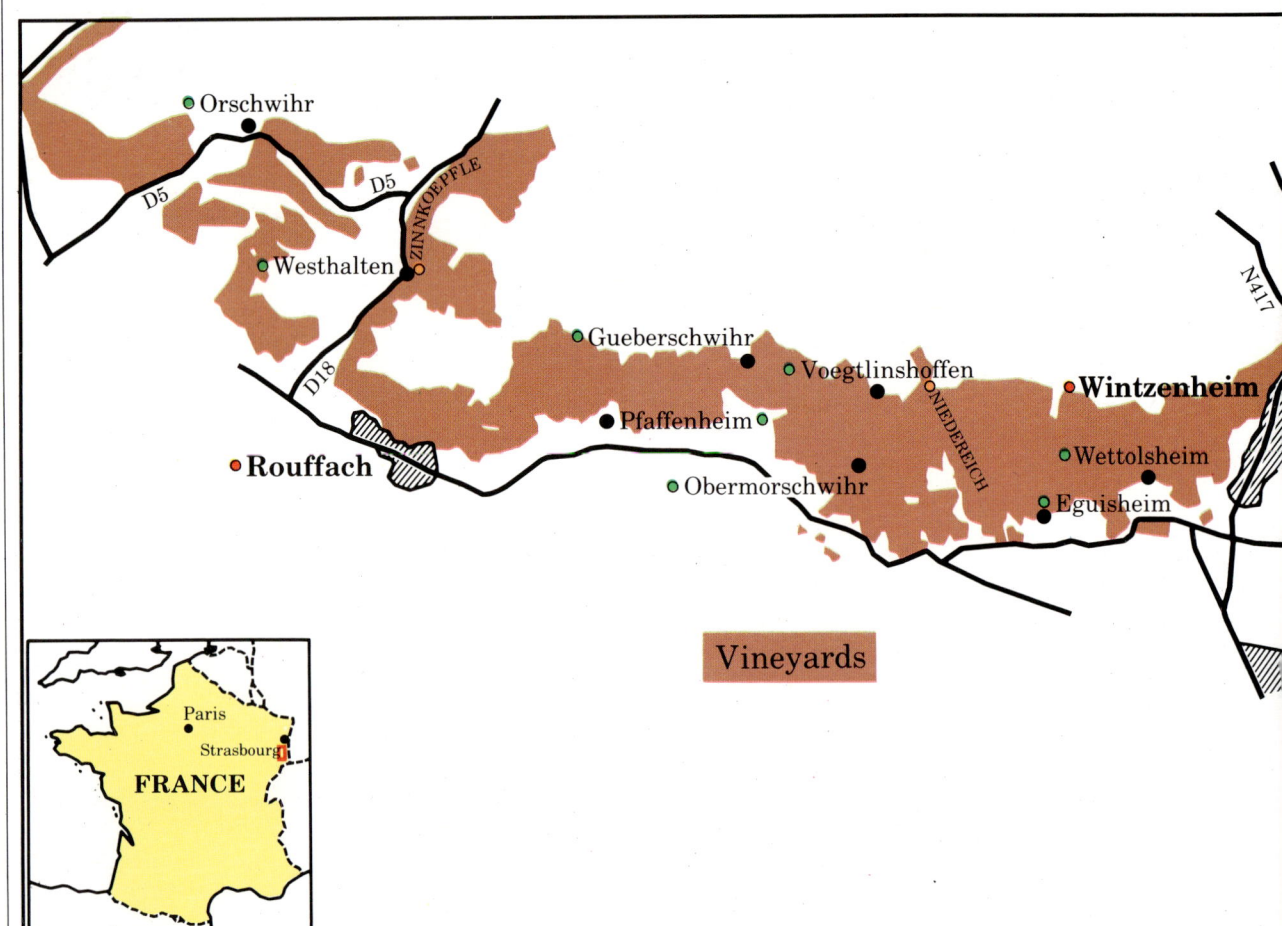

bouquet and flavour, and yet totally dry: an excellent aperitif wine.

PINOT NOIR

Well, as I keep saying, this grape just does not like travel. A comparatively recent arrival to the region, and unfortunately plantings are increasing. The wine is light, almost a rosé, but really is of interest value only. The *vignerons* are most circumspect when discussing the increase in favour; a few have been quite candid and admitted that it is the easiest of all to sell to the huge German tourist market seeking red wine of any description to take home.

PINOT BLANC

Delicious drinking wine. The best of this variety are fresh and fruity with a soft finish, ideal with or without food. These attractions have never really caught on in the export markets, therefore the wine is always relatively inexpensive – the best buy from Alsace.

SYLVANER

The workhorse grape of the region and the most widely planted, accounting for ever 20 per cent of Alsace wines. At times, especially with smaller producers lacking up-to-date equipment, the wine can be fat and a little flabby, but much of the production is racy, instantly appealing, quaffing wine. Léon Beyer makes particularly good wine from this grape.

There is another name common to the restaurants and *winstubs* of Alsace, but one rarely seen

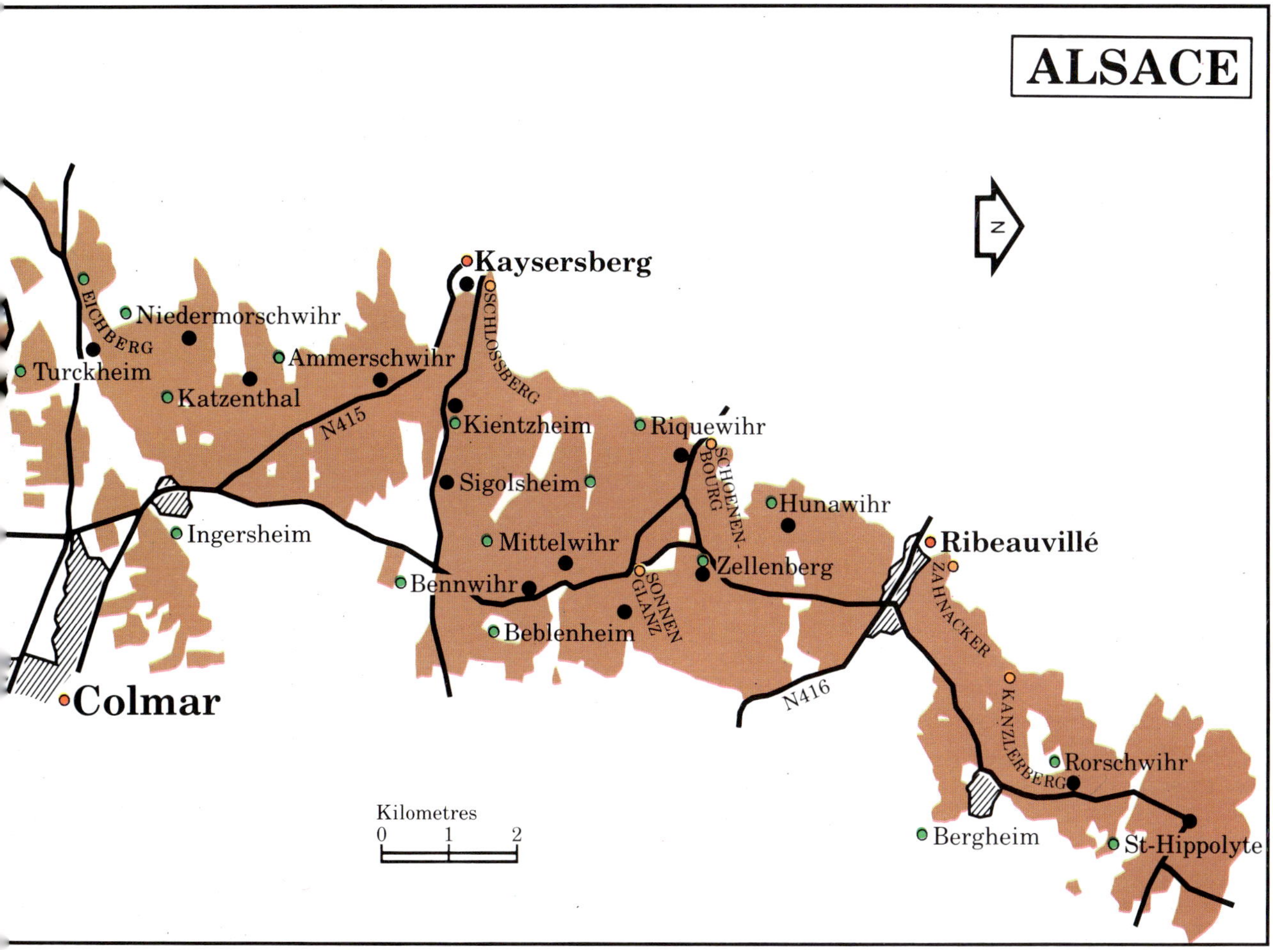

ENJOYING WINE

ALSACE GASTRONOMY

The cooking of Alsace is a by-product of all the historical tug of wars, combining the delicacy of French cuisine and the robustness of German. *Foie gras*, frog's legs, Choucroute Alsacienne, Onion Tart, Baeckeofe, Kougelhopf: the list is endless. Any serious chef, amateur or professional, should possess a copy of the excellent *The Cuisine of Alsace* by Pierre Gaertner and Robert Frederick.

There are superb 'Grand' restaurants: Emile Jung's Le Crocodile in Strasbourg; the Haeberlins' Auberge de L'Ill at Illhaeusern; Schillinger in Colmar and Gaertner's Aux Armes de France at Ammerschwihr.

There are also hundreds of less formal establishments serving delicious everyday fare on the *route du vin*. I normally stay right in the heart of the vineyards at the charming Hotel Arnold at Itterswiller – Telephone (88) 85.51.18.

Strasbourg has many reasonable central hotels and a wealth of restaurants. The *winstubs* are a must. Totally different to even their counterparts as close as Colmar: crowded, noisy, fun places where everyone crams around the tables drinking the jugs of Edelzwicker and eating Gruyère salad, Baked Ham *en croûte* and the superb Tarte Flambée.

---

outside the region: Edelzwicker, a blend of two or more varieties, usually Chasselas and Sylvaner. I consider it by far and away the best carafe white of France. It is normally served extremely young and with a slight, lively prickle on the tongue. I have tried having it bottled and shipped to the United Kingdom the February following vintage, but it just does not taste the same.

Obviously with such limited nomenclature, the name on the label is all important. Vineyard ownership is even more fragmented than in Burgundy. There are so many growers that even the French Government statistics do not tally. It would seem that around 10,000 is an approximate number, of whom only 25 per cent own more than 1 ha (2½ acres)! The cooperatives and large *négociant* houses play a tremendously important role in the socio-economic structure of the region. The cooperatives sell 25 per cent of the total production, and therefore are more important than in many other French wine regions. There are some of considerable repute, particularly for certain wines. Beblenheim makes particularly fragrant and fruity Pinot Blanc; the Eguisheim cooperative is the largest wine establishment in Alsace and its *méthode champenoise* Crémant d'Alsace is most agreeable; Turckheim makes excellent Gewürztraminer. It is rare to find Alsace growers' wines outside France. If you manage to find bottles from Cattin, Faller, Klipfel, Muré, Schleret or Sick Dreyer – grab them!

It is the *négociant* houses, many of whom are also considerable vineyard proprietors, who are responsible for 50 per cent of all Alsace wine and a much more considerable percentage of all exports. Over the years I have consumed more than my fair share of these wines and I have come to appreciate three houses in particular.

LÉON BEYER (Eguisheim)

Established since 1580. Any frequenter of the top restaurants of France will need no introduction: this is very much the prestigious house within France and deservedly so. I adore, in particular, its fragrant Pinot Blanc and steely Riesling Cuvée des Escaillers: not the cheapest wines at any part of the range, but with such delicacy that you do not quibble about the extra few francs.

Léon (left) and Marc Beyer

DOPFF AU MOULIN (Riquewihr)

I am not belittling Pierre and Pierre Etienne Dopff's reputation when claiming that one of the most interesting aspects of this house is that, in my opinion, it produces the best sparkling wine outside Champagne: the Crémant d'Alsace Cuvée Julien. Earlier this century Julien Dopff spent some time in Champagne and returned to inaugurate the production of *méthode champenoise* Crémant from Pinot Noir and Pinot Blanc. The Riesling Schoenenberg and Gewürztraminer Eichberg are superb examples of these grapes at their finest: the house is the largest proprietor in both these top vineyards. A word of warning: I always consider Dopff au Moulin's wines to need a little more bottle age than is normal for Alsace.

HUGEL (Riquewihr)

The name for Alsace around the world – whether you are in Melbourne, Miami or Manila, if you ask for a bottle of Alsace it will invariably be Hugel. This remarkable state of affairs is due to the excellence of the firm's wines, and also the sheer force of the extroverted, amiable personalities of the late 'Papa' Hugel and his son Johnnie, who have continually preached the gospel of Alsace around the world – also ensuring the due prominence of their name. Johnnie quotes his father: 'Since 1923 we have no longer sold, for example, simply Riesling, but only Riesling Hugel to make the consumer understand that there is a world of difference between an anonymous riesling and a fine elegant and typical Riesling Hugel. We have thus followed the Champagne tradition by accentuating the name of the producer, who is responsible for the quality of his wines.'

Hugel's basic wines are all classy; the Pinot Blanc seems to become a wine of superior status. Its Grand Cru wines, especially the Gewürztraminer Réserve Personelle, are wonderfully rich and full. Hugel's outstanding reputation has been enhanced by the attention paid to the limited and only occasional *vendange tardive* (*Auslese*) and *sélection des grains nobles* (*Beerenauslese*) wines.

There are a number of other houses that I class just below the top three: Boeckel, Louis Gisselbrecht, Willy Gisselbrecht & Fils, Kuentz-Bas, Jos. Meyer & Fils who makes a particularly fine Gewürztraminer Les Archenents, Schlumberger the largest of vineyard owners, Trimbach and Zind-Humbrecht.

Johnnie Hugel

CHAPTER FOUR

BORDEAUX

Claret, the Englishman's wine. The tradition dates back to the 12th and 13th centuries when Bordeaux was an English possession. When the English were booted out in 1453, a certain amount of trade disruption followed and restrictive tariffs on French wine led to the growth in sales of Portuguese wine, much to the detriment of claret (the Scots, still an independent nation then, were not so silly – they continued to import vast quantities). But there was still a liking for claret and despite the ups and downs over the centuries, the tradition of claret drinking continued. Life was not too bad for the Bordeaux merchants, many of whom were of British descent. The Napoleonic Wars, preferential duties in Britain for Empire wines, the phylloxera – all these problems came and went, and the Bordeaux trade continued to thrive.

The 20th century brought the inevitable problems common to the other fine wine growing districts of Europe: the Depression and two world wars. By the 1950s the Bordeaux trade was in a bad way: its major customers were recovering from war, the estates were run down and the growers were unable to command realistic prices. February 1956 to the *bordelais* is what 1929 is to Wall Street – a time to be remembered for ever. A relatively warm January had allowed the sap in the vines to begin to rise, and then absolutely devastating February frosts with temperatures down to −20° killed the plants. Some estates were totally wiped out, and the careful ageing of vines and the grape variety balance was destroyed in others. Many owners simply ploughed in their vines and farmed other crops on their land; some merely walked away, never to return. This created obvious problems, but there were rewards that helped gear the region up for the 1960s. The poor, miniscule vintages over the successive years caused a stock shortage and did at least lead to rising prices for the lesser estates, bringing them to something approaching a reasonable return on their outgoings.

The 1960s were great years for the top châteaux as they commanded prices undreamed of a couple of years previously. The rest of the world (particularly the United States) suddenly caught on to what the English had known for the last couple of centuries – the bigger, better estates of the 1855 classification did make very expensive wines, but they were worth it! These châteaux have never looked back. However, things were not so good for the lesser châteaux, or growers, who were simply not able to sell their production at realistic prices. There was continual over-production at the lower levels and many growers were subsidized by the

Annotation to map opposite
The region lies on both sides of the Gironde River – the *Left Bank* comprising Médoc, Graves, Sauternes etc. The *Right Bank* is concentrated with the historically isolated 'Libournais'. Libourne was the port of shipment for St-Emilion and Pomerol.

Bordeaux

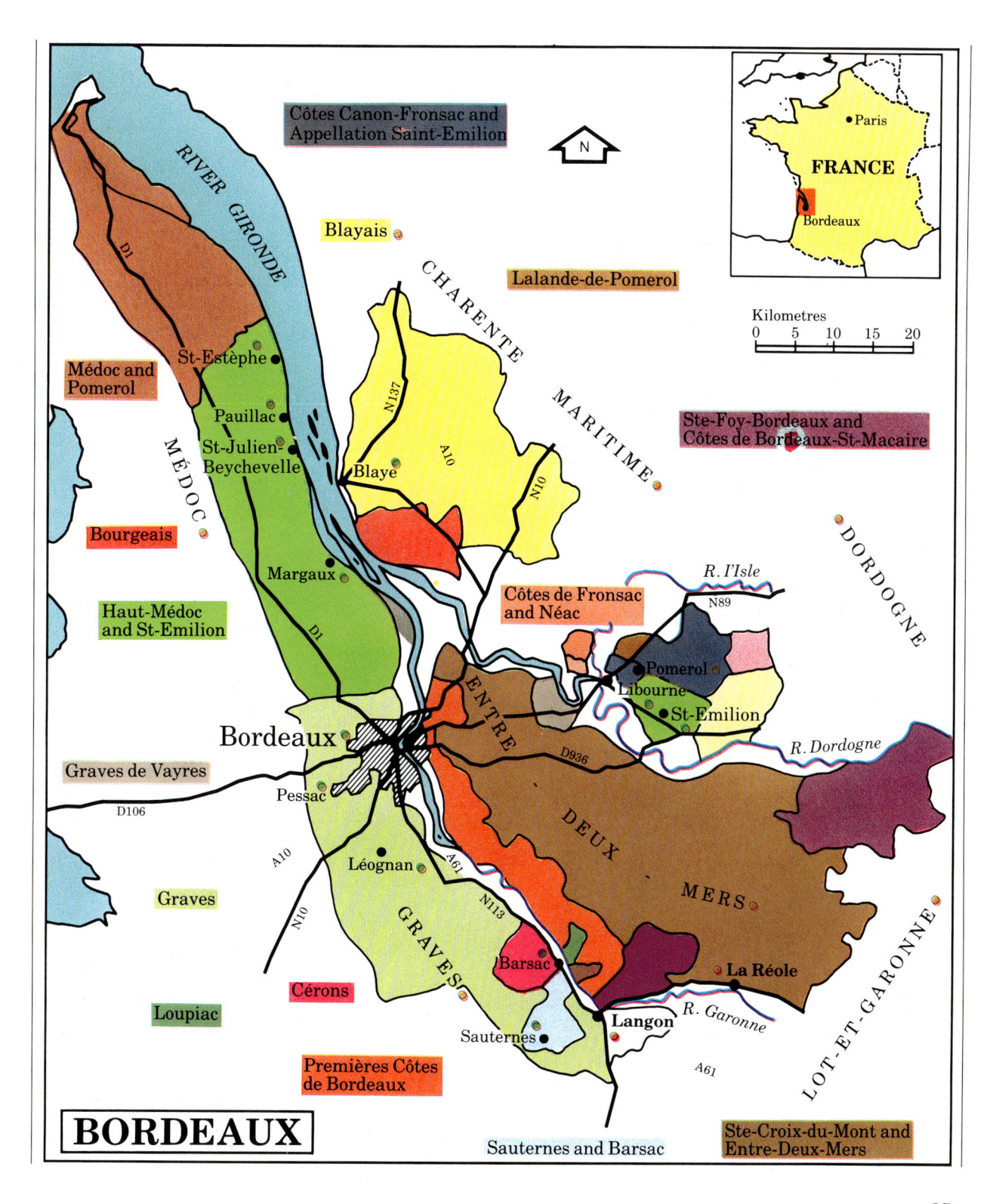

BORDEAUX

Map legend:
- Côtes Canon-Fronsac and Appellation Saint-Emilion
- Blayais
- Lalande-de-Pomerol
- Médoc and Pomerol
- Ste-Foy-Bordeaux and Côtes de Bordeaux-St-Macaire
- Bourgeais
- Haut-Médoc and St-Emilion
- Côtes de Fronsac and Néac
- Graves de Vayres
- Graves
- Loupiac
- Cérons
- Premières Côtes de Bordeaux
- Sauternes and Barsac
- Ste-Croix-du-Mont and Entre-Deux-Mers

Locations: St-Estèphe, Pauillac, St-Julien-Beychevelle, Blaye, Margaux, Bordeaux, Pessac, Libourne, Pomerol, St-Emilion, Léognan, Barsac, Sauternes, Langon, La Réole

Rivers: River Gironde, R. l'Isle, R. Dordogne, R. Garonne

Regions labeled: MÉDOC, CHARENTE MARITIME, ENTRE DEUX MERS, DORDOGNE, GRAVES, LOT-ET-GARONNE

Inset: France, Paris, Bordeaux

Scale: 0–20 Kilometres

ENJOYING WINE

government when they ploughed up their vines. After all, the Bordeaux climate is only marginal with regard to quantity grape growing and there are many other European wine-producing regions better equipped by nature and planted in poorer quality, better cropping varieties, able to produce cheaper, low quality wine – and make a profit.

Many châteaux changed hands and foreign takeovers were commonplace. Even Château Latour was sold to English interests in 1963. Much restructuring of the vineyards and estates took place; some plots were re-established, others transferred title and pedigree and, although purists were sometimes annoyed, this did help the general prosperity of the region. A new breed of château owner emerged, devoted to the pursuit of excellence, and the Bordeaux wine trade began to change.

Previously there was a strictly adhered to social structure of business. The growers and proprietors produced the wine, often keeping a little for themselves, and sold the rest to the Bordeaux *négociants* or merchants. The better quality wines were aged and bottled with the château name; the lesser wines were blended and sold under the shippers' labels. This was the time when names such as Calvet, Cruse, de Luze and Ginestet often meant

The author and Anthony Sargeant with M. and Mme Fougeras, proprietors of Restaurant Le Savoie at Margaux. Comparing Château Tahbilk Cabernet Sauvignon with the local product!

more than the actual *appellation* of the wine. The *négociant* houses were all powerful, and in those days of unrealistically low prices, the only source of finance for wine that needed two years in oak casks alone. The rejuvenation of the estates, mobile bottling lines and higher prices led to a degree of independence for the proprietors previously considered impossible. Some houses (such as Cordier, Eschenauer, J.P. Moueix and Alexis Lichine) still exercise authority – but mostly due to their ownership of important estates.

Now, the future of Bordeaux wines has never looked better, although there are obvious problems. Peter Sichel recently remarked to me, 'We are the only region in a white wine drinking world expanding only red wine production.' If the wine continues to be based on Bordeaux's glorious, intense and rich reds of incomparable quality, I, for one, won't mind!

THE BORDEAUX HIERARCHY

The first important aspect of this region is the definition of 'château'. Châteaux here are not Loire-style palaces with magnificent grounds surrounding a central cellar establishment. The building may be very grand (like Château Margaux), but at the other end of the scale it may just be a collection of functional structures. Some of the medium-sized châteaux are actually more in the normal image, but they are often not even full-time dwellings, merely weekend retreats for absentee owners. Neither are all estates a single conglomeration of vines surrounding the buildings. They may be products of a superior and large-scale version of strip farming: plots, often lying considerable distances apart, with land belonging to other estates in between. For example, Château Prieuré-Lichine, a fifth growth (*cinquième cru*) Margaux (still owned by Alexis Lichine himself, as opposed to everything else with his name which belongs to Bass Charrington, the brewers) has 60 ha (150 acres) spread over 30 plots of land. This, of course, is one of the reasons why the Bordeaux estates show not only regional but also particular characteristics.

There are a host of classifications, patterned on the more rigid class demarcations of society in the previous century, hence such terms as *cru bourgeois*. At the bottom of the spectrum are the *appellation contrôlée* Bordeaux Rouge and Bordeaux Supérieur – the latter being slightly higher in alcohol. These were the quaffing house wines of many better Parisian and British restaurants, but unfortunately they are now being replaced, mostly by more Common Market *vin de table* wines. Agreed these lowly Bordeaux often have an excess of tannin when first sold – that is the nature of the grapes – but at least there is also character, and if the wine has a few months in bottle, it can be as good a buy as any red wine available in Europe.

Petits châteaux are single-estate wines from a varied bunch of *appellations*. Many of these are a result of growers' power and some form part of cooperatives – they are the replacement for the previously widely distributed *négociant*'s blended generic wines. Do not expect too much, but some are excellent. I choose these wines on their *appellation*, as there are too many to try and remember the names. And you are never sure of ever seeing a particular example again. Merchants such as J.T. Davies, a family-owned, London-based claret specialist firm with the 'Davison' shops, tend to follow a château year in year out. If you find a few of these *petits châteaux* you like – follow them!

The lesser *appellations* in many cases involve the *petits châteaux*. Côtes de Blaye, Côtes de Bourg and Premiers Côtes de Bordeaux are in existence on their own geographical terms. Others of them are less favoured surrounding regions of higher class *appellations*, such as Lalande de Pomerol and six versions of St-Emilion – Lussac, Montagne, Barsac, Puisseguin, Sables and St-Georges.

There are two of these lesser *appellations* that stand out as making superior wines, still relatively unrecognized and excellent value for money. The first, Côtes de Castillon, which has recently excited the British wine trade but not, as yet, the customers, is soft, fruity and flavoursome; excellent value as even the better wines, such as Fontenay and de Montdespic, cost little more than Bordeaux Rouge. The second, Fronsac, makes instantly attractive wines. More Cabernet Franc and less time in oak produces a lighter, fruitier, more instantly accessible style. Château Rouet has been exporting for some time but formerly much of the wine was simply sold to the *négociants*. Now more vigorous efforts are being made

ENJOYING WINE

to market the wine in a more positive manner. Much of this dynamism is due to the arrival in 1962 at La Riviera of ex-coffee merchant Jacques Borie, who sees no reason to hide his light under any bushel whatsoever, and has crusaded for his very fine wine in particular, and the Fronsac *appellation* in general. I am sure there are many proprietors in lesser *appellations* who pray for the arrival of such a public relations-orientated dynamo.

THE SUPERIOR APPELLATIONS

THE MÉDOC
The Médoc is divided into six *communes* and is also split into two regions: the area north of St-Estèphe is merely entitled to the *appellation* 'Médoc', whereas the finer producing areas are 'Haut-Médoc'. The region produced the famous 1855

THE 1855 CLASSIFICATION OF RED BORDEAUX OF THE MEDOC

Premiers Crus
Lafite — Pauillac
Margaux — Margaux
Latour — Pauillac
Haut-Brion — Graves
Mouton-Rothschild — Pauillac*

Deuxièmes Crus
Rausan-Ségla — Margaux
Rauzan-Gassies — Margaux
Léoville-Las-Cases — St-Julien
Léoville-Poyferré — St-Julien
Léoville-Barton — St-Julien
Durfort-Vivens — Margaux
Lascombes — Margaux
Gruaud-Larose — St-Julien
Brane-Cantenac — Margaux
Pichon-Longueville — Pauillac
Pichon-Longueville-Lalande — Pauillac
Ducru-Beaucaillou — St-Julien
Cos-d'Estournel — St-Estèphe
Montrose — St-Estèphe

Troisièmes Crus
Kirwan — Margaux
Issan — Margaux
Lagrange — St-Julien
Langoa — St-Julien
Giscours — Labarde
Malescot-St-Exupéry — Margaux
Cantenac-Brown — Margaux
Palmer — Margaux
La Lagune — Ludon
Desmirail — Margaux
Calon-Ségur — St-Estèphe
Ferrière — Margaux

Marquis d'Alesme-Becker — Margaux
Boyd-Cantenac — Margaux

Quatrièmes Crus
St-Pierre-Sevaistre — St-Julien
St-Pierre-Bontemps — St-Julien
Branaire-Ducru — St-Julien
Talbot — St-Julien
Duhart-Milon — Pauillac
Pouget — Margaux
La Tour-Carnet — St-Laurent
Lafou-Rochet — St-Estèphe
Beychevelle — St-Julien
Le Prieuré-Lichine — Margaux
Marquis-de-Terme — Margaux

Cinquièmes Crus
Pontet-Canet — Pauillac
Batailley — Pauillac
Haut Batailley — Pauillac
Grand-Puy-Lacoste — Pauillac
Grand-Puy-Ducasse — Pauillac
Lynch-Bages — Pauillac
Lynch-Moussas — Pauillac
Dauzac — Labarde
Mouton-Baron-Philippe — Pauillac
Le Tertre — Margaux
Haut-Bages-Libéral — Pauillac
Pédesclaux — Pauillac
Belgrave — St-Laurent
Camensac — St-Laurent
Cos-Labory — St-Estèphe
Clerc-Milon-Mondon — Pauillac
Croizet-Bages — Pauillac
Cantemerle — Macau

*A first growth since 1973

Bordeaux

classification of its estates. Denigrators of this effort will always – scathingly – quote the standing of a particular property at the moment in question, forgetting that the rating is an authoritative value judgment based on 19th-century prices and the experienced opinions of 20th-century Bordeaux wine traders.

St-Estèphe is the largest of the Médoc *appellations*. In many ways it presents the image of Bordeaux: acre after acre of non-stop vineyards. Châteaux are dotted all over the area. The wine itself is the least consistent; notice how few St-Estèphes are in the classified growths – Margaux and St-Julien each have as many in second growths alone. The wines lack quite the intense flavour or unique style of the other three: but do not ever let this persuade you to turn down a bottle of Cos d'Estournel or Calon Ségur!

Château d'Issan

ENJOYING WINE

Anthony Sargeant outside Le Moulin de Margaux

Pauillac, home of three of the five first growths: very rich, full-bodied and, of course, aristocratic (if you are fortunate enough to drink a bottle of mature Château Latour you will approve of this term!) It is no disgrace to the others – but when I think of Pauillac, I always relate to the wonderfully perfumed nose of Château Lynch-Bages (often termed 'the claret for Burgundy drinkers'). I cannot think of a non-champagne wine that has given me so much delight over the past 20 years – it rarely disappoints.

St-Julien is my personal favourite of the four major *appellations*. It is the smallest, and yet look at the number of estates in the classification. The overtly attractive fruitiness of the wines is one of the most distinguishing features of Bordeaux. If you do not believe me, try a bottle of Ducru Beaucaillou sometime. If this proves rather expensive, a bottle of the agreeable Gloria will normally show a similar degree of grace.

Margaux The domination of the second and third growths by this *appellation* is sufficient justification of its status. The soil is even more significantly gravelly (*see* illustration p.43), which gives more refined wines enhanced by a pronounced Cabernet content. In the better wines the combination of blackcurrant and a touch of 'cigar box' oak makes Margaux the easiest to spot of the four *appellations*.

Listrac and Moulis In the 1950s the central districts of Listrac and Moulis were added to the four Médoc *appellations*. Things have improved in these regions dramatically as prices have risen. Macaillou and Poujeaux make worthy wines, but the addition of these two regions to the exalted ranks of Médoc *appellations* was rather surprising.

CRU BOURGEOIS OF THE MÉDOC

This is another classification, only finally formalized in 1978 but representing over 30 per cent of the Médoc *appellation* wine production. Some châteaux, for example Caronne-Ste-Gemme (Haut-Médoc), Cissac (Haut-Médoc), Chasse-Spleen (Moulis), Fourcas-Hosten (Listrac), Larose-Trintaudon (Médoc), La Tour de By (Médoc), La Tour St-Bonnet (Médoc), Malescasse (Haut-Médoc), Meynay-St-Estèphe and the already-mentioned Gloria, make excellent quality wines. Some are more modest in their achievements. The rising prices of the classified growths discussed above have now passed on to these wines, but this is not a disadvantage. The better estates have spent realistic sums on replanting and re-equipping and are now being allowed a selective approach to winemaking. These wines are no longer bargains, but the enthusiastic wine lover can still afford to experiment without a phone call to the bank manager.

ST-EMILION

The major right bank *appellation* – in fact its production is larger than that of the Médoc! The most significant difference is that here the Merlot grape produces an aromatic, soft, round, velvety wine at ease in the present-day market with its demands for early maturing, almost instantly attractive wines. It is not that the St-Emilion wines do not benefit from ageing: it is simply that they do not need years and years before showing off their more attractive qualities. The estates of St-Emilion are large and self-contained, not the subdivided plots of the Médoc, but confusion is allowed to reign as there are various estates with similar names: there are four prominent variations of 'Corbin'.

There is a classification, established in 1954, which differs dramatically from Médoc: continual reassessment is one element of it and regular tastings are part of the evaluation. Demotion is not a frequent occurrence. The shock waves lasted for months in early 1985 when it happened to one of the most expansion-orientated properties: Château Beauséjour-Bécot.

There are now eleven St-Emilion 'Premier' *grands crus classés*. Two are in the superior 'A' division – Ausone and Cheval Blanc; nine in the 'B' division – Beauséjour (Duffan-Lagarosse), Bel-Air, Canon, Clos Fourtet, Figeac, La Gaffelière, Magdelaine, Pavie and Trottevielie.

None of these wines are cheap! But they are all relevant ratings of the very best from the region. There are 65 *grands crus classés*, including the redoubtable Canon-la-Gaffelière and Troplong Mondot. An interesting selection of estate wines is marketed through the Association de Propriétaires des Grands Crus Classés de Saint-Emilion. The group's labels bear an easily recognizable red, gold and yellow seal.

POMEROL

A tiny region, smaller in vineyard acreage than St-Julien. Once again the Merlot grape is to the fore, producing concentrated yet early ripening wines. These are the wines I like to put up against the cool climate Californian and Coonawarra (South Australia) wines; they have in common a lack of total finesse and blind tasting becomes even more difficult!

Pomerols are rarely inexpensive (note the price of Château Petrus); the estates are small and for historical reasons they have an automatic market in Holland and Belgium. This precludes them from being classed as relatively good value for money. There is no official classification of the châteaux, but Vieux Château Certan, Latour à Pomerol, Lagrange and Nenin de Sales are good examples of the less exalted wines.

GRAVES: RED AND WHITE

This is *the* region to watch. The really average white wines are giving way and this is the only major Bordeaux *appellation* with relatively unknown, excellent reds at considerably lower than average prices. Of course there is the unique Haut-Brion, the only non-Médoc in the Médoc classification. But there is a wealth of style and flavour elsewhere. The wines do need keeping as they begin adult life still rather hard and dumb. I keep them at least three years longer than other Bordeaux, but when the time finally comes and the deep, earthy but smooth wine is in my glass, I consider for once in my life that patience is a virtue! De Fieuzal, Haut-Bailly, Olivier and, of course, the wonderful Pape Clément are outstandingly good value and often half the retail price of a second growth.

SAUTERNES

Botrytis cinerea (*pourriture noble* or 'noble rot') is the great feature of Sauternes: a fungus growth on the grape which concentrates the sweetness, and it does not come easily! Picking has to be done much later to benefit from it and consequently the entire crop is exposed to the dangers of approaching autumnal weather. All parts of the grapes do not automatically receive this rot at the same time, therefore the harvesters will return again and again, carefully picking the affected parts of each bunch. The yield per acre can be as low as 20 per cent that of a Médoc *cru classé*. Unlike most other white wines, Sauternes also has to be aged before sale: and even that is not guaranteed these days. Nor is the price likely to be correspondingly high (d'Yquem is, of course, an exception). The purchase of an estate in this part of Bordeaux is not guaranteed to interest any bank manager, no matter how friendly! Other winemakers in other countries make *Botrytis* wines (Germany in particular, but also California and Australia), but not as a sole source of income, more as an added bonus.

The Sauternes *appellation* consists of five *communes*: Sauternes, Barsac, Bommes, Preignac and Fargues. The grapes are two-thirds Sémillon and one-third Sauvignon. In no region of Bordeaux is the variation from château to château so apparent as here, where obviously ruthlessly high and often uneconomic standards dictate a small production – and some estates just cannot afford to be quite so self-critical as others. These wines were also classified in 1855 with d'Yquem (Sauternes) in solitary, well-deserved splendour as *grand premier cru classé*. Suduiraut (Preignac), Coutet (Barsac), Climens (Barsac) and Rieussec (Fargues) are my favourite *premiers crus classés*, closely followed by Doisy-Daëne (Barsac), Filhot (Sauternes) and Nairac (Barsac) in the *deuxièmes crus classés*.

These sweet wines do not necessarily need a dessert course; it is fashionable (and delightful) to serve them as accompaniment to *pâté de foie gras* or with the cheeseboard, when there are tangy blue cheeses.

SELECTED BORDEAUX ESTATES

The Bordeaux wine trade constantly talks about estates 'on the way up'. Obviously the problems of producing relatively small quantities of good wine in such a climate involve financial expense that must be matched with high standards. Many properties have varied considerably in the recent past; often they have been shuttled from owner to owner and have suffered. Others have received much needed devoted care and financial attention; some have simply carried on the excellent standards of the past: here are a few of my favourites... some 'household names'; others anything but.

CHÂTEAU LANGOA-BARTON (St-Julien, troisième cru)

It is impossible to talk about this property without including the second growth Léoville-Barton. Although both are totally independent wines from different parts of the *commune*, they are made virtually side by side at Langoa. The estates are owned by one of the grand old men of the Bordeaux wine trade, Ronald Barton, now in his eighties and still flourishing.

In the early 1800s relative peace and stability allowed merchants to start buying up estates, and one of the first to do so was Hugh Barton, the Irish-born partner in Barton and Guestier (now owned by Seagrams), who acquired Langoa in 1822. A portion of the Léoville estate was bought later (the rest was divided into Les Cases and

Poyferré). Over the years the Bartons have kept their Irish nationality, and the château is a delightful blend of the family's countries of adoption and origin. On the reception room table at a recent visit were all the usual magazines, such as *Cuisine et Vins de France, Gault Millau*, but also a pictorial book *Eton Days*!

Ronald Barton is a painstaking craftsman, worried about the fact that 'we are now in an instant world that is beginning to want instant Cabernet Sauvignon'. We were tasting a range of wines from both estates: they were stunning with the intensely fruity, blackcurrant style of St-Julien at its best. The 1984 was surprisingly good and when I remarked to Ronald that the *Daily Telegraph* had printed an article totally writing off that vintage as early as August, he replied, 'How could they possibly know the result two months before picking?' The 1982 and 1983 from the two estates were different in style, but equal in excellence. The real surprise was the high standard of the poorly regarded 1980 vintage – soft and flavoursome. To achieve this standard the estate discarded over a quarter of the total crop. The 1978 vintages were still closed and unyielding, but the fruit was all there – just a matter of time. Ronald went back to his complaint: 'You have to wait for Bordeaux – don't change the blend to suit the people. Tell the people what Bordeaux is all about, and they will wait.'

CHÂTEAU D'ANGLUDET (Margaux)

Peter Sichel has owned this Margaux property since 1961. It was formerly much larger, but when the 1956 frosts took their toll, half of the estate was sold to Château Brane-Cantenac and the other half to Sichel; he now has 30 ha (74 acres) under vine with another 5 ha (12 acres) still to be replanted. The grapes are 50 per cent Cabernet Sauvignon, 35 per cent Merlot, 5 per cent Cabernet Franc and 10 per cent Petit Verdot.

The Sichel family has been steeped in wine, both in Rhineland Mainz and in Bordeaux, and the family tradition of excellence is carried on at d'Angludet. In the early days of ownership, experimental grafting was carried out, but it did not turn out to be totally successful and the estate was therefore replanted at a leisurely pace. I was fortunate enough to be the first outsider to taste the wines from the 1984 vintage before final blending (Sichel waits longer than many: 'You can add to a blend, but you can't take out – therefore it is preferable to wait for developments'). Some of the wine was very good indeed, loads of fruit and tannin, but other casks to be rejected were sharp and sour by comparison. As he said, 1984 would not exactly be a lucrative year for d'Angludet with only 60 per cent of the 1983 harvest produced and, in order to maintain standards, he would be eliminating 40 per cent of that 60 per cent harvest. Obviously the temptation is there to add casks that are not totally poor, but would lower the standard. As Peter Sichel says, 'The grower's economics dictate the wine standards, not the other way around.'

It is a serious criticism of the 1855 classification that such a château should have no status whatsoever. Sichel does not consider d'Angludet a *cru bourgeois* and therefore prefers to remain 'unaligned'.

New vines in Margaux – note the gravel soil

CHÂTEAU LA GARDE (Montillac, Graves)

The firm of Eschenauer was established in 1821 and was one of the first of the major *négociants*. In

ENJOYING WINE

the 20th century the house has had its ups and downs, including the imprisonment of the chairman for collaboration with the occupying Germans. In 1960 Eschenauer sold out to a British company, which promptly set about restoring the estates and promoting the name of the firm – as much as the actual wine. 'Eschenauer' was emblazoned in bold letters on the labels, even of estate wines. Later on it became part of Tiny Rowland's multinational Lonrho empire (once described by Conservative Prime Minister Edward Heath as 'the unacceptable face of capitalism'). Perhaps this progression does not sound particularly wine-orientated, but the inescapable fact is that the company had been heavily fined by the postwar French government and the previous financial stability had disappeared. Considerable investment was needed – and has been provided over the past 25 years.

Much of Eschenauer's reputation has been re-created with its properties in Graves. Château Smith-Haute-Lafitte had been a large-selling sole distribution concern since 1902, but this large estate with 47 ha (116 acres) of vines was only bought for Eschenauer in 1960. The wine has improved immeasurably since the takeover and can now be classed as one of the better wines of the region.

Château La Garde (owned since 1926) is larger at 67 ha (166 acres), and does not possess the same

Peter Sichel at Château d'Angludet

historic reputation. It has only been developed since the 1960 takeover: new vineyards have been planted giving 12 per cent of the production as a white wine with a distinct Sauvignon character. A magnificent underground cellar was built in 1974, one of the largest in Bordeaux with a capacity for 2000 casks. The wine is not particularly refined, but possesses a wonderful earthy fruitiness that softens and becomes quite velvety with age. Not expensive, it is excellent value and well worth searching out.

CHÂTEAU LABÉGORCE-ZÉDÉ (Margaux)
Georges Thienpont, a wealthy Belgian wine merchant, bought Vieux Château Certan in 1924, thereby beginning a new family business tradition. Now a nephew, Luc, owns LaBégorce-Zédé and has rescued a declining reputation. Nothing has been done on the cheap at Zédé. There is a predominance of new oak barrels in a modern, functional cellar (the first year's ageing), and that is not cheap: each barrel now costs over £170. This is followed by rigid selection and ageing in vats for a second year, and the end result is a perfumed, elegant and complex wine. 'A *grand cru classé* wine at *petit bourgeois* price', says Luc. I would not quite agree with his description of the estate's prices, but cannot deny that here is a rising star among the 'non-aligned' estates which deserves recognition somewhere in some classification.

Luc Thienpont and family at Château LaBégorce-Zédé

ENJOYING WINE

CHÂTEAU CANON (St-Emilion, *premier grand cru classé*)
At the risk of inciting civil disobedience, I urge you to buy, beg steal or 'borrow' a bottle or two of the 1982 Canon: a remarkable wine from a remarkable vintage. I have drunk many bottles of many different years of this wine and rarely been disappointed. It is not the most subtle of Bordeaux, but the finest qualities of St-Emilion are apparent – instant warmth and a deep plummy character. Yet it does not quite command the price of better-known St-Emilions of similar classification.

CHÂTEAU DAUZAC (Margaux, *cinquième cru*)
Not one of the best-known estates of Margaux, but as yet it is not one that commands a particularly high price – that is still to come. M. Chatellier purchased Dauzac in 1978 and has spent a large amount of money restoring a rather tired old estate. A few years ago I spent some time in Margaux and brokers, managers and vineyard workers were all talking about the vineyard improvements. M. Chatellier also paid attention to the winemaking and employs the consultant oenological genius of Bordeaux, Professor Emile Peynaud. Beautifully maintained vineyards, newly restored cellar buildings and classically structured, beautifully balanced Margaux wine is the 1980s image of Dauzac.

Finally three 'lesser wines', chosen out of hundreds tasted in the past five years: right up-to-date assessments.

CHÂTEAU LE BOSCQ (St-Estèphe, *cru bourgeois*)
I was a member of the Beaujolais jury at the 1984 Paris Concours Agricole and first tasted this estate, the 1982 vintage, while looking at the gold medal winners from Bordeaux. Le Boscq is a very masculine wine, characterized by intense colour with a solid fruit flavour. M. Durand uses a higher

Château Coutet, left to right 1918, 1934, 1937, 1952, 1971. Note the difference in colours.

BORDEAUX

Phillip Durand of Château Le Boscq

percentage of Merlot than most, yet makes a wine totally different to the right (Libournais) bank. (The actual content varies from year to year on most estates. For example, the 1979 vintage at Le Boscq provided very mature, superbly flavoured Merlot, but not such good quality Cabernet Sauvignon. So, although Durand's vines are only 40 per cent Merlot, this year there was actually a 60 per cent content in the wine.) The property covers only 15 ha (37 acres), therefore it is not exactly easy to find, but he does sell to the United Kingdom trade.

CHÂTEAU TOUR DES TERMES (St-Estèphe, *cru bourgeois*)
An ambitious estate run by Jean Anney and his son, who are 'ploughing their profits back into the vineyard', according to Philippe Dourthe. There

47

are 25 ha (62 acres) growing 55 per cent Cabernet Sauvignon, making a lighter, more fragrant style than Le Boscq. The 1982 was very forward and attractive three years on, whereas the Le Boscq was still totally dumb with intense flavour (Durand harvested later than his neighbours that year). The 1979 was drinking beautifully. Definitely a château to watch – the wines are getting better year by year.

CHÂTEAU HAUT-BERGEY (Léognan, Graves) M. Deschamps makes consistently good wine on a small 13 ha (32 acre) estate (70 per cent Cabernet, 30 per cent Merlot) – once again proving the marvellous value obtained by the keen lover of Bordeaux who searches through the lesser-known wines of Graves. The wine is available in the United Kingdom at a reasonable cost: laying down a few cases of this would not be a bad investment.

ANTHONY SARJEANT

An Englishman based in Bordeaux on and off for the past 25 years, with no previous family trade connections in the region, is unusual. Especially when the years away from Bordeaux were spent in the United States buying and selling French wine (Bordeaux in particular), first as representative of Dourthe Frères and later as managing director of the all-powerful Wildman Company in New York.

Times were good then, with vast sales of top-class Bordeaux and Burgundy all over the States and frequent Atlantic commuting by Concorde. But all good things come to an end and a combination of market collapse and the realization that he was burning himself out led to Sarjeant's opting out of Manhattan and returning to 'Le Moulin' in Margaux: he established a broker's business with all sights set on the British market. In the past few years Sarjeant has become one of the big suppliers to the 'traditional' wholesalers and retailers. He is the middleman with the time, energy and ability to liaise between Burgundian and Bordeaux growers on the way up, and guarantee them a market at the right price, close to home and reliable (it is no secret that the effects of inflation and recession have ravaged the home market for the better wines from both regions).

It all began with his own two wines, La Mouline Médoc and Sauvignon Trois Moulines: the former is a sound, attractive, everyday claret which improves with bottle age (to sound rather perverse, in my opinion that is a criticism of an everyday wine); but it is the latter that has really made an impact. Over 20,000 cases were sold in 1984 (no doubt rather insignificant compared to Mouton Cadet, but still quite an achievement). The wine owes more to the owner's California experience than to Bordeaux. It is a crisp and straightforward varietal style with none of the flabbiness and sulphur problems of most white Bordeaux. Sarjeant terms it the 'poor man's Sancerre'. Its zippy, gooseberry fragrance and style with an appealing fruit–acid balance at a relatively cheap price highlights the potential of white wines from the region.

Obviously this is an excellent long-term plan, but why take on all the problems of production right at the beginning? After all, 'brokering' is actually avoiding all of this part of the wine business. He is quite succinct.

'I am not going to spend the next twenty years building a succession of other people's brands – loyalty is a rare commodity in the Bordeaux wine trade. The estate owner will be delighted if you develop a market for his wine. The trouble is that in the Bordeaux trade most agreements are tenuous and he will blithely ignore your past work and promptly sell to the very first person that comes along offering a higher price!

'And, it is not just the châteaux owners; the growers have been notoriously fickle over the years. Nicholas Faith gives a good example in his book. Years ago Henri Martin of Château Gloria persuaded a *négociant* friend to guarantee his grower contacts a future sale of their wines and better prices so they could improve their product. What happened? The growers thought this guaranteed market was a wonderful way in which to pass off even poorer wines at these higher prices.'

His good and erstwhile employer, Philippe Dourthe, has 'formalized the selling of non-glamour estates' (with the 1982 establishment of a cooperative Des Propriétaires de Châteaux du Bordelais, twenty or so select growers working within the

Philippe Dourthe operation). According to Sarjeant, 'These estates guarantee both prices and wine and their carefully conceived joint marketing operation has performed satisfactorily in France, but has achieved particular success abroad selling to the less sophisticated markets which previously thought of Bordeaux as only the most expensive of red wine.' Sarjeant is trying to achieve a similar operation to Dourthe, not getting involved in the expensive end of the market (as opposed to his Burgundy activities). 'The superstar estates look after themselves, their sales are guaranteed. The Union des Grands Crus travels the world spreading the gospel of their own châteaux – but not of Bordeaux.'

The future Bordeaux sales expansion, according to the Anthony Sarjeant gospel, is with the smaller estates operated by 'people who calculate the price of their wine on a basis of cost and required profit. I am tired of hearing the most overworked phrase in Bordeaux, "Mon voisin il a gagné" [My neighbour has received]. Much of the world has forgotten Bordeaux as a source of good value drinking wine – bottles for the table, not for merely talking about. We produce vast quantities of reasonably priced, individualistic wine and yet we [the Bordelais] have lacked a unified approach – even the wine writers are forgetting about us!'

Obviously many people will disagree, but it cannot be denied that the Sarjeant formula is working for his own operation, and that thousands and thousands of British wine drinkers are being introduced to both his own Mouline wines, plus these smaller estates.

SECOND WINES

Second wines were previously a *bordelais* secret, but now they are becoming extremely well known and therefore possibly open to rather too much commercial exploitation. These wines were the products of 5- to 8-year-old vines, difficult casks and wines almost, but not quite, up to the high standards of the *crus classés*. In the old days they were sold to *négociants* for generic wines or blending purposes. Now they are often given care and attention worthy of major properties, and the wine is of a significant stature.

Ronald Barton casually discusses the discarding of 25 per cent of the 1980 crop. This would have been more disastrous if a certain amount had not been sold as 'Anthony Barton's St-Julien', an excellent wine, well worth the extra cost compared to a straightforward supplier's St-Julien: I should know, I bought as much as I was allowed. Similarly, Château Lascombes has La Gombaude, Lynch-Bages the excellent Haut-Bages Avérous and Pichon-Longueville Lalande has Réserve de Comtesse – and right at the top, and at top prices, there are *Les Forts de Latour* and Pavillon Rouge du Château Margaux.

These wines are *very* good value, while the prices remain relatively low. Unfortunately they are becoming well known and I just 'feel it in my bones' that this publicity and subsequent consumer demand will result in an unjustified price rise: great for the proprietors but bad news for consumers.

RECENT BORDEAUX VINTAGES

Improved viticultural and oenological techniques have eased the problem of many poor vintages, but they still have not reached the dizzy heights of transforming reasonable into great years.

Anthony Barton, Château Langoa-Barton

ENJOYING WINE

1983 and 1982
There is no doubt that these were a remarkable duo of outstanding vintages. Peter Sichel is the only one who claims a similar standard for two other consecutive years – 1928 and 1929 – but this claim does not meet with universal acceptance. The 1982 is the more overtly attractive, with an overwhelming intensity of fruit and character. Prices have escalated since the first sales, yet sales were always buoyant; no doubt a certain percentage of wines will find their way back on to the market when speculators seek to claim their profits via the auction rooms. The 1983 is considered to be excellent and more of a 'true *bordeaux*'. The wines have a similar magnificent concentration of flavour but a slightly less extrovert style: the overall picture is of an outstanding year, which would have had wine writers searching for superlatives – if it had not been preceded by 1982.

1981
In a sense, this vintage is even worse off, comparatively, than the 1983 – this was merely a very good year!

1980
The vintage was totally rejected by the wine trade and yet there was sufficient colour and bouquet in early days to promise better. Wine buyers with independent minds were able to take advantage of very reasonable prices for attractive wines.

1979
Splendid wines (once again, attacked by many – I have never understood why) with a degree of steeliness at the back of the soft, round, ripe fruit flavour.

1978
A very good vintage: classically structured wines destined for a long future.

THE GRAPE VARIETIES

REDS
Cabernet Sauvignon
The grape variety in the region, dominating in Médoc and Graves. Rather condescending in its warmth: it produces over-intense wines in hotter climates, whereas in Bordeaux the wines are almost the opposite of this, being astringent and austere with the need for blending with a softer style, hence the next few varieties.

Merlot
A wonderful variety, generous in both cropping and alcohol – like a favourite daughter, warm-hearted and welcoming. Ripens earlier and therefore there is a greater likelihood of producing wines reeking of ripeness – and that cannot be bad! The dominant variety in St-Emilion and Pomerol.

Cabernet Franc
Planted rather sparingly on the left bank and more prevalent across the Gironde. It produces a lighter wine.

Petit Verdot
Not planted in any quantity but considered a most important element, especially in the Médoc. It is a later-ripening grape which contributes colour, alcohol and acidity.

Malbec
No longer particularly important.

WHITES
Sémillon
An under-achiever for dry white (the wine question of the next few decades is whether this variety will produce good wine anywhere other than Sauternes or the Hunter Valley, Australia).

Sauvignon Blanc
The most important grape for future dry white production. Not the easiest grape to handle, but avoids the sulphury 'old socks' style of traditional regional whites.

CHAPTER FIVE

BURGUNDY

A fascinating region, Burgundy stretches from Chablis in the north, less than 200 km (125 miles) from Paris, right down to Chalon-sur-Saône. When touring this vast region do not expect to see great acreages of vines throughout; as the map shows, wine is cultivated in relatively small, compact pockets of land. Vines were introduced by the Roman legions and later various monastic orders promoted their cultivation. The expansionist 14th- and 15-century Dukes of Valois were able to extend the Burgundian domains to the borders of the Netherlands and, of course, the wines of the

Clos de Vougeot

Duchy followed. Everything was going smoothly and the wines grew steadily in popularity. Then along came the French Revolution. The large vineyards owned by the Church and the Duchy were divided up and handed over as small strips of land to the peasantry. The result was, and still is, a fragmented pattern of tiny vineyard holdings, many of which are too small to be economic. Nothing could be more different from the situation in Bordeaux. The largest single-proprietor Burgundy vineyards are only a matter of a few hectares in area and the famous estates have dozens of owners. For example, Clos de Vougeot, the largest of the Grand Cru vineyards in the Côte d'Or, has an area of 50 ha (124 acres) and around 80 owners – but more about this later.

The region is divided into four main areas:

1. Chablis
2. Côte d'Or
3. Côte de Beaune
4. Côte Chalonnaise

Note that I do not include the Mâconnais or Beaujolais in Burgundy. These regions produce a different style of wine and are closer in character to each other than to these four Burgundy areas: in fact many of their wines are entitled to carry either of the two *appellations*. Neither area was part of the Duchy of Burgundy and in fact, before the Revolution, the Burgundians set up customs barriers to hinder the transport of Mâconnais and Beaujolais wines through to Paris.

CLIMATE

The climate is always difficult, especially in Chablis, where obtaining sufficient heat in summer is always a major factor and late frosts can cause havoc. The other areas are relatively cool, too, hence the emphasis on south- and east-facing slopes. Over the years very localized hailstorms have been extremely destructive. I experienced one of these amazing occurrences in midsummer 1984. The hailstones were larger than golf balls, and although concentrated on only a few of the northernmost villages of the Côte d'Or, they inflicted considerable damage on vineyards (only the car panel beaters are rumoured to have done rather well).

There are essentially only two important grape varieties in Burgundy. The shy, awkward Pinot Noir, which hates travel and has proved very difficult to handle anywhere else in the world; and the incomparable Chardonnay, now producing wonderful white wine in many countries of the world.

Grape varieties and their suitability to other countries are always fascinating, and often a source of gentle humour. It never ceases to amuse me that in conversation with Burgundians about California we will both agree on the poor performance of the Pinot Noir across the Atlantic. Then the Burgundian will inevitably carry on and make a similar statement about the Chardonnay, adding that it does not matter, 'as they make excellent Rieslings!'

Among other Burgundian grape varieties is the prolific Aligoté. It is planted in small areas and occasionally produces a pleasantly fragrant, 'quaffing' dry wine, but all too often the wine is sour and acidic. The Gamay from south of Mâcon is used in a blend with Pinot Noir called Bourgogne Passe-Tout-Grains; this seems to be gradually disappearing, and that is not a bad thing. I have tasted Pinot Blanc from small plantings, and a Chablis sold on the French market with Sauvignon in the blend.

THE SYSTEM

Obviously the Burgundian 'democracy' of ownership causes considerable problems, many of which have been resolved by a series of compromises. There exists a most complex relationship between the grower and the *négociant*. Many growers do not have the facilities for wine making and consequently sell their grapes to the *négociant* houses. Others do actually make the wine, keep some, and sell some to the houses; others will sell some grapes and vinify the rest, some of which they will sell. A large percentage of burgundy does pass through the *négociants*, who are then responsibe for the *élevage* (the maturing of the wine) and, of course, the marketing. The houses are often criticized for tending to blend individualistic wines into a 'house style': hardly the ideal situation for the fine wines, but in my opinion a blessed relief for many of the poorer ones. What cannot be denied, however, is the fact that because of the amazing fragmentation of vineyard ownership, many growers need the houses for both financial and technical reasons. As has been said, the Pinot Noir in particular is a difficult grape requiring considerable technical expertise in vinification and *élevage*; small vineyard owners just do not have the facilities to make the best of the wine.

But things are changing dramatically. There has, after all, been something of a socio-economic revolution throughout the Western world in the past decade. 'Big' is no longer necessarily beautiful (as any student of the history of the large corporation well knows) and the smaller independent producers have now achieved the respectability formerly the prerogative of the more powerful 'establishment' operations. This has affected the wine business in general (growers market their own champagne direct; the 'boutique' wineries of the New World are producing the most highly respected wines) and Burgundy in particular.

Today, some 40 per cent of burgundy is sold without the intervention of the *négociants*, compared to only 20 per cent in the mid-1960s. The whole wine-growing countryside of Burgundy is dotted with signs offering *Vente Directe*, and merchants, hoteliers and restaurateurs are using this purchasing method as well as the general public. Brokers are also selling the growers' wines to the previously traditional customers of the *négociants* (see the Anthony Sarjeant interview in the Bordeaux section, page 48).

There is no doubt that many fine growers' wines that would have previously been condemned to anonymity have received their due rewards. Also it is quite certain that many thin, sour, poorly vinified wines have been sold, wines that would never have been released as such by the houses, who would have used their vinifying and blending techniques to create perhaps a lesser *appellation*, but a much sounder wine.

Another aspect of this change in selling techniques is that the smaller *négociants* are just not able to buy the good wines and are making poorer and poorer ones.

RED BURGUNDY

This brings me to a most important aspect of Burgundy in the 1980s. I was a '60s man, a product of the era that spawned The Byrds, Loving Spoonful, Buffalo Springfield and all that wonderful country-rock music. Equally importantly, you could enjoy frequent helpings of that wonderful, hedonistic *sauce béarnaise* without worrying about the cholesterol count; and there were the unparalleled joys of regularly enjoying reasonably priced attractive, rich and luscious burgundies. A dinner-time bottle of commonplace Côte de Beaune-Villages would ease the worries of the business day: now all a similar bottle does is make

Armand Rousseau, the guru of Chambertin

me annoyed (at the thinness and lack of fruit) and resentful (I will have paid out sufficient money to buy a couple of bottles of excellent drinking claret or Beaujolais). Perhaps my business problems are now of such magnitude that relief can only be obtained from a bottle of 1979 La Tâche Domaine de la Romanée-Conti (sold in Britain at about £60) and considerable after-dinner activity? Or perhaps burgundy no longer tastes like it used to?

In 1968 H.W. Yoxall was able to state without fear of contradiction: 'It [burgundy] is a full wine ... that ranges from the noblest growths, the peer of any region's, to a variety of sound table wines still relatively inexpensive even in these days of inordinate inflation.'

By 1985 burgundy's reputation had declined to such an extent that there is no great surprise at David Wolfe's comments at a recent *Decanter* tasting on Gevrey-Chambertin Premier Cru Les Gazetiers (all wines with a retail price of £10 to £15 per bottle). 'There were no wines in this tasting I would pay my money for ... the general malaise of Burgundy may be summed up as a startling disparity between quality and price.'

Let me assure you that Mr Wolfe is not a cantankerous, aged scribe sitting in a garret bemoaning the fact that life is not what it used to be. He is one of the finest tasters in London and was simply summing up the views expressed by the other eminent palates on the panel.

How has this dreadful state of affairs come about? First of all let me state that I do not expect burgundy to be cheap, nor do I consider 'value for money' to be the most critical aspect. I have indicated the uneconomic vineyard holdings, the unreliable climate and the perversity of the Pinot Noir grape. The wine is always going to be relatively expensive. But must we suffer what Anthony Hanson describes as 'mediocre wines without quality, and poor value for money. Briefly, a rip-off. The Burgundians are coasting along on their reputation.'

Over-production is the main problem. The great vineyards of the Côte de Nuits and Côte de Beaune used to produce powerful, rich, intense wines. The dramatic change in style cannot be explained with a Gallic shrug of the shoulders, and a comment about the 'new' style of burgundy being more genuine as no one is allowed to beef up the wine with a touch of Algerian. No, it has more to do with consistent production of wine from vineyards that are fulfilling the legally allowed crop yield year in and year out, regardless of circumstances. I was amazed at the poor quality of the wines at a recent Chevaliers du Tastevin dinner, and yet the following day tasted some really outstanding *négociant*'s wines with a Côte de Nuits friend. He was most insistent that the present-day problems stemmed from the reluctance of the growers to prune ruthlessly and concentrate their efforts towards maximum quality. These people are now more interested in a guaranteed high yield than the riskier business of making the finest wine ('what happens if I prune heavily and we have a poor summer?').

Fortunately, tastings of red burgundy over the past year have given a clear hint that things are starting to improve; perhaps the poor prices fetched for 1982 *appellation Bourgogne* were partly responsible. The preponderance of really poor, badly made wine seems to be diminishing, and both growers and *négociants* seem to be sharpening up their act ... not before time!.

THE NÉGOCIANTS

One of the most annoying features of Burgundy is the preponderance of the *sous-marques*. Some-

'And the label Sir? Would Sir like it changing for something a little less pretentious?'

BURGUNDY

times these are genuine subsidiary companies, such as Marcel Amance, owned by Prosper Maufoux (Santenay); others are merely one of a number of registered names designed to enable the company to supply a number of agents with 'exclusive' wines – most confusing. I consider there are four great *négociant-éleveur* houses who have produced excellent wines consistently over the years. Interestingly they are all large vineyard owners: as well as offering the standard *négociant*'s wines their lists are crammed with wines made exclusively from their own properties.

Joseph Drouhin My favourite of all. Established in 1880 and one of the very few to concentrate solely on the production of wine from the Burgundy region: no blended *vin de table* nor Côtes du Rhône. The house owns over 50 ha (124 acres) of vineyards in Chablis, Côte d'Or and Côte de Beaune. Its Mâcon Villages Laforêt is simply one of the best

Robert Drouhin at work in Beaune

ENJOYING WINE

wines from the region and the white Premier Cru Beaune Clos des Mouches is consistently excellent. The top-class reds from this house are usually well worth the money but the bargains are among its lesser *appellations*. The Chorey les Beaune, Santenay and Monthélie regularly taste well above their comparatively lowly status; they prove my theory that one can still buy burgundy at a reasonable price by carefully choosing a lesser wine from one of the major houses.

J. Faiveley Whenever I drink a bottle of red from

Not all of Burgundy is cobwebs and damp!

BURGUNDY

Harvesting in the Côte d'Or

ENJOYING WINE

BURGUNDY – NOT ALL GLOOM AND DOOM

Don and I have at least one thing in common. We are both jilted lovers of red burgundy. The difference between us is that while Don is still smarting from the loss of his loved one, I have rediscovered my old flame. Yes there still are major problems – worldwide demand for its famous growths have given rise to the temptation to overproduce. There is a tendency to use high-yield clones. The Pinot Noir is not the most stable grape varieties and tends to mutate quite easily. Put simply cloning is the making of genetically exact copies of vines that are selected because of a particular desired characteristic. If out of say 100 vines, 10 are noted to produce consistently more fruit than others, then cuttings are taken. Over a period of time by further selection and cuttings a new high-yielding clone can be produced. If the grower gradually replaces his vines with the new clone he will dramatically increase the volume of wine made . . . however, the vine produces more fruit at the expense of concentration and thin wines are the inevitable result. Overfertilization also produces quantity at the expense of quality; also underpruning. Replanting can also have a detrimental effect: old vines produce the best wine but their yield is meagre. Quality-conscious growers lovingly maintain their old vines and keep an optimum 'vineyard balance'; quantity-conscious ones replace the older vines with the high-yielding clones.

However, I have toured the Burgundian minefield and have discovered some excellent winemakers. Some are well known, while others are virtually unknown outside their own village. It takes time and patience to find the good guys. I make no claim to having found them all and the situation changes constantly – a great winemaker may retire and his son might opt for quantity.

First of all let me say what I look for in red burgundy. A glorious colour gives pleasure but primarily I desire a bouquet of Pinot Noir – perfumed and a subtle hint of violets. The taste must be rich and full of purity and concentration. If it has the correct fruit and a pleasing balance between acid, tannin and alcohol then I have a winner. The flavour and texture of such wines is a highly sensual experience. Good as the best *négociants* may sometimes be, for me the real superstars are to be found among the growers.

Simon Bize makes wines in the underrated Savigny les Beaune that are a revelation. Complex and concentrated Pinot Noir character yet retaining the lacy elegance of Savigny, Capron Manieux produces gorgeous perfumed Savignys. Domaine Mussy produces wines in Beaune which confounded those who think of this *appellation* of producing merely soft, easy drinking wines; these intense, perfumed wines are more similar to the wines from the Côte de Nuits; the flavour of a recently tasted Epenottes 1981 was memorable. Volnay has an excellent collection of fine winemakers and one of its brightest stars is Michel Lafarge. Drinking his wines is like reading *War and Peace* – hard to get into and you wonder if it will all be worthwhile. In their early years they taste more of raspberryade than burgundy but as they age . . . the intricate strands unfold and the wine is hard to put down! Hubert de Montille, a Dijon lawyer makes incredibly structured, 'big' wines in Volnay and Pommard; once again they take years to develop. A Pommard Les Pezerolles 1969 drunk in Burgundy in 1984 had the stature and nobility normally associated with top quality Bordeaux. The Domaine Henri Gouges has long been famous for its Nuits St Georges, old vintages have a particularly attractive flavour similar to chocolate truffles. More recently the wines of Jacqueline Jayer have caught my palate. Armand Rousseau usually produces the finest of Chambertin but the wines of the late 1970s were disappointing. Alain Burguet makes Gevrey Chambertin that is as good as, and often better than many other *grands crus*; he proves the rewards of dedication to quality. Comte Georges de Vogüé's Musigny has been for many years a shining example to other growers. Alain Roumier is the winemaker and he manages to ally strength and depth with the finesse.

I have reserved for last my favourite grower of all, Jacques Seysses at Domaine Dujac, who makes stunning burgundy from 11 ha (27 acres) of vines in Chambolle-Musigny, Morey-St-Denis and Gevrey Chambertin. His wines are the epitome of pure, concentrated Pinot Noir – a fine depth of colour, fabulous bouquet and a gorgeous flavour. Every aspect of vinification receives meticulous attention – he even dries his own *alliers* oak and makes his own barrels.

Let's hope for a continual improvement in quality of the other Burgundian growers and *négociants*. One of the reasons that some winemakers have been able to succeed while producing poor wine is that the Pinot Noir has not been successful elsewhere, and with no international competition there has been little pressure on the Burgundians. It is perhaps no coincidence that white burgundy is far less often disappointing than red – successful Chardonnays are made in many parts of the world, therefore competition is ever present.

HOWARD RIPLEY

BURGUNDY

Burgundy Labels...What Do They Mean?

There are times when I think the Burgundian labelling laws are attempting to be as difficult to comprehend as the German efforts. There are four actual classifications:

Grand Cru
The absolute top vineyards, mainly in Chablis and the Côte d'Or. Now theoretically these are instantly recognizable – the actual name of the vineyard appears on its own, and really there is no need to mention the name of the village – except of course when the *grand cru* is in Chablis, where a quarter of them reside.

For example: Romanée-Saint-Vivant
Appellation Controlée

Premier Cru
The next best; there are many, many more *premier cru* than *grand cru* vineyards (obviously more accessible in price and quantity). Now you should have no trouble recognizing a mere *premier* because the name of the vineyard appears in the same size lettering as that of the village.

For example 'Nuits Saint-Georges les Vaucrains'

Now just because you have had a bottle of a *premier cru* vineyard and enjoyed the wine, don't think that your next bottle will automatically be of the same status.... many vineyards only have portions classified as this. Now the way you tell this from the label is that the name of the vineyard will be in smaller print than that of the village. What a field day for opticians!

Commune Appellations
Much simpler, usually only the name of a village, for example Pommard or Santenay ... but there may be a vineyard name also.

Generic Appellations
Once again complications reign supreme; this classification covers general wine of an accepted quality, for example Bourgogne Aligoté, Bourgogne Passe-Tout-Grains, Bourgogne Ordinaire and the rather prestigious sounding Bourgogne Grand Ordinaire which is actually the lowest rating of all.

There are also a number of terms that appear with regularity on Burgundy labels; some are important, others meaningless.

CLOS: a vineyard enclosed by a wall (well sometimes the wall fell down a long time ago, but the term stays).
CONFRÉRIE CHEVALIERS DU TASTEVIN: the dinners organised by this order are not serious but the rigorous selection procedures for the wines permitted to bear the 'Tastevin' label are and the wine is normally worth the extra money.
HOSPICES DE BEAUNE: another special label; wine bought at the annual charity auction benefiting this hospital. Not always as reliable a guide to class; look for the grower's name in the smaller type.
MONOPOLE: either a grower or *négociant* has total control of any property with this term; this is no guarantee that the wine will be any better.
NÉGOCIANT-ÉLEVEUR: already discussed.
PROPRIÉTAIRE–RÉCOLTANT: the man who owns and makes the wine.
VITICULTEUR: the same.

---

this house I relax and realize that all is not wrong in Burgundy. It is 150 years old, still in family hands and the largest owner of vineyards in the region. Its estates cover over 100 ha (247 acres), mainly in the Côte de Nuits and Côte Chalonnaise; the single-vineyard Mercureys are outstanding.

Louis Jadot Clean and crisp whites in the lesser *appellations* and magnificent wines at the top, in particular Corton-Charlemagne and Chevalier-Montrachet. A marvellous range of full, fragrant reds including a consistent Corton Pougets.

Louis Latour A major house that has been steeped in controversy since the publication of Anthony Hanson's book *Burgundy* (not a copy to be found in the bookshops of Beaune) when it was disclosed that the reds are 'pasteurized' (heated to 70°C for a brief moment to stabilize the wine). Many people, Hanson included, consider this treatment tends to remove much of the originality of the product, I tend to find a definite 'Latour' house style throughout the reds, perhaps this is the result – but one cannot deny the sheer excellence of the whites.

There are a few other houses well worth searching out:

Coron A small establishment with few vineyard holdings but a considerable reputation for full-bodied, fragrant reds and stylish Côte de Beaune whites.

Dufouleur Père et Fils Produces some excellent wines from its own vineyards in the Côte de Nuits and Santenay.

Jaffelin Owned by Robert Drouhin but run as an entirely separate company. Once again no wine interests at all outside the region. It produces 'serious' wines; the reds benefit from considerable bottle age and in these days of light, insipid wines this cannot be a bad thing! Well worth the money.

Laboure Roi An excellent example of just what can be achieved by a *négociant* house, despite a lack of vineyards. Bought in the early 1970s by Armand Cottin (his brother Philippe is president of Baron Philippe Rothschild, Bordeaux), it has been on a dynamic growth spiral ever since but without any of the quality problems that normally accompany rapid expansion in this region. Its Côte de Nuits wines are excellent and the house also has arrangements with Domaine René Manuel (Meursault) and Domaine Chantal Lescure (Nuits-St-Georges) whereby it tends the vineyards, makes and sells the wines. The house's Bourgogne Blanc Domaine René Manuel produced from a single vineyard just outside the Meursault *appellation* is an excellent buy. Look out for the Meursault Rouge Clos de la Baronne, a flowery, fruity rarity.

Moillard A large house with considerable vineyard holdings, particularly in the Côte de Nuits: Nuits-St-Georges Clos de Thorey, Nuits-St-Georges Clos des Grandes Vignes Premier Cru and Vosne-Romanée Aux Malconsorts are consistently attractive wines, but many of the lesser wines are only average.

Prosper Maufoux The name for Santenay. Pierre Maufoux runs a most reputable house with considerable vineyard holdings around the *appellation*. Both his whites and reds are full of charm and delicacy.

There are other houses often producing class wines – Bouchard Père, Champy, Chanson, Raoul Clerget, Leroy – but they are not always consistent: the less said about most of the other houses the better.

WHITE BURGUNDY

Here the problem is not irregular quality but soaring prices. Throughout this book I have talked about the excellence of 'new world' Chardonnays, especially those from California, Australia and New Zealand, which are attempting to achieve a lightness, but they are just the odd one or two wines. The Côte de Beaune has acres of Chardonnay vineyards producing only the very finest ... but, of course, production is limited and there is a worldwide dry white wine market eager to buy the best. Ironically it is not actually these *grand crus* that are responsible for the sky-rocketing prices, but a humble, average quality *appellation* from the Mâconnais, Pouilly Fuissé. In 1983 the opening price for a *pièce* (the Burgundian term for a barrel; typically they can't agree on size – in the Côte d'Or it is 228 litres, but in the Chalonnais, Mâconnais and Beaujolais it is 216 litres) of Pouilly Fuissé was 6,000 francs and this was considered far too high. But in 1984 the opening price had rocketed to 20,000 francs! Even the growers realize their wine is not worth this, but they are within the *appellation* that is the 'magic name' in the United States, and that country wants to drink virtually only white wine (red wine sales are actually falling): it must be dry, preferably from the Chardonnay grape, and French.

It is not widely known that only 25 per cent of the Burgundian vineyards (I exclude Mâconnais from the region proper) are planted with white wine grape varieties. Chablis produces considerable quantities but whites of the Côte de Nuits are interest-value only rarities, and as I have already said, the Côte de Beaune is not exactly a mammoth production region. One plus point is that every year the wines from Montagny improve; much thanks is due here to the tireless promotional work by Louis Latour. The cooperative at Buxy is also making fine wine and the Saint-Gengoux Groupement de Producteurs is now making an outstanding (dare I say California style?) medium priced Premier Cru Les Loges. They have deliberately adopted a rigid pruning policy, but happily accept the lower yield because of the knowledge of a higher price ... the wine undergoes its first

BURGUNDY

fermentation in new cognac oak casks and is aged in brand new *allier* oak. The result is a well-balanced, flavoursome wine full of character and at a price similar to ordinary Chablis. Saint-Aubin and Saint-Romain, both Côte de Beaune rarities, offer good value wines, but they are obviously difficult to find.

The major source of plentiful, cheapest white burgundy is the Mâconnais. The motorist driving along the A6 sees little evidence of the vineyards of the region as there is not an overwhelming mass of vines in view, but scattered around are vast areas. The southernmost *appellations* produce the finest – the dreaded Pouilly Fuissé, and the much better value Pouilly Vinzelles and Pouilly Loché plus the best value of all – Saint-Véran, which adjoins Beaujolais and actually draws on the *commune* of Saint Amour. If you see wine from M. 'Corsin' or M. Raymond, grab them. Georges Du Boeuf also produces an excellent wine. Mâcon Blanc and Mâcon Blanc Villages offer soft, fresh and fruity Chardonnay at most reasonable prices (still!), but I prefer to spend a little extra for a single village name such as Clesse, Chardonnay (yes there really is a village of this name), Lugny, Prisse and Viré. A large percentage of these wines is made by the dominant, technically advanced cooperatives – the one at Lugny controls the production of approximately 1000 ha (2470 acres) of vineyards.

So there we are. A region producing a style of wine everyone wants, and that most progressive wine regions are determined successfully to emulate. Many of the wines are still very good value, but for how much longer?

ANNOTATION TO MAP OF BURGUNDY
CHABLIS
Produced on the clay soil slopes outside the village of Chablis. The region has had its ups and downs; the harsh frosts of 1956 which decimated Bordeaux also wreaked havoc here. Much anti-frost equipment has been installed and there have been considerable new plantings in the area (Drouhin now owns 30 hectares in the region) and consequently harvest yields have risen dramatically – the average crop in the 1960s was 25,000 hectolitres, now it is 130,000. The result is large quantities of good quality, well made Chardonnay, admittedly without the depth of flavour of the Côte d'Or whites but also without the price. Close to the Chablis *appellation* the vignerons of Saint-Bris have planted Sauvignon Blanc and have VDQS status. The wines are crisp and dry without the charm of their nearby western Upper Loire neighbours.

CÔTE DE NUITS
Here are most of the 'great' names of red burgundy, commanding prices well above the other villages. There are two minor *appellations* Côte de Nuits Villages for general blends of the lesser *'sans appellation'* villages, rather like the curate's egg. Bourgogne Hautes Côtes de Nuits – the house of *Geisweiller* has planted a huge 90 hectare tract of land in the western hills around Bevy. There are also individual growers who sell mainly to the cooperative (the only one in the Côte d'Or). Lighter style wines but quite acceptable as they have reasonable Pinot character at a reasonable price.

CÔTE DE BEAUNE
This other half of the Côte d'Or does not have quite the same social cachet for reds, despite the excellence of Corton, Pommard and Volnay. Value for money is here with Chorey les Beaune, Monthélie and Santenay. But, it is *the* region of the world for production of the driest, rich oaky Chardonnays with all the complex characteristics in subtle harmony.

Côte de Beaune Villages can come from one or more villages except Volnay, Pommard, Beaune or Aloxe Corton. A better bet than its 'Nuits' equivalent.

Bourgogne Hautes Côtes de Beaune similar to Nuits, but without the dynamism of one large house. Not as reliable.

CÔTE CHALONNAIS
The bargains of Burgundy are to be found here, right alongside many of the horrors. By far the largest producer is the village of Mercurey which can make powerful, pungent and fruity reds with real depth of Pinot character; some whites are satisfactory. Faiveley and Protheau reign supreme and some growers make excellent wine, in particular Paul de Launay, Jean-Paul Granger, Michel Juillot (outstanding) and Jean Maréchal. Of course you must organize your Mercurey purchases on the spot, otherwise you will miss out on dining (and staying) at Cogny's Hôtellerie du Val d'Or which offers superb regional cuisine and marvellous wines.

Rully and Givry supply some decent wines, and a lot of poor whites and insipid light reds.

Montagny only produces whites and just has *premier cru* vineyards.

MÂCONNAIS
In my early wine days Mâcon was always red and not too good. Now it is the source of excellent value Chardonnays (with the notable exception of Pouilly-Fuissé).

61

Enjoying Wine

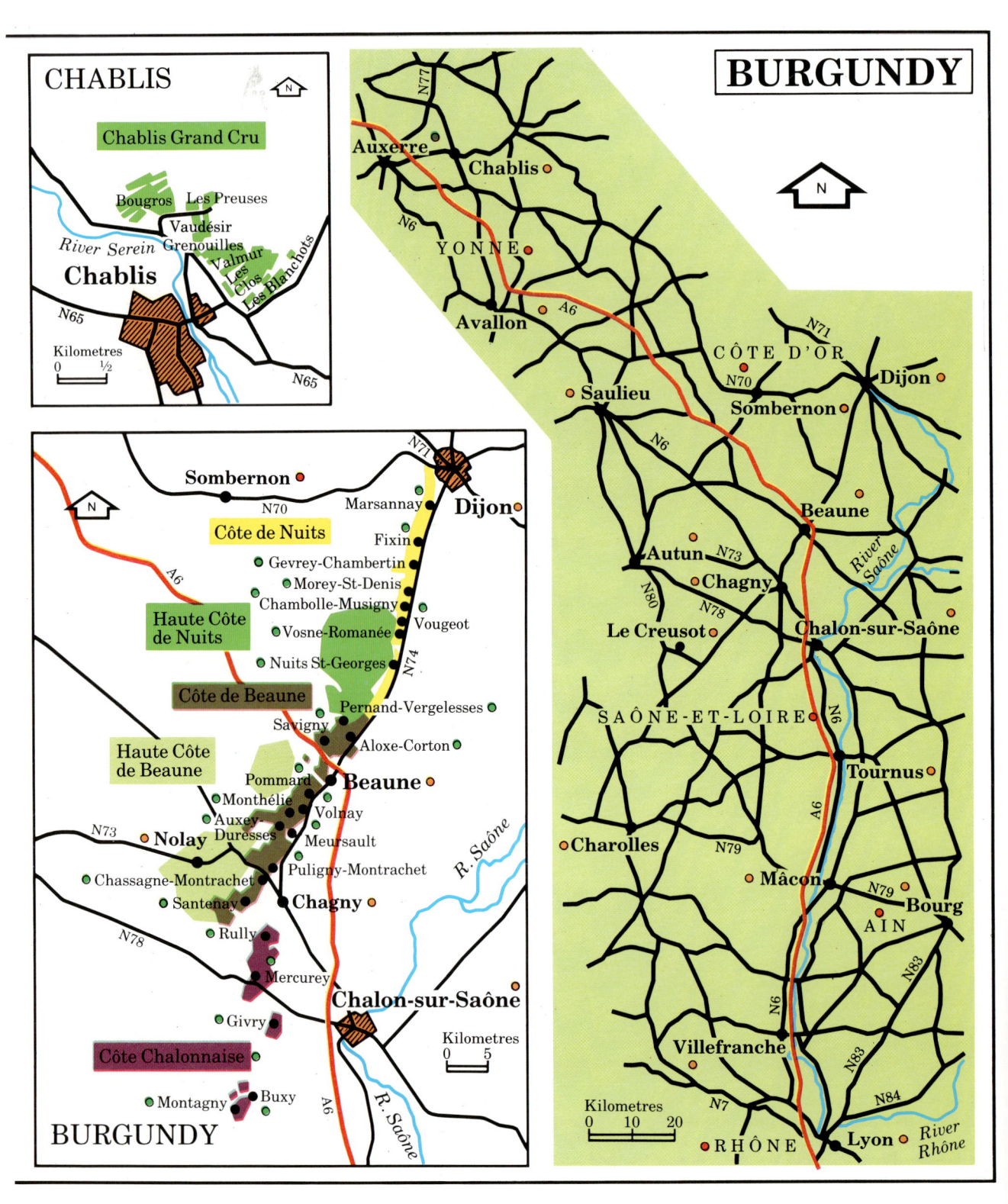

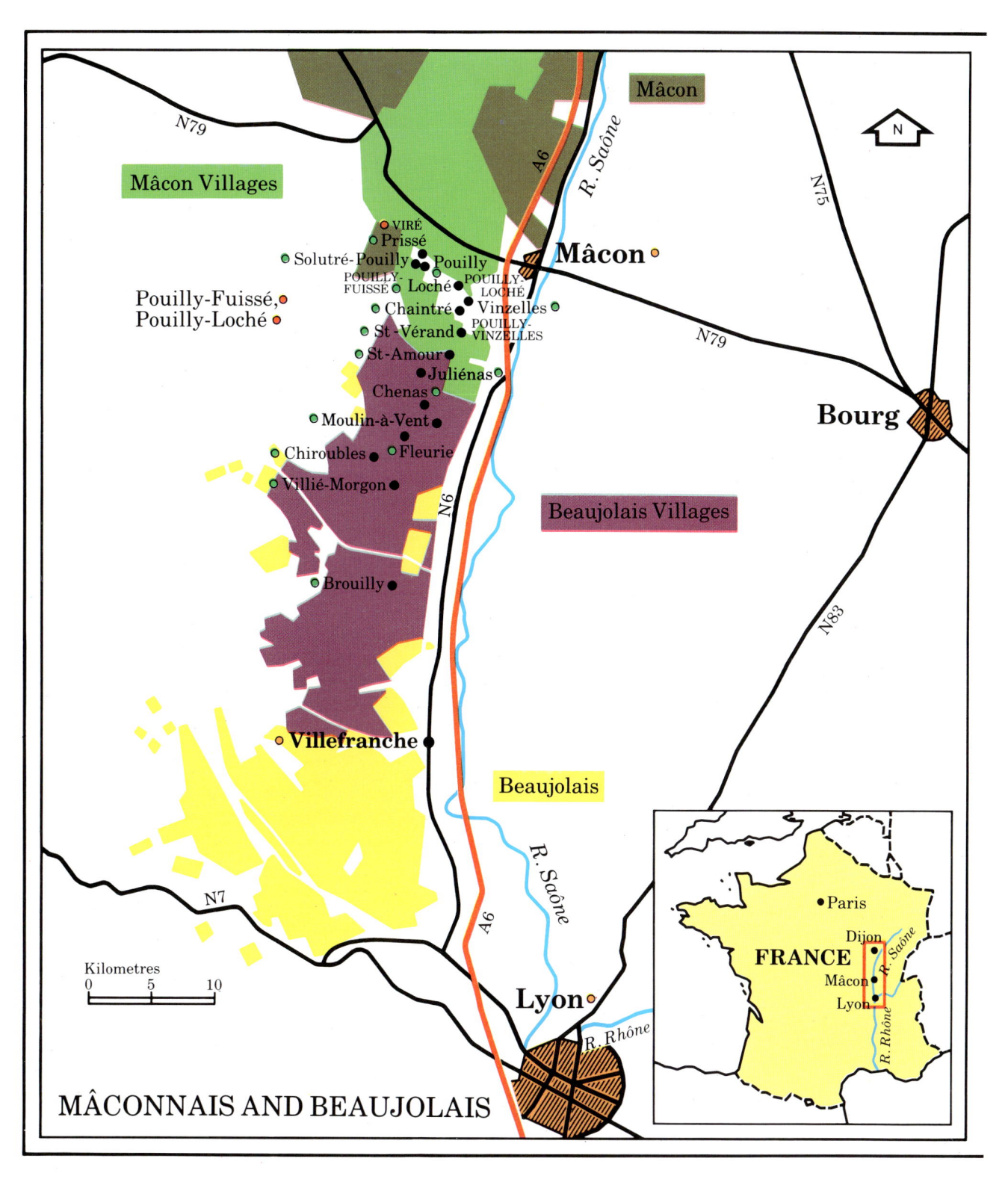

Beaujolais

MÂCONNAIS AND BEAUJOLAIS

CHAPTER SIX

BEAUJOLAIS

THE REGION

The Beaujolais region is not merely an appendage of Burgundy, as students of restaurant wine lists might be led to believe. It is a clearly defined wine area with a character that is unique. The district stretches from just north of Lyon through to the hills south-west of Macon; a considerable area of around 24,000 ha (60,000 acres) of vineyards which in 1982 produced 129 million litres of wine. In Lyon there is a local saying that 'three rivers flow into Lyon: the Rhône, the Saône and the Beaujolais'. The surroundings are totally different to Burgundy (and in fact it was never part of the Duchy of Burgundy), with rolling hills with numerous beautiful, unspoiled villages scattered all around. Church spires are everywhere, as well as countless small tracts of woodland in the valleys, and all this is traversed by narrow, winding roads.

Beaujolais is a hospitable area where there are some 7000 growers, many with their own cellars open to the public. The village cooperatives all have cellars for tasting (you have not lived until you have experienced a Saturday afternoon touring the cellars and finishing at the superb tasting *caveau* at Villié-Morgan!). It seems to me that in August every second Dutch, Swiss and Belgian restaurateur clutches his wife or girlfriend, hops into his Volvo estate and tours the villages tasting and buying. When the car is fully loaded he returns home with sufficient discoveries to keep his wine list interesting until the New Year.

WHY IS BEAUJOLAIS SO POPULAR?

It is without doubt the best known of all French red wine. Indeed it now represents over 20 per cent of all French *appellation controlée* red wine exported to Britain. Beaujolais is the only red wine area in the world producing wine that flaunts gaiety: lightness, youthfulness and extroverted fragrance; the most perfect 'quaffing' wine, equally at home with or without food. It is the most easily digestible of all red wines (this is why Michael Buller, wine consultant to Pan-American Airways, chooses to serve Cru Beaujolais on long-haul flights).

THE BEAUJOLAIS HIERARCHY

The area is dominated by one grape: the Gamay, a variety known throughout the rest of the world for quantity, but only mediocre quality. Here the Gamay comes to life. A combination of granite soil, the hills, together with unique wine-making techniques, produce this very special style of wine.

There are three different levels: Beaujolais; Beaujolais Villages; the nine Cru Beaujolais.
Beaujolais mostly comes from the vineyards south of Villefranche (the Bas-Beaujolais) where the soil is limestone. This wine, at its best, deserves its reputation as the carafe wine of the bars, cafés and restaurants in Paris and Lyon where the lightness of touch and alcoholic content appeal, despite the relative lack of fragrance and finesse characteristic of the 'northern' wines. Until a decade or so ago, this wine was often rather dull and uninteresting, but recent vineyard reforms and application of the most modern of viticultural techniques have improved the overall standard considerably.
Beaujolais Villages This *appellation* produces some of the finest-value drinking red wines of the world. These are wines from the *communes* in the north where the two most important factors of a

BEAUJOLAIS

unique microclimate and the granite soil allow the Gamay to produce individualistic wines with fragrance and finesse. In 1984 I was a member of the jury at the Paris Concours du Vin. With four regional growers I had the delightful responsibility of tasting all the Beaujolais Villages entries and awarding the medals. The standard of the 1983 wines was remarkably high. It was fascinating to note the incredible variety in the wines from the various *communes*: some light, soft and feminine; others full, rich and masculine.

There are many very sound Beaujolais Villages wines from the large *négociants*, but I would recommend searching for the wines produced by individual growers; they cost a little more but the drinker is usually rewarded with a bottling of considerable original style and flavour.

The nine Beaujolais Crus These *premier villages* of the region are the aristocracy of the Beaujolais area. They produce a significant percentage of the area's output, 25 per cent in 1983 (compared to, say, the first and second growths of Bordeaux).

BROUILLY AND CÔTE DE BROUILLY

These were the wines that introduced me, many years ago, to the finer aspects of the Crus. The area produces light, refreshing wines that are easy to get along with. Drink them as young as possible, and never consider keeping them after the next harvest. These two *appellations* account for nearly 30 per cent of the total Cru production and they are, therefore, relatively easy to find, and the prices normally reasonable.

Particularly recommended: Château Thivan, Close de Briante, Château de Grand Vernay, Domaine de Berthaudière, Domaine de Combillaty, Château de la Chaize, Château des Tours.

CHENAS

The smallest production of the nine Crus, growing solid wines with considerable depth. One of the features of the village is the excellent Restaurant Robin (one Michelin star) which serves unforgettable *Andouillette de Chenas*. The Robin family also make, in my opinion, the finest wine of the *commune*, Domaine de Brureau, a rich, velvety mouthful that improves dramatically with a few years in a bottle. Also recommended: Château de Chenas and Domaine de la Combe Remont.

CHIROUBLES

Light and overwhelming with flowery flavour ... this is what Beaujolais is all about! Unfortunately Chiroubles has become the trendy Cru, particularly in Parisian restaurants, so it is difficult to find and consequently a little more expensive. Recommended: Domaine de Moulin, Château de Javernaud, Château Portier.

FLEURIE

One of the largest *appellation* areas and without doubt the best known. The wine is as light as Chiroubles, delicate and feminine – indeed, it has often been classed as 'The Queen of Beaujolais'. The Restaurant des Sports, right on the square close to the large church, is a 'must' for anyone

THE OLD WHITE WINE WITH WHITE MEAT SYNDROME

Many people will advise you to stick rigidly to this maxim, and also of course, red wine with red meat. I recommend that you treat all this with a good deal of circumspection. I once spent a weekend in Paris with a group of French *chef-patrons* whose collective desires seemed to consist of nothing more than continual platters of Belons oysters, yet at no stage was a bottle of Muscadet sighted, nor indeed any white wine. Instead we spent the weekened consuming countless bottles of lightly chilled Cru Beaujolais.

Many great wine and food men and women have considered Roast Chicken *au jus* as the perfect accompaniment to the finest red wines, and yet this is white meat at its most natural. I myself have never considered chicken and white wine a match made in heaven, and always prefer a lightish Burgundy. However, I am not suggesting you serve lightly poached langoustines next time you open a bottle of Domaine Romanée-Conti; but a flavoursome fish grilled with a prominent herb seasoning will be accompanied perfectly with a lightish, young red.

Experiment within moderation; after all, these rules do have some foundation and you will experience some new taste sensations.

ENJOYING WINE

The rolling hills of Beaujolais

BEAUJOLAIS

ENJOYING WINE

touring the Route des Beaujolais. It is a gathering for the artisans who are perfectly happy chatting over a small glass or three or *blanc* as early as 9.30 in the morning. At lunchtime the place is packed with these regulars back again, and also the *négociants*, growers, and transporters, tucking into the best *Coq au Beaujolais* I have ever tasted. The cooperative produces some renowned wine. Recommended estates: Château des Capitans, Château de L'Abbaye and Château des Labourons.

JULIÉNAS

My first visit to this village was remarkable. I frequently annoy my travelling companions with lengthy detours for lunch, and this day was no exception. After driving past Macon I left the *Autoroute du Sud* and joined the RN6, which passes close to Beaujolais, ostensibly to show my passengers the view of the hills and vineyards. As it was lunchtime the challenge proved irresistible and I soon left the RN6 – and by chance ended up at

Fleurie

Beaujolais Nouveau

No analysis of the Beaujolais district is complete without a discussion of this recent phenomenon, which is now accounting for 40-50 per cent of the total production (admittedly most of the wine from the Bas-Beaujolais). I must admit to a certain bias, as I have frequently raced the wine from Fleurie to London (it was not much of a race one year as my means of transport was a 1932 Rolls Royce, which only reached Beaune before spectacularly bursting into giant flames!). I have even raced it by a one-stopover flight from London to Australia: the wine was 'down under' before reaching some of the more isolated parts of Britain.

The Nouveau (or *en primeur*, as it is more often called in France) was originally the rather élitist drink of Lyonnais *boules* players and the patrons of the Lyon and Paris *zincs*. These devotees enjoyed drinking the wine as young as possible when its fragrant, zippy characteristics were accentuated. Suddenly the idea became fashionable and the rush was on to be 'first with the Nouveau' in all the big European cities where the windows of the bars, cafés and restaurants would be plastered with stickers proclaiming 'Le Beaujolais Nouveau est arrivé'. Regular and non-regular wine drinkers suddenly became excited about the verdicts on the new vintage and rushed to buy. Now this has been extended even further afield with merchants chartering jet freighters to fly the wine across the Atlantic.

Why 15 November? This is the date set by the French Government as the first day the new vintage Beaujolais can be sold; it is 15 December for the Cru.

Is Nouveau merely a gimmick? Definitely not! Admittedly it has become a massive public relations exercise, but this in itself is good for the image of Beaujolais which was in need of restoration after much skulduggery (see elsewhere). It has brought Beaujolais in particular, and wine in general, to the attention of a much wider section of the population. There is no doubt that in all but a few years the wine has been eminently drinkable and stunningly different from anything else.

'Beaujolais, Sir? I think we may have one bottle left...'

In years like 1982 and 1983 the wine was glorious – but, much as I like the fun and frivolity of 15 November, the fact is the wine is better for a couple of week's rest after arrival. Beaujolais suffers from travel sickness, especially when shipped immediately after bottling.

Is Nouveau worthless after Christmas? In the poorer years yes, but in better vintages it is excellent to Easter; it loses some of the fruit but also some of the tannin. Because of this fallacy about the short life it is often very cheap after Christmas, and certainly better drinking than the standard Beaujolais of the preceding vintage. (I will often use the Nouveau at this stage to make a 'Cardinal', the local drink in the villages: Beaujolais with a hefty slug of *crème de cassis*.) After all, let us not become too serious about Nouveau – it is a fun wine!

Chez la Rose in Juliénas. On arrival the owner, a lady, informed us that the chef had chopped off part of his finger and was at the hospital, but she was quite happy to offer us what she was cooking for herself. By now my fellow travellers were hungry, it was too late to move on to find another place in another village and so we stayed. It was wonderful! Delicious *terrine de maison* was more than matched by the delicious house white served in the old-fashioned heavy glass bottle. The *Fricassée de Volaille* was wonderful and the local growers' Juliénas even better. My reputation was restored and the fact that we were two hours late for an appointment in Lyon seemed to lose its relevance.

Juliénas wines often offer particularly good

ENJOYING WINE

Moulin à Vent

Beaujolais

What to Buy

Growers and Cooperatives
In the United Kingdom there is a specialist firm (Roger Harris Wines, Loke Farm, Weston Longville, Norfolk), that shops from an amazing selection of growers and represents Beaujolais Propriété, which is the marketing organization formed by ten of the big cooperatives.

Négociants
These are firms whose wines I have particularly enjoyed over the past decade:

Chanut Frères	Loron	Louis Tête
Depagneux	Mommessin	Trenel
Georges Duboeuf	François Paquet	Quinson
Pierre Ferraud	Robert Sarrau	

There have also been a few Burgundy *négociants* whose Beaujolais have been excellent: Louis Jadot (Beaune), Labouré Roi (Nuits-St-Georges), Dufouleur Père et Fils (Nuits-St-Georges) Prosper Mafoux (Santenay), and, in particular, Joseph Drouhin (Beaune).

Super buy: Beaujolais Villages from any of these houses.

value on restaurant wine lists, but it seems that proprietors do not trust the customer to recognize the name (compared with, say, Fleurie). These wines are sturdy and well built, and yet still retain a great deal of fragrance.

Recommended: Château des Capitans, Domaine des Mouilles, Château de Juliénas.

MORGON
A large production offering wines of marvellous value. For years Morgon has had the reputation of needing a few years in bottle, but I find it full of fruit and fragrance and rapidly maturing. In fact I considered that the 1982 and 1983 vintages of this Cru were among the first to be ready for drinking. I have never particularly enjoyed the wines from the cooperative.

Recommended: Château de Pizay, Domaine de Ruyère, Château de Bellevue, Domaine des Pillets.

MOULIN À VENT
Here are found the most full-bodied of all the Crus, the only wines that I would unreservedly recommend for laying down for more than two years. I kept the best of my 1978s for five years. The

Bogus Beaujolais

My first lunch on arrival in London in 1972 was at an attractive Soho bistro. Everything was in the correct French idiom: check tablecloths, candles in bottles, blackboard menu and Edith Piaf on tape in the background (do places like this actually exist in France? I have yet to find one). I ordered a bottle of Fleurie and was horrified at the taste – it had an insidious, soupy, heavy style with a cloying 'hot country' finish. Beaujolais it certainly was not. When I queried the bottle the waiter informed me in a very patronizing manner, 'Of course it is Beaujolais, it says so on the label!' This was my first introduction to 'Bogus Beaujolais' and the then common practice of shipping non-*appellation contrôlée* wines to the United Kingdom, bottling and then labelling them with an *appellation* name, despite the fact that the wine often did not even originate from the same country. Fortunately, Britain's entry into the Common Market in 1974 brought this practice to a halt as the country then had to comply with the French *appellation* laws. Other wines such as Bordeaux and Burgundy (Nuits-St-Georges in particular) suffered the same treatment, but not to quite the extent of Beaujolais.

The other side of the English Channel was also engaged in a similar campaign to destroy the image of Beaujolais. In the 1960s and early '70s it was rumoured that more wine labelled 'Beaujolais' was being sold in Paris alone than was being produced in the whole of Beaujolais! In fact, to be honest, many of the litre bottles of Beaujolais in the cafés of today owe more allegiance to the southern Rhône than to north of Lyon.

Is it any wonder that the reputation of Beaujolais has suffered? This can be overcome nowadays by buying wine that has been bottled in the region of production – be wary if it has been bottled in the Rhône or in Burgundy.

It is not just that they may be 'stretching' the wine; there is also the temptation for the large houses to blend wines for what they consider to be the public palate – then the individuality is lost.

ENJOYING WINE

SOME LIKE IT CHILLED

Another outdated rule is 'all red wines should be served at room temperature'. Not so, particularly with young Beaujolais – this should be served lightly chilled (not ice-cold). This temperature accentuates the fruit in much the same way that chilling brings out the subtle nuances of white wine. Similarly I chill the lighter Italian reds, Provence red and 'new wave' Bordeaux and Rhône. However, if you prefer your Beaujolais at room temperature then carry on, it's your prerogative!

appellation is partly in Chenas and partly in Romanèche Thorins; indeed, some of the finest wine comes from the Château de Chenas (already mentioned). This is an amazing place, full of oak barrels instead of the now usual stainless steel.

Others recommended: Château de Bruyère, Château de Moulin à Vent, Domaine Tagent, Domaine de Champ de Cour, Domaine de Breuil.

SAINT-AMOUR

Not the best known of the Crus (once at a wine trade lunch I challenged the guests to name all nine, and even a Beaujolais-based shipper forgot Saint-Amour!), but certainly some of the finest wines of Beaujolais are produced within this *commune*. Rich and intense wines.

Recommended: Domaine de Billardes, Domaine de Breuil, Domaine des Sablons.

WHITE BEAUJOLAIS

A tiny 5 per cent of Beajolais is white. It is produced from the Chardonnay grape in the northernmost *communes* bordering on the Mâconnais, and the wines are similar in style. I consider that these wines are better in the less than perfect years when the sun has been a little scarce. In excellent years, such as 1983, they tend to lack the acidity necessary for balance and crispness.

Recommended: Château de Chatelard, Château de Loyse

VINTAGES AND WHEN TO DRINK

A simple rule of thumb is to drink Beaujolais and Beaujolais Villages in the year following production: these wines are not made to last and the attractive extroverted fragrance and life tends to disappear after a year in bottle.

The Crus require a little more time and individual attention. I normally drink and sell Chiroubles, Brouilly, Côte de Brouilly, Morgon and Saint-Amour within a year; Juliénas, Fleurie and Chenas within two years; and only Moulin à Vent any later. Of course, there are many exceptions to the rule, especially with growers' wines: for example Robin's Chenas Domaine de Brureau, which peaks at about five years.

There are occasional universally acclaimed vintages such as 1976 and 1978 which produce rich, powerful, solid wines in a 'Burgundian' manner. They benefit from keeping, but are they true Beaujolais?

Gamay grapes at Veaux

Beaujolais

JEAN LOUIS QUINSON

There are easier tasks in the wine trade than that of Beaujolais *négociant*. The most important attributes are a good palate, a wide range of contacts, and the vital ability of being 'fast on your feet'. Deals have to be concluded rapidly, the quantities are large and the margins small. There are also many advantages of course. The Nouveau is often sold before purchase and a large percentage of the rest is sold before the next harvest: the best cash flow of the wine industry!

Quinson Fils at Château de L'Arpaye, Fleurie, is a fifth-generation family firm which has grown dramatically in recent years. It now produces more than 5 million bottles a year, and the renowned *Gault Millau* magazine has rated the firm as one of the top *négociants* of the region (along with Georges Duboeuf, Mommessin and Louis Tête).

Jean Louis Quinson masterminds all this with a degree of authority and experience that belies his relative youth (he is in his early thirties). He is rarely to be found in the office, more often in the vineyards – the firm is also a proprietor – or visiting the numerous grower contacts. Much of the serious business is done over a few glasses at Les Maritonnes (a superb one-star restaurant in Romanèche Thorins where chef and patron Guy Fauvin reigns supreme) or the Restaurant des Sports.

I personally enjoy Quinson wines because of this man's palate. The pale, light, insignificant but technically correct wines are not for Jean Louis. His wines are the earthier 'farmyard' wines with deep colour, pungent bouquet and an abundance of flavour: just what Beaujolais is all about.

Jean Louis Quinson at Les Maritonnes, Romanèche Thorins

CHAPTER SEVEN

Rhône

The Rhône River begins in the Swiss mountains and flows through two serious wine-producing regions – the Valais in Switzerland and Savoie in France – before reaching Lyon and then flowing south. For 210 km (130 miles), between Vienne and Avignon, it nurtures considerable areas of vineyards which produce a huge quantity of wine: some dreadful, some of it excellent value for money, and a few of the truly great red wines of the world.

The Rhône is the only top-quality French wine region to enjoy consistently hot summers. The harvests are abundant and poor vintages a rarity. Most of the region's wine is sold simply as 'Côtes du Rhône', often bottled by national wine merchants as far away as Paris and the north. These large bottles of dull, flabby wine, reeking of sunshine and high alcohol content, are not the ideal introduction and are to be avoided at all costs. There are many fragrant and full-flavoured, individualistic wines of outstanding value available; considerable capital expenditure on the most modern equipment and the accompanying improvement in winemaking techniques has dramatically raised the standards of the better wines of this simple, inexpensive *appellation*. The only problem is sorting out the good from the bad. One useful piece of advice: search out wines actually bottled in the region. There are a number of local *négociants* who never fail to produce wine of a very high standard.

My recommendations are Père Anselme, Jean-Pierre Brotte, Chapoutier, Delas, Guigal, Paul Jaboulet, Gabriel Meffre, Louis Mousset, Claudius Rocher and Vidal Fleury. Many of these houses also produce excellent single *appellation* wines from their own vineyards – particularly Paul Jaboulet and Vidal Fleury.

CÔTES DU RHÔNE VILLAGES

These superior wines come from seventeen *communes* and are the next step up the ladder; Cairanne, Chusclan, Vacqueyras, Valréas, Visan and Beaumes-de-Venise (more about this later) are of particular importance. Just look for the 'Villages' *appellation* on the label – it does mean something, even if the word is on its own (in which case it is a blended product from more than one *commune*), and invariably worth the extra money.

THE SINGLE VILLAGE *APPELLATIONS*

There are two clearly defined vineyard regions: the north, (or Septentrional) around Tain-l'Hermitage and the south (Méridional) surrounding Avignon. As the map shows, there is a considerable non-winegrowing area separating the two, and they vary greatly in climate, geology, land owning and grape varieties.

THE NORTHERN RHÔNE

This area is all about the Syrah grape – you either love it or hate it. When exploring the wines of these *appellations*, forget about the Shiraz of Australia and South Africa, on the Syrah (*Petit* or otherwise) of California, and enjoy these pungent, spicy wines reeking of violets: Syrah at its finest. Lay the wine down for years, or search out older vintages – but whatever you do, don't tell the rest of the world, because at the moment the world has not caught on to their relative value.

Côte Rôtie
This is the 'roasted slope', a small *appellation* with a big reputation. Here the vines cling to incredibly steep cliff faces, suffering intensely cold winters

and very hot summers. The small terraces are extremely difficult to cultivate and harvest, and very labour intensive. In the past this has been disastrous for the growers because rarely has their wine received an adequate price for such labour-intensive viticulture. Fortunately things have improved considerably, and the wines are better for this. A small percentage of white from the Viognier grape is added to the Syrah, a common Rhône tradition which lessens the rather heavy intensity and ensures a fresh, flowery character. The end result is my favourite of the whole region – deep, rich wine with a distinct peppery spiciness, and considerably drier than the southern wines. Around Ampuis are the two most highly respected slopes: the Côte Brune and the Côte Blonde. The finest of all Côte Rôtie is a blend of the two. Top growers are A. Gérin, Marius Gentaz, E. Guigal, Emile Champet, Robert Jasmin and René Rostaing.

Condrieu
A tiny *appellation* of 12 ha (30 acres), basically the continuation of the Côte Rôtie with slopes that are even steeper and terraced vineyards that are even more difficult to work. Only the Viognier grape is planted and it produces a honeyed, luscious white wine, mostly dry; not in the clean, fresh and rather bland style, but a unique fulsome wine that is not to everybody's taste. Château Grillet, the smallest *appellation* in France, is a tiny single vineyard of less than 2 ha (5 acres) within the Condrieu *appellation* area.

Hermitage
The massive vine-laden hill towering over the town of Tain-l'Hermitage is one of the greatest vineyard scenes in the world, rivalling the Mosel for spectacular grandeur. The hill produces outstanding wines with exalted reputations. Before phylloxera, Hermitage was equally renowned with the great wines of Bordeaux and Burgundy. It was also purported to be the source of depth and flavour in the final blends of many a Grand Cru Classé Bordeaux – although many authorities disagree, pointing out that no one would be silly enough to waste such aristocratic wines in this way. Nevertheless, there was a common term for this 'strengthening' of the wine (most probably

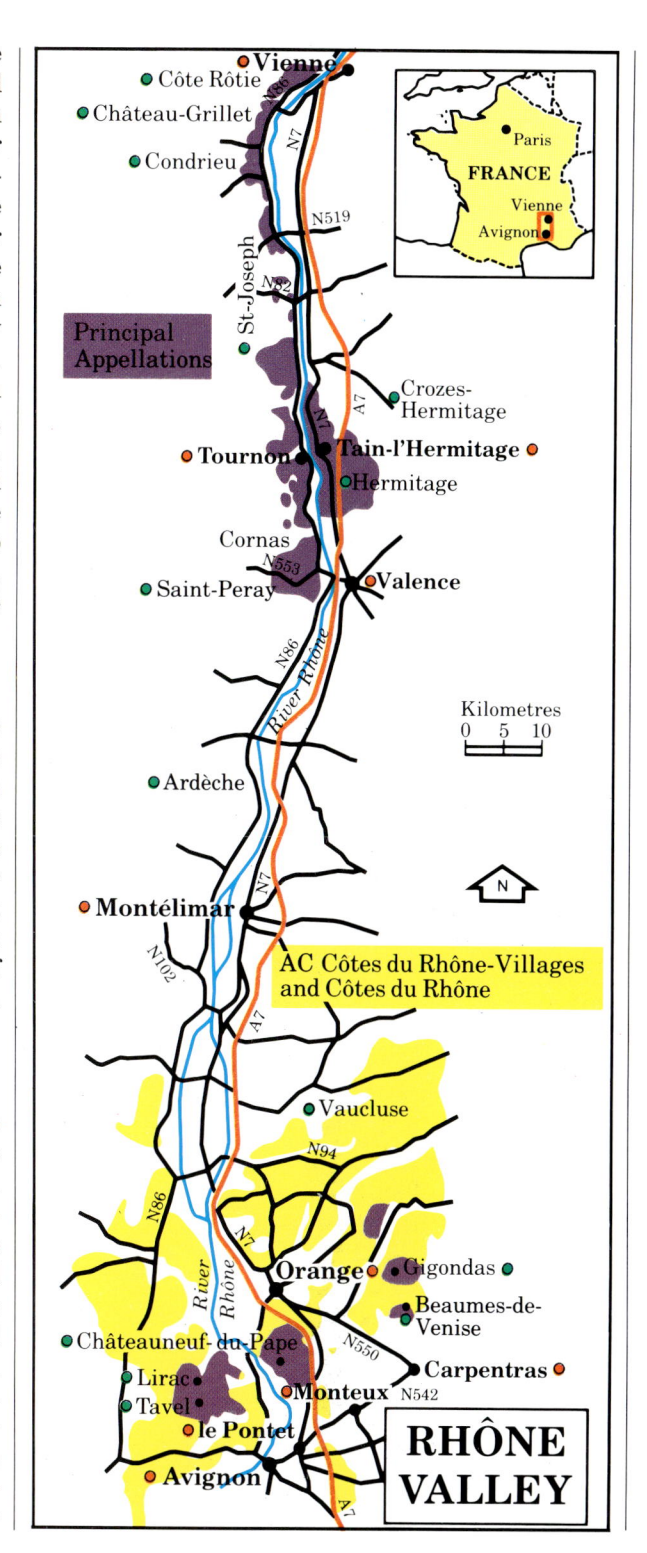

with wine from further south): it was 'hermitaged claret'.

These wines repay keeping; the rich, voluptuous, intense and ripe flavour needs years to develop. Admittedly the very finest wines are by no means cheap, but the buyer is rewarded with magnificence. The doyen of growers in the area is Gérard Chave. His Hermitage is renowned throughout the world – Australian winemakers are remarkably silent when his name is mentioned, and Paul Draper of Ridge Vineyards, California, talked of Chave in reverent tone whenever the Syrah grape is mentioned. Jaboulet Ainé and Chapoutier, too, have superior estates. The *appellation* also produces some of the best white wines of the Rhône Valley.

Crozes-Hermitage
I have fond memories of this wine from the excellent cooperative at Tain-l'Hermitage. It was my introduction to the single village Rhône wines, and even though this relatively modest *appellation* of Crozes-Hermitage, surrounding Hermitage, is not of comparable quality, the better wines still possess some of the qualities of their illustrious neighbour – and at a fraction of the cost. Neither the reds nor the whites need much ageing – in fact with the latter, the younger the better. Over the years I have particularly admired the wines from Delas. The other major *négociants* often make very good wines. Top growers are Joseph Borga, Cave des Clairmonts, Jules Fayolle, Ferraton Père et Fils, Robert Michelas, Raymond Rouve and Charles Tardy et Bernard Ange.

Cornas
The most extroverted of northern Rhône wines, full of attractive fruit and flavour; many can be drunk young, but the very best repay keeping. This is another *appellation* that offers exceptional value for money. Top growers are August Clape, Marcel Juge, Robert Michel and Alain Vogue. The Tain l'Hermitage cooperative also makes a very stylish wine.

St-Joseph
This *appellation* covers 400 ha (990 acres) spread across some 65 km (40 miles). The products are of erratic quality and by no means my favourite Rhône wines. St-Péray and Clairette de Die are best known for sparkling wines of average quality.

THE SOUTHERN RHÔNE

Here the sheer, forbidding cliff faces of the north are replaced by more workable rolling hills; instead of clinging to the hillsides the vines are sprawled across the ground, often on beds of large stones. Viticulture is totally different, with many large estates as well as numerous small growers; the cooperatives are very important in this region. In recent years there has been a dramatic change in the style of southern Rhône wines. Formerly they were big, beefy, and rather obvious and unattractive. Nowadays modern techniques, with shorter fermentation times and less oak ageing, have led to an accentuation of the fruit content. Traditionalists may complain, but this cannot be a bad thing when producing cheap drinking wine! The Grenache is the predominant grape variety, but Syrah is rapidly increasing in importance, and that augurs well for the future. The south does not have the number of big names of the north, but of course it does have one of the best-known of all wines.

Châteauneuf-du-Pape
Whether this wine deserves its status or not is a moot point. There are a number of superb wines produced and there are an equal number of poor ones, but the name is undeniably a magic one. The consequence is that Châteauneuf-du-Pape is the only major Rhône wine that does not always offer value for money: the Pouilly-Fuissé syndrome is repeated (*see* page 60). But make no mistake about it, true Châteauneuf-du-Pape is a magnificent wine: lush, robust and almost overpowering. Up to 13 different grape varieties are used in the blend – mainly Grenache, Cinsault, Syrah and Mourvèdre. This combination of softness, spiciness and tannic depth of flavour produces a unique wine. The only trouble is that the producer does not *have* to use all these varieties to attain *appellation* status. Many are using a preponderance of early maturing Grenache, which makes a soft, lightish wine ready for early drinking but lacking in intensity and that vital depth of flavour. It is ironic that so much harm is being done to this name in the area that in

Rhône

1923 was the initiator of the French *appellation* laws.

The better *négociant* houses, in particular Père Anselme and Jean-Pierre Brotte, make sound wines. There are many excellent estates, of which Château Rayas is the leading light. Others include Château de Beaucastel, Chante Cigale, Domaine des Fines Roches, Domaine Font de Michelle, Château Fortia, Château Moucoil, Domaine Mont-Redon, Château de la Nerte, Close des Papes, Domaine Trintigant and Domain Vieux Télégraphe.

Châteauneuf-du-Pape: the beds of large stones

Gigondas
This nearby *appellation* sometimes produces wines of similar flavour and intensity to Châteauneuf-du-Pape, at a much lower price. Names to look for are Pierre Amadieu, Barroul's Domaine St-Cosmé, Bernard Chuvet, R. Gaudin, Pierre Lambert, Gabriel Meffre, Roger Meffre, Château de Montmiral, Pierre Quiot's Domaine des Pradets and the excellent wines from the cooperative. Tavel is renowned for its full, flavoursome rosé, but I prefer the ones from neighbourng Lirac, which also produces some stunning fruity reds – especially Domaine de Castel-Oualou. There are two new *appellations*, Coteaux de Tricastin and Côtes de Ventoux. I am not sure how they managed to acquire such exalted status.

Beaumes-de-Venise
Ten years ago few dedicated drinkers knew of *vins doux naturels*, sweet white wines made in the same manner as port where fermentation is halted by the addition of alcohol. I remember tasting my first glass of Muscat Beaumes-de-Venise at a 1974 wine trade lunch – only one guest knew what it was. Now the wine is on most restaurant sweet trolleys; it is the 'in' dessert wine, and also a marvellous aperitif wine. One of the main reasons for its popularity is that the higher alcohol content allows the wine to stay fresh well after opening and it is therefore the ideal sweet wine by the glass. The most widely available is the wine from the cooperative in the dreadful bottle reminiscent of a hair oil container. Domaine Bernadins, Domaine Durban and Vidal Fleury are worth searching out.

CONCLUSION

The Rhone is a wonderfully varied region with most of the advantages in favour of the consumer: there is a wealth of interesting individual wines with only Côte Rôtie, Hermitage and Châteauneuf-du-Pape regularly reaching their true market price. A little time spent exploring the villages, preferably in person, is well rewarded.

Hermitage

RHÔNE

CHAPTER EIGHT

PROVENCE

The Provence region is unique, hauntingly beautiful in the hinterland with hillsides covered with dense vegetation and rugged outcrops of rock dotting the skyline. The scorched orange soil and bright light are reminders that Van Gogh's Arles is close by. And there is the smell of the region, a combination of pine and the alluring scent of the ever-present clumps of wild herbs. The beautiful coastal area has wonderful beaches, villages nestling in the hillsides and holiday resorts and towns scattered along its length from Marseille to Nice. The 'Riviera' image of Provence rosé – a few casual bottles by the swimming pool – has belittled the class of both the red and rosé wines (at present the less said about the whites the better). The quality estates have begun to achieve recognition in other parts of France, particularly Paris, and prices have risen as a consequence – but so have standards.

The main grape varieties in Provence are Cinsault, Grenache, Mourvèdre, Tibouren, Carignan, and recently Cabernet Sauvignon. Whites fortunately account for less than 10 per cent of the region's production and are made from Clairette, Sémillon and the Ugni Blanc; experimental plantings of Sauvignon Blanc may help matters. There are three main vineyard regions.

COTEAUX D'AIX EN PROVENCE (VDQS)

This region produces reliable, robust and ripe-flavoured reds with considerable oak and tannin but also soft: not the most subtle of French wines but instantly attractive. They do not benefit much with age as the fruit tends to dry out rather rapidly. Many growers are successfully adding Cabernet Sauvignon to the blends. Château de Fonscolombe, Château de la Garde and Château Grand Seuil are well worth searching out, but the area's superstar is the Château Vignelaure. Its proprietor, Georges Brunet, formerly owned Château La Lagune and now produces a remarkable wine that tastes more Bordelais than Mediterranean. The blend is 60 per cent Cabernet Sauvignon and the remainder Syrah and Grenache. The label proudly states: 'Provenance de vignes cultivées san engrais chimiques, ni herbicides, ni insecticides de synthèse': basically he refuses to use insecticides or artificial fertilizers. This involves planting vegetables and herbs between the vines in spring, and this provides an excellent natural manure, ploughed under before summer, thereby asphyxiating the weeds without the use of herbicides. The work is time- and cost-consuming, but according to Brunet the end result is a 'pure product, a wholesome wine which owes to nature alone the full measure of its flavour and bouquet'.

PROVENCE

Georges Brunel, Château Vignelaure

ENJOYING WINE

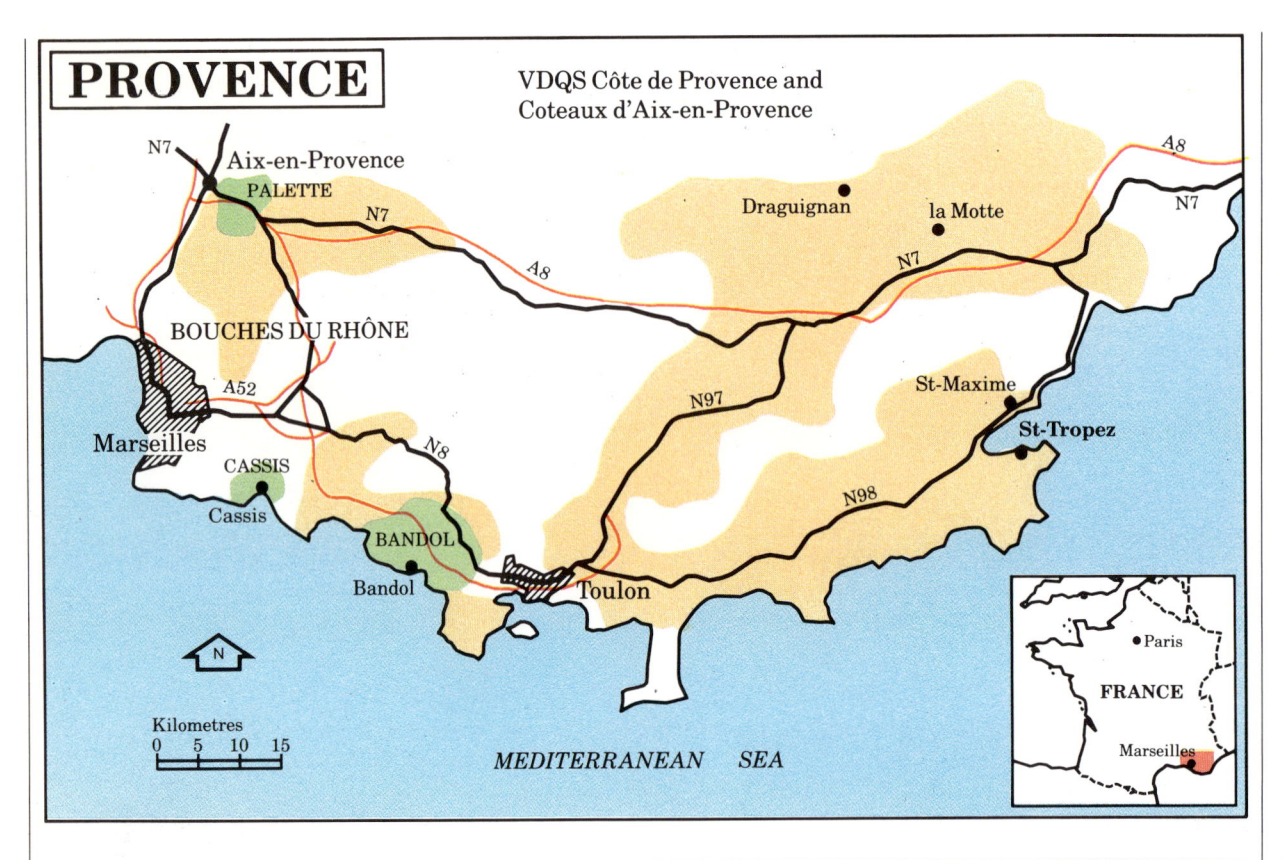

Listel – vineyards on the sand

PROVENCE

Domaine de Belieu, one of the estates of Les Maîtres Vignerons de la Presq'ile de Saint-Tropez

CÔTES DU PROVENCE (*appellation contrôlée*)

Granted full *appellation contrôlée* status in 1977, Côtes de Provence covers three separate areas:

1. The plains surrounding Pierrefeu
2. The St-Tropez peninsula
3. The higher, cooler slopes around Draugignan

Seventy per cent of Provence's production is of rosé and much of this is made in the cooperatives which are scattered all around this region. These wines may lack individual distinction but they are pleasant, cheap and cheerful drinking.

There has been a significant improvement in the standards of the estate-bottled wines of the region, with the Carignan grape reduced in the blends and Cabernet Sauvignon and Syrah gaining in importance. There are two very different styles of red wine. The 'old' Grenache-Carignan blend is soft and fruity, and ideal for immediate consumption: these wines come in the rather fancy club-shaped grower's bottles. Domaine de l'Aumérade, Marius Brun, l'Estandon, Vignobles Kennel and the Maîtres Vignerons de la Presq'ile de Saint-Tropez are well worth trying.

The newer styles with the non-traditional varietals often benefit with some bottle age. They come in 'Bordeaux' bottles. Commanderie de Peyrassol is very good indeed. Winemaker and proprietor Madame Françoise Rigord produces an excellent Cuvée Eperon d'Or which is 40 per cent Cabernet Sauvignon and 20 per cent each of Grenache, Syrah and Mourvèdre: 'new wave' Provence winemaking at its best.

Then there is of course the incomparable Domaines Ott. Château de Selle in the Draugignan area is in a delightful setting of vines among the olive groves and mulberry trees. The red is a delicious full-bodied 'traditional' wine, but it is the delightful rosé which claims the attention. Soft, delicate and fragrant with a beautifully balanced dry finish, it is just the rosé to please white burgundy lovers.

Clos Mireille Blanc de Blancs comes from a vineyard close to the Mediterranean shore in the Pierrefeu area, one of the few white wines to be recommended.

BANDOL (*appellation contrôlée*)

This is the smallest of the major regions, situated on the slopes around the seaside village of Bandol. The main grape is the Mourvèdre which here produces an intense, rich wine with longevity. The dominating forces of the region are the Bunan brothers: Paul, a refugee *vigneron* from Algeria, purchased Moulin des Costes in 1961, and in 1969 Pierre bought Mas de la Rouvière. They run the two properties as a combined operation and now also have Domaine du Bélouve. Paul's son Laurent has joined the family business after studying oenology at Beaune and working in the Napa Valley – there is a considerable Californian influence in the new wine produced at Bélouve, the Vin de Pays du Mont Caume 100% Cabernet Sauvignon. Other significant estates are Château Vannières and the redoubtable Domaine de l'Hermitage. There is really only one problem with the *appellation contrôlée* Bandol – the price. It is worth drinking occasionally, but there are many red wines I would prefer to spend money on.

The adjoining *appellation*, Cassis, is centred around a delightful fishing village crammed with excellent, good value, fish restaurants: but if you drink the overrated, highly priced local white, the meal will no longer be particularly cheap!

Pallette has to be mentioned simply for the fact that the entire *appellation* covers only about 18 ha (44 acres) Bellet is of a little more practical interest, thanks to the efforts of the Bagnis family (of l'Estandon fame). Another tiny region making expensive wine. Well, it is after all close to Nice where the average café on the Promenade des Anglais makes central Paris look inexpensive. All the same, the Bagnis estate of Château de Crémat produces excellent Rosé, Rouge and Blanc.

There are two other important regions close to Provence:

CÔTES DU LUBÉRON (VDQS)

Just to the north of Aix-en-Provence and a source of house wine for many of the restaurants within the region. The cooperative makes inexpensive, pleasant quaffing wines sold under the Cellier du Marrenon label; individual properties such as Château de Mille and Château la Canorgue, and the revolutionary Château Val-Joanis, produce well-structured, soft and instantly drinkable red wines with more in common with Provence than the Rhône just north.

LES SABLES DU GOLFE DU LION (*vin de pays*)

The Compagnie des Salins du Midi produces virtually all of France's salt. It owns huge tracts of land and sand bars around the mouth of the Rhône and across the Gard and Hérault regions, all the way to the environs of the port of Sète. What has this got to do with a book on wine you may well ask. Well, believe it or not, an associated company, Domaine Viticoles des Salins du Midi (Listel) is the largest vineyard owner in France, and right here on the sand!

Here are well over 1000 ha (2470 acres) of vines planted on sand dunes formed by the Rhône river, totally hemmed in by salt water. The plots are actually surrounded by freshwater ditches controlled by sluice gates. Nothing is left to chance: the vines are planted 2.5 m (8 ft) apart to allow mechanical cultivation and harvesting; the most up-to-date winemaking equipment 'processes' the huge quantities of grapes making beautifully clean, crisp white wines totally in line with the modern-day taste, with none of the oiliness associated with the whites of the surrounding Languedoc and Roussillon. The reds are interesting as the firm has planted vast acres of Cabernet Sauvignon. But the most unique wine is the *gris de gris*, a very delicate pink colour with definite flavour, made from very gentle pressing (*à la Champagne*) of Grenache and Cinsault. Only the first half of the pressing is used for this wine.

This may all sound unromantic, but the fact is that an innovative company with technical expertise is producing huge quantities of sound, attractive everyday wine at reasonable prices — and in the dreaded Midi region. It also owns land in the Pierrefeu area of the Côtes de Provence, marketing these wines as Château la Gordonne.

TOURING AROUND PROVENCE

For people travelling from Britain a holiday in the South of France is not the trek it was a couple of decades ago. The main north-south *autoroute* allows a reasonably comfortable drive from Calais to Aix-en-Provence in a day. There is overnight rail travel with accompanying car, and the airlines offer extremely attractive fly-drive packages to both Nice and Marseille. The *autoroute* cuts a swathe through the region allowing Marseilles to Nice in a matter of a few hours, but it is the small roads that offer the interest.

Provençale food is famous for the almost overpoweringly pungent and flavoursome mixture of olive oil, tomatoes, herbs and garlic. *Anchoiade* (pounded anchovies on toast) and *tapenade* (pounded black olives on toast) are the perfect patio hors-d'oeuvres with a glass or three of rosé. The ubiquitous *salade niçoise*, *pissaladière* (onion flan with olives and anchovies), mussels from the St-Tropez bay are all prime examples; and, of course, there is the famous *bouillabaise*. The local markets are crammed with all the necessary ingredients and the locals eat well at home. Unfortunately tourism is responsible for a large number of the restaurants merely serving an unvarying range of grills and *frites* at a fairly basic level: many of the establishments are leased out to different people each season who are only interested in the profit, and neither goodwill nor reputation is of any concern whatsoever.

Of course there are many excellent establishments. Nice is almost an embarrassment of riches, from the modest bistros to the splendid cuisine of Jacques Maximin at The Negresco. Mougins near Cannes has the world-famous Moulin of Roger Vergé. His influence has created a small town of restaurants, all of excellent standards. Lou Capoun in Cogolin, Chez Fuchs in St-Tropez (if you can put up with the insolent service — don't eat anywhere else in the town unless you enjoy wasting money). Chez Camille outside the town on the road to Ramatuelle; the charming, friendly Denise et Michel on Le Lavandou, which has both interesting regional wines and real *poulet niçoise*; and the Auberge Fleurie inland at La Motte — all offer marvellous value for money. There are many more. If I am wandering around the area with no fixed plans, and am unsure of the place, I order a *demi-pichet* of rosé as an aperitif. If it is from Provence I stay, but if it is a blended plonk of dubious parentage I leave before ordering. If a restaurant has little interest in the regional wine, what interest will it have in the cuisine?

CHAPTER NINE

Germany

German wines suffer from an image problem. Most wine drinkers are well acquainted with photographs of breathtaking vistas of the steep hillsides of the Mosel Valley, but few have any knowledge of the finer products of these vineyards. When one thinks of the wines of France, Champagne, Burgundy and Bordeaux immediately come to mind, not *vin de table* from the Midi. Similarly Rioja epitomizes modern-day Spanish wine – not the plonk of La Mancha. With Germany it is all very different; the vast majority of consumers think of Liebfraumilch or wines of similarly low status. There is a 'Germanic' style that is aimed at the most unsophisticated of wine drinkers: sweetish, bland products with little individuality of flavour and no depth of character. They are stunning only in their collective mediocrity. As if this was not bad enough, over a quarter of 'German' wine sold in Britain is not actually made solely from German grapes. In fact, some products may have very little local content! 'Euroblending' was made legal in the country's 1971 wine laws: companies can import the cheapest of wines from eastern and southern Europe, blend with some of the cheapest of the local stuff, add the *Süssreserve* (more about this later), thereby 'Germanifying' the wine. The product is then called by a German title, written in Gothic script, and somewhere on the label *'EEC Tafelwein'* is added – it is hoped that the purchaser will not possess sufficient knowledge of the intricacies of the local grades of quality, and will consider this a bottle of German wine.

Before the 1971 revision of the German wine laws, brought in to comply with EEC regulations, this practice was strictly illegal – now it is encouraged. Also, at this lowly level, it is legal to add sugar, thereby camouflaging poor wine, both local and imported. It does not take much imagination to realize the possibilities for fraud, and there have been many examples of the dishonest minority claiming illegal status for quantities of their cheapest wines, thereby spoiling the reputations of the honest majority. This is verified by the many prominent wine houses at the moment bereft of directors who are unwilling guests of the West German state.

EEC Tafelwein and (*Deutscher*) *Tafelwein*, at the bottom of the categories, are simply not worth the bother. Unfortunately the same is true of much of the QbA – *Qualitätswein bestimmter Anbaugebiete*, or quality wine from a specified area. Topnotch growers and the quality houses sell excellent wine of this status, but the rest is poor and not much of an improvement on the lower categories: in other words, a large percentage of the 'quality wine' controlled by state supervision is anything but. Then again, we are discussing winemaking in a country that allows its gigantic cooperatives to label their wines 'estate bottled'.

NATURAL SWEETNESS

The fact that I dislike Muscadet does not prevent my enjoyment of fine white burgundy. Therefore these dull, uninteresting wines should not stop me and the rest of the world's wine lovers from enjoying the delights of Germany's finer wines, the *Qualitätsweine mit Prädikat*. There are six distinctions, *Kabinett, Spätlese, Auslese, Beerenauslese, Trockenbeerenauslese and Eiswein*, all dependent on the percentage of natural sugar – and here lies the problem for many drinkers. In the 1980s the world is drinking dry white wine, yet in Germany the higher the quality, the sweeter the wine. By way of contradiction the Germans, how-

Germany

THE QUALITY CATEGORIES

Auslese
Spätlese
Kabinett

QmP QUALITÄTSWEIN mit PRÄDIKAT (Quality wine with Distinction)
Eiswein
Trockenbeerenauslese
Beerenauslese

QbA QUALITÄTSWEIN (Quality wine)

LANDWEIN

TAFELWEIN

WEST GERMANY

GERMANY'S ELEVEN WINE REGIONS

The Mosel: ancient villages – modern wines

ever, point to their dryish, austere Franconian (Franken) wines and their *Trocken* and *Halbtrocken* types ('dry' and 'semi-dry') so popular on the home market – but these are not particularly fierce competition for the quality dry whites of the rest of the world. The light *Trocken* wines merely emphasize the need for wines from this northern climate to retain a degree of their residual sugar to enhance the fruit flavour.

Natural sweetness does not include the practice of *Anreicherung* ('enrichment') previously mentioned, where wines of the QbA category and lower are permitted the addition of sugar to increase alcohol content (and mask foul, undrinkable plonk?); but it does include unfermented grape juice, *Süssreserve* ('sweet reserve'), which may be added to the wine shortly before bottling. In the *mit Prädikat* category it is theoretically not needed above the *Spätlese* quality as the wines have such large percentages of natural sugar.

Well-made *Kabinett* and *Spätlese* are the ideal wines for quaffing without food, especially the Rieslings, and are reasonably priced. *Auslese* wines can often be an excellent aperitif – marvellous fruit and low alcohol – but the others are in the dessert wine category, made with similar complications to the best Sauternes. Obviously the best of them have a price to match. I would happily part with the last of my money for a bottle of Riesling *Beerenauslese* and *Trockenbeerenauslese*, but I am yet to be convinced that the *Eiswein* (literally 'ice wine', from frozen grapes – they are the last picked in midwinter) is worth the same or even higher prices. One word of warning: many of the lesser grape varieties are affected by the *Edelfäule* ('noble rot') much more easily – and earlier – than the Rieslings; they will cost considerably less, but lack the all-important rich intensity.

THE MAJOR REGIONS

Mosel-Saar-Ruwer

Without doubt my favourite of all German regions. Forget about your Bernkasteler and Piesporter Michelsberg, and concentrate on single-vineyard Rieslings of *Kabinett*, *Spätlese* and *Auslese* quality – beautifully refreshing, flavoursome wines reeking of appley fruit with a clean acid finish.

Saar and Ruwer

The cold weather with chilly winds and murderous frosts means fewer really first-rate vintages here. Weather permitting, however, the wines can really show their class, as the vintages of 1983, 1976 and 1971 prove. In the Saar, Egon Müller's Scharzhofberg is in a class of its own. Ockfener Bockstein and Henenberg are superb vineyards. The Ruwer has the superb Maximin Grünhäuser owned by C. von Schubert.

Mosel

The most spectacular vineyard scenery in the world. Much of the land around the Mosel, or Moselle, is so ridiculously steep that actual cultivation seems to be out of the question. Nothing exemplifies more the differing aspects of vineyard cultivation than comparing the machine-worked central valley of California and irrigated areas of Australia with these slopes, where individuals somehow manage the mechanics of cultivation assisted by a tractor winch stationed at the top, which simply pulls an iron seat (with vineyard worker) up the slope as he painstakingly tends the vines. The soil, if that is the correct term, on the finest slopes is amazing. It is covered with pieces of slate, and as they slip down to the bottom of the slope they are collected and redistributed at the top, as they play a vital part in heat reflection. The labour costs are obviously extremely high and, as in the Rheingau and Rheinhessen, a large percentage of the vineyards has been recently ripped out and reconstructed, with old terraces replaced by more gentle slopes, allowing easier working conditions. This process (*Flurbereinigung*) has involved both Federal and local governments, and obviously the process of reallocating the land requires considerable diplomacy from the legislators and forethought and pragmatism from the growers: I cannot see such schemes working in some of Germany's neighbouring countries!

As the river twists, turns and flows northeast to its confluence with the Rhine at Koblenz, it passes through a series of towns with familiar and not-so-familiar names: Lieser, Bernkastel-Kues, Graach, Wehlen, Ürzig, Zeltingen, Krov and Traben cover the most famous estates (Germany's vast numbers of vineyards and thousands of producers preclude comprehensive listings in anything other than a specialist book. I have restricted my references to vineyards and growers I know well – some are major names, some are not). The list of great wines includes Trittenheimer Apotheke, Piesporter Goldtropf, Brauneberger Juffer, Lieserer Schlossberg, Bernkasteler Badstube and Graben, Graacher Himmelreich, Wehlener Sonnenuhr, Ürziger Würzgarten, Zeltinger Himmelreich and, of course, the most famous of all, Bernkasteler Doktor. Highly recommended producers are Dr Fischer, Friedrich Wilhelm Gymnasium, von Kesselstatt, SA Prüm, J.J. Prüm, Max Ferdinand Richter, Bert Simon and Dr Thanisch. My favourite of all is a family firm in Bernkastel, J. Lauerberg, who make outstanding, fragrant Mosels with a considerable amount of acidity and depth. Herr Lauerberg is an amazing winemaker – no matter how fine his product, he is always a little critical and seeking perfection. In 1978 I spent a day with him, tasting a series of 30 wines from excellent QbAs of recent vintages right through the range to Bernkasteler Doktor *Auslese* 1971 (not then ready but well on the way to greatness), and a wonderful Doktor *Beerenauslese* 1959: ripe in taste and beautifully balanced. Yet at no time

ENJOYING WINE

Schloss Vollrads, Rheingau

Germany

ENJOYING WINE

was he totally satisfied. He would discuss the relative merits and we would agree on the remarkable standards of excellence, and yet he would always add, 'if just a little more...'.

Rheingau

Between Mainz and Bingen the Rhine turns around and runs southwest instead of north, and thus a small but significant series of sheltered, south-facing slopes bare their grapes to the sun. This micro-climate produces Rieslings of comparable quality to the Mosel: slightly fuller and more flavoursome, with a warm, honeyed richness – wonderful drinking! There are a number of famous estates founded by the aristocratic families from the court of nearby Mainz: Schloss Groenesteyn,

Bernkasteler Doktor, Mosel

Germany

Schloss Johannisberg, Schloss Reinhartshausen, Schloss Vollrads.

The greater Rheingau vineyards are almost totally planted with Riesling. The names are not as well known as their Mosel counterparts and, because of the small output of the area, more difficult to find. Eltviller Sonnenberg, Rauenthaler Rothenberg, Kiedricher Sandgrub, Erbacher Marcobrunn, Oestricher Lenchen, Winkeler Hasensprung, Johannisberger Erntebringer, Geisenheimer Klauserweg and Rüdesheimer Berg Rottland. Top producers are J. Fischer, Königin Viktoria Berg, G.H. von Mumm (yes, the family used to own the champagne house), Dr Heinrich Nagler, Freiherrlich Langwert von Simmern, the Staatsweingut (State Domain), Domdechant Werner and, of course, the previously mentioned estates. Schloss Graf von Schönborn in Hattenheim is one of the largest vineyard owners in the Rheingau with holdings spread all over the region. I have never tasted a poor wine from this house. Its QbAs are delightful and its gorgeous top-quality wines are as fine as the noble Riesling can produce. Oak is still a valued part of Schönborn winemaking, and one result is a superb soft, delicate style, with considerable intensity.

Winemaker Robert Englert is a Hollywood central casting's image of the rotund jolly German winemaker. He will discuss the relative merits of his Hattenheimer Mannberg and the equivalent quality Geisenheimer Schlossgarten for hours, all the time making sure the bottles are kept moving around the table and glasses are continually full.

Rheinhessen

The largest of all the German regions, but more important for interesting crossing of grape varieties than quality. This is the theoretical birthplace of Liebfraumilch and is full of the names best known around the world for inexpensive wines. The cooperatives figure prominently, processing vast quantities of passable wine, and some top-quality ones, often under the labels of prominent shippers. The excellent house of H. Sichel Söhne, best known for Blue Nun, but also one of the big exporters of estate wines, has sold outstanding wines from the cooperative at Nierstein: the Spiegelberg Kabinett 1975 Silver Nun launched to celebrate the silver wedding jubilee of Queen Elizabeth II and Prince Philip was one of the best-value German wines I have drunk. The big district names – Nierstein, Bingen, Oppenheim – tend to swallow up much of the quality individual wines. It is worth searching for grower's wines from smaller villages such as Alsheim, Guntersblum and Nackenheim. Balbach Erben, Franz Karl Schmidt and J. & H. Strub are names to remember. Carl Sittman at Oppenheim is the largest family business in the region, established in 1879. Its *Qualitätsweine mit Prädikat* (QmP) wines are of very high standards. It is indicative of the problems of the German wine industry that managing director Walter Sittman's 1984 harvest report warned trade buyers: 'be on your guard when unusually cheap wines are offered, because there must be a suspicion of illegality'.

Nahe

The Nahe is a smallish tributary that flows through an idyllic, peaceful valley along to the Rhine at Bingen. Thereafter the surrounding vineyard area borders the Rheinhessen, but makes wines of different style – a little more finesse and a drier finish, and yet not the depth of the Rheingau. It is a picturesque countryside, but one to visit during the day and stay elsewhere in the evening. I have had more fun in Britain stranded on a wet public holiday with a broken-down car than on a Saturday night in Bad Kreuznach, and that is the wine capital of the region.

The complexities of German wine labelling are highlighted when considering the main wine towns – another Rüdesheim (this time followed by Rosengarten), appears to offer nothing but confusion to the buyer. Schlossböckelheim and Kreuznach are the other main districts. The most important producer is the immaculate State Domain at Niederhausen; also August Annheuser, Hans Crusius (often imported through Deinhard, but he is acknowledged on the label), Reichsgraf von Piettenberg and Jacob Schneider.

Rheinpfalz (Palatinate)

This is the warmest of all the wine regions of Germany, stretching from the Rheinhessen southwards to the borders with Alsace. Sylvaner is the dominant grape, with much Müller-Thurgau and very little Riesling. There are two distinctly

ENJOYING WINE

Vineyards of Schloss Johannisberg, Rheingau

GERMANY

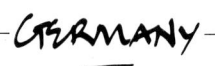

Deinhard & Co, Koblenz

No analysis of German wine would be complete without a description of this remarkable firm.

In 1882 the well-established house of Deinhard purchased the Baron Wetzel-Karben's estates in Oestrich and Rüdesheim. Since then the firm has continued buying, and now it is a major vineyard owner. Deinhard's vineyards are almost a listing of *Who's Who* of the regions, including Bernkasteler Badstube, Bratenhöfchen, Graben and, of course, Doktor (it bought these vines in 1900 for the princely sum of 100 gold marks per vine), Wehlner Sonnenuhr, Kaseler Hitzlay and Nieschen in the Mosel-Saar-Ruwer. In the Rheingau the house has Johannisberger Erntebringer, Geisenheimer Klauserweg and Rothenberg, Oestricher Lenchen and Doosberg, Winkeler Hasensprung, Rüdesheimer Berg Roseneck and many others. In 1973 it bought an estate in the Palatinate with Deidesheimer Herrgottsacker, Forster Ungeheuer and Ruppertsberger Linsenbuch.

Deinhard's everyday wines are most drinkable and well above the average of most other houses, but it is these estates that really show the firm's class: no overt commercialization of style, merely the finest vineyards receiving great care and attention, and winemaking that concentrates on enhancement of the superb fruit.

---

different areas: the northern Mittelhaardt producing excellent quality wines, and the southern Oberhaardt, source of the base ingredient for the blends that actually use the local product.

The better wines possess a spicy richness not seen in the rest of the country – considerable depth of flavour and less acidity. Important estates, all predominantly planted in Riesling, are Bassermann-Jordan, von Bühl and Dr Bürklin-Wolf.

OTHER REGIONS

There are six other German regions, but they are of no great importance on the export market. Ahr, a small valley south of Bonn, is known locally for the production of light red wines from Spätburgunder (Pinot Noir) and Portugieser grapes: they taste reasonably good when you are touring Germany and exposed to a surfeit of white wines, but only then! Baden, the southernmost region, is dominated by huge cooperatives producing vast quantities of anonymous, dull wines. The locals are proud of the fact that the cooperative at Breisach is the largest winery in Europe. Its statistics may impress the mind, but the wine does not excite the palate. Franken (Franconia), another small region growing mainly Müller-Thurgau and Sylvaner, produces dryish wine that commands a premium price on the local market; it is easily recognizable by the squat, dark-green 'Franconian flask', the *Bocksbeutel* (and you all thought that Mateus invented its own bottle shape!). Hessische Bergstrasse is a mere 380 ha (940 acres), the smallest region, producing Riesling and Müller-Thurgau. Virtually all wine is sold to the cooperatives. Mittelrhein, between Bingen and Bonn, is a long stretched-out region, with only 700 ha (1730 acres) of vineyards, mostly planted in Riesling. Württemberg, east of Baden, has a national reputation for its red wines – once again, more out of desperation of claret-starved wine drinkers than any inherent quality factors of their own.

GERMANY – AT THE CROSSROADS

Readers will realize that I *do* enjoy German wines, but only the quality ones. The rapid and recent demise of the Riesling grape in favour of less shy-bearing, easier cultivated grapes with more 'instant fruitiness' does not augur well for the future. German winemakers are renowned for their skills – witness the worldwide spread of graduates of the Geisenheim Institute – but are they becoming too clever? There is no doubt their skilful ways are contributing to the steadiness in prices of the *Kabinett, Spätlese* and *Auslese* categories, but I for one would pay more for the retention of some of the admittedly expensive traditions. I find it difficult enough to select with confidence the better wines from the better producers – even the small Rheingau has over 2000 growers, 1800 with less than 1 ha (2½ acres), and over 400 bottle their own wine – without having to worry about the burgeoning trend towards blander, more commercial wines. But do not give up: try a few of the *Kabinett* and *Spätlese* wines mentioned and then experiment with a few of the thousands that are not. Yes, maybe they are a little sweet, but the end result is a vivacious and yet crisp finish – and with a *very* low alcohol content.

CHAPTER TEN

ITALY

The quality of Italian wines is beginning to shine through; you just have to know where to look.

GENERAL

Italy is a country of excess: life, love, art, food, music – she never does things by halves, and especially so with wine. The country is the biggest producer in the world, 3.6 million ha (9 million acres) of cultivation yielding an oceanic 8 billion litres of the nectar (although not all can be safely labelled as divine). Italy can lay some claim to be the cradle of winemaking, for it was the builders of the Roman empire who encouraged its production throughout much of Western Europe, and the worship of Bacchus which continues in its various forms to this day. Much of this vast output is exported, finding its way into its EEC partners' bottles at the lowlier end of the market, and onto the tables of Manhattan restaurants at the other. Germany, where it bulks out the Euroblends, consumes huge quantities. France imports an excess according to native growers, but some thin French table wines need the enrichment of the full-bodied Italian reds. In Britain, Italian wine is often dismissed by the serious consumer as a shoddy tipple. This is a great shame, as with a little exploration the buyer will find great rewards at a far lower price than for a comparable wine from, say, France. Rest assured that within that sea of 8 billion litres are some very fine drinking wines.

WHY THE BAD REPUTATION?

Until recently laws did not ensure a proper standard of quality control. However, new laws have come into force with some degree of success. Italy's reputation in the past suffered due to a flood of sour whites and enamel-dissolving reds onto the shelves of British off-licence shops. This has changed, since new labelling practices have been adopted to ensure quality in the bottle.

Yet it was only in the not-so-far-off sixties that some hair-raising scandals hit Italian wine imports. The 'Great Banana skin' swindle did untold damage to the reputation of the wines when huge consignments were found to contain anything but grapes!

It seems, too, that the proprietors of countless Italian restaurants are responsible for inflicting even more wounds on the tottering reputation of this great wine-producing nation. Why is it that the expatriate citizens of that often fervently nationalistic country (look at the way they support

'In the time it took for me to establish whether the wine was *"Denominazione di origine controlla e garantita"* or not, my minestrone's gone cold!'

ITALY

their soccer and opera) subject us, once captive at their tables, to such unspeakable house wines? The average Italian restauranteur is the worst possible ambassador for his country's wines, and in my experience merchants around the world bemoan the fact that they are only interested in price.

However, the DOC regulations have at least put an end to the prospect of a bottle of fermented unimaginables! But here again we are soon floundering in confusion. The labelling is not the easiest of systems to follow. Apart from DOC, we now have a more stringent classification, namely DOCG: *denominazione di origine controllata e garantita*. This was introduced in 1984 as a government guarantee of authenticity for five wines: Barbaresco, Barolo, Brunello di Montalcino, Chianti, and Vino Nobile di Montepulciano. What impact this may have has yet to be seen. But apart from these five illustrious wines, the vast outpouring of Italian wine is badly regulated to this day. The DOC formulae are often so rigid that growers decline to involve themselves in it, as in the case of Sassicaia and Tignanello, the highly praised Cabernet Sauvignon blends from Tuscany. Indeed, many great Italian wines do not carry the DOC tag but instead are labelled under the umbrella term *Vino da Tavola*, simply because either they are situated outside the DOC zones, or rather, the producers deliberately shun the regulations, because they consider their wines too special to be labelled by a common denominator.

There are further distinctions indicated by Riserva, a specified age or maturity; and Classico, wine from the heartland of the particular area.

The rule is to identify the producer and know his reputation first. This involves familiarizing yourself with a great number of Italian names, a worthwhile occupation with the added bonus of some excellent wine drinking.

The DOC does help as a basic guideline providing you bear in mind the individuality inherent in Italian wine production. There are, after all, some 210 DOC zones, producing more than 500 wine types; yet DOC applies to only 10 per cent of Italian wine.

Start with a region and proceed from there. There are some 19 regions of production, and it is an explorer's market, so put on your ten-league tasting boots!

THE REVOLUTION

The changes in technique and expertise of recent years are making Italy the country of the future with regard to middle-range wine production. With the introductions of exciting new grape varietals, in particular Chardonnay, Italian whites are due for a major reassessment, and for vastly increased availability around the world.

Now that France has, theoretically, exhausted its potential for further Chardonnay plantings, the extensive growing potential of the Italian slopes is coming into its own. At the same time the Italians have at last come to terms with the Chardonnay grape, the most sought-after white wine varietal in an increasingly white-wine drinking world. Xavier Loron from Beaujolais has told me recently that restricted Chardonnay plantings were curtailing French production. Moreover, the price of white Burgundies had doubled just before the 1984 harvest because of increased demand and limited supply. The latter is due to market factors, a poor harvest and a strong US dollar hitting a weak franc. I could not purchase enough for my 1985 requirements. So where do we go to buy our classic whites?

Well, northern hemisphere wine buyers can buy southern hemisphere Chardonnay, but the price is high because of the distances travelled and the premium price fetched at home. Therefore we look to Italy to fill the gap in the market and we find some excellent new wave whites beginning to arrive.

At a recent *Decanter* magazine tasting, Italian whites were given high praise. For example, the Artesino Alois Lageder Chardonnay from the South Tyrol region was particularly lauded. Yet these wines have only been in production since 1982-3. Sometimes the wine is slightly *spritzig* and maybe offends the traditional anticipation of more mature Chardonnay but let's face it, we have often drunk dull, flat, life-bereft white burgundies in our time; perhaps we shall profit by this new style, reasonably priced treatment. As the writer and Burgundy expert Christopher Fielden said of the Artesino Chardonnay, it 'tastes like a good Mâconnais'. Given time, the dramatic arrival of Chardonnay on Italian soil may yet produce fireworks in the worldwide market for white wine.

ENJOYING WINE

ITALY

Map of Italy showing wine regions:

- **VALLE D'AOSTA**
- **PIEDMONT** — Turin; Barbaresco, Asti Spumante, Dolcetto, Barolo
- **LOMBARDY** — Milan
- **TRENTINO ALTO ADIGE**
- **FRUILI VENEZIA-GIULIA**
- **VENETO** — Venice; Valpolicella, Amarone, Bardolino, Soave
- **LIGURIA** — Genoa
- **EMILIA-ROMAGNA** — Bologna; Lambrusco
- **TUSCANY** — Florence; Vernaccia di San Gimignano, Chianti, Nobile de Montepugano, Brunello di Montalcino
- **THE MARCHES** — Verdicchio
- **UMBRIA**
- **LATIUM** — Rome; Frascati
- **ABRUZZI** — Montepulciano
- **MOLISE**
- **CAMPANIA** — Naples; Taurasi, Lacrima Christi
- **APULIA** — Castel del Monte
- **BASILICATA**
- **CALABRIA**
- **SICILY** — Palermo
- **SARDINIA** — Cannonau, Torbato
- **CORSICA** — Patrimonio, Coteaux d'Ajaccio
- **ELBA**

Surrounding countries: FRANCE, SWITZERLAND, AUSTRIA, YUGOSLAVIA, ALBANIA

Seas: LIGURIAN SEA, ADRIATIC SEA, TYRRHENIAN SEA, IONIAN SEA, MEDITERRANEAN SEA

Kilometres 0 100 200

Italy

Castello di Vicchiomaggio, Chianti

However, the biggest distributors in Britain have said that as yet these wines have made little impact. There is a huge demand as ever for the basic generics such as Soave, Valpolicella, etc.

The wine box has caused a slight decrease in bulk. But it is the Italians' own fault: they do nothing to promote their own wines.

This wind of change has been blowing throughout Italian wine growing. In Chianti the introduction of new varietals to blend with the existing grape formulae is producing a whole new wave of reds.

And so the story goes on. Italy may be the country of the future for middle-range wine production. In a world where more and more people are beginning to drink wine, watch out for the rise of the Italian reputation from the ashes, as it were, of past scandals.

ENJOYING WINE

Torgiano, Umbria

NORTHERN ITALY

Piedmont

Great oaky reds, mouth-filling flavour and strength, robust, blood-rich accompaniment to food: these are the epithets ascribed to Piedmont wines. The great names such as Barolo and Barbaresco, which roll off the tongue and equally easily slide down the throat, are wines to be wary of. They are made from the noble grape Nebbiolo, which comes from the Italian word for fog: and this great sea mist rolls in every autumn and makes these wines susceptible to vintage years. And note that these wines taste anything but 'nebulous'.

The wines spend a good many years in cask (often far too long) and require considerable bottle age. Barbaresco is theoretically lighter and more fruity, but often excessive oak ageing results in thick, soupy wines with little charm. If only the winemakers would remove the wine from cask and bottle when it is ready, reather than leave in oak until an order arrives!

Gaja is the most innovative and largest producer of Barbaresco, with ridiculously high prices closer to *premier cru* Burgundy; definitely *not* worth the money. Fratelli Baraco, Bersano, Paolo Cordero di Montezemolo, Bruno Giacosa, Maccerini and the excellent Pio Cesara offer much better value.

Other wines worth tasting from the region are Barbera d'Alba, Carema, the excellent value and

ITALY

underrated Dolcetto, Fara, Ghemme and Siano. Cortese di Gavi is the pick of the white wines. I particularly like the crisp, flavoursome wines from Bersano, La Scolca and Tenuta San Pietro.

Lombardy

The alpine slopes and valleys produce Valtellina DOCs and carry delightful names such as Inferno, Grumello, Valgella and Sassella. Expect to see DOC on the bottle from this region. Lombardy wines are not normally capable of greatness: workhorse reds from the Oltrepo Pavese DOCs are adequate.

The Nebbiolo arrives drier in the bottle hereabouts. For a raisiny glass, check out Sfurzat, a heavyweight of the fairground class, high in glycerine.

Fortunately, the Chardonnay grape is beginning to arrive and the whites generally are well made, particularly from Lake Garda's southern shore, where the Luguna is stylish white, deliciously dry and goes well with the fish of the lake.

Names to rely on are Rainoldi, Tona, Negri, Bettini, Pavese (these wines are always identified by the grape variety on the label) and Pellizzatti. Frecciarosso is renowned. Also, to be drunk young, Riviera del Garda Bresciano, both red and rose.

Alto Adige (Sud Tyrol)

Not the most easily understood of Italian wines, but this hybrid Italian-Germanic region (the northernmost province) hosts most of Italy's really exciting developments with classic grape varieties. Previously this region's wines were light and Germanic. Now Chardonnay, Gewürztraminer (the traminer grape originated here), Sauvignon, Sylvaner, Cabernet Sauvignon, Merlot and Pinot Noir are captivating the hearts and palates of wine drinkers throughout Europe and the United States who are searching for clean, stylish wines of pedigree at a reasonable price. Taste a bottle or three of these whites and discover just how difficult it is to revert to the more ordinary but better-known names!

Tiefenbrunner is the super star of the region. Hofstatter, Altois Laegeder, Pojer & Sandri and Zeni are also highly recommended.

Veneto

The mountains in the north of the Venetian basin slope down to the Adriatic and the sublime city of Venice, where on deserted winter afternoons I have enjoyed the tiny warming glass of local Amarone, and congratulated myself on coming at just about the only time of the year when you can avoid the tourist hordes. Sample this rich, ruby wine with the Venetian speciality of *carpaccio*: thin slices of raw fillet served with olive oil and lemon and a fiery relish made from whisky and horseradish! The distinctive meaty flavour of Amarone comes from the *recioto* method of selecting the 'ear of the bunch' (*recce* = 'ear') which has received more sun than the rest, so the grapes are riper, then semi-dried on racks to concentrate the sugar further and produce this austere, yet comforting wine.

Veneto wines are the ones we all know best — and often worst: Valpolicella, Bardolino, Soave. Yet this region also has been in the vanguard of the changes sweeping through Italian wine production.

French grape varieties are being established: especially Merlot, Cabernets Sauvignon and Franc, and both white and black Pinots.

Each season Veneto opens the sluice gates and some 10 million hectolitres of wine gushes out. Do not be put off by the odd disappointment, for there are increasingly fine wines to be found within this vast industrial output.

Friuli-Venezia-Giula

Here grow Italy's finest and most expensive whites. Pinot Grigio is outstanding and there are Chardonnays and Sauvignons, but these are not so easy to find outside the domestic market. Much of this white wine is consumed locally, and only a certain amount finds its way onto the world's shelves. What good white is available is not yet in demand. It is the same old story of the Italians being their own worst enemies, and failing to promote their wines in the manner of the French or Spanish.

Names to look out for: Collio and Colli Orientali del Friuli; and check Count Formentini wines; Bollini, Giacomelli and Jermann for excellent Pinot Grigio; Marco Felluga and Livio Felluga for Tocai del Collio.

ENJOYING WINE

The village of Carema

Friuli is in many ways like the Alto Adige in that it should soon be coming into great international prominence. The whites are clean, fresh, fruity and there is a silky finish to their considerable depth.

CENTRAL ITALY

Tuscany

The superb Tuscan landscape produces the three historic greats of Italian red wine: Chianti, Vino Nobilo di Montepulciano and Brunello di Montalcino.

Chianti is steeped in history. They have been making wine in the rocky, unfertile soil of the gentle Tuscan hills for many, many centuries. Fossilized remains of an ancestor of the wild vine have been found here, which suggests that the grape predates man in this part of the world.

However, not all bottles labelled Chianti contain the real thing. To define Chianti we can go back as far as Baron Bettino Ricasoli, who became Prime Minister in 1861, for his classic definition: a blend of Sangiovese and Canaiolo red grapes with the addition of Trebbiano and Malvasia del Chianti white. This basic formula was adopted some years ago for the DOC regulatory laws, in order to control the problem of bogus Chianti. Chianti is now in the throes of change and innovation, as in other areas of Italian wine making, and that basic formula is undergoing some revision. Producers like Piero Antinori explain it thus: in the past the Sangiovese grape was usually fermented with the stem and needed the addition of Malvasia to soften the wine. Nowadays growers favour new varieties like the Cabernets, both Franc and Sauvignon, which adapt well to Etruscan terrain and 'can complement Sangiovese, support it, and make up for its shortcomings, especially with regard to colour, aroma and body'. New oak and ageing in the bottle combine to develop the final bouquet of modern Chianti. All the processes from vine to wine bottling 'are now in full evolution. We are only at the beginning. A new era and therefore a new tradition is perhaps beginning for Chianti'. Tradition is the keyword in this ancient wine-growing region.

Selecting the best from Chianti is not easy as there is a large amount of rubbish produced and sold to the unsuspecting public. One cannot use price as a guide as much of the more expensive wines are poor ... but there are many reputable names, including Antinori, Berardenga Capezzane, Frescobaldi Montalbano, Monte Vertine, Pasolini, Querceto, Riecine, Rocca della Macie, Volpaia and Vicchiomaggio.

Brunello di Montalcino is reputed to be Italy's most expensive wine – yes, even more pricy than Gaja Barbaresco! They are no better value for money.

Vino Nobilo di Montepulciano is a different story. The best are full of fruit and delicate flavour. The Fognano Riserva is particularly good – a product of a large 100 acre estate where quality of fruit is paramount. If the DOCG laws can be used to ensure standards of more wines like this, then long may they flourish!

Sassicaia is a superb Cabernet Sauvignon, but no DOC status. The white Vernaccia di San Gimignano is a full flavoured wine more akin to Meursault than Italian wines. It was the first wine to be given DOC status.

Emilia Romagna

The region is notable for the production of Lambrusco, the red fizz to be found in the kitchen at parties, which is now undergoing some reassessment through the worthwhile efforts of the drier Secco Lambrusco. Grasparossa di Castelvetro is slightly drier, and Giacobazzi and Cavicchioli also come with recommendations.

There is a highly drinkable white from this region: Trebbiano di Romagna.

Not all Lambrusco is bad and you can be pleasantly surprised.

The Marches

Verdicchio to be drunk young, from Castelli di Jesi, and Santa Chiara.

Latium

Why is it that when you sit in a cantina in Frascati, you will be served a delicious, soft, light white wine that bears no resemblance to the stuff called Frascati and sold around the world?

What I substitute for it is the ever-dependable Marino Superiore from Castelli Romani, more like the local Frascati than the exported wines. Gotto

ENJOYING WINE

Soave

d'Oro is reliable.

Look out for: EST! EST! EST! and Colli Albani, both good blends of Trebbiano, Malvasia and other varieties; good Frascati from Colli di Catone and Velletri.

SOUTHERN ITALY

Campania
Mastroberardino produces the venerable and traditional Taurasi, a dry red made from the Aglianico vine. The Riserva is recommended.

Lacrima Christi from the slopes of Vesuvius is a wine to try from Saviano in all varieties: dry, medium, sweet and *frizzante* whites, and reds and sparkling rosé. Also the dry whites: Greco di Tufo and Fiano di Avellino.

The Abruzzi
Tough, hilly terrain produces such wines as

ITALY

Montelpulciano d'Abruzzo, a packed fruity red, and the white Trebbiano d'Abruzzo. The Monteculpianio has a smooth, mellow finish and is good value. Look out for Valentini, Illuminati and Pepe.

Apulia
Here in the southern heat grow vast quantities of hearty red which go into many another labelled bottle in many another country. However, they are not to be easily dismissed by those who want their red wine meaty.

There is some elegance here, too, with a surprising dry white Alsace grape variety, the Pinot Blanco Favonio.

Leone de Castris produces the sublime Salice Salentino, a red and rosé choice, both made from Negro Amaro grapes.

Five Roses from de Castris is recommended for laying down: unusual but definitely worth seeking out.

San Severo, Castel del Monte and Il Falcone should also be tried.

Calabria
The toe of Italy with its Ciro in all colours is changing with the times and producing less hard-tasting wines.

See Ciro; and also a dessert wine, Greco di Bianco, gold and smooth.

Basilicata
Make a quick detour around the area to sample its one renowned wine, the Aglianico dei Vulture, a huge red that will not disappoint.

Sicily
Apart from the recipe wine Marsala, which has some very pleasant after-dinner effects, Sicily produces a number of excellent modernist wines.

Look out for: Corvo, Moscato Passito di Pantelleria, Regaleali Rosso del Conte, and a clean white, Rapitala.

Sardinia
The changes are being rung here as everywhere else in Italy, and Sell and Mosca make two contemporary triers: Cannonau, a dry, red worth waiting some years for; and Torbato di Alghero a balanced white of some refinement.

VILLA BANFI INNOVATION
In a parallel development the recent $100 million investment by Villa Banfi, the New York-based firm of wine merchants in the Tuscan hillsides, is causing great discussion in the wine-producing world. At Montalcino, just south of Siena, the largest and most technically advanced winery in Europe has been developed; it is a hi-tech viticultural assembly line without equal. The owners, John and Harry Mariani, had a dual purpose behind this multi-million dollar investment: to expand their line with Banfi-made world-class offerings, and at the same time to take an active part in the current movement to modernize the Italian wine industry. High-quality wine alongside fine, high-volume beverage wines is their goal. 'Our objective is to grow the healthiest of noble grapes scientifically and then extract their maximum potential.'

This may seem a far cry from the peasant toiling on the verdant slopes under a Tuscan sun – and it is. The development looks like a steel mill, and from the point of view of the vinous traveller who wants to drink his wine in the vernacular, perhaps it is to be hoped that not too many of these monsters will grow on Italian soil. But in one way or another we have to find the wine to assuage the seemingly endless thirst for wine in North America and throughout the northern hemisphere.

As for the blends, here the changes that are already happening in Chianti are taken into consideration. Interestingly, in order to safeguard the exclusivity of the *brunello* Sangiovese grape, only 10 per cent of the acreage will be devoted to production of that variety. For the rest, Cabernet Sauvignon and Chardonnay will each be allotted 15 per cent, while Pinot Grigio and Sauvignon Blanc will share 5 per cent each. The remaining 50 per cent will be devoted to Moscadello production and aimed at the Italian domestic market.

Not that foreign buying-in is so revolutionary in Tuscany – after all, Seagram Distillers owns vineyards in the region, as do others – it is rather the scale and, therefore, the anticipation of such a huge supply-and-demand situation that is breathtaking.

Again the emphasis must lie on waiting and seeing. However, New York wine merchants must

105

ENJOYING WINE

know the kind of consumption they are expecting to meet. They have chosen Italy as the place to spend their dollars. At present production levels Banfi turns out two million cases of wine a year. This is expected to rise within a few years.

We have seen the future – let us hope it tastes good!

Chianti

> But if you come, I shall pour for you,
> Etruscan Chianti, like ruby, that
> kisses you and bites you
> and makes you shed sweet tears...
>
> Fulvio Testi, Poet (1593-1646)

Chianti is steeped in history. They have been making wine in the rocky, unfertile soil of the gentle Tuscan hills for many, many centuries. Fossilized remains of an ancestor of the wild vine have been found here, which suggests that the grape predates man in this part of the world.

However, as mentioned already, not all bottles labelled Chianti contain the real thing. To define Chianti we can go back as far as Baron Bettino Ricasoli, who became Prime Minister in 1861, for his classic definition: a blend of Sangiovese and Canaiolo red grapes with the addition of Trebbiano and Malvasia del Chianti white. This basic formula was adopted some years ago for the DOC regulatory laws, in order to control the problem of bogus Chianti. Chianti is now in the throes of change and innovation, as in other areas of Italian wine making, and that basic formula is undergoing some revision. Producers like Piero Antinori explain it thus: 'in the past the Sangiovese grape was usually fermented with the stem and needed the addition of Malvasia to soften the wine. Nowadays growers favour new varieties like the Cabernets, both Franc and Sauvignon, which adapt well to Etruscan terrain and can complement Sangiovese, support it, and make up for its shortcomings, especially with regard to colour, aroma and body.' New oak and ageing in the bottle combine to develop the final bouquet of modern Chianti. All the processes from vine to wine bottling 'are now in full evolution. We are only at the beginning. A new era and therefore a new tradition is perhaps beginning for Chianti.' Tradition is the keyword in this ancient wine-growing region. We have seen the hi-tech manifestation of the Villa Banfi New Yorkers; but better still, perhaps, is to look at a traditional Chianti vineyard and see just how it is welcoming the new age.

ITALIAN GLOSSARY.

abboccato: semi-dry, very slightly sweet
amabile: semi-sweet, gently sweet
amaro: bitter
bianco: white
classico: from the heart of region
cantina: winery
casa vinicola: wine house
chiaretto: pale pink red
consorzio: growers' association
dolce: sweet
fattoria: producer
fiasco: flask
frizzante: semi-sparkling, effervescent
imbottigliato all'origine: estate-bottled
liquoroso: fortified wine
morbido: soft, mellow
riserva: matured for a specified number of years
rosato: rosé, pink
rosso: red
secco: dry
semplice: simple; category of non-DOC *vino da tavola*
spumante: sparkling, *méthode champenoise* Charmat
stravecchio: very old
superiore: selected grapes, higher degree of alcohol, greater age
vecchio: old
vendemmia: vintage
vino da tavola: sound, honest wines from non-DOC sources
vino santo: strong wine from dried grapes, also vino pasito
DOC: Denominazione Origine Controllata – placename and zone, controlled production and regulated conditions
DOCG: *DOC e Garantita* – five wines with a more stringent classification (see above)

Badia a Coltibuono

On the ruins of a 3rd-century BC Etruscan city called Cetamura stands the thousand-year-old monastery of Badia a Coltibuono (the Abbey of the Good Harvest). Here where the borders of Siena and Florence met, there has been winemaking in this beautiful farm since feudal days of the Barons Ricasoli. Even the great and powerful Lorenzo de Medici drank the wine and patronized the Abbey. He received a bottle of wine and a letter from the Abbot's brother Baccio Ugolino in July 1476 (the letter still exists today, but not, alas, the wine).

The monastery was secularized in 1810 under Napoleonic rule and the estate sold off. However, in 1846 the grandfather of the present owner bought up land and renovated the old structures, and production increased. The Second World War left the abbey unscathed, but changes were taking place. The traditional peasant share-cropping disappeared and many of the original farms were unable to survive the arrival of the latter half of the 20th century. Coltibuono, with its vast lands, was able to sell off some property and reorganize to survive. Uniquely in Tuscan history, the Abbey stands today, still making wine in the finest traditions of Chianti Classico, and yet turning itself willingly to face the winds of change. The Abbey encapsulates all that is great about Chianti.

Within this medieval setting stainless steel fermentation tanks replace the old wooden ones. There are refrigeration units and new vats of Slavonian oak have been introduced and small French wine barrels lie hidden behind the ancient stone walls. Red Chianti Classicos, Rosatos, Biancos and a pure Sangioveto red are produced. Vino Santo, a semi-dry dessert wine, aged for four years in oak, is made in very limted quantities. There is also the traditional by-product of the Riserva Chianti wine grapes: Grappa.

Coltibuono is hugely popular throughout the world, with exports to the United States and Britain, and it can generally be relied upon to be superb drinking Chianti, of which I have enjoyed a great deal; ruby-red (still), fruity, fleshy and robust, a great Chianti.

Badia a Coltibuono

ENJOYING WINE

NEIL EMPSOM

Well, it takes a New Zealander to pioneer the production and marketing of single variety Italian new-wave wines. Empsom is a car-crazy globetrotter who settled in the land of Ferrari via the United States and England. Initially he and his wife Maria represented a select group of growers and shipped respectable quantities across the Atlantic. Empsom saw the marketplace opportunities for 'everyday varietal wines', and in 1980 was one of the people who persuaded the Italian Government to pressure the EEC into rescinding a regulation preventing Italian wine houses calling their Chardonnay by its simple, correct name.

By this time he had contracted a smallish Alto-Adige cooperative to supply the wine (previously erroneously called Pinot Bianco) . . . no oak, but a crisp, clean new-wave style. The next significant decision was to join forces with the marketing whiz kid who persuaded the American public to drink millions of bottles of Perrier water. Bollini was launched, and the excellent value Chardonnay, Pinot Grigio and Cabernet Sauvignon are some of the few wine success stories of the 1980s.

The labels are stylish, the names are comprehensible, and the price is right.

Neil and Maria Empsom, négociants for Bollini and many of the better growers

CHAPTER ELEVEN

SPAIN

I have a friend who lives in a small village near Nerja on the Esta Costa del Sol. He is most graphic in his description of the wine made and consumed by the locals: 'Total brain damage, one small glass and they are "out to lunch", but they can't have any worries thanks to this stuff, they can't remember anything – and they live to a ripe old age.' University students of my era will understand this rather well as they remember the feeling of the morning after a night out on 'Spanish Burgundy', shipped in bulk and bottled (adulterated might be a better term) in Britain; and for those who could not face the red, there was always a white equivalent labelled 'Chablis' or 'Graves'.

Nowadays things have changed dramatically. Vast new wineries crammed with stainless steel have been built, new grape varieties have been planted and the shipping of wine in bulk has virtually ceased: the peasant may look on with bewilderment and reach for another glass of his own 'brain damage', but the technocrats have finally grabbed the Spanish winemaking industry by the scruff of the neck and hauled it into the 20th century. Without doubt the Spanish wine exports are the success story of the past decade, whether it be a shipping of Rioja and Penedès to the wine drinkers of the world, or the ups and downs – mainly ups – of Sangria sales to North America.

The country is the third largest wine producer in Europe and offers an amazing range of styles: the unique sherry; full-bodied, oaky whites and racy, refreshing dry ones; elegant fulsome reds reeking of their ageing in oak, and light fruity ones that have never seen wood; underestimated fragrant rosés worthy of any patio; and inexpensive, well-made sparklings. Admittedly you still need to choose with care as not every winemaking operation has mastered the new techniques and some have not even tried. After all, the *mañana* attitude does not disappear overnight. A visitor to this wonderful country can wake up in the morning wishing that wine had never been invented, but most of the export product is of a remarkably high standard. Some of it offers remarkable quality at a most reasonable cost. Nowadays a fine mature Rioja, such as Berberana 1975 Gran Reserva, will be treated by experts with the degree of respect due the finest of reds from Bordeaux, Burgundy or California. Try a bottle of this or something similar, and you will enjoy the great oaky richness with a beautifully scented vanilla finish: it is as though on opening the bottle the sunshine of the Ebro Valley has entered the room (obviously the perfect winter wine), and all this at a comparatively modest cost. How do they do it?

ENJOYING WINE

Vineyards in Rioja

SPAIN

ENJOYING WINE

Enthusiastic group of local growers waiting for the opening of the wine festival in Cenicero, Rioja Alta

RIOJA

The aristocracy of Spanish winemaking is to be found in the small northernmost wine region, only 100 km (62 miles) long and 40 km (25 miles) wide along the Ebro Valley. Surprisingly there are few vast expanses of uninterrupted vineyards. Most are scattered plantings. Much of the viticulture is in the hands of the peasantry with average vineyard holdings a mere 4.5 ha (11 acres). It is little wonder that this all-important region produces only 5 per cent of the national wine output.

There are three Rioja regions: the Alta, Altavesa and Baja. The first two are subject to Atlantic climatic conditions, with cooling autumnal winds and a summer that is not excessively hot. The Baja has a much more Mediterranean climate with the consistent heat and sun producing coarse, sugary wines. Very little Rioja is produced that is not a blend of the regions. Principal grape varieties are the Garnacho (the local form of Grenache), Tempranillo, Graciano and Mazuelo for reds; and Vivra, Malvasia and Garnacho Blanco for the whites.

The development of the unique soft, oak style of Rioja goes back to 1860 when the Marqués de Riscal and a couple of other wealthy landowners decided to improve their winemaking and hired a Bordelais, Jean Pineau, who devised the first *bodega* using the most advanced designs of the Bordeaux region. He also introduced Bordeaux methods of tanks and ageing in the Bordelais 225-litre (50 gal) oak *barriques*. The next important development factor came about thirty years later: the phylloxera problem, but this scourge had not reached Spain. The Bordeaux *négociants* were desperate for wine and came to Rioja for supplies. Many set up *bodegas* and expanded the number of establishments making the 'new' style wine. When phylloxera finally arrived, it was not with quite the same disastrous effect as elsewhere and was dealt with.

Winemaking carried on in much the same tradition throughout the first 70 years of this century. The *bodegas* acted as the *négociant* firms in the Burgundy manner, buying the produce in the form of either grapes or wine, vinifying, ageing and marketing. There were two major problems, especially with the cheaper wines. The winemakers tended to over-oak and over-age much wine that was patently unsuited to the process, and therefore most of the fruit was lost. Also, attitudes to vintages on labels was rather cavalier, with vast quantities of the superior harvests around for years, and it seemed that no produce was ever made, let alone sold, from the poorer years. It was rather like film stars' ages – think of a good year and stick to it!

Everything changed in the 1970s. Vast stainless-steel wine factories with computer-controlled vinification were introduced and placed alongside the traditional oak-filled cellars. The winemakers were becoming aware that fruit was a crucial aspect of their product. It was not so much simply a need for less ageing, but more a case of how much wine in oak and how much in bottle. Regulations were tightened regarding vintage claims and over the decade a set of classifications was established. Unfortunately these have changed many times: but here is the very latest list of up-to-date decisions straight off the press. Do not expect to see the status on the label itself. It will more likely appear overprinted on the coloured map back label.

CLASSIFICATIONS

San Crianza Basic wines with no wood ageing.
Vino do Crianza A minimum of one year in cask. Cannot be sold before the third year after harvest.
Reserva The numerous changes in this classification offer a fascinating insight into the desire to produce fruitier, fresher wines. Before 1979 the wines were matured for at least six years in cask and bottle. This was then reduced to two years in cask and one in bottle. This was then reduced to two years in cask and one in bottle, and it has just been changed to one year cask and two in bottle.
Gran Reserva Has also been altered three times in the past six years (at least the powers that be are consistent in their inconsistency!). Formerly there was a minimum of 8 years age; now all that is required is two years in cask and three in bottle.

However, just because I point out the vacillations of these wine authorities this does not mean I am ultra-critical, merely that I am amused at the number of attempts at change. Recent tastings of the last two classes of Rioja have proved the benefits of less ageing. Most Gran Reservas used to be well 'over the top' before bottling, let alone by the time the wines had reached the consumer. I have much more faith in the gradual ageing potential of the top Riojas from the more recent vintages.

The name of the *bodega* is all-important when selecting Rioja, as the better houses have consistent styles. Among the names to look for is Berberana, founded in 1877 and controlling nearly 50 per cent of its grape production. Its Carta de Plata and Carta de Oro are sound basic wines, full of character and excellent value. Berberana's Gran Reservas are superb. Watch for the 1975 in particular: beautifully balanced, full-flavoured and with vanilla oak; it will live for a good many years. Campo Viejo is a huge house, making pleasant wines in the basic categories – the most common restaurant wine of Spain it would seem. CVNE (Compagnia Vinicola del Norte de España) is my favourite *bodega*. The company owns over 50 per cent of its own grape production and makes a wide range of styles, from light extroverted wines, full of fruit and flavour, to the delicious silky Imperial Reserva, which must rate as one of the most outstanding value-for-money red wines of the world. CVNE also makes Viña Real Reserva, in a Burgundian bottle, a fatter, more robust wine from the Alavesa region. There are also Gran Reservas in both styles. An added bonus is that CVNE is very export-orientated, therefore supply of these excellent wines should prove no problem. Faustino makes dependable, tannic wines which always seem to need a little more bottle age. Rest assured the wine is better than the terrible bottle and packaging! Lopez de Herida Viña Tondonia makes very good San Crianza, even if a little lacking in subtlety. Marqués de Cáceres is the ultra-revolutionary *bodega* established relatively recently by Enrique Forner who, although Spanish, lived for years in Bordeaux and with his brother owns Château de Camensac and Château Larose-Trintaudon. The reds are made more in the Bordelais tradition with an absolute maximum of two years in oak, but usually less. The result is pleasant, soft wine but without the distinctive regional characteristics.

Marqués de Murietta and Marqués de Riscal are the two oldest-established *bodegas* and they are the super traditionalists, making very rich, oaky old-fashioned no-compromise wines – if you like this style of wine, these are the very best. Montecillo is another of the older houses, established in 1874. It makes lightish wine, but with lovely fruit and beautifully balanced and ready for immediate drinking. Finally Muga, the *bodega* revered by Rioja fanatics, and there are many. Its wines are definitely unique with less of the Rioja richness and depth of colour, more pale and elegant, and yet still full-bodied.

WHITE RIOJA

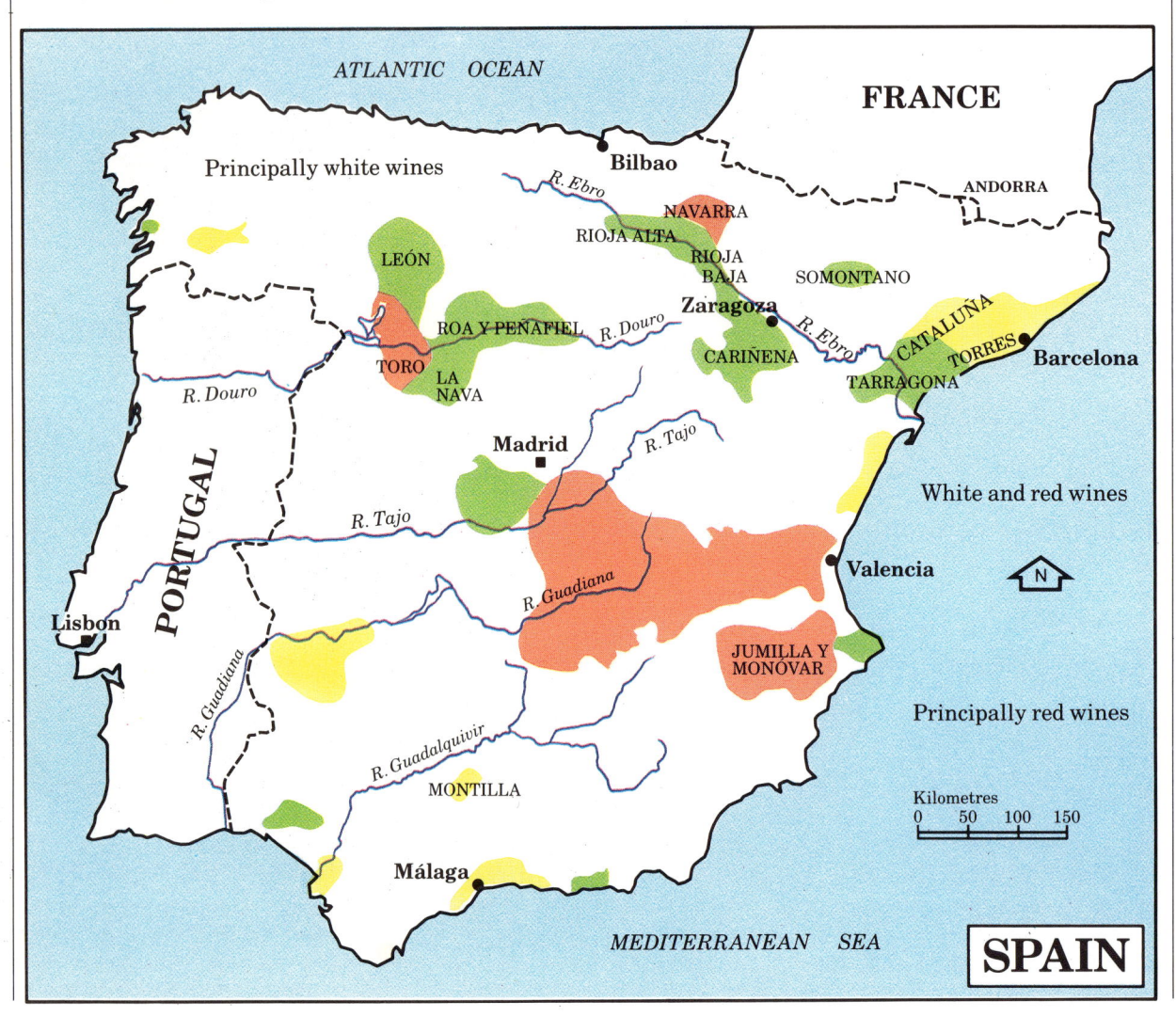

White Rioja represents the most exciting transition in winemaking techniques, with many houses changing styles almost overnight. In the old days the whites were fat, blowsy, over-oaked, often slightly maderized wines. The hardest part of dinner in Spain was not staying awake until the late hour of serving (normally around most other Europeans' bedtime), nor the caramelized Spanish brandy at the end – it was the white Rioja with the first course! I can remember my first dinner, and trying to smile in appreciation as the host watched my first sip of something that was out of condition a year or so before bottling.

There were many houses who understood that oak and white wine could be balanced, but needed different techniques of winemaking and ageing. They are still making wines reminiscent of Meursault, but at everyday prices – Marqués de Murietta, CVNE's Monopole and Tondonia's Blanco immediately come to mind. But even these are still only enjoyed by the small band of devotees.

The 'new' style of white Rioja, as pioneered by Forner at Cácares, has caught the imagination of the world's rapidly expanding white wine market. He established a 'space age' winery in the village of Cenicero in the Rioja Alta, for white wine production only. All stainless steel, no ageing of the wine. The result is beautifully fragrant, crisp-drinking wine. People talk about the Cáceres Blanco being of similar style and standard to Loire white, but I have not drunk any from that region in this price range that are anywhere near as attractive! Many other houses have followed suit as this is obviously a very profitable exercise. Montecillo is making a delightful white and Faustino and CVNE are also improving. Who knows just how great the future is for these wines?

PENEDÈS (PANADÉS)

Penedès is the story of three ultra-modern innovators working among the traditional peasant wine growers whose methods are as old as the surrounding Montserrat Hills some 750 m (2450 ft) up from the Mediterranean village of Sitges. Torres, Jean Leon and Raimat produce a very small but internationally significant part of Penedès wine. The Catalans have been making wine for centuries and theirs is that happy bravado which dares the tourist to attempt drinking from the *porron* – the fat-bellied bottle is held high and the long spout is aimed with crack precision at the gaping mouth – it is all fun for the local with unerring aim. For the tourist this is a source of wine-splattered fun which may or may not be remembered the next morning. The Catalans do love their wine and the drinking thereof. In autumn they have the festival of the vine in Sitges and a fountain of freely flowing wine is set up on the esplanade. Tourists, many of whom have travelled hundreds of miles for a night of free wine, mix with the locals: it all seems rather out of place with the serious blessing of the vintage at the beautiful church the next morning.

Torres
Miguel Torres Jnr studied oenology at Montpellier University in the 1960s before returning to his native Penedès and planting a host of classic grape varieties. Some thrived, others did not. Instant recognition came when performance of the 1970

Rocket for diversifying hailstones in the higher altitude Torres vineyards

Enjoying Wine

Miguel Torres

Black Label Coronas scooped the pool in the Cabernet Sauvignon section of the Gault Millau Olympiad at Paris. The Torres winery is now a mass of stainless steel and oak. Many new vineyards are planted in the previously ignored high altitude, cooler areas, with Gewürztraminer, Muscat d'Alsace, Chardonnay, Sauvignon Blanc, Cabernet Sauvignon, Cabernet Franc and Merlot. But these new grape varieties are complemented with the area's traditional kinds: Parrellada for white wines and Garnacha, Cariñena, Ull de Llebre (the Tempranillo of Rioja) and Monastrell.

I must confess to no great fondness for the three staple wines of Torres, Viña Sol, Coronas and Tres Torres Sangredetoro. These are the wines available in most countries in the world. They are made from the traditional grapes, are technically sound and distinctive: but for the same price I prefer the cheaper Rioja wines. There is no doubt that these are the wines of commercial success for the company, but it is the wines made from the new varieties that have actually pushed the name Torres to the forefront with the wine-drinking public. Gran Viña Sol is a delightful blend of Parellada with 30 per cent Chardonnay; Green Label Viña Sol is the same Parellada with 30 per cent Sauvignon Blanc; Viña Esmeralda is 60 per cent Muscat d'Alsace and 40 per cent Gewürztraminer; Gran Coronas 55 per cent Cabernet Sauvignon and 45 per cent Ull de Llebre; Viña Magdala 51 per cent Pinot Noir and 49 per cent Cariñena; and the already legendary Black Label Gran Coronas 90 per cent Cabernet Sauvignon and 10 per cent Cabernet Franc. An added bonus for rosé lovers is the excellent de Casta Rosado with 65 per cent Garnacha and 35 per cent Cariñena with a mere 24 hours skin contact – a superb wine that I have unerringly picked three times in blind tastings as the 'finest from Provence'.

Miguel Torres was at the forefront of the revolution, but there were two other big producers following the same principles.

Jean Leon
This man, a native Catalan, owned the La Scala Restaurant in Beverly Hills, Los Angeles, and returned to his homeland in 1962 with background expertise gained at Davis College courses in oenology. He planted only classic grape varietals and rapidly built up a formidable Stateside reputation

for his Chardonnay and Cabernet Sauvignon.

Raimat
Situated on the western borders of the region, Raimat has the considerable financial might of the Cordonvi empire as backing. The company has had its ups and downs over the years. In 1920 the land was transformed from saltpans and scrubland to fertile vineyards. The years came and went, and took their toll, but in the 1970s the grandson of the founder planted Chardonnay and Cabernet Sauvignon and blends including these wines are now readily available. Some of the other products still remind me of the 'bad old days' of Spanish winemaking, so I will wait a few more years before making total judgment, but the sheer size of the estate – almost 1000 ha (2470 acres) under vine – and the high standard of the quality wines are very exciting.

The bulk of Penedès wine production
The inescapable fact is that I have talked about a minute percentage of production and the rest of the still wines of the area are quite frankly unexciting. Yes, many producers do have the up-to-date technique equipment, but they are using it on the old style grape varietals.

Sparkling wines
The region is also the home for the massive sparkling wine industry of Spain. One of my friends used to claim that Spanish sparkling was 'only suitable for car shampooing your worst enemy's coachwork'. Things have changed and they have done so drastically; gone is the earthy 'old socks' taste. Instead *Cava* (the term given to the wines produced by *méthode champenoise*) is usually clean, refreshing with a crisp well-balanced acid-fruit finish. I must confess I don't like them but 100 million bottles are drunk each year and all those customers can't be totally wrong (or can they?).

The two largest houses are Freixenet, who are reputed to sell more bottles in the United States than the whole of Champagne does, and Codorniu. Segura Viudas makes a reasonable wine, as does Peralada, and at least these wines are relatively cheap. If bubbles are required and the budget is modest, they are a much better source of sparkle than are most of the expensive 'Champagne' substitutes that are produced in France.

ALELLA

A tiny region just north of Barcelona: it has long been the object of scorn and derision from wine-loving tourists of the 1950s and early 1960s, when the white wines were anything but refreshing. There is a new company marketing Marqués de Alella; a beautifully fresh, crisp wine with a hint of residual sugar. Very, very drinkable and a firm favourite of many a British MP at a certain wine bar close to Parliament Square!

NAVARRA

Northeast of Rioja, another region of change. The tendency was to plant the same grapes as in Rioja, with emphasis on the Garnacha. Now they are planting more of the lighter, fruitier Tempranillo and one *bodega*, De Sarria, is making a Sarria Tinto, very fresh and very fruity: a Spanish red wine that has never been near oak.

RUEDA

This region hit the headlines when Marqués de Riscal decided to transfer its white winemaking here where it was easier to produce the more modern style. There is also a most prestigiously labelled Marqués de Grinon (numbered labels always annoy me – any pretentious winemaker can organize a printing plant with the necessary equipment), but the wine has real style: no oak but an attractive depth of flavour.

OTHER AREAS

Spain produces much more wine in many more areas (of course there is the unique Vega Sicilia from just east of Vallodolid) and the dreaded gut-wrenching products of La Mancha, Tarragona *et al*. I have concentrated on simply the best, offering a wide range of incredibly good-value-for-money wines.

THE SPANISH QUALITY CONTROL SYSTEM

There are 24 specifically defined regions, each given a *denominación de origen*, governmentally controlled by the regional committee, the *Consejo Regulador*.

Chapter Twelve

Central and Eastern Europe

BULGARIA

Bulgaria is the pace-setter for Eastern European wines. Its wines offer good value and are dependable. There is a rising standard of red wine production, especially of Cabernets, which are regarded very much as the wine of the future from this part of the world.

Although only in existence, as a state-run monopoly, since the end of the Second World War, Bulgarian wine-growing has ancient roots. In Ancient Thrace, roughly where Bulgaria is today, was some of the earliest wine-making in civilization.

The Bulgarians have a most efficient industry and you will find their wines at supermarkets and off-licence shops all over the world. They have captured a share of the world market with their classic wines displaying the great varietal characteristics: in particular the Cabernets, Merlots and Chardonnays. At the 1983 New York Food Fair the Bulgarian Merlot won the Gold Medal for 'Best Wine'.

Gone are the old labels in Cyrillic script which confused the Western consumer and often led to a quick replacement on the dusty shelf. Nowadays the labels show the grape variety or brand names. There are three main areas of production: the Black Sea coast, where the Chardonnays thrive; the Danube plains; and the Maritsa valley.

Reds: Cabernets and Merlots are attractive, the more traditional wines less so . . . avoid Maurud and Gamza.

Whites: Chardonnay is the wine of the future; a firm classic flavour and an, occasionally, popular grape. Riesling is scented, with a charming acidity. Others are Sauvignon, Misket (Muscat), Sylvaner, and Dimiat.

HUNGARY

This country produces an enormous range of wine from the ubiquitous and inconsistent Bull's Blood to the delectable Tokays, of which the 'Wine of the Emperor', Tokay Aszu Eszencia, is one of the most sought-after (and expensive) wine experiences going. This wine is made entirely of grapes affected by noble rot and crushed by their own weight in the vats. It is then matured for many years in special tunnels hewn out of the volcanic mountainside. Remarkable curative properties are ascribed to this wine: apparently one emperor was kept alive on his deathbed by administration of regular, large draughts! Preachers ranted against its aphrodisiac powers, and there are still in existence bottles of the almost divine nectar dating from the 17th century which are sold at auction for astronomic prices!

But back to earth and the huge output of Hungarian good value wines. These include the ordinary Tokay, a rich, dessert-style wine; Tokay in distinctive ninepin-shaped half-litre bottles – very good value; Bull's Blood, a blend of Kadarka, Pinoit Noir, and Merlot and sometimes other varieties. Look out for the domestic brand Egri Bikaver: more age, and body.

Some supermarkets stock the recently introduced Cabernet Sauvignon and Chardonnay. Both cheap, well-made wines offering good value. Olasz Riesling comes as dry, medium and sweet whites. Kadarka is also available as a rich, punchy red that is good with meats.

Generally, Hungary lags behind the other Eastern bloc countries in technique and organization. However, things are beginning to improve in this direction. A great deal is expected from the next few seasons, and a higher quality is to be

CENTRAL AND EASTERN EUROPE

Tokaj, Hungary and the River Tisza

'We won't be needing the corkscrew, Framlington...'

hoped for. Sadly, the Bull's Blood, of old always dependable, has recently been inconsistent.

YUGOSLAVIA

A nation as diverse as this – it is a pot-pourri of six different republics – produces correspondingly diverse wines. Sadly, most of these fail to reach our shelves. The Lutomer Rieslings that flood the world's markets along with Cloberg, almost as common, and Laski Riesling, a retailer's brand, belie the true quality and depth of Yugoslavian wines. The staggering difference between the 'Party member' winemakers and the independent 'non-Party' growers is best summed up as the gulf between rich, resinated whites and sweet reds on the one hand, and fresh, fragrant Rieslings and clean, modern reds on the other.

Most of the bulk goes to Russia and Germany for 'industrial' wines. Yet among the new wave, young non-Party growers some fascinating wines are made. Successive tastings have proved this great divide. As a general rule, avoid the supermarket brands; these are brought over in bulk and bottled in Britain and bear absolutely no resemblance to the base product that can be sampled at home in the villages of Yugoslavia's different areas of cultivation. There are currently two of these new wave producers who are graduates of the Davis U.C. system and they are making superior wines.

Look out for (although uncommon): Merlot, Cabernet and Pinot Noir varieties from Macedonia: Vranac, the powerful red from Montenegro, which is available worldwide from Vitkovitch.

Slovenia produces some of the better whites along with the Lutomers and Laskis. Look out for Slovenian Traminer, Sauvignons, and Penski Riesling.

ROMANIA

Not so widely available as yet, the wines of the Carpathian mountain slopes have a tendency towards sweetness, including the reds. Wines are marketed under varietal names.

Merlot (slightly sweet), from Dealul Mare, and Tarnave, from Transylvania, a medium-dry white (not the blood-rich red you might expect) are good value and consistent. There is a good quality Cabernet Sauvignon.

Aromatic whites made from Traminer, Muskat Sylvaner and Walschriesling varieties, sold under the brand name Perla, are worth checking out.

CHAPTER THIRTEEN

ENGLAND

The Romans were not content with introducing the vine to France; they even brought it with them to Britain. Later, in medieval times, vines flourished in the south of England under the care of the monasteries. Over the centuries two major factors contributed to a total decline: Henry II married Eleanor of Aquitaine and the prolific wine producing Bordeaux region came under the control of England; and later Henry VIII closed down the monasteries. By the present century, hardly any wine was made in England and commercial winemaking did not exist until 1952 when Sir Guy Salisbury Jones planted a vineyard at his home in Hambledon, Hampshire: 2 ha (5 acres) of the hybrid grape Seyval Blanc. Gradually many dedicated, if amateurish, enthusiasts followed suit and by 1967 there were sufficient of them to form the English Vineyards Association. Suddenly vineyards were being planted all over Suffolk, Norfolk and the more southern counties of England. By 1984 there were 230 vineyards producing commercial quantities of wine, spread over 400 ha (1000 acres).

The results in the years up until the 1980s were not exactly awe-inspiring. England is hardly ideally situated: north of the 50th parallel and only saved by the warmth of the Gulf Stream. There is too much rain, therefore rot is a problem; there is too much wind, so only the most sheltered of sites are practical; and there are many years when the all-important mild, sunny autumn just does not happen! The wines tended to be harsh and uncompromising, with considerable technical defects masking any traces of pleasant flavour – definitely unacceptable. One of the most obvious problems was the almost consistent need to make wine with unripe fruit.

Things have improved dramatically. Experimentation with earlier-ripening grape varieties has helped, and many winemakers have become aware of the virtues of using German *Süssreserve*. This is the EEC-approved additive so important in the quality wines of that country: unfermented grape juice, literally 'sweet reserve', that is added in tiny quantities to the base wine in order to complement the acidity and allow the true flavour of the grape variety to dominate. In April 1984 I participated in a tasting of English wines for *The Times* where the best wines were extremely attractive, easy drinking, flowery whites with delicate balance between fruit and acid. Richard Barnes's Biddenden Vineyard Ortega 1983 from Kent was the outstanding wine of the tasting. It has an individualistic and alluring fresh fruit style really crammed with flavour and with a lingering finish: a beautiful summer wine. (It had already won the Gold Medal at the 'English Wine of the Year' competition.) Biddenden was established in 1969 and, with 7 ha (18 acres) under vine, is one of the largest vineyards in England. It was formerly an orchard, but apples became more and

ENJOYING WINE

Richard Barnes, Biddenden Vineyards

more unprofitable and Barnes realized that the south-facing slopes in a shallow sheltered valley were suited to vines. He initially planted sample sections of the varieties most common in England. Some, such as the highly popular Madeleine Angevine, 'simply didn't work', while Müller-Thurgau and Ortega, early ripeners, flourished. Biddenden also grows Huxelrebe, rarely seen outside England, which when on form is attractive with a ripe grapefruit style, and Reichensteiner.

The problems of winemaking in England are exemplified by Barnes's experiences with the classy Scheurebe grape variety, which can produce excellent wine in bountiful quantities, but needs really outstanding years to shine as it does not ripen until early November. Most years I have taken my overcoat out of summer storage by then!

Despite the use of all these German grape varieties (mainly crossings with obscure members of the Müller-Thurgau family), English wine does have a real style of its own. The clean, delicately scented freshness is in fact quite unique.

Other names to look for are Wootton (Somerset – possibly the county with the best climatic conditions); Barton Manor (Isle of Wight); Carr Taylor (Sussex); Highwayman's Vineyard (Suffolk); Staple St James (Kent); Lamberhurst (Kent); Cavendish Manor (Suffolk); Magdalen (Norfolk); and Monnow Valley from Monmouth in Wales.

> **DON'T CONFUSE ENGLISH WINE WITH BRITISH!**
>
> Carrow Prior, Country Manor – British wines. They sound like the real stuff but beware: they are anything but. Inept legislation allows factories to import concentrated grape juice, produce a fairly average 'plonk' with a passing resemblance to wine – and call it 'British'. Of course, England is renowned as a country of eccentricity, but isn't this carrying the tradition too far?

CHAPTER FOURTEEN

CALIFORNIA

Spanish missionaries introduced wines to California in the late 18th century. The grape they planted was the 'mission' and the product was definitely not for connoisseurs of the finer things of life. A much more important development was the planting of European varieties by immigrants – in particular the important pioneering work by the Hungarian founder of Buena Vista Winery, who toured the finest vineyards of France in 1861 and returned with more than 100,000 first-rate vines and cuttings. The rest of the century saw dramatic vineyard expansion, and many of the earliest firms are still well-known names today: for instance Beringer, Inglenook, Charles Krug, Korbel and Wente. The only trouble was that these classic varieties (*Vitis vinifera*) suddenly developed the same scourge as their European counterparts, the phylloxera. As every serious student of wine knows, the New World saved the Old World vineyards as well as its own: it was discovered that the hybrid (*Vitis labrusca*) vines native to the East Coast had been subjected to the virus for countless years and were totally immune. Phylloxera-resistant stocks were shipped to both California and across the Atlantic, and the most serious disaster in the history of wine was overcome.

Even after this, things never exactly proceeded smoothly. There is no doubt about it, pioneering winemaking is a 'boom or bust' business. Overplanting and market recession (due to both poor economic conditions and resistance to poor quality products) had their effects, but there was nothing to match the problem that affected only one major winemaking nation.

PROHIBITION

The writing had been on the wall since 1900 when militant temperance leader Carry Nation began her saloon-raiding campaign, a Bible in one hand and an axe in the other. By the First World War 70 per cent of the States were already legally dry. But the 18th Amendment to the Constitution, making production and sale of intoxicating liquors illegal, still caught most of the 700 California wineries unprepared. Many, such as Simi, initially refused to sell off their stocks within the deadline and continued to work the vineyards in the belief that such a law would be short-lived. Others, like Wildwood Vineyards, simply closed shop, turned to other crops and returned to grape growing after the repeal – but never to actual winemaking again.

There was a wonderful loophole for growers which actually increased the prices of grapes and trebled American wine production – home wine making was perfectly legal! Huge quantities of grapes were shipped across country to the immigrant communities in New York State. The better varieties were delicate travellers, therefore they were ripped out and replanted with Carignane and Alicante Bouschet – which made awful wine, but their thick skins were more suitable for long-distance travel. It is rumoured that thirsty, skilful winemakers could produce huge quantities of 'Dago Red' from a small amount of grapes – no great threat to the status of Château Latour, but presumably better than nothing in these desperate times. Another product in great demand was Grape Concentrate, carefully labelled 'Do not dilute with water, add sugar and yeast, nor leave standing for seven days ... otherwise you will produce an alcoholic beverage ...' Louis Martini delightfully named its product Forbidden Fruit. Medicinal wine was another source of alcohol but required a doctor's prescription. Tonic wines were much easier to obtain and refrigeration would remove the foul-tasting medicinal additives. Sacramental wine was allowed to be produced under strict government supervision and kept many a winery afloat – Beringer, Beaulieu, Christian Brothers, Eschol and Simi were some that managed to keep their plant working making considerable quantities of this. An amusing aspect of sacramental wine was that at no other time in American history has conversion to Judaism been quite so frenetic. Unfortunately after the repeal the 'converts' seemed to lose interest! Of course there were other wineries who carried on making wine as normal, and flouted the law which allowed them to produce 200 gallons a year for family use. They would often have storage facilities holding the regulation 200 gallons – but also hidden tanks keeping the supply topped up.

The repeal in 1933 saw a few of the remaining 160 wineries, especially those involved in sacramental wine, in reasonably good order, and with large stocks of aged pre-1920 wines ready for immediate sale. For most of the others it was a time of serious problems: the wrong grapes planted, out of condition equipment (casks do not take kindly to 13 years of disuse) and the Depression restricting financial support for reorganization. Also the educated market had almost been swallowed up in a sea of filthy, rich, strong wine: considerable re-education was needed. The Prohibition era was over, but the effects were felt until the Second World War.

THE POSTWAR PERIOD

The 1950s and '60s saw considerable industry expansion, but under the control of the big companies, with the necessary sources of finance. Gallo, which now makes approximately 40 per cent of the total California production, expanded rapidly; Seagrams purchased Paul Masson in 1943; United Vintners (later part of the giant Heublein Corporation) bought Inglenook in 1963. The nadir was 1966 – there were 25 Napa Valley wineries in existence, compared with 143 in 1889 – but it was also the year that the industry began a radical change. It was not coincidental that this was the year that Robert Mondavi departed the family firm Krug and established his own winery in Oakland, Napa. Individual small wineries began to appear, but they were still very much a gamble. Janet Trefethen talks of her family's arrival in the Napa in 1968: 'When we purchased the ranch even the thought of planting grapes as a crop was a major decision.'

The 1970s was the decade that the 'small is beautiful' revolution really took effect. Hundreds of wineries were established, not only in the Napa and Sonoma Valleys, but also in many previously underrated regions such as Mendocino, Santa Clara, Santa Barbara and Monterey counties – the last-named had a mere 600 ha (1500 acres) under vines in 1960 and 21,000 ha (53,000 acres) by 1980. No longer were the wine store shelves stocked with dozens of products from a few large firms – there seemed to be an insatiable market for all these new wineries. Suddenly the subject of wine was an important facet in every 'upwardly mobile' middle-class household. New labels appeared on the wine scene every week; many 'single varietals' (by US law containing 75 per cent of the stated grape) appeared at much higher prices than the traditional blended wines. 'Chenin Blanc' was a much more stylish alternative to 'Chablis' (how do you like it – dry white, medium white or pink?), and 'Burgundy', with considerable quantities of residual sugar, fought for a market share with dry, fruity and clean Zinfandel and

CALIFORNIA

Cabernet Sauvignon. There was still much poor wine, but as long as the label was right and one of the dozens of newly established authorities wrote something complimentary, success was assured.

Suddenly the unbelievable occurred: there were just too many new wines and many of the new entrants to the winemaking business, hampered by spiralling land costs and high interest rates, suddenly discovered that their break-even sales figures were considerably higher than the amount the public was prepared to pay. The more traditional companies (including those of the '60s) with their cheaper wines, plus inexpensive and prestigious European imports, were fulfilling the wine consumption needs of most of the slowly expanding market. The 1980s is definitely the decade for consolidation: overproduction of grapes is rife (some figures quote up to 20 per cent in 1985); Lambrusco drinkers, quaffing sufficient quantities to keep many an Italian winery afloat financially, account for well in excess of the total Napa Valley wine production (and that is including industry giants such as Christian Brothers, Domaine Chandon, Charles Krug and Inglenook). At present the market for expensive wines is actually decreasing and only inexpensive whites and sparkling wines are on the up. The top-quality California wines are better each year, but can they afford to continue the price spiral?

WINE REGIONS

NAPA VALLEY

This is the most attractive of all the regions, wending its way from Napa city along the Silverado trail (a hint of the past) through acre after acre of beautifully tended vineyards surrounded by gently rolling hillsides. The valley abounds with microclimates. Frost-free vineyards nestle side by side with others just a few feet higher that require extensive use of anti-frost equipment every few years: surprisingly the southern end is the coolest and the north the hottest, but there are no totally valid generalizations. Over the years trial and error plus technical expertise have resulted in a gradual acceptance of the suitability of the various areas to only certain grape varieties. Lack of water is the main problem, hence the drip irrigation.

The Napa produces a mere 8 per cent of all California wine, but it is *the* image of the Golden State's wine industry with a host of well-known wineries including Beaulieu, Beringer, Caymus, Chapellet, Chateau Montelena, Clos du Val, Grgich Hills, Joseph Phelps, Stag's Leap and Sterling. It was the first area to concentrate on quality grape varieties and to promote itself as an independent, high-class region. Of course it possessed the great advantage of Robert Mondavi, who has tirelessly promoted the cause of California wines worldwide and nationwide, but in particular the Napa and his own outstanding products. The early variety favourites of the past decades are well on the way out and Chenin Blanc is following rapidly. Much of the Valley concentrates on Chardonnay, Sauvignon Blanc, Pinot Noir and Cabernet Sauvignon, with some significant plantings of Merlot.

Growers in other regions often complain about the higher prices paid for Napa grapes, but both the growers and wineries of this valley have been well ahead of the other areas, creating the superior wines and individual images.

SONOMA-MENDOCINO

Sonoma lies east of the Napa Valley on the other side of the Mayacamas Mountains. This region was planted with vines at the same time as the Napa but has never been the front runner. Even as recently as the 1960s the main concern was the production of cheap 'jug' wine from unfashionable grapes – but that has all changed. Classic Cabernet Sauvignon (especially from the Alexander Valley) and some of the most promising Pinot Noir, Zinfandel, Chardonnay and superior Chenin Blanc are produced by top names such as Clos du Bois, Dry Creek, Foppiano, Gundlach Bundschu, Hanzell, Iron Horse and Kistler.

This is the land of opportunity. The Sonoma has a similar acreage under vines to the Napa, but this could easily double: the sheep and cattle would just have to graze elsewhere. The southernmost area, the Carneros Valley, is a unique micro-climate – below sea level and fanned by cooling fog and sea breezes which filter in a gap in the coastal ranges. 'On a clear day you can see right through to San Francisco ... at least that's what they tell me,' says Doug Davis, executive winemaker of Sebastiani, who spends a considerable amount of time in the area. This is the up and coming region for

ENJOYING WINE

Wildwood Vineyard winery (Sonoma Valley): abandoned with the advent of Prohibition but still standing!

CALIFORNIA

ENJOYING WINE

Frost protection equipment, Napa Valley

CALIFORNIA

Drip-feed irrigation. 'European wine authorities are inclined to denigrate any region that uses irrigation, but all we are doing is compensating for lack of rainfall. After all the Burgundians add sugar to compensate for lack of sunshine' – Janet Trefethen

ENJOYING WINE

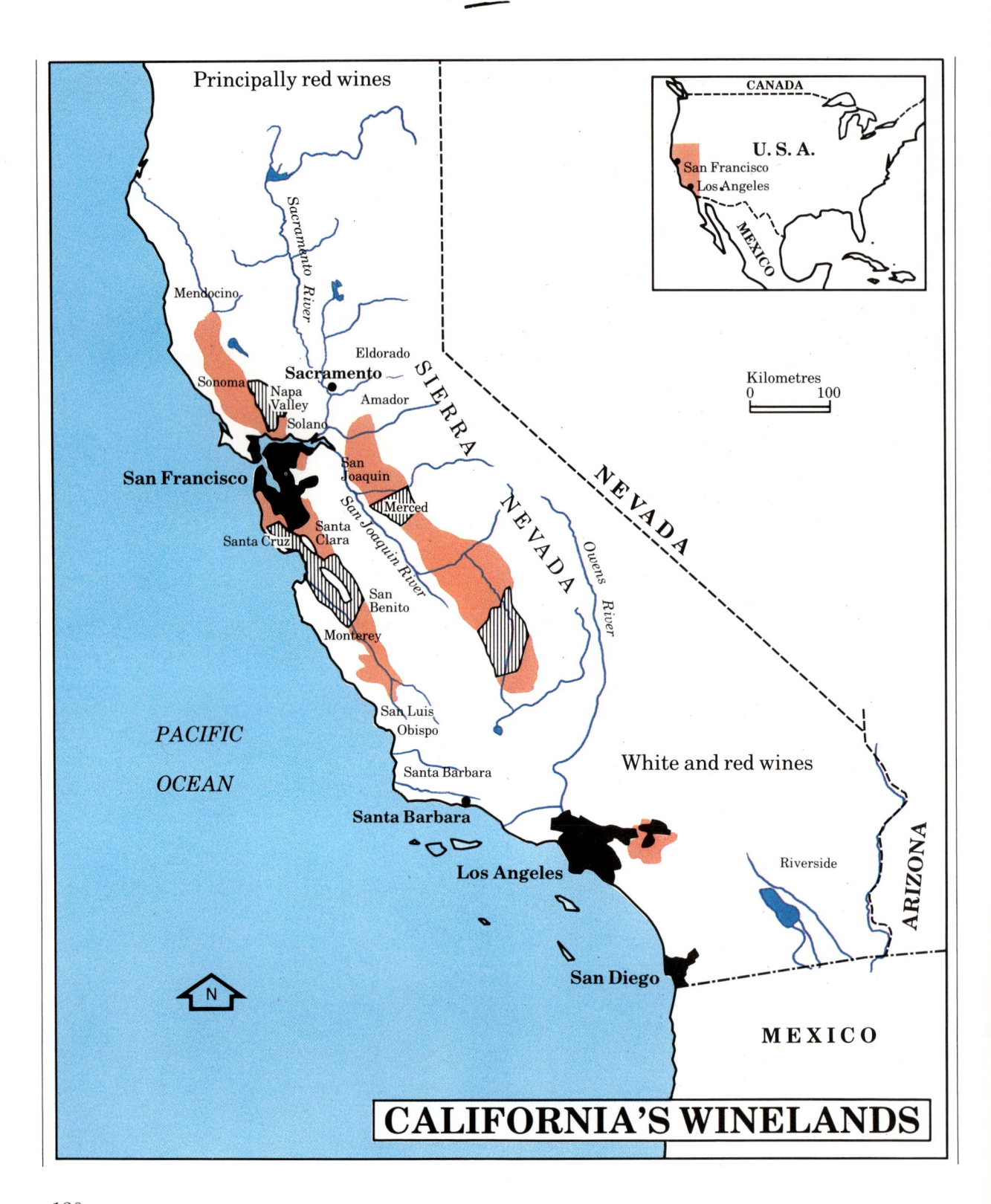

CALIFORNIA'S WINELANDS

CALIFORNIA

Joe Heitz

sparkling wine production: even the Spanish Cava giant Freixenet has joined in the modern-day gold rush.

Mendocino has been a late developer, but pioneers such as Fetzer and Parducci have done sterling work in the cause of better winemaking in the area.

CENTRAL COAST
This covers the important coastal regions south of San Francisco from Almada County, just alongside the bay, and on for miles through San Mateo, Santa Cruz, Santa Clara, Monterey, San Benito, San Luis Obispo and Santa Barbara counties. These are by no means the best-known premium wine areas of California, but they are developing steadily and some excellent wines are being produced, often at more advantageous prices than similar wines from the more prestigious areas further north. Some of the best names here are David Bruce, Chalone, Concannon, Firestone, Jekel, Mirassou and Zaca Mesa.

CENTRAL VALLEY
The Sacramento and San Joaquin Valleys produce over 60 per cent of California's wine. A plane trip over these vast expanses is quite an experience; drinking the products of the vines below is not quite as spectacular. The ubiquitous Thompson Seedless, which is suitable for table grapes, dried raisins, table wines, sparkling wines, fortified wines and even brandy, is gradually being phased out in favour of Colombard, Chenin Blanc and Barbera, which are much more suited to the main task: the making of good quality, inexpensive 'jug' wine. The region is the home of E. & J. Gallo, a company that specializes in these very wines and produces a mere 250,000 or so cases each day.

GRAPE VARIETIES
There are three varieties of major importance today: Cabernet Sauvignon, Chardonnay and Sauvignon Blanc (also known as Fumé Blanc). These are the varieties for which *aficionados* around the nation are prepared to part with large numbers of dollars; they are the magic names, and the first two deservedly so. The rich, perfumed Cabernets, often with a distinctive 'minty' flavour, are without doubt the finest wines the region produces, especially those blended with a proportion of Merlot. As the California wine tradition became more established, so did the realization that the 'blockbusters' of old are better replaced with lighter, less alcoholic and more refined wines. Chardonnays are still a mixed bag — some are big, fat, blowsy wines, reeking of oak and alcohol, wines for talking about but not really drinking. There are many promising glimpses of the future, with many winemakers now preferring full yet stylish, more delicate wines, made on the principle 'If you want oak, go bite a tree.' The wineries still have not made up their minds about Sauvignon Blanc. They either soften the tart gooseberry flavour too much, or beef it up with a considerable amount of oak and turn it into a second-class Chardonnay. Much of this is due to attempts to use the variety for making an aperitif wine for the cultivated palate. If the wine tastes like the Raymond Sauvignon Blanc 1983 (crisp, delightfully fragrant with just the right amount of 'grassy' character) than that is fine – but if it is blended with 20-30 per cent Semillon, forget it.

Merlot is often used for blending *à la Bordelais*, but rarely shown as a straight variety, which is a pity. Watch out for the few that are. Zinfandel is the most widely grown grape variety, with a host of personality problems (*see* Ridge Vineyards page 136). Some areas in particular Sonoma and Monterey, are doing reasonably well with Pinot Noir. Petit Syrah is no longer considered the true Syrah of the Rhône Valley – it certainly does not taste like it. Barbera and Gamay de Beaujolais are planted in singificant quantities, as is the dreaded Carignane (in the Central Valley), but that is mercifully declining in popularity.

The relative importance of white wine varietals has changed with the times. The average American wine drinker quaffs white and whichever is in fashion; but it must be admitted that the finer varieties are the ones that have survived. Colombard is by far the most frequently planted, but now mainly used for blending. Chenin Blanc makes some excellent quaffing wines, but is out of favour. The case is similar with Grey Riesling and Johannisberger Riesling (no relation). Gewürztraminer is produced with usually an attractive flowery style, but lacking the necessary acid finish. Of course in recent years a tremendous amount of increased Sonoma plantings of Chardonnay, Pinot Blanc and Pinot Noir have been started for the flourishing *méthode champenoise* industry.

THE WINERIES

Over the years I have enjoyed hundreds of wines from many Californian wineries. I have chosen a few of the most interesting to discuss in detail. They vary greatly in size and style, but all have impressed me over the years with their high quality wines and degree of consistency.

HEITZ WINE CELLARS (St Helena, Napa Valley)

Joe Heitz worked at a number of big wineries before he and his wife Alice bought their own in 1961. They do not own a large amount of land: a vineyard next to the winery planted with Grignolino (the only in California) and Zinfandel, plus two plots of Chardonnay. A recent purchase of a 32 ha (80 acre) ranch with some areas suitable for Cabernet Sauvignon should increase Heitz Vineyard acreage. When questioned on his policy of buying in grapes, Joe has a cryptic answer: 'I grew up on a farm in Illinois and when out on the horse-driven plough, I hated the feeling of sweat running down my back; I much prefer the coolness of the winery!' Be that the truth or a part thereof, there is no doubt about his ability to buy the right grapes, often from single vineyard sources which receive due label recognition.

Heitz Chardonnays are elegant and delicate and yet with characteristics that improve dramatically with age. In 1985 I tasted the 1973 and 1974 vintages and they were a revelation – real depth of flavour with a rich, almost sweet, style and yet a bone-dry finish. The Napa Valley Cabernets are some of the better value wines of the region: by no means cheap, but they receive the legendary Joe Heitz care and attention, which is the total opposite of present-day California winemaking techniques. The wine is aged for 2½ years in large oak vats, and then for 18 months in *barriques*: 'I don't like new oak, I "run it in" on my cheap wines, but then my Cabernet has already been in large casks for a long time first.' The results are the most individualistic wines of California, intense, complex blends of rich, soft fruit flavour, oak and tannin.

Martha's Vineyard Cabernets are in a class of their own, and with a price to match. In these wines the mint flavour is really predominant (the trendy description beloved by West Coast wine writers is 'eucalyptus', but mention this in front of Joe only if death by strangulation seems OK at the time!) These wines are for keeping and the Heitz family policy (dictated by Joe, Alice, winemaker son David, marketing daughter Kathleen Heitz Ryan and finance-orientated Rollie) is to age large quantities in the cellars and have as many as six vintages on sale at once. Joe laughs about this rather unappreciated attitude: 'We have sweated through the years, scrimped and saved, kept the Bank of America off our backs ... to build up a backlog of wines. People come into the tasting room and see the 1976 Martha's Vineyard listed and immediately comment "What's the matter, don't people like these wines?"' I have an important hint for those fortunate enough to have access to Heitz wines (only 40,000 cases per annum) – the Bella Oaks Vineyard Cabernets are wonderful. The vineyard is only 3 miles along the road from Martha's and was planted by the same man, yet the wines are considerably lighter but also more elegant – just as good if not better and only half the price.

I really admire this man. His sometimes brutal honesty and apparent lack of patience with pretentious members of the wine press, trade and drinking public, has created a somewhat false impression of tetchiness – he is simply devoted to the pursuit of excellence. Industry guru André Tchelistcheff sums him up perfectly: 'You might find one, maybe two, great winemakers in a generation, and today you can take my word that Joe Heitz is the best in California ... he has the gift, the natural talent and is an innovator.'

JORDAN WINERY (Healdsburg, Alexander Valley, Sonoma)

Tom Jordan has become a California wine legend in a matter of a few years. A quiet-spoken, engagingly friendly Denver oil geologist, who has made a fortune 'Dallas-style' (more in the manner of Bobby Ewing than J.R., I hasten to add), he is annually listed in *Fortune* magazine as one of

ENJOYING WINE

America's 200 wealthiest people. A dedicated lover of fine Bordeaux, he decided in the early 1970s to buy a top château (Margaux?) and began serious negotiations. The French government was reluctant to sell to a foreigner and nothing much happened. Also Jordan began to wonder whether he really wanted an estate across the other side of the Atlantic: 'I would have been an absentee landlord, and with the strict *appellation contrôlée* laws my task would have been carrying on tradition, not creating my own series of challenges.' In 1972 he looked around the Napa but there was not much left and, once again, not a lot of challenge – but the Alexander Valley, now that was different. 'My consultant oenologist, André Tchelistcheff, told me the site I had chosen was fine soil and climate and promised that the wine would be good. The Alexander Valley was more bucolic and less developed, therefore more attractive to me.'

The 625 ha (1300 acres) were bought that year. Much of the area intended for grapes was covered in prune trees – all were ripped out and Cabernet Sauvignon was planted, with a small percentage of Merlot. For Jordan 1975 was the year he had either to commit himself totally to the vast expense of building château, winery and a name (estimates vary between US$15 and 25 million), or merely remain a grape grower – but then again, the latter choice is not the style of the man. In 1980 the first vintage, the 1976, was released to instant acclaim (a small amount of grapes was bought in for this initial wine; since then all wines have been produced from the Jordan estate, a very uncommon practice in California.) The 1976 Cabernet impressed critics and public alike on two major counts: it was soft, rich and full of subtlety, yet low in alcohol character (more similar to classic Bordeaux than to its neighbours), and it was ready for drinking on release – not an esoteric wine needing another decade in the cellar.

Jordan Winery has not looked back since. Tom admits he lost his nerve a little in the middle of the white wine boom of the late '70s and grafted 32 ha (80 acres) of Chardonnay, but no matter – the wines are superb with a delicacy of style expected of the house.

The young winemaker, Rob Davis, is now a superstar. The Cabernet is justifiably commanding high prices and on strict ration to distributors

Jordan Winery; Healdsburg, Alexander Valley

CALIFORNIA

Tom Jordan

throughout the United States and Britain. Vast sums of money and quality winemaking have not always proved ideal partners in California, but this one has worked. The winery operation is working in the black; perhaps even the château will do the same over the years – it will not be for lack of trying. As Tom Jordan recently remarked to me, 'If the winery hadn't worked, the loss of money would have been tough, but the personal ignominy of the failure would have been worse!'

RAYMOND VINEYARD & CELLAR (St Helena, Napa Valley)

The Raymonds are the oldest winemaking family in the Napa. Winemaker Walter and vineyard manager Roy Jnr, are fourth generation descendants of the Beringer family, and with their father, Roy Snr, worked for the family company. The fifth generation, in the person of Roy Jnr's son Craig, is now working in the winery: quite a family affair.

The 32 ha (80 acre) vineyard was planted in 1971 and a small winery with more similarity to a garage than a Napa establishment was built – just in time for the 1974 harvest, which produced a mighty 2400 cases. They now produce 75,000 cases a year from a spacious ultra-modern winery.

Progress has been gradual, nothing too hectic and no changes for change's sake. I have already mentioned the firm's 1983 Sauvignon Blanc, which was its first-ever vintage of this variety. The Chardonnays account for nearly 60 per cent of the output and it has been a pleasure to watch them develop over the years. Three styles are now made: California Chardonnay, made from grapes bought in from regions other than the Napa, it is light, fresh with only four months in oak; Napa Chardonnay, more buttery and flavoursome, with eight months in oak; and Napa Valley Private Reserve Chardonnay, superb full-bodied, rich and toasty wine with a beautiful depth of style and yet a totally dry finish, with ten months in oak.

Raymond Cabernets are full of blackcurrant flavour and softened with 18-20 per cent Merlot. They are normally ready for drinking on release, but age well with a very smooth oak and tannin balance.

RIDGE VINEYARDS (Cupertino, Santa Clara)

This enterprise was one of the very first of the new style medium-sized wineries, established as long ago as 1959. When it started, each year there were fewer wineries; it did not turn around for years. The initial partners were four Stanford University research scientists and at first the vineyards were treated as a part-time hobby, albeit a very serious one; the winemaking received painstaking attention and the Cabernets of the '60s received considerable acclaim. In 1969 Paul Draper joined the group as a principal shareholder and winemaker, and the whole operation suddenly changed gear.

The firm's own vineyards and winery buildings are 700 m (2300 ft) above sea level on the Monte Bello Ridge of the Santa Cruz mountains, high above the urban sprawl of San Francisco. In the 1880s the French settled in the Santa Clara Valley then moved up the mountain, attracted by the unique red soils with excellent drainage, and by one of the few areas in California that had poor soil offering low yields – ideal for vineyard cultivation.

CALIFORNIA

By the turn of the century eight wineries were established. In the 1890s an expatriate Alsace *vigneron* was sending his best Cabernets across to the Paris Exhibition and regularly winning medals. The LaCuesta Vineyard, established from 1822 to 1944 produced, in Draper's opinion, 'some of the greatest Cabernets in California'. Unfortunately only two wineries survived Prohibition – but at least the lower vineyards were replanted with Cabernet in the '40s, one of the major attractions in the purchase of Ridge.

As the Ridge expanded and searched for grapes to buy in, it was difficult to find Cabernet of suitable standards. This was, after all, well before the planting boom of the last 15 years, and there certainly were no spare vines with any age (Cabernet was such an insignificant planting in the early days that the Californian Agricultural Department did not even bother to report the acreage statistically until 1936). But there was a wealth of Zinfandel: old vineyards with big vines producing low yields of intense small berries. This was exactly what Draper desired and after initial experiments, he decided to go ahead and pioneer this grape as a producer of premium wine.

Even now many people are still writing about the manner in which the style varies so dramatically from area to area. Consequently the majority of the public is unsure what to expect from this grape. As Draper explains, 'There was a real problem – the makers didn't identify what style of wine Zinfandel was meant to be. This is a unique California grape variety, but there was no discipline. The fruit was used to make everything from Rosé, light Beaujolais style, deeper more tannic Claret style, port . . . you name it. There was no careful attention with cultivation. It received no priority and was picked when it suited the grower, not the grapes. Then the winemaker would crush these overripe grapes, age in the nearest stainless steel tank, bottle and sell – and then wonder why the public never rated it as a quality grape!'

Well, there is no doubt about Ridge's reputation for this grape, plus its Cabernets, in particular 'Monte Bello' from its own vineyards. The most modern equipment is in use but the techniques are traditional. 'I am the iconoclast of California – I have turned backwards and asked what the past

Paul Draper, Ridge Vineyards

Rutherford Hill Winery, Napa Valley

has to teach us. After Prohibition the big boys were in, and out went the small boys, along with centuries-old traditions. Suddenly everyone was filtering right after fermentation; very convenient but the wine loses complexity.' The Draper system is to clear the wines through natural settling in barrel and careful racking; filtration is used only as a last resort for problem casks.

The exterior of the Ridge establishment is more Wild West than California winery. The money has been spent on barrels and the intensive labour needed to work them. The wines speak for themselves. The Cabernets possess deep aromas of currants and oak *à la Bordelais* and an intense but warm flavour. They need considerable bottle age. I recently tasted a 1971 Monte Bello that was delicious but still about five years away from perfection. The Zinfandels are everything Draper claims – rich, robust and reeking of fruit; instantly attractive luscious mouthfuls of flavour – the ideal introduction to real red wine drinking.

RUTHERFORD HILL WINERY (St Helena, Napa Valley)

Rutherford Hill was established in 1976 as a partnership of growers and experienced wine people. They are financially tied with the older and smaller Freemark Abbey just along the highway. All grapes for the considerable production (130,000 cases and growing) are from the partners' vineyards in the Napa. I have been following this winery for years because of winemaker Phil Baxter's devotion to Merlot and the delightful wines he has produced from this variety. Not only does it drink well on release, but it confounds the 'experts' and ages gracefully. I recently drank a 10-year-old bottle, and it was a real education: subtle and soft, yet possessing considerable depth of harmonious oak and tannin. Rutherford Hill makes sound, attractive oaky Cabernets, but it is the Merlot that steals the show.

The Chardonnays are also excellent, being light and fragrant with considerable elegance and no over-oaking, and yet enough depth of flavour for ageing. A tasting of a lively 10-year-old was a revelation – still full of buttery fruit and a delicate, clean finish. Baxter says he would eventually like to hold back stocks in the best years and release five years later – I hope that financial considerations allow him to do so. The Sauvignon Blanc does not quite have the extrovert varietal style I prefer, but it is attractive, fresh and clean.

At a time when many California wineries are desperately looking for means of cutting costs, it is reassuring to note the dynamic expansion programme at Rutherford Hill: a brand new computer-controlled fermentation room and the recent construction of a huge 65,000 barrel capacity underground storage cellar, 'the largest in the States' according to Baxter. Definitely a winery to watch.

SEBASTIANI VINEYARDS (Sonoma)

Sam Sebastiani has chosen an eagle for the crest on the labels because he considers a symbol of an endangered species is appropriate for a family-owned company producing more than 4 million cases a year – mixing it with the big boys.

The vineyards were established in 1904, survived Prohibition and over the years built a reputation for inexpensive wines made in the 'Italian' tradition: soft and full of oak and age. Sam's father August was the driving force over the first three postwar decades and towards the end of his reign there was a gradual lightening of style. Executive winemaker Doug Davis, a Sebastiani veteran with 30 years of service, points out that Sam's degree is in business administration, not oenology – 'because that is where August needed help'. Sam's influence was crucial in 1980 when his father died: 'Sam realized that survival would be conditional upon a reputation for quality as well as quantity. The wines were bottled younger and varietal character was intensified.'

Classy 1.5-litre 'Country Varietals' were inaugurated: the Chardonnay Sauvignon Blanc and Cabernet Sauvignon may not be the cheapest jug wines on the market, but they offer some of the best value. The Eye of the Swan (pure Pinot Noir Blanc) commands attention, as does a serious, full fragrant Pinot Noir, but the outstanding Sebastiani product is the Proprietor's Reserve Cabernet Sauvignon: a lovely, delicate and flavoursome wine. Thanks to Sam's influence, Sebastiani is one of the California wineries producing individualistic wines with character.

SIMI WINERY (Healdsburg, Alexander Valley, Sonoma)

Ask people in the wine trade on both coasts for their favourite winery and a vast number of different names will be mentioned; some are featured in this book. But request their opinion on the most improved winery in recent years, and the name Simi crops up time and time again. Considering the ups and downs of this winery over the past two decades, this is nothing short of remarkable.

Before Prohibition the winery was one of the largest in the area, with 280 ha (700 acres) of vineyards – but although the winery survived, forced sales and foreclosures took care of the land. After the Second World War, things gradually declined until 1970, when an oil executive bought the property and began bringing it into the 20th century. However, it took him only four years to tire of these heavy demands. Simi was sold to Scottish & Newcastle Vintners, a subsidiary of the

Michael Dixon, Simi Winery Alexander Valley

Excavation of Rutherford Hill Winery's ageing caves, the largest underground storage cellar in the States

British brewing group. Its chairman, Michael Dixon, was convinced of the necessity of broadening the spirits sales base of the company. Two years later it pulled out of the States, but Dixon was 'hooked' and stayed on as president under the ownership of New York-based wine and spirits importers Schieffelin & Co. (now part of the Moët-Hennessy Group).

Two major decisions were made in the late '70s. The first was to invest $5.5 million in expansion and re-equipping. The decaying historic stone cellar building was renovated and the most modern winemaking equipment organized to fill one half. The other part was ready to accommodate 7000 oak barrels. The other crucial decision was the appointment of Robert Mondavi's head oenologist, Zelma Long, as Vice-President Winemaker. Just as a chef works better in a kitchen of his own design, so does a winemaker prefer a free hand in winery planning. Production has now reached 150,000 cases, and yet the wines receive all the care and attention they would in the smallest wineries – in fact probably more. Ms Long has installed computer controls to allow winemakers to attend to many of the basic, but crucially important, tasks often delegated to casual labour at harvest and fermentation time.

There are five styles of wine now produced, the first two accounting for 70 per cent of production:
Cabernet Sauvignon These wines possess the *cassis* flavour of the Alexander Valley, but also a delicate cedarwood hint of Margaux. Superb fragrance and really stylish; 10 per cent Merlot.
Chardonnay These are of the 'new style'. Intense, lean but with a rich flavour and a delicate touch of acidity. The Reserve wines are outstanding.
Sauvignon Blanc First released in 1982. The Sauvignon Blancs are lower in alcohol and crisper than most others, with a beguiling hint of gooseberry.
Chenin Blanc No oak, with a little residual sugar and a hint of *spritz*. A wine of much higher quality than most others produced under this name.
Rosé de Cabernet Sauvignon I must state that this is simply the finest rosé, apart from the very best from Provence! Delicate strawberry colour, well-balanced and lively fruit flavour with a crisp finish – a most attractive wine that should convert all wine lovers with preconceived ideas of the perils of this much-maligned type.

In 1982 Simi purchased 42 ha (105 acres) of uncultivated land in the Chalk Hill area of the Alexander Valley – off the floor on the slopes, and ideal for Cabernet. They have been planted and in part an experimental trellising system developed in New Zealand by Dr Richard Smart is in use. More vineyard plantings are planned and it is anticipated that soon two-thirds of Simi's Cabernet requirements will come from its own sources. Michael Dixon is an optimist: 'Although excellent grapes are on sale now, we believe that this will not always be the case in such a booming industry.'

TREFETHEN VINEYARDS (Napa Valley)
The *Gault Millau* 'Olympics' offended a number of French wine personalities, none more so than Robert Drouhin. He was aghast at the comprehensive defeat of the French in the Pinot Noir and Chardonnay sections and, with the cooperation of the magazine, the foreign competitors and a new jury, he organized a 'retrial' of burgundy – but this time with top-class wines of his choice from his own firm (let's face it, the initial home team selection was not exactly crammed with superstars). The burgundies fared better this time, but in the white section the same Stateside wine repeated the triumph: Trefethen Vineyards Chardonnay 1976. This would have been an amazing feat from an old-established vineyard, even if one from the other side of the Atlantic – but this family-owned operation had been in the grape-growing business for only 11 years, and had been making its own wines for only 3 years by 1976! This is rapid social climbing, even by Californian standards.

The Trefethen presence in the Napa can be summed up as the 'right people in the right area at the right time'. Gene Trefethen was a farmer looking for a new ranch; urban sprawl had taken care of his original one. In 1968 he bought the derelict Eschol vineyard at the southern end of the Napa Valley, plus the adjoining 154 ha (380 acres), thereby creating the largest 'contiguous' (what a lovely American word!) vineyard in the valley. I have previously mentioned what a major decision it was to use land for grape growing instead of other agrarian pursuits, but once this was finalized a meticulous planting operation was instituted with considerable attention to soil and the tremendous micro-climatic difference within the property. Initially he was worried about the Cabernet Sauvignon grapes ripening in such a cool part of the valley, but the research proved worthwhile and Trefethen Vineyards steadily progressed. At first the family were only grape growers, until son John returned from graduate studies and decided to use a percentage of the grapes to make wine. Nothing was done on a particularly grand scale: the first year the Trefethens made a mere 3000 cases; even now they sell 50 per cent of their crop as grapes, to Domaine Chandon and Schramsberg, high-class sparkling wine producers.

The winery building has been lovingly restored to the initial glories of the turn of the century when an oddball farmer, J. Clark Farrer, owned Eschol – he never even drank the stuff but carried on making and selling wine until his death in 1940. The latest stainless steel equipment produces a delightfully fragrant White Riesling, and there are hundreds of *barriques* for the ageing of their superb Chardonnay and Cabernet Sauvignon: some of the finest products of the Napa Valley.

THE FUTURE

Paul Draper posed the question 'Americans are only consuming 2 gallons of wine each year, 10 per cent of the Australian total, and this figure isn't increasing ... yet all the time more and more wine is being made. Are we destined to spend our time all chasing the same market?' Others, such as Michael Dixon and Doug Davis, are confident of a positive future; and the spirit companies are certainly worried about the threat of wine – a significant amount of their advertising is now aimed at keeping their customers away from it with claims of less calories and less alcohol in 'long' drinks. Obviously with such a large population a modest increase in wine consumption will have a significant effect. The 'French invasion' is well under way with Moët & Chandon, Piper Heidsieck, Burgundian Jean-Claude Boisset, and, of course, Baron Philippe de Rothschild, firmly established, and G.H. Mumm and Louis Roederer coming up – they must be confident. The wineries certainly excel at doorstep public relations. Sebastiani staff guide 250,000 tourists around their winery annually and an estimated 10 million people will soon tour the Napa Valley each year.

I recently stood in the cashier's queue in an upmarket New York kitchen equipment shop and

ENJOYING WINE

Trefethen Winery, Napa Valley

CALIFORNIA

ENJOYING WINE

the lady behind me confided to her friend that 'food and wine was now in and replacing sex as the focal point of the male New Yorkers' life!' Perhaps she was a sociologist airing her latest theory, but there seem to be more food periodicals on the bookstall shelves than sex magazines these days. The 'New American Cuisine' is 'in' and hamburgers and pastrami sandwiches are 'out' – surely increased wine drinking must follow. White Zinfandel is a fashionable drink now; it is most pleasant, rather innocuous and pale pink, charmingly referred to as 'blush wine'. Perhaps this will achieve something that Lambrusco has never managed: increased awareness of the subtleties of wine as both a drink and an accompaniment to food. Then the United States wine market will fulfil its potential.

OTHER WINEMAKING AREAS

New York State

There is one big drawback to this region: the extremely harsh winters, hence the planting of sturdy hybrid grape varieties (*Vitis labrusca*). Baco Noir, Chancellor, Concord, and Delaware sometimes make sound, drinkable wine and the Seyval Blanc is capable of a considerably higher standard, but most of the wines are unrewarding. They are often described as having a 'foxy' taste; I know this is a strange term to apply to wine, but it refers to the harsh, unsophisticated style of these 'wild' or 'fox' grapes. Often the more drinkable of these wines have been produced with full use of the liberal state laws regarding the significant allowable percentage of out-of-state (i.e. Californian) grape content. Sparkling wine production is enormous and the word 'Champagne' is liberally featured on the labels. The wines so labelled are no better than one would expect from companies who, lacking the courage of their convictions and any real faith in their products, pass them off as one of the greatest styles of wine in the world.

However, things are improving and there is a new generation of wineries producing very, very stylish white wines from classical grape varieties. Gold Seal Chardonnay and Johannisberger Riesling have created a considerable reputation, and Wagner Vineyards have a deliciously fresh, fruity Riesling. But the really outstanding wine I have tasted is the Hargrave Vineyards Chardonnay, which has a varietal character, and a rich delicate finish, more similar to Australia than California.

The Pacific Northwest

Oregon is producing wines of considerable quality, especially Pinot Noir from Knudsen Erath, The Eyrie Vineyards and Tualatin. Washington State has a large operation, Château Ste Michelle producing high quality wines, in particular its Cabernet Sauvignon. Idaho has the Château Ste Chapelle Vineyards situated in a high – 760 m (2500 ft) above sea level.

Texas

Believe it or not there is a winemaking boom down in the Lone Star State with cotton farmers, cattle ranchers, university professors, financiers, and the inevitable doctors and lawyers, joining the new industry with a degree of enthusiasm previously reserved for striking oil. The recent planting of vines was initially a university experiment in a search for a new agrarian cash crop that did not require a great deal of their precious water. There are now well over 1000 ha (2470 acres) of vineyards and the total is rising rapidly. Some people are turning out rather weird concoctions ('Nouveau Barbera'?), but there are a number of well-financed, well-organized wineries producing more than acceptable Chardonnay, Chenin Blanc, Sauvignon Blanc and Cabernet Sauvignon. Dick Gill's Llano Estacado (Spanish for 'staked plains') has been the pioneer operation making large quantities of the better varieties, and he has now established a mammoth joint venture with two French companies, Cordier (Bordeaux) and Richter (Montpellier), which is expected rapidly to become one of the largest wineries in the whole country. Other names to look for are Fall Creek, Pheasant Ridge and Sanchez Creek.

The main problem the quality wines from all these regions face is lack of public awareness: the finer New York State wines receive scant recognition even in the Big Apple. Texas wines are not exactly filling the shelves of retailers across the country. Ironically most of these wines mentioned (including the last three Texas vineyards named above) are available across the Atlantic in Britain – a good example of the country's role as 'Capital of the Wine World'.

Chapter Fifteen

AUSTRALIA

The first white settlers in this vast continent were not exactly imbued with the idea and spirit of colonizing a new land. As they were in fact convicts condemned by the magistrates of Mother England to a life of penal solitude in the harsh conditions of early New South Wales, the only spirit that interested them was the type that came out of a bottle, and in plenty. Residents of the inner West London districts who have lived near the pubs frequented over the years by expatriate Australians will not be surprised to learn that the colony had a serious drinking problem right from the start! Winemaking was encouraged from the earliest days as a moderating influence; if the residents were determined to blot out the realities of life at least they could do it in a moderate manner – with wine.

Captain Arthur Phillip, the first governor of New South Wales, brought out the first fleet in January 1788 and founded the settlements. The eleven small ships had taken nine months to traverse the world and had stopped at the Cape of Good Hope in South Africa for stores. While there it was decided that some vine cuttings should be bought for the settlement and these were duly planted in new South Wales, and by the early 1800s winemaking was firmly established. Many history books refer to the British desire for Australia to be the wine producer for the Mother Country, and in 1822 a Mr Blaxland exported a pipe of red wine to the United Kingdon where it won a silver medal in the exhibition of the 'Society for the Encouragement of Arts, Manufactures and Commerce'. The wine was fortified with brandy to ensure a carefree passage around the world. A few years later Mr Blaxland repeated the exercise with even better results, received more widespread approval, and the 'Empire Wine' tradition was born.

VINEYARD EXPANSION IN THE 1800s

Vines were initially planted in areas that are now suburban Sydney. The cuttings were cultivated wherever was convenient for the settlers, with scant regard paid to climatic and soil conditions. It was an 'anything goes' operation until the arrival of James Busby, the father of Australian viticulture. This canny Scot was either a remarkable visionary, or a man of blessed luck, because even before leaving Europe he decided that this new, rugged penal colony was ideal for viticulture. He therefore went to France and studied both viticulture and winemaking before travelling to Australia. He received considerable government grant money and in 1825 established the first vineyard proper: Kirkton Estate in the Hunter River area, 160 km (100 miles) north of Sydney. By the 1830s the intrepid settlers had carved a road through the mountainous terrain from Sydney to the Hunter

ENJOYING WINE

Southern Vales – South Australia

AUSTRALIA

ENJOYING WINE

Valley and considerable areas were planted; in 1850 there were more than 200 ha (500 acres) under vine. Meanwhile, in the newly settled Victoria, cuttings from Sydney were planted by a William Ryrie at Yerring, near Yarra Glen. This man was a real character. In 1839 he was an elder of Melbourne's Presbyterian Church, but he blotted his copybook in January 1840 when he was involved in a very public duel. A few years later he returned to his native Ayrshire and his property was sold to a Swiss grazier, Paul de Castella. Wine was the last commercial operation in de Castella's mind but the quality of the existing vines and their product persuaded him to treat this aspect of the farm most seriously. Bordeaux friends shipped 20,000 cuttings from Château Lafite Rothschild and a firm basis for quality winemaking was established in Victoria as respectable Cabernet Sauvignon was produced.

South Australia, the first non-convict settlement, was established and in 1840 a group of Adelaide citizens subscribed to a fund for the purchase of cuttings from the Cape of Good Hope. These were distributed to all members, but, most importantly, a specimen of each was planted in the Botanical Gardens. Considerable planting followed in two areas: Southern Vales just outside Adelaide, and the newly discovered Barossa Valley. Vineyard development in the latter region was helped considerably by the influx of Silesian Lutherans who were encouraged to flee the religious persecution back home and seek their freedom and fortunes in this colony.

Obviously there were many trials and tribulations, but there was certainly established a national industry of considerable strength – until the economic depression of the 1890s, which bankrupted many of the wineries. By this time it was also apparent that the short-term interests of the rapidly expanding South Australian industry were against the long-term interests of the others. This province had expanded too fast and too far, and there were considerable over-production problems which led to problems in the burgeoning exports to Great Britain as these winemakers began to dump their large parcels of inferior wine on this important market. However, all credit to the industry: the people that mattered in South Austalia saw the problems and took positive steps.

THE 1900s

The early years of the century saw continual expansion, especially in South Australia, whose growers had many advantages: higher yields, considerable state subsidies and an absence of the dreaded phylloxera, which was ravaging Victoria. A final bonus was the political decision to federate all the states, which allowed the South Australians free access to the more heavily populated markets of Sydney and Melbourne. They certainly made the most of their advantages and severe price cutting was rampant ('So what's different these days?', I hear my Victorian friends commenting). This state of affairs was disastrous for the Hunter and Victorian producers and, to make matters worse, along came the First World War accompanied by the decimation of the British and home markets.

There is no doubt about it, the Australian wine industry was persistent and never stayed down for long. No sooner was the war over than expansion was in fashion again, and returned servicemen with government grants were planting large holdings in the irrigated regions surrounding the Murray and Murrumbidgee Rivers (encompassing all three states). South Australia continued expanding: the 1920 vintage produced 20 million litres; four years later it had rocketed to 50 million! The inevitable had happened, and production was suddenly discovered to be greatly exceeding demand. things looked bad, but worse was to come in the form of the worldwide Depression. Both overseas and local sales fell even further and very many acres of vineyards were simply ploughed under. Things stayed this way for years and consumption only began to rise with the influx of visiting armed forces in the Second World War (with a little help from local servicemen).

It must be said at this stage much of the wine produced was rather horrible. The previously mentioned semi-fortified, sweetish 'Empire wines' (still available today in the less sophisticated areas of Northern England) could transport drinkers from harsh reality through ecstasy to oblivion within the space of a few glasses. But they did not exactly stimulate the palates of the more sophisticated wine drinkers either at home or abroad.

AUSTRALIA

> ## CLOSER TO GOD
>
> HEGGIES Vineyard stands so high that it sometimes disappears into the clouds altogether.
>
> They say that's when the saints come and steal the grapes.
>
> At least they don't steal the wine, the heavenly Heggies Rhine Riesling, the fruit of the altitude, the soil and the specially selected vines.
>
> That's strictly for the worldly.
>
> HEGGIES RHINE RIESLING

Things began to improve in the postwar years. Australian society was still rough and ready but extremely affluent compared to war-torn Europe. The 'New Australians' flooded in from the Mediterranean and Eastern European countries and brought their own food and wine values. The roast leg of mutton and bottle of beer began to share the nation's dining table with tagliatelle and vino rosso. More and more respectable table wines were being made. I have tasted some remarkable Cabernet Sauvignons of these years: a bottle of 1959 Rosewood (Rutherglen) drunk in 1978 with Melbourne restaurateur Siggy Jorgensen was the finest bottle of wine I tasted that year.

THE 1960s

The 1960s were an amazing decade for wine production and consumption. At the beginning of the decade the promise was evident, but suddenly the revolution really arrived. One wine obviously cannot take sole credit for this amazing development in local drinking habits, but it did have three aspects that are crucial to an explanation of this boom: technical innovation, mass market appeal and price. Barossa Pearl was first produced by the South Australian firm of Orlando in 1956, and by the early 1960s it was the unchallenged market leader for table wine. It was the first Australian wine to retain the natural *spritz* of the fruit and accentuate it with the use of cold fermentation techniques (all very run-of-the-mill nowadays, but remember we are talking about nearly 30 years ago).

To be honest, it was everything the 'real' wine drinker disliked: naturally sweet, carbonated sparkling white, packaged in an awful bottle (reminiscent of a smooth pineapple), reeking in bad taste but loaded with brand recognition – and it was cheap. The public loved it! Non-wine drinkers were converted in their thousands and this dynamic preaching to the unconverted was just what Orlando's shareholders and the national wine industry needed. Many companies in the more traditional wine-producing countries of the world have attempted to emulate Barossa Pearl, but none with the same dramatic effect.

At the same time a host of other influences were involved. Australia had 'never had it so good' and there was plenty of disposable income – the local businessman was not so much concerned with mortgage payments as the size of the newly installed swimming pool. Graham Kerr, TV's 'Galloping Gourmet' was no rival to Escoffier but introduced a captive audience to many of the finer aspects of eating and drinking. Wine columns suddenly appeared in all serious magazines and 'Dining Out' became an integral part of social life.

THE 1970s

The revolution was under way, everything was primed for the explosion. The industry at this stage was confidentially described to by a very senior executive as 'about to overcome the problem of producing wine from the wrong grapes planted in the wrong areas'. This was a rather harsh evaluation, but the fact of the matter was that Australia was producing sound, workmanlike wines, rather solid and dependable but lacking the finesse of their European counterparts.

Furious planting occurred, still not always in the correct areas but mostly of classier varietals. Wineries stopped labelling their Shiraz as either 'Claret' or 'Burgundy' according to the demand of the moment. New wineries sprang up everywhere

ENJOYING WINE

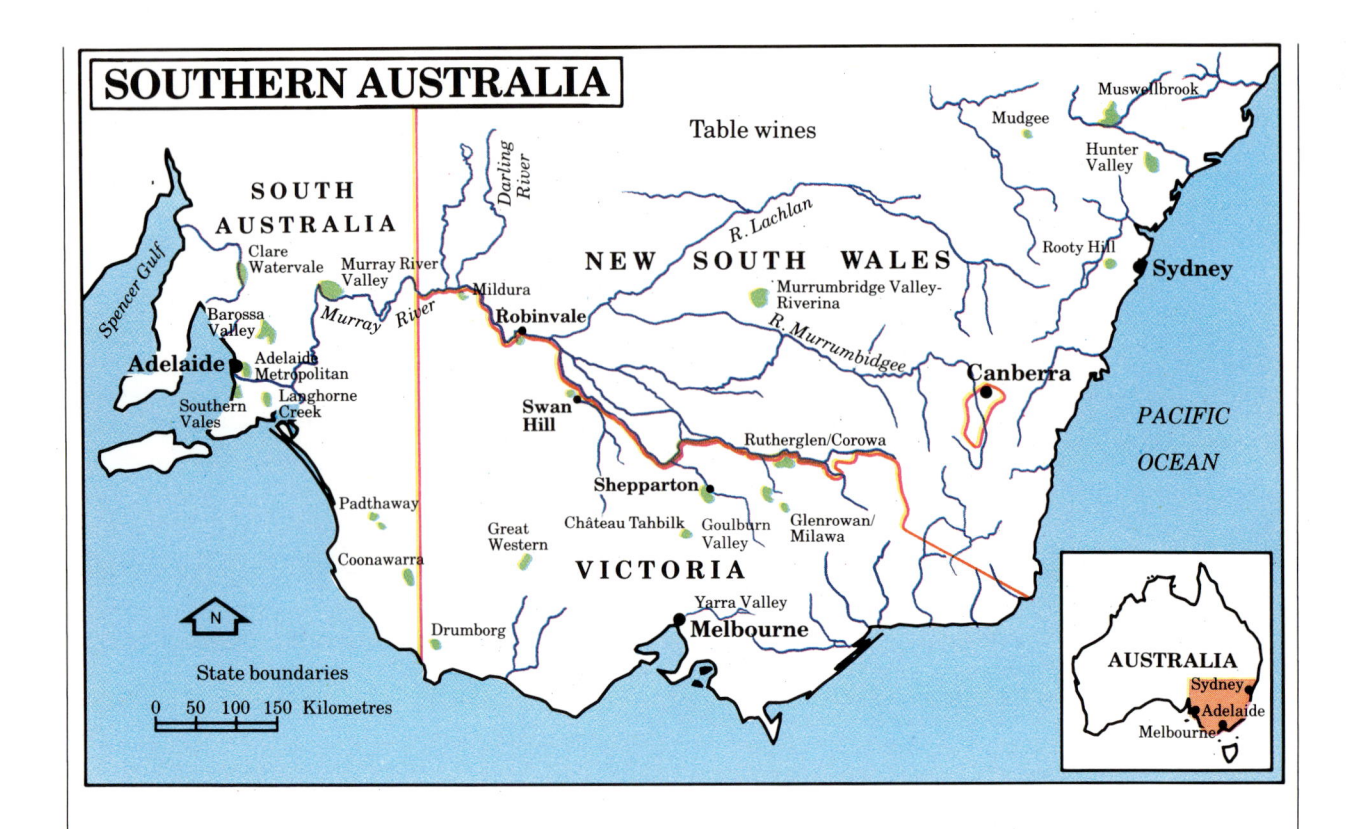

SOUTHERN AUSTRALIA

NEW SOUTH WALES

HUNTER VALLEY
The oldest wine growing area proper and also one of the real quality ones. Not the easiest region for wine producing ... cool sea breezes in summer accompanied by much cloud cover and a continual threat of rain at harvest time; all this adds up to low yields and uneven vintages. The region has had its fair share of financial 'ups and downs' but the best vineyards produce delicate European style reds and soft flavoursome whites.

MUDGEE
Further west and on higher ground. Many of the vineyards are relatively recently established therefore they are planted with mostly 'new wave' varietals, i.e. Chardonnay, Traminer, Cabernet Sauvignon.

RIVERINA (Murrumbidgee Irrigation Area)
Large, flat and hot terrain; formerly planted exclusively with the old style grapes for making of fortifieds but cold fermentation has offered new hope and the huge yields are turning out vast quantities of cheap drinking wine. Griffith, the central town of the area, now seems better known for marijuana cropping and murders!

SOUTH AUSTRALIA

The largest producing state; in downtown Adelaide they never tire of reminding you that they produce more wine than all other states put together.

ADELAIDE METROPOLITAN AREA AND THE SURROUNDING HILLS
Suburban sprawl has taken its toll of many of the grand old establishments but a token amount is still left, especially at Penfold's Magill, the birthplace of Grange. Further out Petaluma has defined a new area as 'Piccadilly' by sheer virtue of its presence.

SOUTHERN VALES
A trip through this area is not to be missed, but hire a teetotal chauffeur with a good sense of direction! Reynella, Coromandel Valley and McLarenvale are only just south of Adelaide but the dozens and dozens of hospitable wineries are dotted around the hillsides, ranging from small part-time ones to 'Hardys', one of the largest in Australia. Extremely hot summers and mild

AUSTRALIA

winters (sunburnt grapes are the problem, not frost) tend to produce fat 'old fashioned' shiraz and over-ripe Cabernets. The whites can be excellent nowadays. Lunch at 'The Barn' restaurant at McLarenvale is not to be missed.

BAROSSA VALLEY
The most famous Australian wine region claiming to supply 10 per cent of the nation's wine (but . . . see 'Sheppard's Creek' page 161). A narrowish valley more like a Down Under Côte d'Or than Bordeaux . . . the lack of a vista of nothing but vineyards is rather perplexing on first visit . . . it makes superb Rhine Riesling and rather heavy, obvious reds which for some reason always seem to have a slight aftertaste of salt. Many of the large companies have their headquarters here and their technical resources will accelerate the already obvious gradual improvements.

CLARE VALLEY – WATERVALE
Higher ground producing the finest of all Rhine Riesling and luscious, fruity reds.

COONAWARRA
The most unusual vineyard area in the whole country. At first glance it seems a mere few strips of vines on a short, thin stretch of bright red volcanic loam interspersed with a few old shacks – you almost expect to see Gary Cooper on patrol! But it is the combination of this 'terra rossa', the cool climate (mainland Australia's southernmost vineyard area) and proximity to the ocean which produces the super, highly rated Cabernets. Close by is Keppoch, a newer area, similar climate but different soil.

MURRAY RIVERLAND
The cooperative wineries here are some of the largest producers in the country. The Berri Coop alone crushes more than three times the whole of Coonawarra. Much of the wine is sold in bulk and marketed in the flagons and casks of well-known names.

VICTORIA
It is difficult to specify vineyard areas in this state; there are a number of well established areas . . . but in the past fifteen years there has literally been an explosion of vineyards all over the state. Ten years ago there were 40 vineyards within the boundaries of the state, now there are 150!

NORTH EAST
Hot, dry area famous for fortified wines, in particular the unique Liqueur Muscats. There is some table wine expansion . . . but mainly at Milawa with the dynamic 'Brown Brothers'.

GOULBOURN VALLEY
Formerly solely inhabited by Château Tahbilk, but now significant new vineyard plantings.

SOUTH WEST
Old established area initially well known for Seppelt's sparklings. Now there are many small vineyards in the general area plus a large Remy Martin investment in sparkling and table wines.

YARRA VALLEY
As already seen in the initial winemaking history, this was a flourishing vineyard area but over the years economic vicissitudes forced a return to grazing. In the past couple of decades much has changed and vineyards are being planted furiously . . . and with the correct grape varieties. I once attended a function with a group of these 'new' Yarra *vignerons* and they are as diverse a bunch of people as one could imagine ranging from quiet, serious introverts and total extroverts bordering on controlled lunacy (is there such a state of being?). Many vineyards are still run on a part-time basis.

GEELONG was a considerable area but ravaged by phylloxera and is now on the way back. Bendigo has the remarkable Stuart Anderson . . . the list could go on and on.

Harvesting, Barossa, South Australia

ENJOYING WINE

offering a vast range of styles of wines at reasonable prices, to the delight of the public. Wine drinking was no longer the occasional bottle with Sunday lunch, it became an everyday occurrence, with or without food.

There was much bad wine made at this time as often untrained enthusiasts grappled with something they really did not understand, but this was counteracted by the graduates coming from the famed Roseworthy Oenological College (founded in the 1930s) and Brian Croser's first students who emerged from the newly founded Wagga Wagga School of Oenology in the mid-1970s.

The country even possessed an oenophile Prime Minister!

THE WINEMAKERS AND THEIR WINES

Nothing changes more rapidly in this world than the Australian wine scene. No sooner has one winery established itself as the paramount force in the area than another couple spring up with aspirations to change the state of play; some succeed, some fail abjectly. Winemakers are national superstars and change firms as regularly as British football managers change clubs – and often for as much money. The increasingly demanding, but often fickle, buying public seem always to be waiting for 'something old, something borrowed, something new', to paraphrase a popular song. As a Melbourne winebroker friend always reminds me, over 60 per cent of the total wine production comes from only 12 companies; but this has not hindered the continual expansion of either the medium-sized, often family-owned, establishments or the small boutique wineries.

The reader will have already gathered that I am reasonably opinionated about the wines of the world and I must point out that the following listing of the major Australian wineries has nothing to do with size, ownership, market acceptance or area. These are my personal preferences gathered in 15 years of regular tastings and vineyard visits.

Wine Festival Downunder Style

AUSTRALIA

The First Division
This comprises the larger companies (and some not so large) who make consistently fine wines year in, year out; often they are technically superior to the less financially resourceful small wineries. They are listed alphabetically, not in order of preference.

Brown Brothers (Milawa, northeast Victoria)
A remarkable family firm established in the 1880s. John Brown senior is a third generation winemaker from this region; all his four sons are in the business providing the vineyard management, production, sales and marketing. Over the past 15 years they have planted a bewildering range of varietals: Rhine Riesling, Frontignan Blanc (labelled Muscat Blanc for export markets), Croucher Riesling, Chenin Blanc, Colombard, Gewürztraminer, Chardonnay, Cabernet Sauvignon, Shiraz, Mondeuse and so on. Many of the scattered vineyards are in the cooler areas and with dynamic technical innovations (including night-time harvesting) the wines all possess considerable depths of individual flavour and delightfully pure varietal character. I once showed Brown's Individual Koombahla Cabernet Sauvignon to American first-class passengers on a Pan Am flight from Los Angeles to Sydney and their reactions were amazing. Most were businessmen with regular Australian dealings and were used to the national reds with more oak and tannin: this clean, European-style Cabernet amazed them. I would actually pick two whites as the outstanding Brown Brothers wines: the superb Chardonnay and the unique rich, Late Picked Muscat Blanc.

Château Tahbilk (Goulurn Valley, Victoria)
Here I have to declare an interest: I am the European representative for this unique winery. I had been appreciating the fine Tahbilk reds since 1965 (my very first year in the restaurant business). Indeed, when tourist customers, soon tired of the poor New Zealand wines of those days, yearned for something better but still reasonably local, I would serve them Tahbilk Shiraz, or 'claret' as it was called then. Therefore when I decided to import Australian wines into Britain the Purbrick family seemed the obvious choice of suppliers. The estate has been in existence since 1860 when vines were planted and considered ancillary to the grazing. Later an undergound winery was established. Phylloxera ravaged Victoria in general and Tahbilk in particular, where 60 per cent of vineyard land was lost. A myriad of other problems beset the vineyard for year after year, the inevitable result of having English absentee owners. In 1925 the Purbricks bought the estate and in 1931 Eric, then 25, agreed to take over its management and rehabilitation. His qualifications for the task were somewhat minimal, being a law degree from Jesus College, Cambridge, and frequent trips around Europe; in fact he had only visited Tahbilk once.

The Depression, the degeneration of vine stocks and the total deterioration of vineyard equipment were only a few of Eric's problems and they were tackled with the forthright attitude still evident nowadays. There are many tales in Melbourne regarding Eric's legendary visits to town to insist on people buying his excellent bulk wine, just to keep sufficient money coming in to the house of Purbrick.

Since those days the estate as a whole has been built up with almost 1500 ha (3700 acres) of grazing land and 70 ha (175 acres) of vineyards. In the 1950s and '60s a solid reputation was established for the two reds. The soft, buttery Shiraz was one of the most consistent Australian reds of those decades and the Cabernet Sauvignon was absolutely superb: a firm, aromatic wine with a complexity that develops over the years. In 1980 I attended a family dinner at Tahbilk and brought over a few bottles of very fine claret from London. My bottles were served, and then with the cheese Eric offered the finest wine of the night. I pronounced it a first growth Bordeaux at least 20 years old and in peak condition: it was his 1953 Cabernet!

Today son John is involved with much of the general management of the estate and wine sales. Grandson Alister, a Roseworthy College graduate, is now winemaker. His arrival in 1978 led to a considerable transformation in the white winemaking — without any lowering of the standards of the reds, thankfully. A new cool fermentation cellar was built and the fresh, fruity whites have been consistent gold medal winners at the big shows. The Marsanne is of particular interest, a minor white Rhône variety normally used for blending but here produced on its own, making a soft, flavoursome wine with a delicate hint of honeysuckle (I realize this sounds pretentious, but it really is like this). I have tasted very promising experimental bottlings of Sémillon and look forward to the future.

Lindeman (Hunter Valley, Coonawarra)
The establishment of this company in 1843 was the beginning of the Australian medical profession's close involvement with the wine industry. Dr Lindeman planted Cawarra in the Hunter, and despite the inevitable problems the company flourished and by 1870 was firmly established with headquarters in Sydney. As the doctor's family expanded, so did the vineyards, and the sons continued the tradition; even the daughter had the good grace to marry the nephew of James Busby, thereby bringing the original Australian vineyard of Kirkton into the family fold. Serious financial problems in the 1930s and '40s did not prevent the firm from making many of the absolute classic wines of the time; in fact many older generation wine personalities claim the Lindeman reds of this time, along with Maurice O'Shea's Mount Pleasant Hunter wines, to be among the finest ever made in Australia.

The 1950s and '60s saw a host of reliable drinking wines. I remember with affection the Cawarra Claret and Cawarra Hock. In 1965 the company took over Rouge Homme Wines in the Coonawarra and the result has been the dependable Rouge Homme Cabernet Sauvignon. In 1971 Lindeman was taken over by the American tobacco company, Philip Morris, and the expansion has continued with much wine being trucked to the Hunter for blending. Mention must be made of the tremendously popular Ben Ean Moselle, a natural successor to Barossa Pearl as the home market became more sophisticated.

Today Lindeman impresses me as a maker of sound, attractive, value-for-money wines. I am very fond of Nyrang Hermitage, a Shiraz grown from grapes from the Hunter, Clare and Coonawarra. The Bin 45 Claret and Coolalta Hermitage are perfect 'barbecue reds', smooth, aged wines with an attractive fruit finish, and very easy to drink.

Orlando (G. Gramp & Sons; Barossa Valley)
Much has already been written about the contemporary influence of this firm. Perhaps I have given the impression of a relatively recent winemaking establishment but this is not the case. Johann left his natuve Bavaria at the tender age of 18, arriving in South Australia in 1937. Within a few years he had moved from Adelaide and planted the first vineyard in the Barossa Valley.

I am not belittling the early years and the Gramp influence on South Australian wine production when I state that one of my first tasks on retiring from my present business would be to write a book about Orlando – but it would begin in 1953 when temperature-controlled fermentation was introduced there. For some time the company was unfairly denigrated because of its 'Pearl' image, which was obscuring the fact that the expensive technical equipment was also producing a revolutionary fresh, fruity Barossa Rhine Riesling (perhaps a less lurid label would have helped!). This has become better and better over the years. I would now rate it as quite the most consistent

Château Tahbilk, Victoria. A National Trust building

white wine in the whole country.

Orlando was also the first to market Late Picked Rhine Riesling with a pronounced *spätlese* style. There are some particularly interesting Gewürztraminer blends, and a pleasant drinking inexpensive Riverland Chardonnay made totally from irrigated vineyards.

Former winemaker, and now Managing Director, Gunter Prass has been at the forefront of these developments and the progress continues. Jacob's Creek Claret, a consistent blend of Cabernet, Shiraz and Malbec, is the largest selling bottled red in Australia, and the best selling imported wine in New Zealand. Orlando's Cabernet-Shiraz and Shiraz-Cabernet (the dominant part of the blend is always stated first) have softened over the years and are now superb examples of winemaking at its finest, although no longer particularly 'Barossa' in style.

Orlando has been owned by Reckitt and Colman since 1970. This has been a financial advantage for Orlando but nothing short of disaster for the British wine-buying public, as the parent company for years ignored the sales possibilities of their acquisition. Once many other such firms were selling to the British market they reluctantly began and promptly put most of their effort into a red and white blend, shipped over in bulk and bottled in Norwich: hardly the right image for such a superb company.

Penfold Wines (South Australia)
Once again, another doctor appears in Australian wine industry history. Christopher Penfold was a Sussex general practitioner who believed in the healing effects of wine. On arriving in Adelaide in 1844 he built his house and promptly planted a small vineyard at Magill. He then planted more vines, and more and more again, eventually giving up his medical practice. His wife carried on the management and expansion after his death and by 1880 Penfold owned a third of the total wine stocks in South Australian cellars. By the turn of the century the emphasis was on planting grapes suitable for table wine, and the in-laws now running the company were busy expanding into the McLarenvale, Nuriootpa (Barossa) and Eden Valley. After the First World War considerable areas of vineyards were established in the Murrumbidgee irrigation area and existing Hunter Valley vineyards were bought: definitely a dynamic company.

In the first years of the wine boom Dalwood Hermitage Claret and Dalwood White Burgundy were two ot the stalwarts of the table wine business, but in the latter years many other companies have been more positive in the development of white wines. Red wines are the mainstay of the Penfold reputation with St Henry Claret and Bin 389 Cabernet Shiraz and Kalimna Dry Red 28 Shiraz. Nothing matches the internationally renowned Grange Hermitage, the most famous Australian wine of all. The great winemaker Max Schubert began producing this rich, intense Shiraz with an amazing purple colour in the 1950s but the wine really came into its own in the 1960s. I still have a few bottles of the 1966 vintage, courtesy of my brother, in the Cork and Bottle cellars and will drink them on their 20th birthday.

Penfold has been owned since 1976 by the New South Wales brewers Tooth & Company and has recently taken over the larger Kaiser Stuhl Barossa Cooperative, which now makes the company the largest wine operation in Australia.

Petaluma (Piccadilly, South Australia)
This is a totally different style of operation from the rest of this 'First Division'. The Petaluma label has been in existence only since 1976, and in fact the wines were revered and a reputation was established well before there was a winery or vineyards. This sequence of events may sound unusual, or even irregular, but Brian Croser is without doubt the technical overlord of the modern Australian wine industry. This young man was at Davis University, California, and has been winemaking at Hardy's, and a teacher of oenology at the Riverina College, Wagga Wagga. He has kept moving on, establishing new concepts and setting new standards. A man of dynamic technical innovation, he has pioneered the concentration of fruit flavour with a clean finish so that more of the actual quality of the grapes crushed come through in the wine than the techniques of the winemaking: 'over-oaking' is not a criticism ever to be applied to a Croser wine!

While he was teaching, he formed a company, named it Petaluma and produced wines, initially using the winemaking facilities at the college. But as the medals and plaudits rolled in (and, presumably, the orders) a winery was needed and this was duly built in the area of Piccadilly with its cool climate in the Adelaide Hills, in partnership with Len Evans and Leeuwin Estate owner Dennis Horgan. Croser also bought land himself and planted Chardonnay grapes. In the meantime all his grapes, Cabernet Sauvignon, Rhine Riesling and Chardonnay, were purchased from the finest of sources: the first two will continue to be bought in from the Coonawarra and Clare Valley respectively.

There is also a winemaking consultancy business, Oenotec, established by Croser and fellow oenological academic Dr Tony Jordan, which advises wineries up and down the country, from the smallest boutiques to the biggest concerns. Champagne Bollinger has made its first investment outside France and a joint venture with Petulama will be turning out a top-class product by the *méthode champenoise*, using Chardonnay of course.

No one achieves this amount of success in such a short time without gaining a few detractors. Some wine people talk disparagingly of wines from Oenotec's clients as having been 'Crosered', i.e. they all taste very similar no matter what the label. It cannot be denied, however, that Croser and his disciples offer the most positive vision of the future of the Australian wine industry.

Rosemount Estate (Hunter Valley)
At last we come to one of the brash young upstarts of the industry, a company founded in 1969 by multi-millionaire coffee trader Bob Oatley. An initial planting of 55 ha (135 acres) – 'it was to have been a small venture, to provide a weekend retreat and interest for my two sons and daughter' – rapidly developed into a serious venture after the Hermitage, Cabernet Sauvignon, Traminer and, in particular, Rhine Riesling received more than favourable recognition.

Such were Oatley's business flair and enterprise that within the space of a few years he had bought the Penfold Dalwood Estate, Edinglassie Estate and Rosenglen (all Hunter vineyards) and the last 26 ha (65 acres) of suitable grape-growing land in the Coonawarra

Lest this sounds like a simple exercise in the power of money, it should be pointed out that the company had a number of problems at this stage and its image suffered considerably. Chris Hancock, trained in marketing and also winemaking, was brought in and had considerable influence in rectifying the company's quality image and then proceeding with a carefully conceived export programme.

The Rosemount Show Reserve Chardonnay has received considerable international acclaim. The 1983 vintage beat 50 others into first place in a competition organized by Terry Robards of the *New York Post*. Wines such as David Bruce 1982, Raymond 1982, Château St Jean, Trefethen 1982, Bâtard Montrâchet Domaine Leflaive 1982, Corton Charlemagne Bonneau du Martray 1981 were among those others: the competition was certainly keen! These tasting results are not, of course, the definitive assessment of a wine's quality, but it was virtually as successful in a *Decanter* panel tasting in 1984 (and, interestingly, was beaten only by a fellow Australian, Leeuwin Estate).

I am not so convinced about the standards of the reds, which do not at present match either the Chardonnay or the Sémillon. The Coonawarra Cabernet Sauvignon 1982 shows much promise; only time will tell with the others.

Tyrrell's Vineyards (Hunter Valley)
Australian wine rocketed to international stardom in 1979 at the Gault Millau Paris Wine Olympiad. Much to the bewilderment, and the chagrin, of the French. Murray Tyrrell's Pinot Noir 1976 was awarded first place. Despite the problems of the 1970s in Burgundy, it is an acknowledged fact that the Pinot Noir is an even more difficult grape away from its native slopes. And here was an unknown wine from an almost unknown wine country beating a host of the biggest names in Burgundy!

Tyrrell had already made his reputation locally through his devoted efforts in the 1960s, after taking over his uncle's sound but average vineyard in 1959 and transforming the production to such an extent that within a decade the better wines were the yardstick by which all other Hunter wines were judged. At the time of writing the Sémillon,

Pinot Chardonnay Vat 47 and, of course, the Pinot Noir are of exceptional merit. However, it is difficult to discuss Tyrrell wines in terms of permanence and tradition because Murray himself is dedicated to change and constant improvement.

Yalumba (Hill Smith Estates; Barossa Valley)
It has been a long-standing tradition that the Australian and English teams spend the rest day in the Adelaide Test Match together enjoying the hospitality of 'Windy' Hill Smith.

There is, however, far more to Yalumba than its great hospitality. This is the largest Australian winery still totally controlled by the original family: the sixth generation of Hill Smiths are now actively involved. Samuel Smith, a Dorset brewer, arrived in South Australia in 1848 and within a year had wandered along the Barossa Valley to Angaston, bought 12 ha (30 acres) and planted his first vines. Like other pioneer Australian *vignerons*, Smith was no ordinary man. Three years later Victorian gold fever proved tempting and he was off, leaving his wife to look after Yalumba (the Aboriginal word for 'all the country around') and the children. He returned four months later with sufficient money to treble the vineyard, and the winery never looked back. By 1866 he was making wine of sufficiently high standard to collect a medal at an international exhibition in London.

Development continued with successive generations of Hill Smiths. An important source of revenue was added in 1940 when production of brandy was begun. The postwar years saw much expansion in both the Barossa Valley and the Murray River area. The very latest technical equipment has been installed to enable the company to crush huge quantities of bought-in grapes and become a truly national enterprise.

I consider Yalumba's inexpensive Carte d'Or Riesling as one of my favourite Yalumba wines, in fact one of the most dependable cheaper wines of the world, full of clean, attractive fruit with a slightly steely finish. Pewsey Vale Rhine Riesling and the Heggie's Rhine Riesling are two excellent wines produced from cooler climate, high altitude vineyards. As I prefer the lighter styles I am less keen on the Yalumba red wines, which possess the Barossa intensity. I have enjoyed many of the reds the company calls its Signature Series, which are either Cabernet Sauvignons or Shiraz, considered special and labelled with the names of Yalumba personnel or other local, and not so local, personalities.

The Second Division
There are a few old-established wineries of significant size who produce certain wines that I have regularly enjoyed over the years, but who do not have a sufficiently interesting range of well-structured products to merit inclusion in the premier division.

Leo Buring (Barossa)
This subsidiary of Lindeman was responsible for my youthful conversion to wine. Its 'Rhinegolde' semi-sweet table white in an unusual Mateus-style bottle was a sure way of impressing equally unsophisticated fellow university students of the opposite sex, and it tasted great too. Since then my taste buds have improved and so have Leo Buring wines. The Rhine Riesling Bin 33 is a most dependable, refreshing and typical South Australian Rhine.

Thomas Hardy & Son (Southern Vales, South Australia)
The founder has been termed 'the father of the South Australian wine industry', and there is no doubt that over the years the continual expansion of this family firm has been a considerable force in the prosperity of the Southern Vales. I find the reds rather tough and unrewarding but am very fond of the two best-known whites (which, ironically, do not come from the region): the popular, blended Old Castle Riesling, and the more expensive, but also more refined Siegersdorf Rhine Riesling from the Barossa.

Quelltaler (Clare)
Situated in my favourite wine region of Australia, this is one of my favourite sources of readily available, sound and flavoursome drinking wines. The firm was run by the Sobel and Buring family for nearly one hundred years and then bought by the Melbourne liquor merchants Nathan & Wyeth. It is now owned by Remy Martin. Edmund Peat, one of the true gentlemen of the Australian wine trade, presided over the changing fortunes of

Quelltaler, maintaining its reputation for consistency and honesty. All that might be regretted is the 'generic' labelling of its standard bottlings.

Rothbury Estate (Hunter)
Founded in 1968 by Len Evans, an important figure in Australian wine, together with a group of investors. Consultants include Murray Tyrrell. Over the years, during which Rothburg has had more than its share of financial difficulties, the wines have developed nicely and the Sémillon is without doubt the finest from the Hunter. Oddly enough the wines are dificult to obtain in Australia but are readily available in Britain.

Tulloch (Hunter)
This winery's Private Bin Riesling is good enough to dispel my dislike of the nomenclature, and I have fond memories of the Pokolbin Dry Reds of the past. However, I must state that I am not so keen on the recent vintages.

Wynn's (Coonawarra)
Now owned by Toohey's Brewery in New South Wales, this is a 1960s trendsetter that seems to have slipped back – except for its uniformly excellent Coonawarra Cabernet Sauvignon. Recent tastings of the Chardonnay and Ovens Valley Shiraz augur well for the future.

Good Smaller Wineries
Although I do not believe that 'small' invariably means 'best', I do enjoy the products of the individual approach to winemaking. The fanciful term 'boutique winery' is used by the popular press today, especially in the United States. If this means simply a small operation, producing wine only from the company's own vineyards, with total individual control, then the term 'smaller winery' is preferable. Not all the crush of the following

The Gramp family – early days, South Australia

wineries is their own grape production, and on many occasions consultants such as Oenotec may have exerted considerable influence on the winemaking.

In the old days the small winemakers were not only ignorant of the techniques, trends and tastes of the northern hemisphere; they were unaware of the goings on twenty miles away. Times have changed and many of the present owners and winemakers have studied abroad, have toured and tasted extensively, and are right up to date with what is going on in the wider world of wine.

Allandale (Hunter Valley)
Winemaker and partner Ed Joualt is almost unique in Australia in his mode of operation, but in New Zealand many dynamic concerns are working in a similar way. For Allandale is almost exclusively supplied in small quantities by top class growers whose grapes in return receive separate crushing, fermentation and winemaking. The result is an indvidual wine bearing the name of the grower (what could be done with this approach in parts of Burgundy?).

Brokenwood (Pokolbin, Hunter Valley)
These wines are big, tough brutes produced from the Cabernet and Shiraz (in the Hunter, the latter grape is called the Hermitage), full of depth and intensity. There are a number of partners, including James Halliday, Nick Bulleid and John Beeston, a solicitor, actively involved – even to the extent of helping with the harvest as tends to happen in Australian small 'weekend' wineries.

Coonawarra and the Lindeman Connection (South Australia)
After Owen Redman had sold the Rouge Homme winery to Lindeman in 1965 he set up along the road and began producing the highly esteemed Redman Claret. Eric Brand, who had worked for Redman, bought the vineyard next door, grew grapes and sold them to other Coonawarra wineries until 1966, when he began making his own Laira wine. I am still enjoying the voluptuous 1976 Cabernet Sauvignon and the lighter 1977 Shiraz. Doug Bowen came to the Coonawarra as a winemaker for Rouge Homme. At the same time he too bought land and, in his spare time, planted Cabernet Sauvignon and Shiraz. Eventually he left and the Bowen Estate has since been producing attractive, soft wines.

Enterprise (Clare Valley)
Enterprise wines come very close in quality to those of the 'first division'. They are the product of another splendid winemaker, Tim Knappstein, who created superb individualistic wines for the Stanley Wine Company in the Clare. He left this company not long after the Heinz Corporation had taken it over and founded Enterprise. From very humble beginnings Enterprise has progressed to producing significant quantities of some of the finest of all Clare Valley Rhine Riesling and Cabernet Sauvignon.

Fergusson's Winery (Yarra Valley, Victoria)
Peter Fergusson is extrovert and forthright in a characteristically Australian way and handles all his own public relations and sales operations, runs a successful restaurant on the vineyard, acts as courier for overseas 'wine enthusiast' tours and runs an 11 ha (27 acre) vineyard, which has a consistent output of award-winning wines.

Fergusson offers an interesting comparison to many of the smaller wineries now in financial trouble in Napa Valley, California. He bought the land when the price was realistic and made wines which, in the early days, were not particularly good. However, they did have character and through this, and his own personality, they sold well. As the money came in, so did the more expensive equipment. Now the winery is equipped totally and every year the quality of the wines becomes better. The recent vintages of Rhine Riesling and Cabernet Sauvignon have been very good, interesting wines with an unmistakable Fergusson style.

Lake's Folly
It is hard to imagine what persuaded an eminent Sydney surgeon, Max Lake, to search the Hunter in the early 1960s and, in 1963, buy 18 ha (44½ acres) of land, the first new land purchase for the purpose of grape growing in years and years? Hence the name Folly. Max was the pioneer small *vigneron*, professionally trained in another discipline but dedicated and talented; both the

ENJOYING WINE

Australian and American sections of this book have very many such enthusiasts. Marvellous Chardonnay and Cabernet Sauvignon.

Marienberg (Coromandel Valley, South Australia)
Once again I have to declare an interest: I represent this winery in Europe. Ursula Pridham and her stockbroker husband bought an existing 6 ha (15 acre) vineyard as a weekend interest. Her wines were a bewildering rapid success at the wine shows and production was increased – the hobby had become serious. Out went some of the areas of older style plantings and another vineyard, Bethany, was bought. Ursula's personal preference for a 'soft' style is evident in her wines; the Rhine Riesling in particular has freshness, but underlying depth. I enjoy showing her oaky, pungent yet lightish Shiraz 1979 to British *aficionados* of this Syrah grape.

The Marvels of the Margaret River (Western Australia)
The famous Robert Mondavi of Napa Valley, California is involved in this area as a consultant. This has no doubt increased nationwide interest in the Margaret River wines in general, along with the excellent products of Vasse Felix, Cullens, Cape Mentelle, Moss Wood, and the Leeuwin Estate in particular.

These small wineries, from a brand-new area (most were only really coming on stream at the end of the 1970s), have begun to scoop the medals all over the country – and many are commanding the highest retail prices.

Wantirna Estate (Wantirna South, Melbourne)
Reg and Tina Egan's 6 ha (15 acre) vineyard within the Melbourne metropolitan area has been established since the mid-1960s, well before the Victorian wine boom. Obviously they planted all the usual grapes of that time, but have now replanted with Rhine Riesling, Chardonnay, Cabernet, Merlot and Pinot Noir. They produce the best Australian Pinot Noir that I have tasted, apart from Tyrrell.

My customers can drink the excellent, complex, graceful Cabernet Sauvignon-Merlot. Reg is a full-time and busy city lawyer, running the estates as a sideline.

Wirra Wirra (McLarenvale)
Wirra Wirra was originally established in 1893 by Robert Wrigley, a law student and drinker supreme whose antics are said to have been far too outrageous for Adelaide society. The family made efforts to move him as far away from the genteel city as possible, but they must have provided finance because he and his brother bought 97 ha (240 acres) of land and planted 40 ha (100 acres) in vines, and were soon active in both the home and export trade. Despite his drinking, Wrigley was a prodigious worker and the life suited him. After his death in 1924, however, the winery fell into disuse as the family disposed of the property in parcels.

In 1969 Gregg Trott and his cousin bought some of the original estate, planted Cabernet Shiraz and Rhine Riesling, and Wirra Wirra was back in business. The Rhine Riesling is excellent and I also have fond memories of a very limited release Late Picked Rhine Riesling; both wines showed a definite Oenotec influence. The Cabernet Sauvignon has more delicacy than most in the area. A certain amount of wine was exported to Britain by Winebrokers International of Melbourne, but the extremely 'Australian' name was a stumbling block.

Yarra (Victoria)
Siggy Jorgensen and my brother Iain were the first Melbourne restaurateurs actually to attach importance to the promotion of their own Victorian wines and it is through them I have had the good fortune to meet so many of the state's winemakers.

Yarra Yerring is a 12 ha (30 acre) vineyard planted in 1969 by a botanist, Dr Bailey Carrodus, near the original Castella vineyards. The two main reds are labelled simply Yarra Yerring Dry Red No 1 (Cabernet with Malbec and Merlot) and Yarra Yerring Dry Red No 2 (Shiraz). I have enjoyed these but missed what is obviously the star of the show. If James Halliday is to be believed in *Decanter Magazine*, December 1984, 'Yarra Yerring Pinot Noir confirms ... that the Yarra Valley really can produced a Pinot Noir worth the name.'

Just down the road Guillaume de Pury, a descendant of the founder of the third vineyard in Victoria, has a mere couple of hectares making

AUSTRALIA

Some Australian Wine Terms Explained

Bin Numbers on Labels
Australian wine labels have tended to go from the unpretentious to the verbose, and many bin numbers to what should be straightforward varietal names; for example Leo Buring's Bin 22 Rhine Riesling. Thanks to the law I know this must contain at least 80 per cent Rhine Riesling, but Bin 22 does not mean a thing, although in the past a bin number often signified a special bottling of selected casts.

BYO
A term first encouraged by Melbourne's antiquated and repressive licensing laws. It refers to 'Bring Your Own' restaurants, very popular in the Victorian capital but less common in the more liberal states. Theoretically the diner benefits by either taking a really fine bottle or two from home, or saves money by avoiding the restaurateurs wine mark-ups, or both. There is always the problem of getting the bottles to the restaurant in the right condition; the better BYOs charge highly for their food to make up for the loss of beverage revenue.

Casks ('Bag in the Box')
Pioneered in Australia in the mid-1960s and now widely copied around the world, even in France. Normally there are 3 to 4 litres in a wine sac with a valve, which is put inside a cardboard box. The valve is pressed for an instant glass and, most importantly, the wine sac collapses as the wine level goes down. This prevents the intake of air and oxidization. Unfortunately very poor wine is mostly used for these containers as the actual method of packaging is not cheap and the cheap wine market is extremely price competitive. Orlando's Coolabah is extremely consistent and the white (13 million produced last year!) in particular has always been good.

'Champagne' (Australian)
Some day the Australians will have to come into line, but at the moment the name can be used on any product made by the *méthode champenoise*, no matter what the grape varieties used. Most are dreadful, some are merely poor. The better Australian sparkling wines avoid false claims, for example Yellowglen Brut Nature *Méthode Champenoise*.

A London wine merchant friend has a hilarious story of the old days before there was any restriction on the term 'champagne'. He was visiting a Sydney liquor wholesaler and asked to answer the telephone and take a message. The caller was a winemaker apologizing for the non-delivery of the standing order of a pallet of 'champagne'. 'The wine isn't made yet, but don't worry . . . you will have it by first thing tomorrow morning!'

'Chablis'
One of the most abused terms in the whole of Australian wine in the old days; and unfortunately it is on the way back and misuse is likely to continue.

Flagons
These have a capacity of 2 litres. As the packaging cost is cheaper the wine is often a little better than that in casks. The only problem is that you need to drink the wine faster as it deteriorates more rapidly.

Medal winners
All Australian state capitals and Canberra have annual wine shows, and many of the individual wine-producing areas have their own. Consequently there is a proliferation of medals. Winning these awards is often significant and a reliable indication of quality, but not always. Controversy regarding the likes and dislikes of the judges is not unknown.

Out of State
Normally to be heard from the lips of dinner guests in South Australia and New South Wales when they are asked for an opinion on some new, highly regarded wine, that has been produced outside their states.

PLO
An irreverent wine trade term describing the 'Big Three' of the industry: Penfold, Lindeman and Orlando.

Sheppard's Creek
This is one of the most delightful terms in the whole world of wine. 'Trucking' wine from state to state is permissible in Australia and has many beneficial effects, but there is no doubt things get out of hand and there is a significantly larger amount of Barossa Rhine Riesling sold than could ever be produced in the area. The locals wryly call this the production from Sheppard's Creek. 'Sheppard's' is the large interstate haulage company specializing in bulk wine transport; Sheppard's Creek is the road from the irrigated regions of the Murray River to the Barossa.

161

ENJOYING WINE

VICTORIA MUSCATS

This is not a book about fortified wines; enough has already been written on the subject. But mention must be made of the glorious Liqueur Muscats from northeast Victoria. These are totally unique wines made from the Frontignan: rich, luscious and yet with a delicate finish. Unfortunately, as they have become more and more fashionable, the old stocks have dwindled. Beg, steal or borrow a few bottles. Names to look for are Bailey, Bullers, All Saints, Chambers, Morris and Brown Brothers.

Brown Brothers, Milawa-Victoria. Mechanical harvesting at night to avoid excessive heat

AUSTRALIA

Yalumba Winery, South Australia

an especially stylish Cabernet wine.

Another couple of miles away is Mount Mary, which does not in fact sell to the public, so knowledge of this winery is of no use whatsoever to the average Londoner, Parisian or New Yorker. The owner, Dr John Middleton, is absolutely determined to produce the most technically perfect Australian Cabernet (Bordeaux blend) and Pinot Noir. I have tasted a few vintages which show promise, but they are not quite to the intended standard as yet.

There are dozens of other excellent wineries – Huntingdon Estate, Stuart Anderson's Balgownie, Taltarni, Cambrai – just to name a few, but in any attempt to discuss them lie the making of another book.

THE FUTURE

I love the country, the people, the sunshine and the accompanying outdoor eating; and most of all the variety and almost bewildering pace of change in the standards and styles of the wines. But it is not all a bed of roses. Most Australians drink a reasonable quantity of their own wines (as opposed to the Americans), but production is growing rapidly and an increasingly large percentage of the market is in cash and flagon wine: analysts forecast 80 per cent within a few years and yet in 1978 it was only 30 per cent.

It has been suggested that some of the old 'cheap wine source' districts will disappear with the new plantings in more suitable areas producing better fruit cheaper, but that is simply agrarian economics. What is more depressing to the wine lover is that some of the real quality areas may suffer another downturn, given the swings and roundabouts state of the industry. That fine Australian wine writer James Halliday is most depressed about the fate of the Hunter Valley. In a recent article in the *Australian* he quoted the dramatic rise in vine plantings there in the 1970s. In 1969 592 ha (1460 acres) were under vine and by 1976 the total was 4000 ha (9885 acres). The fact is that much of the planting was on unsuitable land producing unsuitable yields (of either uneconomic or indifferent grapes). An increase has followed; in 1984 the figure was down by a third and still falling.

I am not despondent, however; if the wineries concentrate on quality wines from low-yield vineyards and forget about trucking blending wines from outside the region, then a range of stylish wines with definite regional characteristics will emerge and the public *will* pay the price needed. They are already doing so for Leeuwin Estate Chardonnay and many Yarra Valley wines.

And finally, contrary to the general pessimism, or perhaps unwillingness to become involved in the inevitable complexities, there *is* an export market waiting for the better Australian wines – but not only for dumpings in surplus years. The government seems to have done very little despite the existence of the Wine and Brandy Corporation. Little New Zealand, for example, has provided a much more consistent and visible showcase for its wines in London.

The wines are excellent, and around the world wine enthusiasts have their pocketbooks ready.

MAJOR GRAPE VARIETIES: RED

Shiraz
This is the predominant red (and fortified) wine grape. The wine was often called 'Hermitage' or, with less scrupulous *vignerons*, anything from 'claret' to 'burgundy'. This is the well-known Syrah grape of the northern Rhône. It was a favourite varietal with the growers of the past two decades: a dependable, high-yielding grape that thrived in the local conditions and produced a rich, luscious wine reeking fruit. At times this overpowering intensity can be over-oaked and, particularly in the hotter areas of Australia, the wines show a no-compromise style. The Hunter Valley did not plant any other red wine grapes until the mid-1960s; the Shiraz there, when handled correctly, makes a much lighter, elegant wine.

Cabernet Sauvignon
As we have seen, much of the first plantings was of this varietal. Captain Phillip's South African cuttings classed as 'claret' were undoubtedly Cabernet. The first large Victorian plantings were definitely so, and much of the original South Australian purchase was Cabernet. The 1970s saw a marked increase in plantings, some successful, some not.

The Cabernet has flourished particularly in the

AUSTRALIA

Ursula Pridham, Marienberg Winery, South Australia

ENJOYING WINE

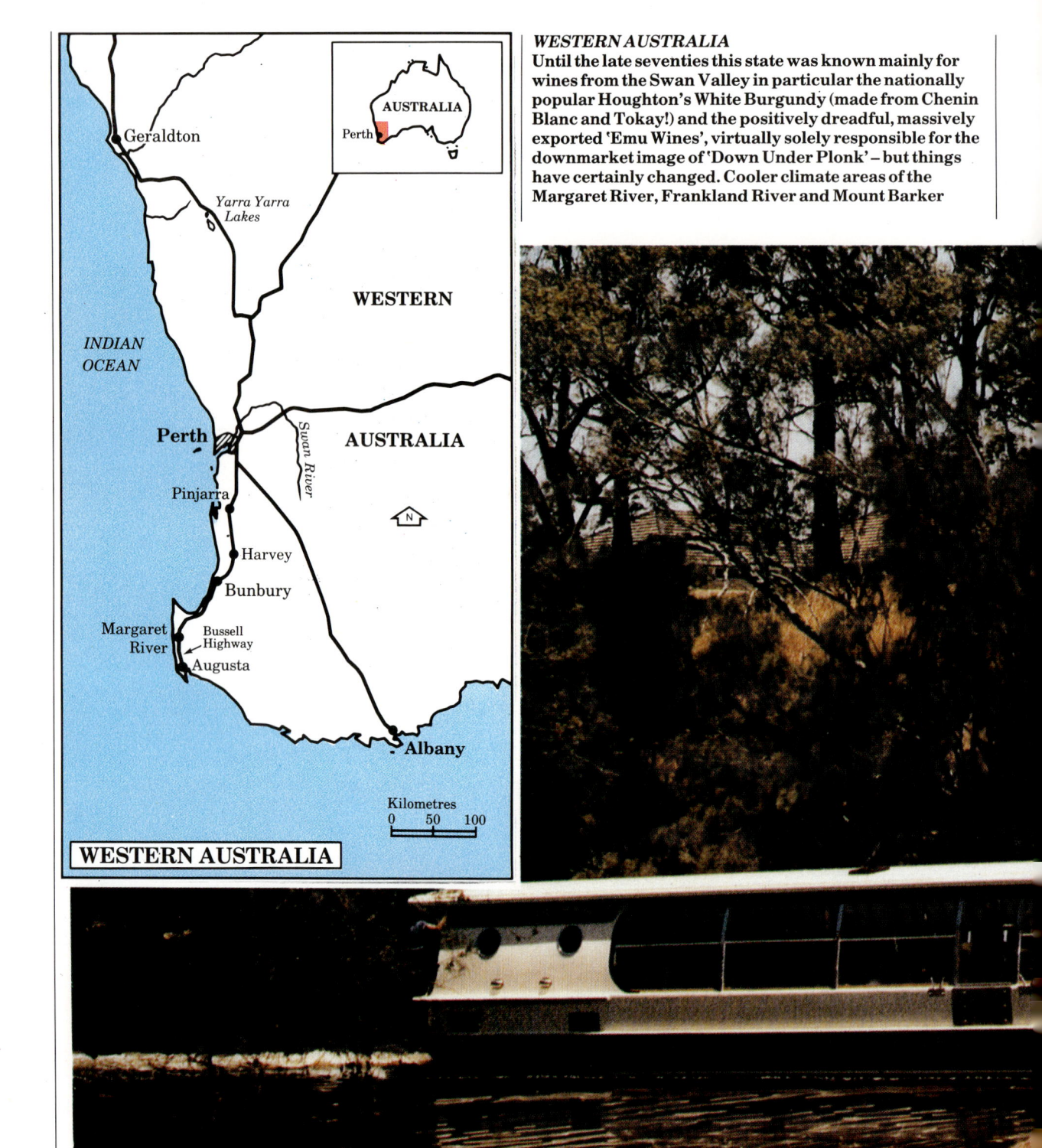

WESTERN AUSTRALIA
Until the late seventies this state was known mainly for wines from the Swan Valley in particular the nationally popular Houghton's White Burgundy (made from Chenin Blanc and Tokay!) and the positively dreadful, massively exported 'Emu Wines', virtually solely responsible for the downmarket image of 'Down Under Plonk' – but things have certainly changed. Cooler climate areas of the Margaret River, Frankland River and Mount Barker

Wine cruising Western Australian style

AUSTRALIA

have been planted; in the space of the last few years this southwest corner of the state has excited wine judges and public alike and is now producing some of the finest and certainly most expensive Chardonnays (and the Cabernets aren't too bad either!).

TASMANIA
There are a number of newly established vineyards producing wines in a climate previously considered too cold and wet. If the quality of Dr Andrew Piries's Pipers Brook Cabernet Sauvignon and Rhine Riesling is continued then perhaps mainlanders will have to acknowledge certain climatic merits!

QUEENSLAND
There are a number of small wineries in the hills beyond Brisbane. I have not tasted any products, but the press critical judgment has been rather mixed.

cooler climate South Australia district of the Coonawarra.

Grenache
This was once a major source of cheaply produced South Australian red 'plonks' and fortifieds, but as tastes became more refined and sales competition intensified, this varietal fell from favour. In the late 1970s, just after harvest, acres and acres could be seen with all the fruit left rotting on the vines.

Pinot Noir
This grape is around in small quantities, mainly in the Hunter, with promising parcels in Victoria. Whatever reservation one may have about this grape when it strays from the Côte d'Or, there are a few promising exceptions, and they are in Australia.

Malbec
This has been planted in small quantities and in fact its contribution to the blend of Orlando's Jacob Creek Claret is significant.

MAJOR GRAPE VARIETIES: WHITE

Rhine Riesling
The 'cold fermentation' Barossa Valley Rhine Riesling were good in the 1960s and they have got better and better. If only the Germans could make inexpensive quaffing wine like these – fresh and fruity, full of character and flavour with just a hint of residual sugar backed with a firm but well-balanced acid finish. The bulk of Rhine Riesling plantings are in South Australia, but interesting developments are afoot in Victoria.

Sémillon
The second most widely planted varietal, especially prevalent in the Hunter and irrigated areas where it produces wines labelled anything from 'Chablis' to 'Hunter Riesling'. The wines are actually often very good and quite capable of standing up on their merits.

Trebbiano
This grape is another source for the ubiquitous 'Chablis' or 'White Burgundy' (it is a wonder no one has thought of 'Le Montrachet').

Traminer
A relatively small acreage of this Alsace grape has a certain amount of significance because it is often blended with Rhine Riesling to produce a palatable, commercial wine which is pleasant, if no more.

We now come to the two grape varieties that are completing the revolution and forcing wine lovers and producers alike to re-evaluate all previous white wine making in Australia.

Chardonnay
Robin Young of the London *Times* recently pondered the question 'How on earth do they actually do it?' He was referring to the standard and relatively inexpensive cost of Rosemount Estate's Show Reserve Chardonnay 1984. Time and time again he had tasted this wine alongside the finest of whites that the Côte d'Or could offer and not only did the Rosemount equal most in performance, it was also much much cheaper.

Suddenly every second grower is planting Chardonnay, but many seem to be more influenced by the developments in California than the traditions of Burgundy.

There is no doubt about it, this is what the 1980s wine-drinking public desires for the dining table. People realize it will not be cheap and still have the good sense to be happy to pay the price and treat the best bottlings as 'special occasion' wines.

Sauvignon Blanc
The other 'new' variety of the 1980s, and once again important more because of its relative stature in California. There are already some excellent examples of refined, if rather thin character, but so far these wines are not up to the high standard of the finest from either France or New Zealand.

Chenin Blanc
This is developing along with the new white winemaking industry of Western Australia.

It is still too early to judge what effect this rather ordinary varietal will have on the Australian market; certainly there are not many promising signs.

Chapter Sixteen

New Zealand

The New Zealand wine industry makes a fasincating story. Wine has been produced since the early days of colonization. In 1833 an intrepid Glaswegian, James Busby, arrived in New Zealand as British Resident bringing with him a considerable collection of European vine cuttings. By the turn of the century the government had shown considerable interest and an experimental nursery had been established at Te Kauwhata. In 1902 Romeo Bragato was brought over from Australia as 'Government Viticulturist'. In 1908 a wine from Te Kauwhata was awarded a gold medal at the Franco-British Exhibition in London.

We should not be too carried away by the idea of such an award: most of the wine was rather ordinary, produced by immigrant Dalmatian gum diggers who planted vines more on the basis of proximity to the gum fields than out of any vitivultral idealism. Coupled with this 'mixed farming' were some more professional operations. In 1902 Stephen Yelas established Pleasant Valley Wines, and Abraham Corban planted grapes; both in the Henderson area.

At this stage everything looked rosy. About 240 ha (600 acres) were under vine and the government was committed to a positive approach to the future of the industry; and yet by 1930 less than 80 ha (200 acres) was still planted. Winemakers had been bedevilled by their two greatest scourges: phylloxera and prohibition. The former was obviously not easily defeated, but was less difficult to counter than the latter. By the beginning of the First World War New Zealand actually had 'dry' electorates, one of them including parts of the Henderson area. In 1914 the Prime Minister Mr Massey attacked the Dalmatian winemakers and described their products as 'a degrading, demoralizing and sometimes maddening drink'.

The future was obviously beginning to look rather grim! Worse was nearly to come, and total prohibition was only just avoided in 1918 thanks to the overseas votes of soldiers away at war.

No doubt the remaining enthusiasts told themselves things could not get much worse – but they did. The Depression followed. Many Europeans have the idea that because the Antipodes were remote and their economies were agrarian-based, the forces of economic disaster were not significant there. Rest assured the period produced the same folk memories in New Zealand as in Europe, my grandfather was a district postmaster responsible for handing out the little amount of social security and his stories were very grim. The end result was lack of sales and interest, vividly reflected in the

'He says it was thrust upon him by an immigrant Dalmatian gum digger . . .'

ENJOYING WINE

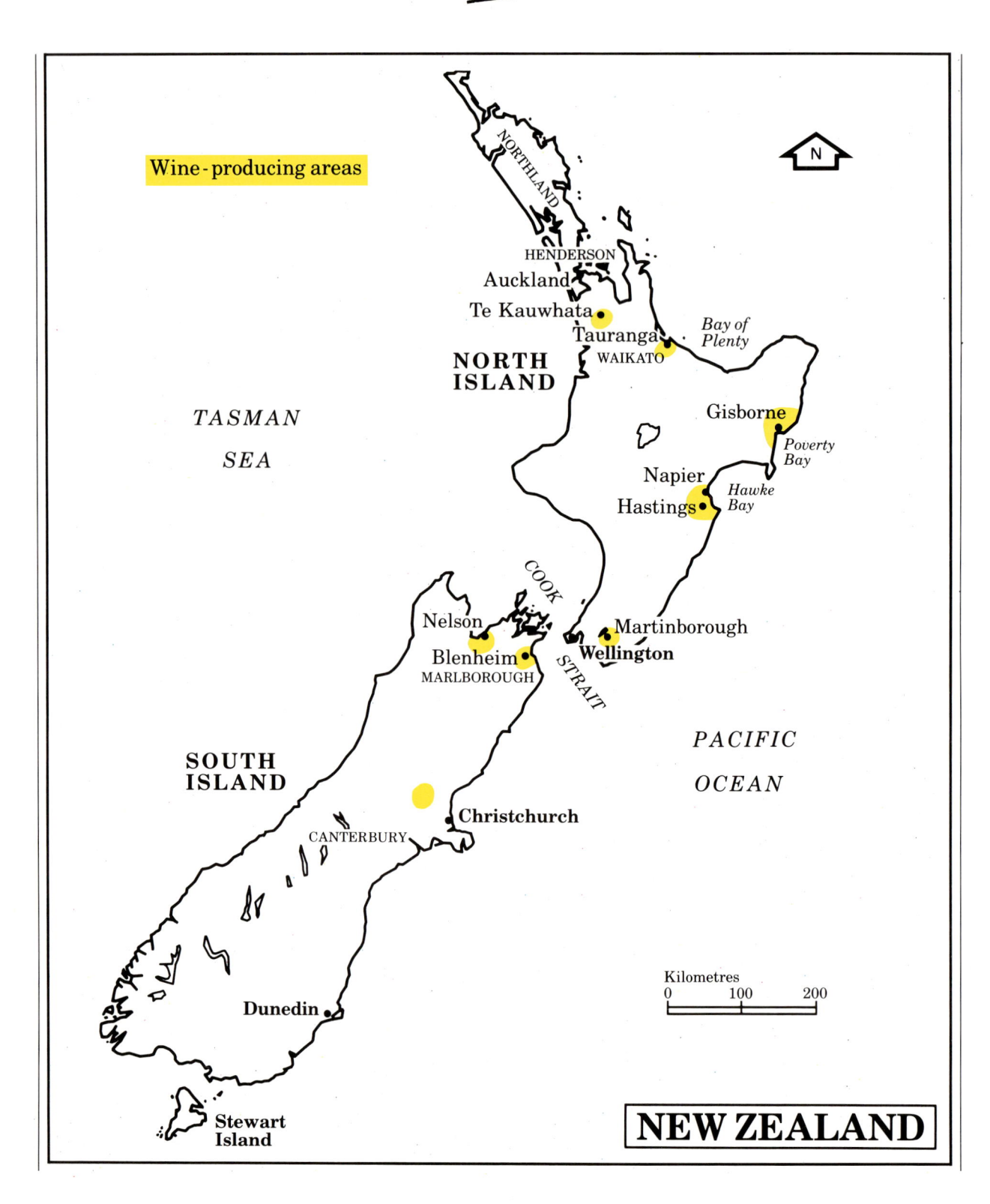

Wine-producing areas

NEW ZEALAND

- NORTHLAND
- HENDERSON
- Auckland
- Te Kauwhata
- Tauranga
- WAIKATO
- Bay of Plenty
- **NORTH ISLAND**
- Gisborne
- Poverty Bay
- Napier
- Hastings
- Hawke Bay
- TASMAN SEA
- Nelson
- Martinborough
- **Wellington**
- Blenheim
- MARLBOROUGH
- COOK STRAIT
- **SOUTH ISLAND**
- PACIFIC OCEAN
- CANTERBURY
- Christchurch
- Dunedin
- Stewart Island

Kilometres 0 100 200

NEW ZEALAND

HAWKE BAY AND GISBORNE
These East Coast areas produce two-thirds of the country's grapes. The big companies all have wineries in the region and the vineyard expansion has been dramatic – Gisborne increased from 600 ha (1480 acres) under vine in 1975 to 1900 ha (4695 acres) in 1982. Initial plantings of Müller Thurgau have been complemented with all the 'new wave' varietals: Chenin Blanc, Chardonnay, Gewürztraminer, Sauvignon Blanc and Cabernet Sauvignon. Vines flourish in the fertile loam soil. Well-established companies, new large companies, small individualist wineries, contract grape growers are all here.

WAIKATO
Te Kauwhata is the home of Cook's New Zealand Wine Company and of the governmental research station.

WEST AUCKLAND
This is basically the Henderson area described in the history. It is nowhere near the force it once was within the industry. Some companies have kept their head offices in the region but have expanded their facilities elsewhere. Judging on recent tastings the smaller wineries are starting to concentrate on producing quality wines from the grapes suitable to the area. Areas further north are being planted and are already showing considerable promise.

SOUTH AUCKLAND
A small area under vines, but the right varietals including, interestingly, Sémillon.

BAY OF PLENTY
One of the classic illustrations of the fact that historical vineyards were mostly planted in the wrong places. Grapes thrive here in the sunshine and warmth of the region, and the fast-draining volcanic ash soils, but it was not until Morton Estate was established that there was much vine cultivation.

MARLBOROUGH
Long, dry summers and cool autumns are ideal for grape growing and yet there was nothing until Montana planted extensive vineyards in the mid-1970s. Others have since arrived on the scene.

Grapes are also planted in limited quantities in Waikanae, just north of Wellington, Nelson and in Canterbury, close to Christchurch.

Pioneering agricultural days

ENJOYING WINE

Cook's New Zealand Wine Company (Te Kauwhata)

attempted sale of the Te Kauwhata in 1933: fortunately no one could afford to buy it.

How did anyone in his right mind stay in this business, in a country that regarded alcohol as evil? Fortunately the winemakers continued and the public began to accept wine as a part of life, albeit only the fortified products: and pretty awful they were, too. The 1940s and '50s saw what was basically a winemaking culture with the wrong grapes planted in the wrong areas producing downmarket, fortified plonk sold mainly to customers searching for a cheap form of alcohol. The 'wino' image was paramount and the serious wine drinkers tended to ignore the local products and search out the limited supply of imported tables wines from Australia and Europe. Winemakers producing reasonable quality table wines were few and far between.

At this stage the Hawkes Bay area was the focal point of the small amount of quality production. The tradition was really started here by a group of Marist Fathers who established the Mission Vineyards at Greenmeadows. They were followed very much later, in 1927, by the man who in my opinion is the most important figure in the pre-1970s wine industry, Tom McDonald. His initial venture, McDonalds Winery, was later incorporated in the much larger McWilliams Wines Ltd and Tom became Managing Director, producing and successfully marketing readily available and sound table wines alongside the fortifieds. He also produced limited quantities of wine under the old McDonalds label. I remember particularly his Pinot Blanc in the 1960s.

The first hint of things to come was the release of McWilliams Cabernet Sauvignon 1965: at last, an elegant, well-made wine with rich varietal flavour. Up until then even most table wines had been the product of hybrid grapes which had offered the wine makers resistance to disease and higher yields; but here we were into the 20th century at last.

This 'hybrid' factor is very important. Not only does it explain much of the public's antipathy towards the local product, with its harsh unclean taste; but if the winemakers were going to improve they literally had to start all over again. The New Zealand public was becoming more and more aware of wine (and sophisticated dining), and was beginning to demand better products, and the necessary capital investment began to look attractive. The Siebels, Bacos and Chasselas grapes were uprooted and replaced with Muller Thurgau, Chenin Blanc and Cabernet. New areas such as Marlborough were planted for the first time, at last areas were being established for only one reason: the best possible grape growing.

Suddenly the boom was in full swing. The giant North American distilling company purchased 44 per cent of market leaders Montana. Cook's Wine Company was formed by independent businessmen with no previous wine connections and no great desire to produce fortifieds. Rothmans International bought Corban's; and importantly, a large number of small independents set up their own estates and wineries with the aim of growing their own grapes and vinifying other 'bought-in' produce.

By now the sheer variety of wines being made in New Zealand is amazing. There is still a large amount of inferior wines for the unsuspecting market (in 1984 a visit to a provincial wine store offered the delights of a 'Corban's Beaujolais Nouveau 1980' and a series of mass-produced poor wines). But diligent searching is rewarding: already Montana, Cook's, and others are producing excellent varietals in commercial quantities, and more and more boutique wineries are releasing more and more outstanding wines. The only cloud on the horizon is the problem of overproduction. In the simplest of terms, part of the consumption boom has stopped before it has really begun, and the makers of large volume, poorer wines are now discounting at uneconomic prices. These are not the ideal market conditions for further experimentation and expansion. A few statistics emphasize just how rapid these developments have been. Without doubt New Zealand is the newest of all 'emergent wine nations'.

In time the New Zealand scene will all settle down, and the large houses offering the right products for the market will flourish along with the medium-sized independents, and I see nothing but success for the best of the small 'individualist' wineries: the public is there waiting for the wines. Export markets are always an attraction, especially to a country with such an agrarian export heritage. Britain and Canada show considerable

ENJOYING WINE

Storage tanks, Cook's New Zealand Wine Company – Te Kauwhata

AREAS PLANTED IN VINES

	Hectares (acres)	Classic varieties %	Hybrids %
1960	388 (959)	41	59
1970	1,468 (3,628)	57	43
1975	2,351 (5,809)	72	28
1980	4,853 (11,992)	91	9
1986*	5,550 (13,714)	95	5

(Source: MAF Vineyard Surveys)
*Wine Industry Development Plan prediction

interest, and Australians are starting to be attracted to the whites: their aromatic styles and low-alcoholic delicacy have not gone unnoticed.

I have tasted literally hundreds of New Zealand wines in the past few years, both in their native land and in London. Eight establishments stand out to me as the finest and I have divided these into an upper and a lower group with four in each. It is interesting that only two large wine companies feature in my list of eight, but they are both in the top group.

NEW ZEALAND

The first four

Cook's New Zealand Wine Company (Te Kauwhata)

The youngest of all the bigger winemakers, now merged with McWilliams Wines. Some of the grapes are grown on land surrounding the winery, but most are drawn from the East Coast. The company was the first to concentrate almost exclusively on table wine production. Pioneering is never easy, however, and because of a lack of direction and consequent public apathy, it has had a rather chequered career. The firm was initially known for large amounts of very cheap plonk; and yet – a fact that only a knowledgeable few were aware of – it was also making the forerunners of the country's commercially available classic varietals. Recent releases of Chardonnay Rhine Riesling, Gewürztraminer and Cabernet Sauvignon have shown the company is producing better wines than ever: it is to be hoped that all the teething troubles are well and truly over.

Montana Wines (Auckland)

It is difficult to specify where this giant of the industry is based as it is established all over the country. Montana was initially a small family company, one of the many Henderson immigrant wineries. In the 1960s it suddenly blossomed forth and expanded at a rate that had never been seen before (nor since). Suddenly Montana wines were everywhere, but the less said about the quality the better. Seagrams bought the majority of its shareholding in 1973, the same year that Montana pioneered winegrowing in the substantial Marlborough region, and in 1974 the last of the original family departed. The better varietals were planted, overseas winemakers exerted their influence, and a well-balanced combination of commercially required drinking wines and top-class wines were marketed. Thanks to the Marlborough plantings, the latter are available in sizeable quantities and therefore the local wine drinker can actually buy a bottle of Montana Chardonnay or Cabernet Sauvignon instead of simply reading about it.

Morton Estate (Bay of Plenty)

A really small winery: 10 ha (25 acres) were planted as recently as 1979. John Hancock, a graduate of Roseworthy College (Australia), has already reached a superstart status in New Zealand resembling the glamour and fame accorded his fellow professionals across the Tasman Sea.

I have been most impressed with the excellent Chardonnays and their variations in style. The 1983 is oaky, with the intensity and the buttery

Morton Estate, Bay of Plenty

flavour of the Napa; very good wine but lacking finesse. The 1984 is different altogether and much closer to Hancock's personal liking, with more acidity in the form of a delightful tart fruitiness and elegance – the best New Zealand white wine I have tasted. The same vintages of Gewürztraminer are also quite different: the 1983 soft and elegant in the national varietal style and the 1984 more powerful and pungent with a sweetish finish, just how a good Gewürztraminer should be!

Morton Estate also buys in considerable quantities of grapes from Gisborne and Hawke Bay and therefore the production is of a significant size as well as quality: this will not be an élitist operation selling only to the chosen few. Export plans are being formulated at the time of writing, so in time the rest of the wine world should be able to buy these fine wines.

Te Mata Estate (Hawke Bay)
John Buck worked in the London wine trade before returning to Wellington in the 1960s and partnering Graham Kerr in a food and wine promotional venture. Over the years he became New Zealand's first-ever wine personality: author, columnist, wine merchant and radio and television broadcaster. He was an outpsoken critic of the standards of most local wineries, but an enthusiastic supporter of those attempting to improve their product. I knew John in these days (he was the man who introduced me to Joseph Drouhin wines) and it would not be an exaggeration to say that he did not appeal to a considerable percentage of the old-style winemaking brigade devoted to their hybrid varieties.

In 1974 John and Michael Morris, a Wellington accountant, bought a TMV Vineyard, renowned for little other than the cheapness and the alcohol content of its bottlings. Development of Te Mata has been relatively gradual by New Zealand standards. A winery was restored and equipped, new vineyards were planted – some by Te Mata and much by shareholder local growers. I have tasted three recent releases and all have been excellent: Castle Hill Sauvignon Blanc 1984; Cape Crest Sauvignon Bland 1983 (interestingly, when the wine is the product of a single grower's crop, the due acknowledgment is given on the label); and an outstanding Coleraine Cabernet Merlot 1982, a most positive assertion of the Hawke Bay's potential in red wine making: superb flavour with ripe fruit and oak prominent, and yet nothing overdone.

The second four

Collard Brothers, Sutton Baron (Henderson)
A family concern run by Lionel Collard and his two winemaker sons. The produce of their small 10 ha (25 acre) vineyard is augmented by grapes brought in from Te Kauwhata and Auckland, and many of the better Collard wines of recent vintages (in particular the Chenin Blancs) have been made with a significant percentage of non-Henderson grapes. The company has recently bought 60 ha (150 acres) further north, close to the Matua Valley, and has planted Rhine Riesling, Gewürztraminer, Cabernet Sauvignon, Merlot and Cabernet Franc. Collard will be a name to be taken very seriously when these come 'on stream'.

Matawhero Wines (Gisborne)
It seems rather as if the British wine trade has been talking about Dennis Irwin's Gewürztraminer for decades, but in fact it is only a matter of years. The wine is rich and flavoursome, and it rivals many of the better wines of Alsace. The 1982 Traminer/Riesling Sylvaner is an excellent example of fine grapes and fine winemaking: a beautiful, authentic nose, intense fruity style and a lingering aftertaste.

Matua Valley Wines (Waimauku)
The Spence brothers have done it 'Australian style'. They established their vineyard on a part-time basis and developed classic varietals as their expansion programme gradually took shape. Ross, the winemaker, studied oenology at Fresno State University and was responsible for the introduction to New Zealand of Sauvignon Blanc and Sémillon. Grapes are also brought in from Gisborne, and whenever relevant the grower is acknowledged. The Judd Estate Chardonnay 1984 is one such wine: soft and stylish with a beautiful balance between fruit and oak.

Selak's Wines (Kumeu)
I well remember 1965 when motorway development wiped out Selak's Vineyard at Te Atatu –

much of New Zealand felt a sense of outrage. Fortunately Mate Selak, nephew of the founder, saved the company from extinction by moving to Kumeu. The wines subsequently produced continued to suffer from the general problems of the area and I, for one, lost interest as other more progressive wineries arrived on the scene.

However, things have changed dramatically and recent tasting of Selak's quality varietal wines (in both Auckland and London) have confirmed a new dimension, due to superior winemaking and Hawke Bay grapes. The company's Rhine Riesling is attractive, but the real stunner is the Sauvignon Blanc: it is delightful to drink such a wine, crisp and fresh with a low (10 per cent) alcohol content.

Some Other Winemakers

There are many other wineries, large and small, making classy wines. Babich (Henderson) consistently wins awards. Délégats (Henderson) is one of the older-established wineries suddenly to find a new lease of life, Cooper's Creek Vineyard (Kumeu) is another from the area to show considerable promise, but with Hawke Bay grapes. Eskdale (Hawke Bay) whites are rather oaky but impressive; the unique St Helena Estate (near Christchurch) is 'flying the flag' down south with attempts to nurture Pinot Noir and very presentable Pinot Blanc. San Marino Vineyards (Kumeu) is run by the friendly, extroverted Mate Brajkovich. He has handed over the winemaking to son Michael, who topped his year at Roseworthy College, and things are moving in the right direction.

There are many large winemaking firms I have deliberately chosen not to mention as their wines have just not improved at the general New Zealand rate. Also it is noticeable that I have made scant reference to red wines; however, Marlborough and the Hawke Bay area have produced some excellent wines and I am convinced that it is only a matter of time before real recognition is achieved. One must always remember just how recent the changes are, not only in winemaking but also in social attitudes in New Zealand to drinking (the notorious 'six o'clock swill' law under which all drinking establishments closed at 6 pm was only repealed in the 1960s.)

Licensing laws still hamper the industry and a large percentage of liquor outlets are controlled by a few brewery-owned companies: but the future is there.

Tradition and innovation. John Hancock of Morton Estate surrounded by Nevers oak casks and stainless steel

Enjoying Wine

Trucking the wine across country

NEW ZEALAND

CHAPTER SEVENTEEN

SOUTH AFRICA

In the 1960s Cape wines were right up to date with the rest of 'new world' products – inexpensive cold fermentation medium whites had arrived to complement the bruising, robust reds, often named 'claret' or 'burgundy' but remarkably similar. True, these reds may have been a bit overbaked and solid, but they were a reasonable glass of wine. As highlighted in this book, changes swept the wine world in the 1970s – but not in South Africa, which is still known for these same basic wines. The South African Airways Rhine Riesling and Cabernet Sauvignon both scored rather poorly in the 'Business Traveller Wine on the Wing' tasting and no one was very surprised. Jane McQuitty of *The Times* summed it up: 'South African wines always taste fine against each other but rate poorly in international competitions.'

Has the political isolation affected the South Africans' contact with the rest of the winemaking world? Have they carried on making relatively unsophisticated wines for an 'unsophisticated' market? Are there any glimmers of hope for the future? The answers to all these questions is 'Yes'.

The South African wine industry is dominated by three giants: the KWV (Kooperatieve Wynbouwers Vereniging), the most powerful company – all 6000 growers in the Republic have to be a member of this export organization, which also determines grape prices; the Oude Meester Group, the huge organization selling mainly in South Africa the well-established mass-market Fleur du Cap and Grunberger ranges of wines; and Stellenbosch Farmers' Winery, known throughout the Republic and overseas for its dependable Nederburg wines.

It is all rather cosy having these powerful companies with considerable financial resources controlling the selling of wine both at home and overseas, but it has been the source of stagnation as the good old faithfuls have been cultivated year in, year out. The KWV 1983 statistics are illuminating reading: 'new wave' grape varieties of Cabernet Sauvignon, Rhine Riesling, Sauvignon Blanc and Chardonnay accounted for less than 2 per cent of total plantings. Over 50 per cent of the acreage was still planted in the dull, but heavy-cropping, Chenin Blanc, Palomino and Cinsau: hardly the basis of a really fine winemaking industry.

Admittedly there is a rigid classification of these wines. In 1973 the Wine of Origin Law came into operation with strictly designated grape-growing regions being allowed to class their wines as WOS (Wine of Superior Origin). A wine of specific varietal nomenclature must contain at least 75 per cent of that grape, and most importantly for the future, a number of smaller farms with individual winemaking facilities processing only grapes grown within their boundaries have been classed as 'Estates'. All of these various levels of classification are detailed on the Wine and Spirit Board seal on the bottle.

These 'Estates' are beginning to buck the trend of mass mediocrity, and some are making really stunning wines right up to the class of the rest of the world's top wine countries – and the best thing of all is that many are available in the United Kingdom. Henry Collison and Sons in London is a specialist South African wine firm owned by Oude Meester, which has an exciting selection of the finest estates.

De Wetshof (Robertson)
Danie de Wetshof was the first Cape winemaker to produce the three classical varietal whites: Rhine Riesling, Chardonnay and Sauvignon Blanc. His

SOUTH AFRICA

Boschendal Estate: The Homestead

Chardonnay shows particular promise as the vines gather a little more age: well-balanced and not excessively high in alcohol.

Le Bonheur (Stellenbosch)
Michael Woodhead was originally a soil scientist who bought an existing vineyard called Oude Weltrede, renamed it and then set about changing the soil, raising the calcium content to a level more common with the better European vineyard regions.

It has certainly worked. He makes one of the world's finest Sauvignon Blancs, a delicious grapy freshness with perfect gooseberry flavour and beautifully balanced acidity.

L'Ormarins (Franschhoek)
A new super-modern winery belonging to the multi-national industrialist Dr Antonij Rupert (his company also owns Oude Meester) and run by his son Tony. The estate has been replanted with Chardonnay, Sauvignon Blanc, Rhine Riesling, Pinot Noir, Cabernet Franc and Merlot. The delightful, clean and fragrant 1983 Rhine Riesling, only the second vintage, augers well for the future.

Meerendal (Durbanville)
The only estate in this classified area. Proprietor Koos Starke concentrates on red wine, Shiraz and Pinotage – the latter is a South African native originating from the crossing of Pinot Noir and

ENJOYING WINE

SOUTH AFRICA

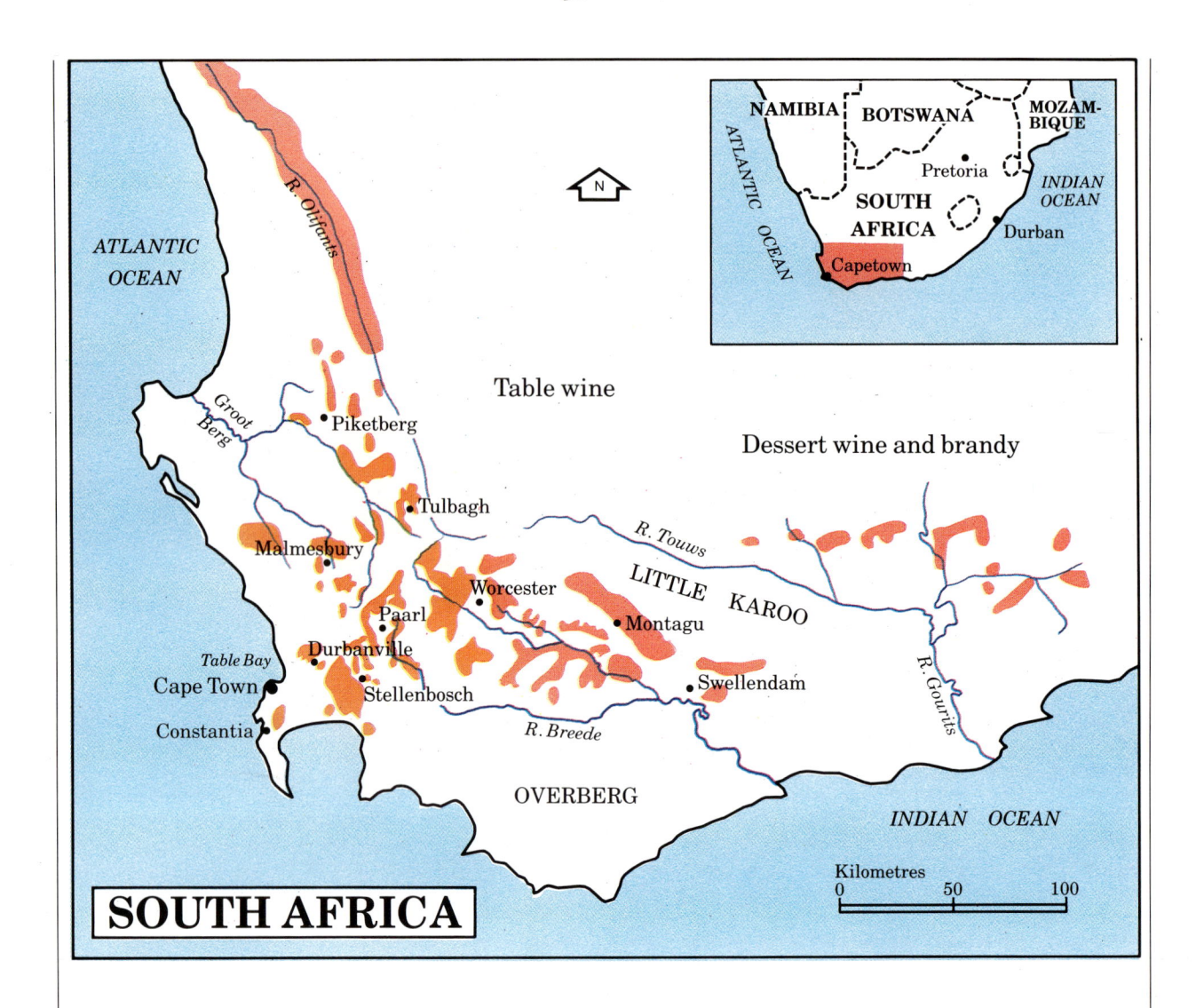

Hermitage (Cinsaut). Not the most delicate of wines, but full of flavour and individuality.

Meerlust (Stellenbosch)
Nicholas Myburgh is the eighth-generation owner of this estate; it has been in the family since 1756. The 250 ha (620 acres) under vine offer considerable quantities of grapes and yet the production and handling is very much *à la bordelaise* with small oak *barriques*. The wines are remarkable – the classic Cabernet Sauvignon, so unlike the heavy-handed efforts of most others in the Republic. Rubicon is a beautifully balanced, rich and complex blend, 45 per cent Cabernet Sauvignon, 35 per cent Merlot and 20 per cent Cabernet Franc. I have also tasted some Pinot Noir from relatively young vines which shows considerable promise.

Zandvliet (Robertson)
This estate is reputed to make the best Shiraz in the Cape, full of flavour. I feel that after a bottle of this you do not need to worry about vitamin pills!

QUESTIONS OF WINE

Is wine tasting a natural gift or is it a learnable skill?

Any experience we encounter in life has certain significant sensations which we can easily commit to memory if we wish. All you have to do is concentrate! This is true of wine tasting, once you have decided to approach the experience in a basic, serious way.

The question was prompted by a recent wine tasting at which I acted as quizmaster in a contest between wine trade professionals and a select group of top restaurant personalities. The professionals overwhelmed the restaurateurs. The trade tasters knew their varietals, and when they did not know, they made calculated, intelligent guesses. The restaurateurs were not assessing wines through their colour or nose, and ended up making wild stabs in the dark. Why was there this shocking gulf?

It was simply a lack of memory on the part of the losers. Memory is one of the keys to wine tasting. Since the professionals have to taste wines, sometimes three or four times a day, nearly every day of the year, their memories are superb and in constant training. The restaurateurs had no memory worth speaking of simply because they were restricted to their own wine lists, however varied, and for reasons of economic common sense, they are not likely to be constantly experimenting.

Yet even given the trade's unfair advantage in this contest there is no real excuse for their opponents' abysmal performance, because anyone can taste wine. They simply were not concentrating.

All you need is to make your own simple judgements on the basic elements that make up the wine: colour, bouquet/scent, taste – and memorize. Having made a basic assessment and noted down your reactions, you have tasted wine.

Of course, the subject begins to become more complicated, which is where the lay person tends to shy away from further experimentation. For one thing, the language used by tasters to described their reactions is specialized, almost a private language (which lay people, understandably, are quick to ridicule) and has to be learned. Here, you are developing a basic skill to a greater level of expertise. But even without fluency in this specialized language, there is nothing to prevent you being as much a judge of wine as the next expert.

Basic approach

First ensure the cleanliness of the room, glasses and taster. By this we mean it should be odour-free (particularly the taster – no tobacco smoke, no perfumes, or aftershave, no boot polish; you do not have to be a scruff, just clean and neutral!).

1. Colour

A glance through the wine at a white surface or a candle flame will show whether the wine is cloudy or clear. Cloudy is a negative; brilliant, at the other end of the scale, is a star rating. (Over-simplification is dangerous, but for whites a general rule is to reckon that the paler the colour the drier the wine, the more honey-coloured, the sweeter. For reds, purple means youth, and brown-brick means age.)

2. Smell

Very important. Swirling the wine for a few seconds helps to enable the wine to interract with the oxygen in the air and release the various elements and alcohol, and allows the smell to rise.

3. Taste

Take a small sip of wine onto the tongue to assess the sweetness and the acidity. Then breath some air through the wine by reverse whistling: holding the wine in the mouth and exhaling through the nose. This conveys the whole taste of the wine to the various parts of the taster's sensory equipment.

Note down your comments in basic, honest reactions, such as sweet, sour, burning, bitter, etc. Memorize and concentrate, lodging that particular glass in your memory banks. You have the first entry in your own personal mental wine catalogue. And so it goes on.

Because there is a certain degree of pomposity with regard to the finer wines, with a reverence of approach that is sometimes almost religious, people tend to be put off. There is some magic in some wines, no doubt about it; some of my experiences verge on the supernatural, but we will not dwell on those here.

Do not let yourself be put off. Persevere with various wines from different areas with striking characteristics to see how much contrast there can be between wines. Commit to memory each experience so that next time you can trace the wine back through your mental catalogue and log it.

So whether you are a company director, circuit judge, oilman, restaurateur or building supervisor, whatever your professional occupation, remember wine tasting is a developed skill. Be honest. Do not be afraid of making mistakes. It is timidity and the fear of being wrong that makes for bad wine tasting. You have your tongue as much as the next man, so use it and concentrate on your reactions. Describe them as they are, not how you think they ought to be. You will probably find yourself making some very decent assessments. Good luck and enjoy!

What is a Wine Bar?

Wine bars are certainly not the passing phenomenon predicted by many of their mid-1970s critics. They have

ENJOYING WINE

been around the City of London, since the days of the Great Fire of 1666. Before the 1960s they were bastions of male drinking – traditional wines, many fortified, and basic snacks. Then along came one of the great characters of the wine trade, Jack Denovan, 'the founding father of the modern wine bar movement'.

Jack was employed as a consultant to Searcey's, upmarket Knightsbridge caterers who occupied premises in Pavilion Road, just behind Harrods. He noticed a vacant space and with muted support from the board established a wine bar with a difference: it would serve mostly table wine, offer a wider range of snacks and, most importantly, it would welcome women. No one thought it would work – but it was a roaring success!

Others followed with varying degrees of success. I was able to buy *The Cork & Bottle* in 1972, a mere ten months old and already insolvent. A wine company opened a London-wide chain which came and went before the public were properly aware of the new eating and drinking revolution.

Gradually wine bars were accepted as alternative venues to both the pub and the trattoria – and how they have boomed! There are now more than a thousand in Britain that describe themselves as wine bars.

What should these places offer? Obviously a decent and interesting selection of the products of the noble grape. The list does not necessarily have to be all-encompassing, as financial restrictions and storage problems often prevent this. But it must offer excitement, something other than a selection of readily available mass-market plonk. These should be the places to sample the occasional glass of something you have heard about but have never been able to find in shops.

Food is important; after all drinking wine is really just half of the total enjoyment. It does not need to be elaborate, but should be innovative. Look for the establishments with enough enthusiasm to offer a wide range of unusual cheeses – marvellous accompaniment for wine slurping. In Britain it is wise to avoid places that offer only the regular routine of pâté de campagne, smoked salmon pâté, lobster bisque, chicken Kiev, veal cordon bleu, duck à l'orange, Black Forest gâteau etc. These are a few items from the repertoire of the 'boil in the bag' catering suppliers.

When is a Wine Bar not a Wine Bar?

The trouble with bandwagons is that everyone wants to hop on. I recently visited a town 30 miles west of London which boasted a wine bar. I suggested to the group of professionals I was meeting that we should lunch there and the response was revealing: 'Definitely not, you know what wine bars are like outside London.' Well, what a dreadful place it was! There was no wine list because, basically, there were no wines. The reception was distinctly frosty as I had entered with a few of the basic assumptions mentioned above, and the manager obviously did not believe in any of them and found it difficult to bother talking to me. And when he did it was in a most condescending manner.

I was finally offered a bottle of Côtes du Rhône proclaimed 'very nice': it turned out to be a totally over-the-hill 1979 Côtes du Fronton. We did not stay for this – or for the hamburgers.

What was most annoying was that this alleged member of the wine bar fraternity was ruining our reputation in the town. Britain has many dozens of absolutely superb provincial wine bars fulfilling all the prerequisites. I have particularly fond memories of The Georgian Wine Lodge in Bradford-on-Avon, Wiltshire, which has a wine list second to none and food to match; Llangollen in Wales is fortunate to have Gales; Epworth, South Yorkshire, has the highly rated Epworth Wine Bar: the list could go on and on. What a pity that many others spoil the name!

Are Branded Wines to be avoided?

Wine snobs will answer this question with a resounding 'Yes!'. (Every wine lover with a sense of humour should have a copy of Leonard S. Bernstein's hilarious book, *The Official Guide to Wine Snobbery*.) But I answer this question with an equally affirmative 'No!'.

At the risk of sounding like a marketing executive I must point out that a respectable percentage of branded wines did not obtain pre-eminence in the 1970s by accident. Certainly, they were helped considerably by mass advertising and a captive audience loving wine but lacking knowledge. But there is no doubt about it, the market leaders are sound, well-made wines. I have tasted Mateus Rose and Liebfraumilch Blue Nun regularly in blind tastings and they always perform with credibility. The individuality is lacking, but they do taste pleasant and are reliable.

These wines, and others (Liebfraumilch Black Tower and Bernkastler GreenLabel from Deinhard are two notable German brands of quality) are like manna from heaven when the intrepid traveller is stuck in the back of beyond, staying in an appalling hotel and suffering the equally repugnant delights of the dining room. Believe me, this is when the devil you know is a far better proposition than the remainder of the list which has languished upright on the shelf untouched for years.

Can wine complement an Asian meal?

Yes. Champagne is excellent. Alsace whites are ideal, especially Gewurztraminer; their spiciness and full flavour matches the food, they are rarely overpowered.

QUESTIONS OF WINE

Similarly a young, Syrah flavoured Rhone red or lightly chilled Provence red will stand up to the most fiery dishes without dominating the food.

What is Crémant Champagne?
This is made with considerably less pressure than normal therefore it is less sparkling, more 'foaming'. The style is more delicate and softer, epitomised by GH Mumm's *Cremant de Cramant* from the Cotes des Blancs.

Wine faults
Wine is a living product with many individual parts working together to constitute the whole. At times, often in youth or old age, there is an imbalance – too much or too little tannin, loss of fruit, excess acidity. With well structured wines these parts are working well and complementing each other for their drinking life.

There are two major faults that can destroy all the careful attention. *Maderisation* occurs inside the bottle when the alcohol oxidises and produces an insiduous smell and cloying taste. It is not common in well made wine. *Corked Wine* is *not* when pieces of cork are discovered floating in the first glass, irritating as this may be. It is the 'off' flavour of a faulty cork tainting the taste of the wine. It is relatively easy to pick on the nose. Beware, despite great technical improvements in other aspects of winemaking the incidence of corked wines is growing.

SPECIALIST WINE MERCHANTS

The United Kingdom is the centre of the world of wine. There are dozens of specialist wine merchants who will send catalogues and provide a standard of individual service seldom seen in other consumer businesses these days. Here are a few:

Beaujolais
Roger Harris Wines
Loke Farm, Weston Longville, Norfolk
Burgundy (and many other regions of France)
Laytons
20 Midland Road, London NW1
Champagne
The Champagne House
15 Dawson Place, London W2
Loire (and Rhone)
Yapp Brothers
The Old Brewery, Mere, Wiltshire
Rhone (and Germany)
O.W. Loeb
15 Jermyn Street, London SW1
Spain
Laymont and Shaw Ltd
The Old Chapel, Millpool, Truro, Cornwall
Italy
Cynthia Bacon
Ffowlers' Bucke, South Harting, Petersfield, Hants
South Africa
Henry C Collison & Sons Ltd
7 Bury Street, London SW1
United States
The Wine Studio
9 Eccleston Street
London SW1
Australia (and France)
Alexander Findlater & Co Ltd
77 Abbey Road, London NW8

There are many outstanding general wine merchants who offer a bewildering range of wines, Lay and Weeler, 6 Culver Street, Colchester, Essex are my favourites. Close by are Adnams, Sole Bay Brewery, Southwold, Suffolk. Nick Davies is a young wine man in a hurry and his Hungerford Wine Company, 128 High Street, Hungerford, Berkshire is particularly active on the 'opening price' claret market. The Wine Society, Gunnels Wood Road, Stevenage, Hertfordshire is in a class of its own – but you have to be recommended by a member. Avoid the mail order specialists who advertise in the colour supplements.

Supermarket Wines
There has been a revolution. Approximately half of all wine drunk in the United Kingdom is purchased in supermarkets, Sainsburys alone account for 15 per cent. Gone is the image of shelves stacked with tired, anonymous plonk. The major firms (Sainsburys, Tescos and Waitrose in particular) are actually creating the new wine drinking trends as they introduce their customers to the delights of the more unusual products of the South of France. Spain, New Zealand, California, Bulgaria . . . and also classed growth Clarets and Premier Cru Burgundies. Some of the best Champagne buys are to be found on their shelves.

ENJOYING WINE

THE WINE YEAR

Preparatory pruning at Domaine Dujac, Morey St. Denis

THE WINE YEAR

Champagne vineyard in winter

ENJOYING WINE

Pruning and training of the vine in March – Médoc

Flowering in spring – Médoc

Two weeks before harvest in Provence

Spraying at Listel. Golfe du Lion

Picking at Chambolle Musigny

The Wine Year

Traditional press, Nuits-St-Georges

Fermentation tanks, Loire

Bottling line at Sauvion, Loire

INDEX

Numbers in italics refer to illustrations

Aglianico dei Vulture, 105
Ahr, Germany, 95
Alella, Spain, 117
Alexander Valley (Sonoma), 133-6, 139-41
Alicante Bouschet, 124
Aligoté grape, 52
Allandale (Hunter), 159
Alsace, 28-33; cooking and restaurants, 32; cooperative and *négociant* houses, 32; map, *30-1*
Alto Adige (Sud Tyrol), 101
Amance, Marcel, 55
Amarone, 101
Anderson, Stuart, 151
Anjou, 24
Anjou Rosé, 24
Anjou Rouge Logis de la Giraudière, 24
Anney, Jean, 47
Anselme, Père, 74, 77
Antinori, Piero, 103, 106
Artesino Alois Lageder Chardonnay, 97
Australian wines, 6, 41, 60, 145-68; grape varieties, 164, 168; maps, *150, 166*; regions, 150-1, 166-7; wine festival, *152*; winemakers and wines, 152-60, 164; wine terms, 161

Babich (Henderson), 177
Baden, 95
Badia a Coltibuono, 107, *107*
Bagnis family, 84
Bandol, 84
Barbaresco, 97, 100
Barbera d'Alba, 101
Barbera grape, 132
Bardolino, 101
Barnes, Richard, 121-2, *122*
Barolo, 97
Barossa Pearl, 149, 154
Barossa Valley, 148, 151, *151*, 154-5, 157
Barsac, 37, 42
Barton, Anthony, *49*
Barton, Ronald, 42, 43, 49
Bass Charrington, 37
Baumard, Jean, 24, *25*
Baxter, Phil, 138, 139
Bay of Plenty (New Zealand), 171, *175*, 175-6
Beaujolais, 52, 60, 61, 64-73; bogus, 71; growers and cooperatives, 71; hierarchy, 64-5; map, *62*; *négociants*, 71, 73; the region, 64; served chilled, 72; vintages and when to drink, 72; white, 72
Beaujolais Nouveau (*en primeur*), 69
Beaujolais Villages, 64-5, 71, 72, 73
Beaulieu, 124, 125
Beaumes de Venise, 74, 78
Beaune, *55*, 58
Beaune Close des Mouches, 56
Beblenheim cooperative, 32
Bella Oaks Vineyard Cabernets, 133
Bendigo (Australia), 151
Ben Ean Moselle, 154
Benson, Anthony, 54
Berberana, 113; Gran Riserva, 109, 113
Beringer, 123, 124, 125
Bernkasteler Doktor (Mosel), 89, *92*, 95
Beyer, Léon (Eguisheim), 32
Beyer, Marc and Léon, 31, *32*
Biddenden Vineyard Ortega, 121-2, *122*
Bize, Simon, 58
Blue Nun (H. Sichel Sohne), 93
Boisset, Jean-Claude, 141
Bollinger (Ay), 12, 16, 24, 156; R.D., 13, 16; vintage rosé, 16
Bommes, 42
Bonnet Blanc de Blancs champagne, 18
Bourgueil, 25
Bordeaux, 34-50; *châteaux* and *petits*

châteaux, 37; grape varieties, 50; hierarchy, 37-42; map, *35*; recent vintages, 49-50; second wines, 49
Borie, Jacques, 38
Boschendal Estate: The Homestead, *181*
Bourgogne Blanc Domaine René Manuel, 60
Bourgogne Hautes Côtes de Beaune, 61
Bourgogne Hautes Côtes de Nuits, 61
Bourgogne Passe-Tout-Grains, 52
Bowen, Doug (Bowen Estate), 159
Boyer, Gerard, 20
Bragato, Tomeo, 169
Brajkovich, Mate and Michael, 177
Brand, Eric, 159
Branded wines, 185
Breisach cooperative, 95
British wines, 122; *see also* English wines
Brokenwood (Hunter Valley), 159
Brotte, Jean-Pierre, 74, 77
Brouhin, Joseph, 55-6
Brouilly, 65, 72
Brown Brothers (Milawa-Victoria), 153, *162*
Brunello di Montalcino, 97, 103
Brunet, Georges, 80, *81*
Buck, John, 176
Budin, Michel, 16
Buena Vista Winery, 123
Bulgarian wines, 118
Buller, Michael, 64
Bull's Blood, 118, 120
Bunan, Paul and Pierre, 84
Burguet, Alain, 58
Burgundy, 51-63; climate, 52; labels, 59; map, *63*; *négociants*, 52, 53, 54-60; red, 53-60; the system, 52-3; white, 60-1
Buring, Leo, 157
Busby, James, 145, 154, 169
Buxy Co-operative, 60

Cabernet Franc grape, 24, 25, 37, 43, 50, 101, 103, 106, 116, 118, 176, 181
Cabernet Sauvignon grape, 6, 43, 47, 48, 50, 80, 84, 85, 97, 101, 103, 105, 106, 116, 117, 118, 120; Australian, 148, 153, 156, 157, 159, 160, 167; Californian, 125, 132, 134, 139, 140, 141, 144; New Zealand, 171, 173, 175, 176; South African, 180, 182
Californian wines, 6, 60, 123-44; drip-feed irrigation, 215, *129*; the future, 141-4; grape varieties, 132-3; map, *130*; postwar period, 124-5; prohibition, 123-4; wine regions, 125-32; wineries, 133-41
Calon Ségur, 39
Campo Viejo, 113
Canaiolo grape, 103, 106
Carema, 101, *102*
Carignan grape, 80, 84, 124, 132
Cariñena grape, 116
Cassis, 84
Casta Rosado (Torres), 116
Castella, Paul de, 148
Castello di Vicchiomaggio, Chianti, *99*
Castle Hill Sauvignon Blanc 1984: 176
Cellier du Marrenon, 84
Cenicero wine festival, *112*
Chabernaud, Marcel and Dominique, 25
Chablis, 51, 52, 55, 59, 60, 61; 'Australian', 161
Chalonnais, 60
Chambertin, *53*, 58
Chambolle Musigny, 58, *188-9*
Champagne, 7-21; ageing, 9, *11*; blending, 8, 9, 15; crémant, 185; crown corks, 7, 9, 11; cultivation, 8-9; *cuvées de prestige* (premium), 12-13, 14-15; dégorgement, 10-11; dosage

added to, 11; harvest, 7-8; houses, 15-18; map, *10*; remuage, 9-10, *17*; rosé, 12, *14*, 16; secondary fermentation, 7, 9; vineyard in winter, *187*; vintage, 11-12, 15
Champagne Charlie (Heidsieck), 15, 17
Chardonnay (grape), 8, 27, 52, 60, 61, 72, 97, 101, 105, 116, 117, 118, 125, 132, 133, 136, 138-9, 140, 141, 144, 153, 156, 160, 164, 167, 168, 175, 180, 181
Château Canon, 41, 46
Château Coutet, *46*
Château d'Angludet (Margaux), 43, *43*
Château Danzac, 46, *46*
Château de Chenas, 65, 72
Château de Crémat, 84
Château de Selle, 84
Château d'Issan, *39*
Château de Mille, 84
Château Gloria, 41, 49
Château Grillet, 75
Château Haut-Bergey, 48
Château La Bégorce-Zédé, *44*
Château la Canorgue, 84
Château La Garde, 43-5
Château la Gordonne, 85
Château Langoa-Barton (St-Julien), 42-3, *48*
Château Lascombes, 49
Château Latour, 36, 40
Château Le Boscq, 46-7, *47*, 48
Château Lynch-Bages, 40, 49
Château Margaux *see* Margaux
Châteauneuf du Pape, 76-7, *77*, 78
Château Prieure-Lichine, 37
Château Rayas, 77
Château Ste Chapelle Vineyards, 144
Château Ste Michelle, 144
Château Smith-Haute-Lafitte, 44
Château Tahbilk (Victoria), 153-4, *154*
Château Tour des Termes, 47-8
Château Val-Joanis, 84
Château Vannières, 84
Château Vignelaure, 80, *81*
Chave, Gérard, 76
Chenas, 65, 72
Chenin Blanc grape, 24, 124, 125, 132, 140, 144, 153, 166, 168, 171, 173, 176, 180
Chianti, 97, 99, *99*, 103, 106, 107
Chinon, 25, *26*
Chiroubles, 65, 72
Chorey les Beaune, 56, 61
Christian Brothers, 124, 125
Churchill, Sir Winston, 16
Cinsault grape, 76, 80, 85
Clairette, 80
Claret *see* Bordeaux
Clare Valley (Australia), 151, 156, 157-8, 159
Cloberg, 120
Clos de Vougeot, *51*, 52
Clos du Papillon, 24
Clos Mireille Blanc de Blancs, 84
Codorniu, 117
Coleaux de Tricastin, 78
Collard Brothers, Sutton Baron, 176
Collison & Sons, Henry, 180
Colombard grape, 132, 153
Commanderies de Peyrassol, 84
Condriau, 75
Cooks New Zealand Wine Company, 171, *172*, 173, *174*, 175-6
Coonawarra (S. Australia), 151, 154, 156, 158, 159
Cooper's Creek Vineyard (Kumeu), 177
Corban, Abraham, 169, 173
Cordier (Bordeaux), 37, 144
Cornas, 76
Coron, 59-60
Coronas (Torres), 116
Cortese di Gavi, 101
Cos d'Estournel, 39

Côte Blonde, 75
Côte Brune, 75
Côte Chalonnais, 52, 59, 61
Côte de Beaune, 52, 54, 55, 60, 61
Côte de Beaune Villages, 61
Côte de Brouilly, 65, 72
Côte de Nuits, 54, 58, 59, 60, 61
Côte de Nuits Villages, 61
Côte d'Or, 52, 55, *57*, 60
Côte Rôtie, 74-5, 78
Coteaux d'Aix en Provence (VDQS), 80
Côtes de Blaye, 37
Côtes de Bourg, 37
Côtes de Castillon, 37
Côtes du Luberon (VDQS), 84-5
Côtes de Provence, 84, 85
Côtes du Rhône, 74
Côtes du Rhône Villages, 74
Côtes de Ventoux, 78
Cottin, Armand, 60
Coulée de Serrant, 24
Crémant d'Alsace (Eguisheim), 32
Crémant d'Alsace Cuvée Julien, 33
Crémant de Cramant (Mumm), 17, 185
Croser, Brian, 152, 155-6
Crozes-Hermitage, 76
Cru Beaujolais, 64, 65-72
Cuvée des Escaillers (Riesling), 32
Cuvée Eperon d'Or, 84
Cuvée William Deutz, 16
CVNE (Compagnia Vinicola del Norte de España), 113, 115

Davies, J. T., 37
Davis, Doug, 125, 139, 141
Davis, Rob, 134
De Castellane champagne, 18
Deinhard & Co., Koblenz, 95
Delas, *négociant*, 74, 76
Délégats (Henderson), 177
Deutz et Geldermann (Ay), 16
De Wetshof, Danie, 180-1
Dixon, Michael, *139*, 140, 141
Dolcetto, 101
Domaine Bernadins, 78
Domaine Chandon, 125, 141
Domaine Chantal Lescure, 60
Domaine de Belieu, *83*
Domaine de Brureau, 65, 72
Domaine de Castel-Oualou, 78
Domaine de l'Hermitage, 84
Domaine du Bélouve, 84
Domaine Dujac, 58, *186*
Domaine Durban, 78
Domaine Henri Gouges, 58
Domaine Mussy, 58
Domaine René Manuel, 60
Domaine Viticoles des Salins du Midi, 85
Domaines Ott, 84
Dom Pérignon champagne, 12, 13, 18
Dopff au Moulin (Riquewihr), 33
Dourthe, Philippe (Dourthe Frères), 47, 48, 49
Draper, Paul, 76, 136, *137-8*, 141
Drouhin, Robert, *55*, 60, 61, 141
Dufouleur Père et Fils, 60
Durand, Phillip, 46-7, *47*

Edelzwicker, 32
EEC *Tafelwein*, 86
Egri Bikaver, 118
Eguisheim cooperative, 32
Emilia Romagna, 103
Empson, Neil and Maria, *108*
Englert, Robert, 93
English wines, 121-2
Enterprise (Clare), 159
Epenottes, 58
Epernay, 15, 20
Eschenauer (Bordeaux), 37, 43-4
Eschol (Napa Valley), 124, 141
Eskdale (Hawke Bay), 177
Eye of the Swan (Sebastiani), 139

Index

Eyrie Vineyards (Oregon USA), 144

Faith, Nicholas, 49
Faiveley, J., 56, 59, 61
Fargues, 42
Farrer, J. Clark, 141
Faustino, 113, 115
Fauvin, Guy, 73
Fergussons Winery, 159
Fielden, Christopher, 97
Fleurie, 65, 68, *68*, 71, 72, 73
Fleury, Vidal, 74, 78
Folle Blanche grape, 23-4, 27
Forner, Enrique, 114, 115
Fougeras, M. et Mme, *36*
Franken (Franconia), 88, 95
Frankland River (Australia), 166
Frascati, 103
Frecciarosso, 101
Freemark Abbey (Napa Valley), 138
Freixenet, 117, 132
French wines, 7-85; Alsace, 28-33; Beaujolais, 64-73; Bordeaux, 34-50; Burgundy, 51-63; Champagne, 7-21; Loire, 22-7; Provence, 80-5; Rhône, 74-9
Friuli-Venezia-Giula, 101, 103
Fronsac, 37-8
Fumé Blanc *see* Sauvignon Blanc

Gaja (Barbaresco), 100, 103
Gallo, E. J., 124, 132
Gamay grape, 52, 64, 132
Garnacho grape, 112, 116, 117
Geelong (Australia), 151
German wines, 86-95; categories of wine, 86, 87-9; 'enrichment' of wines, 86, 88; major regions, 89-95; map, *87;* natural sweetness, 86, 88-9; 1971 wine laws, 86; *Süssreserve*, 86, 88
Gevrey-Chambertin, 54, 58
Gewürztraminer, 28, 30, 32, 33, 101, 116, 132, 153, 171, 175, 176, 185
Gill, Dick, 144
Gisborne, New Zealand, 171, 176
Gogondas, 78
Gold Seal Chardonnay, 144
Goulbourn Valley, 151
Goulet, Georges, 18
Graciano grape, 112
Gramp & Sons, G., 154-5, *158*
Grange Hermitage, 155
Granger, Jean-Paul, 61
Grape Concentrate, 124
Grappa, 107
Gratien, Alfred, 24
Gratien & Meyer, 24
Graves, 42, 44, 48, 50
Greco di Bianco, 105
Greco di Tufo, 104
Grenache grape, 76, 80, 84, 85, 168
Grey Riesling grape, 132
gris de gris (Midi), 85

Halliday, James, 160, 164
Hancock, Chris, 156
Hancock, John, 175, 176, *177*
Hanson, Anthony, 59
Hardy & Sons, Thomas, 157
Hargrave Vineyards, 144
Haut Bages Avérons, 49
Haut-Brion, 42
Haut-Médoc, 38
Haut-Poitou (VDQS), 27
Hawke Bay, 171, 173, 176, 177
Heggies Rhine Riesling, *149*, 157
Heidsieck, Charles (Reims), 15, 17, *19*, 21
Heidsieck Dry Monopole, 17
Heidsieck, Jean-Marc Charles, 21, *21*
Heidsieck, Piper (Reims), 17-18, 141
Heitz, Joe, *131*, 133
Heitz Wine Cellars (Napa Valley), 133
Hermitage, 75-6, 78, *78-9;* Australian,

154, 155, 156, 159, 164
Hessische Bergstrasse, 95
Heuenberg, 89
Hill Smith Estates, 157
Horgan, Dennis, 156
Houghton's White Burgundy, 166
Hugel, 30, 33
Hugel, Johnnie, 33, *33*
Hungarian wines, 118-20
Hunter Valley, 145, 150, 154, 155, 156-7, 158, 159, 164-5

Inglenook (California), 123, 124, 125
Italian wines, 96-107; Badia a Coltibuono, 107, *107;* Central, 103-4; Chianti, 103, 106; classifications, 97; DOC and DOCG regulations, 97, 103, 106; glossary, 106; map, *98;* Northern, 100-103; Southern, 104-5; Villa Banfi, 105-6
Italvini, 99

Jaboulet Ainé, 76
Jaboulet, Paul, 74
Jacob's Creek Claret, 155
Jaffelin, 60
Jadot, Louis, 59
Jayer, Jacqueline, 59
Johannisberger Riesling, 132, 144
Jones, Sir Guy Salisbury, 121
Jordan, Tom, 133-4, 136, *136*
Jordan, Dr Tony, 156
Jordan Winery (Sonoma), 133-4, *134-5*, 136
Jorgensen, Siggy, 149, 160
Joualt, Ed, 159
Juillot, Michel, 61
Juliénas, 68, 71, 72

Kadarka, 120
Kaiser Stuhl Barossa Co-operative, 155
Keppoch (Australia), 151
Kirkton Estate (Hunter Valley), 145, 154
Knappstein, Tim, 159
Knudsen Erath, 144
Krug, Charles (California), 123, 124, 125
Krug (Reims), 12, 21; Grande Cuvée, 14, 21
KWV (Kooperatieve Wynbouwers Vereniging), 180

Laboure Roi, 60
Lacrima Christi, 104
Ladoucette wines, 27
Lafarge, Michel, 58
La Gombaude, 49
La Grande Dame 1979 (Veuve Clicquot), 13
Lakes Folly, 159-60
Lalande de Pomerol, 37
Lambrusco, 103, 125, 144
La Mouline Médoc, 48
Langlois-Château, 24
Lanson (Reims), 17
La Tâche Domaine de la Romanée-Conti, 54
Latour, Louis, 59, 60
Lauerberg, J., 45
Launay, Paul de, 61
Laurent Perrier (Tours-sur-Marne), *11*, 17, *17*, 18; Cuvée Grand Siècle, 13; Cuvée Rosé Brut, 12
Le Bonheur (Stellenbosch), 181
Leeuwin Estate, 156, 160, 164
Léon, Jean, 115, 116-17
Les Forts de Latour (Margaux), 49
Les Griottes (Pouilly), 27
Les Sables du Golfe du Lion, 85
Libournais, 34
Lichine, Alexis, 37
Liebfraumilch, 86, 93
Lindemans (Hunter Valley), 154, 157,

159
Lirac, 78
Listel, *82*, 85, *188*
Listrac and Moulis, 41
Llano Estacado (Texas), 144
Loire, 22-7, *189*
Lombardy, 101
Long, Zelma, 140
Lopez de Herida Viña Tondonia, 113, 115
L'Ormarins (Franschhoek), 181
Loron, Xavier, 97
Luguna, 101
Luguy Co-operative, 61
Lutomer Riesling, 120

McDonald, Tom, 173
Mâcon Blanc and Mâcon Blanc Villages, 61
Mâcon Villages Laforêt, 55-6
Maconnais, 52, 60, 61, *62*
MacQuitty, Jane, 13, 180
McWilliam Wines Ltd, 173, 175
Madeleine Angevine grape, 122
Maîtres Vignerons de la Presqu'île de Saint-Tropez, *83*, 84
Malbec grape, 50, 155, 168
Malvasia grape, 103, 106, 112
Maréchal, Jean, 61
Margaret River (Australia), 166
Margaux, *36*, 37, 39, 41, 43, 45, *45*, 46, 48, 49
Mariani, John and Harry, 105
Marienberg (Coromandel Valley), 160, *165*
Marino Superiore, 103
Marlborough, 171, 173, 175, 177
Marqués de Alella, 117
Marqués de Cáceres, 114, 115
Marqués de Grinon, 117
Marqués de Murietta, 114, 115
Marqués de Riscal, 114, 117
Marsala, 105
Marsanne (Tahbilk), 153-4
Martha's Vineyard Cabernets, 133
Martin, Henri, 49
Martini, Louis, 124
Mas de la Rouvière, 84
Masson, Paul, 124
Matawhero Wines (Gisborne), 176
Matua Valley Wines (Waimauku), 176
Maximin Grünhäuser, 89
Mazuelo grape, 112
Médoc, 38-41, 50, *188*
Meerendal (Durbanville), 181
Meerlust (Stellenbosch), 182
Mendocina, California, 124, 132
Mercier champagne, 16, 20
Mercurey, 59, 61
Merlot grape, 41, 47, 48, 50, 101, 116, 118, 120-2, 125, 132, 134, 138, 160, 176, 181, 182
Méthode champenoise, 15, 32, 33, 117, 133, 156, 161; *see also* Champagne
Meursault, 60
Meursault Rouge Clos de la Baronne, 60
Middleton, Dr John, 164
Mission Vineyards, Greenmeadows, 173
Mittelhein, 95
Moët and Chandon, 12, 13, 15-16, 18, 20, 141
Moillard, 60
Monastrell grape, 116
Mondavi, Robert, 6, 124, 125, 140, 160
Montagny, 60, 61
Montana Wines (Auckland), 173, 175
Monte Bello (Ridge Vineyards), 137, 138
Montecillo, 115
Montepulciano d'Abruzzo, 105
Monterey (California), 124, 132
Monthélie, 56, 61

Montille, Hubert de, 58
Montlouis, 25
Morey St Denis, 58
Morgon, 71
Morris, John and Michael, 176
Morton Estate (Bay of Plenty), 171, *175*, 175-6, *177*
Moscadello, 105
Mosel, *88*, 89, 92, *92*
Moueix, J. P., 37
Moulin è Vent, *70*, 71-2
Moulin des Costes, 84
Mount Barker (Australia), 166
Mount Mary (Victoria), 164
Mount Pleasant Hunter wines, 154
Mourvèdre grape, 76, 80, 84
Mouton Cadet, 48
Mudgee (New South Wales), 150
Muga bodega, 115
Müller-Thurgau grape, 93, 95, 122, 171, 173
Mumm, G. H. (Reims), 13, 15, 17, *18*, 20, *20*, 93, 141, 185
Murray Riverland, 148, 151, 157, 160
Muscadet, 22-4, 86
Muscat, 30-1, 116
Musigny, 58
Myburgh, Nicholas, 182

Nahe, 93
Napa Valley (California), 124, 125, *126*, 136, 138-9, 141, 159, 160
Navarra (Spain), 117
Nebbiolo, 101
Nederburg wines, 180
New South Wales, 150
New York State, 144
New Zealand wines, 60, 141, 164, 169-79
Nierstein, 93
Nuits St Georges, 58, 60, 71, *189*
Nyrang Hermitage, 154

Oatley, Bob, 156
Ockfeuer Bockstein, 89
Olasz Riesling, 118
Oltrepo Pavese, 101
Orlando (Barossa), 149, 154-5, *158*
Ortega, 121, 122
O'Shea, Maurice, 154
Oude Meester Group, 180

Pacific Northwest, 144
Pallette, 84
Papa Clément, 42
Parrellada grape, 116
Pauillac, 40
Pavillon Rouge (Margaux), 49
Peat, Edmund, 157-8
Penedès, 109, 115-17
Penfold Wines (Australia), 155, 156
Peralada, 117
Perignon, Dom Pierre, 7
Perrier, Joseph, 18
Perrier-Jouet (Epernay), 16, 17
Petaluma, 155-6
Petit Syrah grape, 132
Petit Verdot grape, 43, 50
Peynaud, Professor Emile, 46
Phylloxera, 27, 34, 112, 123, 148, 153, 169
Pichon-Longueville Lalande, 49
Piedmont, 100
Piettenberg, Reichsgraf von, 93
Pineau, Jean, 112
Pinot Blanc, 52, 101, 133, 177
Pinot Blanc (Alsace), 28, 31, 32, 33
Pinot Blanco Favonio, 105
Pinot Grigio, 101, 105
Pinot Meunier, 8
Pinot Noir, 8, 27, 31, 33, 52, 54, 58, 95, 101, 116, 125, 132, 133, 139, 141, 144, 156, 157, 160, 168, 177, 181, 182
Pinot Noir (Alsace), 31, 32, 33

INDEX

Pleasant Valley Wines, 169
Pol Roger (Epernay), 16
Pol Roger Cuvée Sir Winston Churchill 1975: 13
Pomerol, 41, 50
Pommard, 58, 61
Pommard Les Pezerolles 1969: 58
Pommery et Greno (Reims), 18, 20
Pouilly Blanc Fumé, 25, 27
Pouilly Fuissé, 60, 61, 76
Pouilly Loche, 61
Pouilly Vinzelles, 61
Pourriture noble (Botrytis cinerea), 24, 42
Prass, Gunter, 155
Preignac, 42
Pridham, Ursula, 160, *165*
Prosper Maufoux (Santenay), 55, 60
Provence, 80-5, *188-9;* food and restaurants, 85; *gris de gris,* 85; map, *82;* white wines, 80, 84
Purbrick family, 153
Pury, Guillaume de, 160

Queensland, 167
Quelltaler (Clare), 157-8
Quincy, 27
Quinson, Jean Louis, 73, *73*

Raimat, 115, 117
Raymond Vineyard and Cellar, 132, 136, 156
Redman, Owen, 159
René Lalou 1979 (G.H. Mumm), 13
Restaurants and Hotels: Alsace, 32; Boyer 'Les Crayères', Reims, 20; 'Chez la Rose', Juliénas, 69; Cogny's Hostellerie du Val d'Or, 61; 'Hotel Cheval Blanc', Sept Saux, 20; 'La Briqueterie', Vinay, 20; 'Le Savoie', Margaux, *36;* 'Les Maritonnes', Romanèche Thorins, 73, *73;* Provence, 85; 'Restaurant des Sports', Fleurie, 65, 68; 'Restaurant Robin', Chenas, 65; 'Royal Champagne' hostelry, 20
Rheingau, *92,* 92-3, 95
Rheinhessen, 93
Rheinpfalz (Palatinate), 93, 95
Rhine Riesling, 149, 153, 154-5, 156, 157, 159, 160, 168, 175, 176, 177, 180-1
Rhône, 74-9, 85
Ricasoli, Baron Bettino, 103, 106
Richter (Montpellier), 144
Ridge Vineyards (Cupertino), 136-8
Riesling: Alsatian, 28, 30, 32, 33; American, 141, 144; German, 88, 89, 92-3, 95; Yugoslav, 120; *see also* Rhine Riesling
Rigord, Mme Françoise, 84
Rioja, 109, *110-11,* 112-13, 116; classifications, 113-15; white, 115
Riquewihr, *29,* 33
Riverina (New South Wales), 150
Riverland Chardonnay (Orlando), 155
Riviera del Garda Bresciano, 101
Robards, Terry, 156
Roederer, Louis (Reims), 17, 141; Cristal, 13, 17
Romaneche Thorins, 72, *73*
Romanian wines, 120
Rosemount Estate (Hunter Valley), 156
Rosemount Show Reserve Chardonnay, 156, 168
Rosewood (Rutherglen), 149
Roseworthy Oenological College, 152, 175
Rothbury Estate (Hunter), 158
Rothschild, Baron Philippe de, 6, 60, 141
Rouge Homme Wines, 154, 159
Roumier, Alain, 58

Rousseau, Armand, *53,* 58
Rubicon (Meerlust), 182
Rueda (Spain), 117
Rutherford Hill Winery (Napa), *138,* 138-9, *140*
Ruwer, 92
Ryrie, William, 148

Saar, 89
Sacramento Valley (California), 132
Saint Amour, 72
Saint Aubin, 61
Saint Bris, 61
St Emilion, 37, 41, 46, 50
St-Estèphe, 38, 39, 46, 47
Saint Gengoux Groupement de Producteurs, 60
St Helena Estate (New Zealand), 177
St-Joseph, 76
St-Julien, 39, 40-1, 42-3, 49
Saint-Nicholas-de-Bourgueil, 25
Saint Romain, 61
Saint Veran, 61
Salice Salentino, 105
Sancerre, 25, 27
Sangiovese grape, 103, 105, 106
Sangria, 109
San Joaquin Valley (California), 132
San Marino Vineyards (Kumeu), 177
Santa Barbara (California), 124, 132
Santa Clara (California), 124, 132, 136-8
Santenay, 56, 60, 61
Sardinian wines, 105
Sarjeant, Anthony, *36, 40,* 48-9
Sarria Tinto, 117
Sassicaia, 103
Sauternes, 42
Sauvignon Blanc (Fumé Blanc), 25, 27, 42, 50, 61, 80, 101, 105, 116, 125, 132, 136, 139, 144, 168, 171, 176, 177, 180, 181
Sauvignon de Touraine, 25
Sauvignon Trois Moulines, 48
Sauvion (Loire), 23, *189*
Savennières, 24
Savigny les Beaune, 58
Saumur, 24
Scharzhofberg, 89
Scheurebe grape, 122
Schloss Graf von Schönborn, Hattenheim, 93
Schloss Johannisberg, Rheingau, 93, *94*
Schloss Vollrads, Rheingau, *90-1,* 93
Schubert, Max, 155
Scottish and Newcastle Vintners, 139-40
Seagrams, 105, 124, 175
Sebastiani Vineyards (Sonoma), 125, 139, 141
Segura Viudas, 117
Selak's Wines (Kumeu), 176-7
Sémillon grape, 42, 50, 80, 132, 154, 156-7, 158, 168, 176
Seysses, Jacques, 58
Seyval Blanc grape, 121
Sfurzat, 101
Shiraz grape, 79, 149, 153, 154, 155, 156, 157, 159, 160, 164, 181, 182
Sichel, Peter, 37, 43, *44,* 50
Sichel Söhne, H., 93
Sicilian wines, 105
Silver Nun (Spiegelburg), 93
Simi Winery (Sonoma), 123, 124, 139-41
Sittman, Carl, 93
Smart, Richard, 141
Soave, 99, 101, *104*
Sonoma Valley (California), 124, 125, *126-7,* 132, 133-6, 139-41
South African wines, 180-2
South Australia, 148, 149, *150,* 150-1, *151,* 155-6, 157, 159, 160
Southern Vales, *146-7,* 148, 151-2, 157

Spanish wines, 109-17; map, *114;* Penedès, 115-17; Rioja, 112-15; sparkling wines, 117
Spence Brothers, 176
Stanley Wine Co. (Clare), 159
Stellenbosch Farmers' Winery, 180
Strasbourg, 32
Süssreserve, 86, 88, 121
Swan Valley, 166
Sylvaner grape, 31, 32, 93, 95, 102
Syrah grape, 74, 75, 76, 79, 80, 84, 160, 164, 185

Tain l'Hermitage Cooperative, 76
Tattinger (Reims), 18, 20; Comtes de Champagne 1976: 13, 18
Tasmania, 167
Taurasi, 104
Tavel, 78
Tchlistcheff, André, 133, 134
Te Kauwhata (New Zealand), 169, 171, *172,* 173, *174,* 175
Te Mata Estate (Hawke Bay), 176
Tempranillo grape, 112, 116, 117
Texas, 144
Thienpoint, Luc and Georges, *45,* 45
Thompson Seedless grape, 132
Tibouren grape, 80
Tiefenbrunner, 101
Tocai del Collio, 101
Tokay Aszu Eszenzia, 118
Tokay d'Alsace (Pinot Gris), 30
Tokay, Hungarian, 118, 120
Torgiano, Umbria, *100*
Torres wines, *115,* 115-16, *116*
Trebbiano grape, 103, 106, 168
Trebbiano d'Abruzzo, 105
Trebbiano di Romagna, 103
Trefethen Winery (Napa), 141, *142-3,* 156
Trott, Gregg, 160
Tualatin (Oregon, USA), 144
Tulloch (Hunter Valley), 158
Turkheim, 32
Tuscany, 103, 105-6, 107
Tyrrells, Vineyards, 156-7
Tyrrell, Murray, 156-7, 158

Ugni Blanc grape, 80
Ull de Llebre, 116
United States, 6, 123-44; California, 123-44; New York State, 144; Pacific Northwest, 144; Texas, 144
United Vintners, 124
Upper Loire, 25-7

Vacheron, Jean, 27
Valpolicella, 99, 101
Valréas, 74
Valtellina, 101
Vega Sicilia, 117
Veneto, 101
Verdicchio, 103
Vergé, Roger, 85
Vernaccia di San Gimignano, 103
Veuve Clicquot (Reims), 13, 18
Victoria (Australia), 148, 151, 153-4, 159, 160, 164; Liqueur Muscats, 162
Villa Banfi, Montalcino, 105-6
Viña Real Reserva, 113
Viña Santo, 107
Viña Sol (Torres), 116
Vino Nobile di Montepulciano, 97, 103
Vino Santo, 107
Vins Doux Naturels (VDN), 78
Viognier grape, 75
Visan, 74
Vitis vinifera and *Vitis labrusco,* 123, 144
Vogue, Alain, 76
Vogue, Comte Georges de, 58
Volnay, 58, 61
Vosne-Romanée aux Malconsorts, 60
Vouvray, 24
Vranac, 120

Wagga Wagga School of Oenology, 152, 155
Wagner Vineyards, 144
Wantirna Estate (Melbourne), 160
Western Australia, 160, 166-7, *166-7*
Wildman Co. of New York, 48
Wildwood Vineyards (Sonoma), 123, *126-7*
Wine bars, 184-5
winstubs of Alsace, 31, 32
Wine-tasting, 183-4
Wirra Wirra (McLarenvale), 160
Wolfe, David, 54
Woodhead, Michael, 181
Wrigley, Robert, 160
Württemberg, 95
Wynns (Coonawarra), 158

Yalumba (Hill Smith Estates), 157, *162-3*
Yarra Valley (Victoria), 148, 151, 159, 160, 164
Yelas, Stephen, 169
Young, Robert, 6, 168
Yoxall, H.W., 7
Yugoslav wines, 120

Zandvliet (Robertson), 182
Zinfandel grape, 125, 132, 137, 138, 144

Illustration sources
The publishers would like to thank the following:
Australian Information Service, London: 51
The Australian Trade Commission, Manchester: 146-47, 158
Badio a Coltibuono: 107 (below)
Berkmann Wine Cellars, London N7 9NH (Stuart Miller): 83, 189 (centre right), 189 (below right)
David Charles, The Kirkham Studios, Midhurst, W. Sussex: 10, 22-23, 30-31, 35, 62-62, 75, 82 (above), 87, 98, 114, 130, 150, 166, 170, 182
Mick Dean: 14
Joseph Drouhin: 55, 56
Margaret Harvey: 172, 175, 177
Charles Heidsieck: 19
Percy Hennell: 26, 29, 40, 51, 66-67, 68, 70, 72, 77, 110-11, 187, 188-89 (below)
Herschel Dee Williams, Jr. All rights reserved: 140
Laurent-Perrier (UK) Ltd: 11, 17
Hervé Lefebvre: 36, 39, 43, 44, 45, 46, 47, 48
Listel: 188 (below left)
Noelene Moss: 73, 122, 188-89 (above)
G.H. Munn et Cie: 18, 20
Pol Roger & Co: 8
© QED Publishing: 24, 78-79, 88, 90-91, 92, 94, 99, 100, 102, 104, 181, 186
John Rapp: 127-27, 128, 129, 131, 137, 142
Mark Reynier: 25, 53
© David B. Simmonds: 154
Bill Stott: 9, 34, 54, 69, 80, 96, 109, 119, 120, 121, 123, 145, 169, 184
Nick Tresidden: 189 (above right)
Vinos de Espana, Jan Read: 112, 115
Western Australia House, London: 152, 166-67
© David Williamson, 68a Recliffe Square, London SW10: 119

192